# Mr. Jingle Bells

## (Mr. Christmas #3)

## By Leta Blake

An Original Publication from Leta Blake Books

Mr. Jingle Bells
Written and published by Leta Blake
Cover by Dar Albert
Formatted by BB eBooks


First Print Edition, 2021
ISBN: 978-1-626226-5-48

# Other Books by Leta Blake

Any Given Lifetime
The River Leith
Heat for Sale
Smoky Mountain Dreams
Angel Undone
The Difference Between
Omega Mine
Bring on Forever
Raise Up Heart

## The Mr. Christmas Series
Mr. Frosty Pants
Mr. Naughty List
Mr Jingle Bells

## The Training Season Series
Training Season
Training Complex

## Heat of Love Series
Slow Heat
Alpha Heat
Slow Birth
Bitter Heat

## Stay Lucky Series
Stay Lucky
Stay Sexy

## '90s Coming of Age Series

Pictures of You

You Are Not Me

**Co-Authored with Indra Vaughn**

Vespertine

Cowboy Seeks Husband

**Co-Authored with Alice Griffiths**

The Wake Up Married serial

Will & Patrick's Endless Honeymoon

**Gay Fairy Tales**

**Co-Authored with Keira Andrews**

Flight

Levity

Rise

**Audiobooks**

Leta Blake at Audible

**Free Read**

Stalking Dreams

**Discover more about the author online**

Leta Blake

letablake.com

# Gay Romance Newsletter

Leta's newsletter will keep you up to date on her latest releases and news from the world of M/M romance. Join the mailing list today.

# Leta Blake on Patreon

Become part of Leta Blake's Patreon community in order to access exclusive content, deleted scenes, extras, bonus stories, rewards, prizes, interviews, and more.
www.patreon.com/letablake

# Acknowledgements

Thank you to the following:

PC for talking with me about his gambling issues. Mom & Dad, without whom I couldn't be following this dream of being a writer. Brian & Cecily, my lights to travel home to. All the wonderful members of my Patreon who inspire, support, and advise me. Keira Andrews for the editing work, handholding, and long-lasting friendship. Lori Parks for proofing. Sean & Cindy for use of their vacation condo so I could write during a crowded, locked-in 2020. Kim V for her loving friendship and hours of listening. Holly & Sabrina for cheerleading. My home of Knoxville, TN for the setting inspiration.

Most of all, thank you to my readers for making all the hard work worthwhile.

*To Brian for everything and always*

**Opposites attract as frosty business partners become fake boyfriends in this Christmas gay romance!**

*Christmas love will heal their wounded hearts*

After an emergency forces Ashton Sellers from his apartment, all he wants for Christmas is new lipgloss, zero contact from his abusive family, and a place to stay for the holidays. Cue his business partner begrudgingly taking him in.

Walker's a fuddy-duddy with no sense of fun, but he does have a safe, warm home with four adorable dogs and delicious food on the table.

If it turns out Walker's also a secret softy with a tender side and a hot body beneath his endless parade of golf shirts? Great, good, cool. And if Walker wants Ashton to pretend to be his boyfriend for his sister's Christmas-themed wedding? Awesome, amazing.

Could Walker be the safe haven Ashton missed out on as a child? Could they be falling in love for real?

But when Ashton uncovers a painful mistake in Walker's past, it hits too close to home. As the jingle bells quiet and the snow settles, will Ashton be able to forgive Walker, or will their relationship be over before it ever truly begins?

*Mr. Jingle Bells* is a gay Christmas story by Leta Blake featuring forced proximity, opposites attract, fake dating, office romance, steamy scenes, and a taffy-sweet happy ending. It's set in the *Mr. Christmas* universe, which began with *Mr. Frosty Pants*, but **can be read as a standalone.**

Content warnings for childhood abuse, past addiction issues, PTSD episodes, and gambling.

# Chapter One

*A*SHTON SELLERS.

Walker Ronson stared at the tiny slip of paper he'd pulled from the office's candy bowl. Normally, it perched on the edge of their receptionist Kayla's desk and contained lollipops to tempt clients on their way in or out. But today the bowl was full of small, folded rectangles, each sporting a name in Kayla's loopy writing, and everyone in their small advertising agency was expected to take one.

Walker didn't even want to do this Secret Santa thing. It seemed frivolous to him, buying and giving cheap presents to each other. It would all just wind up in a landfill, wouldn't it? But Nicole, their office manager, had argued for it vociferously during SRS Advertising's November management meeting.

She insisted Secret Santa, decorations, and a Christmas potluck luncheon kept employees happy and loyal. Walker suspected Nicole just really loved Christmas. He was no Grinch, but he worried forcing staff to buy gifts was unfair. She'd agreed to make it voluntary at least.

His business partners, Casey and Ashton—yes, *the* Ashton—had been on board for Secret Santa too. No, "on board" was too staid a term for what Ashton had been. He'd been *outrageously* enthusiastic in championing Nicole's suggestion, even getting up to do an excited Snoopy dance to encourage Walker to "lighten up" and "live a little."

Weirdly, that dance had made Walker's blood race and his hands sweaty. Even now he couldn't begin to understand why. There was nothing sexy about the Snoopy dance, but apparently his body didn't agree. By that point, Walker had been willing to do anything to make Ashton sit down and stop being so…so…

*That.*

So he'd caved.

At the time, it'd seemed harmless enough. Especially if Nicole was right and Secret Santa truly made everyone else in the office happy. How hard could it possibly be to get a Secret Santa present for an office assistant? He'd buy a pretty coffee mug, slap a red bow on it, and call it a day, right? Or so he'd thought as Nicole and Ashton had solidified the plans for the event, stipulating a price limit and a rule prohibiting gift cards.

Now, as he blinked down at the slip of paper in his hand, he cursed his lack of backbone.

Because he, Walker Alan Ronson, had turned out to be the unlucky bastard who'd drawn Ashton Middle-Name-Unknown Sellers.

*Not* an office assistant.

And not an easy person to shop for either.

A pretty coffee mug was out because Ashton only drank one cup of coffee per day, brought directly from Starbucks every morning and still steaming in its paper cup when he arrived at the office. After that he switched to water, citing "hydration and beauty." Hand to God, Walker had heard the man say those exact words to Taylor, one of their best copywriters, in all seriousness as his reason for snubbing additional caffeine. Hydration and *beauty.*

So, yeah, Ashton was the kind of man Walker couldn't relate to at all: gorgeous in an almost inhuman way with shiny green eyes the color of moss, and dark, almost-black, curly hair that fell over a pale face that Ashton always perfected with a hint (or more) of makeup.

Plus, the man wore, well, *fashion.*

Where did a six-foot-tall man even buy soft, flowery, silk shirts, and cream-colored tight pants? Or all that pretty makeup? Did Ashton go to the Sephora counter in the mall like Walker's older sister always had? Or did he get his eye shadow somewhere else? What did Walker know about all that? Maybe there *were* special men's makeup brands! And if there weren't, there should be, because that could make some asshole a fortune.

Note to self.

"Caught yourself a difficult one, have you?" Kayla asked with a laugh, jolting him out of his Secret Santa induced misery.

"Difficult?" he repeated.

She pointed at the paper in his hand.

"Oh." He blew out a breath. "I guess."

Kayla pushed her brown, softly curled bangs off her forehead and grinned at him. She had a great smile. That was half the reason they'd hired her for the receptionist position. The other half being that she was organized, enthusiastic, and responsible—and her cute, quirky clothing choices were always fresh, fun, and on brand for their office.

Today, Kayla wore a pink sweater with silver snowflakes on it, and her skirt was a spring green, like Easter and Christmas had had a baby. Walker thought she looked like a gorgeous doll; at another time in his life and if she weren't an employee, he might have been interested in her.

"Is the name you drew a problem?" she asked.

"No. It's fine," Walker muttered, rubbing a hand across the back of his sweaty neck. Why did he get Ashton of all people for Secret Santa? He fought the urge to pluck at the front of his navy-blue golf shirt to fan some cool air under his collar.

"No takebacks." Kayla winked, holding the clear bowl containing all the other, non-Ashton names away from him, as if he might stick his hand back in and pull out another. Like she could read his damn mind.

She spun on her sharp heel and grinned wickedly at Joe Warner, SRS's art manager. He was a tall, skinny guy, currently contemplating the spread of fresh donuts on the break room table like he might give in and shove them all in his mouth at once. Joe was a garbage disposal like that. Walker briefly considered grabbing a chocolate frosted one just in case Joe gave in to his need to feed and left nothing for anyone else who came in later.

Lightly jabbing Joe with her elbow, Kayla instructed him to draw a name too. "No trading and no switcheroos," she warned, swinging her long, pink fingernail between the two of them like they were co-conspirators in a plan to cheat at Secret Santa.

Joe's hungry gaze turned away from the donuts and onto Kayla instead. Those two had been sleeping together for a month now, and Walker wasn't supposed to know. In fact, he wished he *didn't* know. He was pretty sure SRS's attorneys would say inter-office romance was deeply problematic, but Joe didn't have any sway over Kayla's job, or vice versa, and so Walker had chosen to look the other way. So had Casey and Ashton.

The microwave dinged. Walker moved to grab his banh mi breakfast wrap as Joe let out an aggravated little huff.

"Let me choose again," he begged.

"Now, now, fair is fair," Kayla said, laughing lightly at his groan of frustration. "Isn't that right, Walker?"

Walker shrugged, placing his wrap on a paper plate. "Whatever you say, Kayla." He had an older sister. He knew better than to argue. But he couldn't help feeling there was little fair about having been stuck as Secret Santa to *Ashton Sellers*. He had no clue what a man like that might want. None at all.

Why couldn't one of the girls in design have drawn Ashton instead? They all liked lip gloss, nail polish, and the color pink. They had a ton more in common with Ashton than Walker did.

Kayla winked at Joe before leaving the room to distribute more Secret Santa despair.

"Uh, Walker?" Joe asked.

Walker hunted through the break room's silverware drawer for a clean fork. He found one as he replied, "What's up?"

Joe held his slip of paper up with a mournful expression. "Who'd you get?"

"I got—"

"No trading!" Kayla crowed again from just outside the break room door, where she was now allowing Anna and Jamal, two recently hired artists, to pull names from the bowl. "No discussion about who you got either! It's called *Secret* Santa, Joe. Got it?"

Joe cast a worried glance toward the door. "Who did you get?" he whispered.

Walker shot him a pained look.

"That bad?"

"Yup."

"I got…" he inclined his head in the direction of Kayla's cheerful voice babbling on with Jamal about their Secret Santa experiences of years past. If nothing else, it seemed Nicole was right, and most of the employees enjoyed this game. "Kayla," Joe mouthed. "And if it's not perfect, she'll have my balls for breakfast."

Hope filled Walker's heart. "Wanna switch?" He held up his slip of paper with Ashton's name facing Joe.

Joe's eyes went wide and then he laughed. "Oh. I see. Um, *hell* no. Good luck, man." He patted Walker on the arm and scooted past him. "I think I'll just keep the one I got."

Sighing, Walker stepped into the hallway carrying his wrap and spoon. He preferred to eat in the privacy and quiet of his office.

"Ashton!" Kayla called out.

Hearing Ashton's name, Walker froze in place. When he looked up, he almost couldn't breathe. Ashton wore a pair of tight, black pants that cupped his ass and package, and a soft-looking, gold blouse beneath a black, faux-military jacket covered with gold and red trim.

He carried a Starbucks cup, like every morning, and, in the winter light from the big windows, he looked stunning. Absolutely breathtaking. What with his pale skin, dark hair, and all that black, gold, and red contrasting so perfectly. He looked like a model. Or a famous actor. He looked *unreal*. It was maddening.

Walker wished they'd instituted a dress code back when he, Casey, Ashton, and Nicole had met with their business attorney to draft all their other office policies. At the time, he'd barely known Ashton and hadn't realized they'd need to prohibit Ashton's entire wardrobe due to the risk of it sending Walker into a dazed and confused state nearly every single day. For fuck's sake! How the man dressed, how he talked with that little lisp, the way he held his hands and moved his hips…none of that was Walker's business. Why couldn't he stop noticing it?

"Come here! You have to draw for Secret Santa!" Kayla said.

Ashton released a soft squeal of joy and rushed forward to shove his free hand into Kayla's proffered bowl. Walker stayed only long enough to witness the overly dramatic production Ashton made of swirling the remaining four papers around before choosing one. Without waiting to see Ashton's reaction to the name he'd chosen, Walker stalked off, his skin prickling with unwarranted irritation.

Once safely inside his lightly cluttered office, Walker shut the door and dropped his breakfast on his desk. Settling into his ergonomic chair, he folded the piece of paper with Ashton's name on it into a tiny square and slipped it into his desk drawer. He couldn't quite bring himself to throw it away. It felt rude somehow. Ashton might make Walker feel confused and agitated but he still deserved better than the trash can.

Hoping the spicy banh mi wrap would distract him, Walker took a bite. Unfortunately, his tension didn't dissipate, but at least he was sweating now from the spice and not from a riot of unwanted emotions over Ashton Sellers.

*Why* did he feel this way?

It wasn't as if he were attracted to Ashton. Walker could never want a man like that—all feminine and glamorous, all gut-churningly beautiful. No. Walker liked women who were stereotypically feminine, and men who were, well, stereotypically, *masculine*. Thickly muscled. Hairy in the right places. Button-ups during the week, and Polo shirts and golf shorts on the weekends. A beer drinker. A golfer.

Always a golfer.

Walker winced. His last boyfriend had been a traveling golf pro. Sebastian had spent most of their short relationship on tour. He'd never been around when Walker wanted him, much less needed him. He'd been only so-so in bed. But he'd ticked most of Walker's boxes of someone worthy of interest, and they'd had a good run. Until it was over. That was always the way with the men Walker dated.

Not much work but not much reward either.

The point was, Walker had a well-established type and Ashton Sellers was *not it*. So why did everything about Ashton make him anxious? He brought back awkward memories of high school and Walker's first, itching awareness of just how much he'd liked Justin Gregg's sweaty body in his skimpy track uniform. He'd despaired to realize he liked it even more than he'd liked Layla Bautista's smooth, sweet legs stretching out endlessly from her cheerleading getup.

Those had been confusing, awkward years of surprise boners and fear. Just before graduating, he'd finally admitted to himself and his family that he was bisexual. That'd gone about as well as expected: his mom and sister were fine with it, but his dad had chafed under his queerness for a long time. Eventually, his father had accepted Walker, telling him, *"At least you don't like pansies, son. If you have to fuck a man, at least fuck real ones."*

Which, Walker knew logically, was seriously messed up. Ashton and men like him were just as much "real men" as the guys his dad approved of, yet those words lived on in the back of Walker's mind. Even if he did find Ashton attractive (and he didn't), how would being with him—or someone like him—look to his father? Not that Walker cared what his father thought of the men he dated.

And not that Ashton would ever want to be with Walker. He was so gorgeous. There had to be men lined up around the block to try their luck with him.

Whoa. What was he even *thinking* about? His mind was out of control today.

Determined to shake free of all that shivery weirdness, Walker consulted his upcoming schedule for the month.

The next few weeks were going to be hectic as hell, what with the office Christmas party, Christmas itself, and then his sister's wedding coming up the following weekend. And then there would be New Year's Eve to navigate.

Maybe he'd stay in and watch the Times Square ball drop on the TV, safe in the comfort of his living room this year. His former golfing buddies wouldn't miss him much. They'd all have their wives along at the country club party. If he joined them, his friends there would try to set him up with their sister's cousin's best friend, or their coworker's hairdresser's brother. Others would try to tempt him into a game of cards or get him to commit to a round of golf...

Yeah. It would be better to have a quiet night at home. Less tempting in a lot of ways.

Walker glanced at the list of wedding-related activities coming up. Why Evelyn had decided to go and get married in December, he didn't know. But at least most of his work for SRS's clients was wrapped up for the season. They were already designing Valentine's Day pushes and spring marketing plans, but he had a few weeks to breathe before everything at work escalated to full steam ahead again.

Or he *should* have had. If it weren't for his sister's wedding, and the office Christmas party, and all the rest. Oh, and he couldn't forget Secret Fucking Santa.

Dammit.

SOMETIMES ASHTON HATED being an adult.

For one thing, it came with a ton of responsibility. Like bills and cleaning and grocery shopping. Like having honest-to-heaven employees who worked for him because he was somehow the third partner in an up-and-coming advertising firm. Like having to pretend to be excited for Secret Santa in front of said employees when he'd pulled the name of the one man he'd least wanted to get. The one man impervious to Ashton's charms in every way.

Ashton leaned back against the closed door to his office and pondered.

What was he supposed to buy *Walker Ronson* for less than $25 dollars?

Frowns were free, right? Ashton could put one of those on Walker's face without even trying. All he had to do was show up at work for Walker's face to contort miserably before he darted off to hide in his office. Gift achieved. You're welcome.

Yeah. He'd just have to suck it up. Be a grown-up about it. Which *sucked*. Kids just didn't know how great they had it. Childhood was easy street. Ashton huffed. Hashtag not-all-kids. Hashtag not-his-childhood.

A memory came to him unbidden: Cassie—the nice, chubby social worker with serious eyes who'd stood over him calmly as he'd sobbed and packed all of his meager belongings into a big, black, plastic trash bag. She'd clucked soothingly at him as he'd climbed into her shiny hatchback before taking him by McDonalds to grab a bite to eat. As soon as he'd finished the last French fry, she'd driven him to his grandmother's house over in South Knoxville to live for good.

Another betrayal. Though Cassie hadn't known it of course.

*"You ain't Ashton Sellers no more. You're Ashton Hudson."*

Ashton took up the name plaque at the end of his desk. He *was* Ashton Sellers. He owned the last name his mother had put on his birth certificate, the name of his father. He'd hated having that piece of his identity stolen away and a lie shoved into its place. It'd almost broken him. But he'd remedied *that* situation as soon as he'd turned eighteen.

Pen to paper. Money in hand. Boom.

He was Ashton Sellers. He was safe and he was grown.

With a shaking hand, he sipped his coffee. Maybe caffeine wasn't a good idea now but tasting something was the last step in breaking himself out of the early stages of a panic attack. He found himself fully present again as the bittersweet, nutty flavor rushed over his tongue.

Yeah, okay. Given what he recalled of his own childhood? Never mind. Kids had it rough. He never wanted a repeat of that experience. By comparison, Ashton loved, loved, *loved* being an adult. Even when it was hard. Even when it flat-out sucked. As an adult, no one scolded him for smiling or lisping or laughing or being himself.

Yeah, okay. Being an adult was pretty great like that.

The only time being a grown-up *really* sucked was when he had to admit to himself that even adults don't always get what they want. And what Ashton wanted right now was to have never drawn Walker Ronson's name for Secret Santa, and since *that* was obviously impossible, he wanted to make Walker Ronson smile at him. Genuinely. Just once.

Bah.

It wasn't fair. Walker was guaranteed to hate whatever Ashton got him. If he'd drawn the name of one of the girls in design, he'd have bought them an Urban Decay makeup palette, gone a bit over budget, and been greeted with squeals of joy. Now he'd be greeted with a glare no matter what he bought.

A golf shirt maybe? Polo brand? In a boring color? Like navy blue?

Usually Ashton loved Secret Santa. He'd never been allowed to play Santa *anything* growing up—since Santa Claus wasn't Jesus and presents were demonic, or something. He hadn't listened much, because even as an abused and neglected kid he'd been determined not to let his grandmother crush *all* his joy. So it stung extra badly to know he wasn't going to satisfy his Secret Santa recipient this year. After all, half the fun was in the giving.

At least *he'd* still receive a gift from someone. And maybe it would even be a good one!

Ashton closed his eyes and crossed his fingers, making a wish (he didn't do prayers anymore) that Ruby, Casey's assistant, had drawn his name, because she knew he was dying for new Fenty lip gloss. A single vial was just under the maximum budget, so it could work. And Ruby was a good egg. He could count on her.

Wrapping up his angst and wishing, Ashton crossed to lift the blinds in his office to allow the flat, winter light to spill in over the smooth wooden floor of his rather empty space. He peered out at the view of Gay Street bustling with cars and a few pedestrians and took a deep, cleansing breath.

It was two weeks before Christmas. He would buy a tree to decorate on Friday after work and splurge on some shiny, new ornaments for it after he got his next paycheck. And he'd play Christmas music while he worked today! Yes! The sound of jingle bells alongside chorusing, angelic voices were just what he needed to lift his spirits.

So what if he'd drawn a dud for Secret Santa? So what if he'd tripped into dark memories again for a bit? It'd be fine. He was *always* fine. Ashton was determined. It was still going to be a good day.

Sitting back down in the fancy roller chair he'd bought himself just before his not-insubstantial, but now entirely spent hunk of savings had run out, he scooted up to the desk he'd approximated out of a small table. He'd found it by a dumpster behind an apartment building near the Old City. It was a little beat up, but it had that one, all-important advantage over any other desk: it was free!

Back when they'd started SRS, money had been tight, so Ashton, Casey, and Walker had agreed to buy their own personal office furniture. That way they could spend company funds on employee salaries and making the common areas their clients *would* see as nice as possible. No one important came to Ashton's private office. He met with clients in the SRS conference room or at a client's place of business. So who would he need to impress with a big fancy desk? His assistant? He gave Damien a paycheck. As far as Ashton was concerned, he should be plenty impressed with that.

Plus, bonus points: the table-desk allowed him to get his chair at the right height for his knees not to bang, something he'd always struggled with. Heck, he might never replace it.

Waking up his computer, Ashton opened Spotify and cued up some Christmas joy. A little Mariah, a little Jackson 5, a little Nat King Cole, and a lotta Ella. Perfection! His spirits rose with the sweetness of the Christmas spirit as he clicked on his email icon.

"Crap."

There, one right after the other, were two messages that he really, really could have done without.

*Justin's account at Oaks Rehab is overdue.*

And:

*When you repent, you'll be welcome home for Christmas again.*

Ashton leaned back in his chair and shook out his tingling fingertips. Holiday messages from his family. Great. Cool. Love it.

After closing his eyes and breathing in and out on slow counts of five, Ashton swung his chair around to a small filing cabinet tucked behind his table-desk. From the mostly empty top drawer, he removed an engraved pocket mirror and his second favorite lip color (Zip by Glossier), and applied it carefully. This was fine. He was okay. There was nothing to worry about. He was safe. He was grown. It was *all fine.*

Calmer, he capped the lip color and ran his fingers through his hair. He checked out his reflection. Beautiful as always—though little good that had done him over the years. He cleaned a little pink from his front teeth and practiced a smile. Ella crooned from his computer speakers. Festive, festive, festive. He crinkled the edges of his eyes to make the smile appear more genuine.

There. Back to happy.

Just as he returned the mirror and lip color to the filing cabinet drawer, his phone binged with an incoming message. One glance at the text from his building's superintendent was enough for his recently established and far too fragile bubble of sanguinity to pop. He grabbed a tissue from the Kleenex box at the edge of his table-desk and furiously scrubbed off the newly applied lip color.

"Fuck."

Quickly, Ashton squeezed his eyes shut and fought the urge to plead for forgiveness. He was an adult. He could curse if he wanted. It just so happened that he didn't usually want to. But first emails from his family and now this? Bed bugs and fumigation now? Now? At *Christmas?*

"Fuck, fuck, *fuck.*"

Ashton tugged at his hair. Why didn't he have a sugar daddy? Didn't he deserve one? After all he'd been through in his life? Why wasn't there some man out there who thought he was adorable? Who thought he had a smile like sunlight on water? Who wanted to take him in his arms and protect him forever from all this nonsense? A man—one single, solitary man—who thought he'd be worth it?

Ugh. It was unfair. All he'd wanted from his morning was to listen to Mariah Carey's "All I Want for Christmas Is You" and Ella's "Jingle Bells" and feel the Christmas spirit in his soul. All he'd wanted was the joy of getting to plan a *great* Secret Santa gift for a happy, smiling recipient. All he'd wanted was to forget about his childhood forever! That was all he'd wanted for the whole damn day, but no! Noooo!

Desperate for a distraction—good or bad, he didn't care—Ashton opened up Facebook, a near-giddy resentment rising in him.

*Look at all these happy people with all their happy lives on display. Houses decked out for Christmas. Toy elf shenanigans designed to make cute kids scream with joy. Great, good, love it,* he snarled internally.

Ashton scrolled his timeline, staring at all the smiling families of his friends, co-workers, and clients. Gawky teenagers holding awards or singing at Christmas recitals with their dozen pimply-but-beautiful peers. Aging moms looking tired but proud and dads looking like they knew what it was to be a grown man.

Like they never doubted their choices or wondered where they were going with their lives or felt lonely and lost. Or got horrible emails from their family. Or had bed bugs in their apartment building.

Ashton opened his own profile.

No happy kids. No husband. Just a lot of carefully posed shots of him looking amazing: yoga poses by waterfalls, a wide grin at the Orange & White game with a client last summer, and several of him, Casey, and Walker in suits, shaking hands and looking proud in front of the doors to their office space.

Ashton Sellers was packaged and branded.

All of it real, but none of it *really* real. The only pictures that were more than three years old were a handful where he'd been tagged by old friends. He usually untagged those as quickly as possible, horrified by the memories they evoked. That beautiful-but-miserable kid was his past. Not his present. *Never* his future.

Ashton clucked his tongue, thinking. It'd been a while since he'd posted anything to Facebook that really stood out. He focused so much of his creative energy on his clients these days, and so rarely took any time to waste it on himself. His Facebook statuses had devolved into business announcements and observations about the weather. Boring stuff.

What was he always saying to his clients? Generate clicks, likes, *engagement*—that's the ticket! Create positive feelings by being fun and fresh, post things that may even seem risky or dangerous. Make your clients remember you later! That's more than half the battle. They'll come to associate you with that feeling of fresh surprise and want that again and again. They'll ask you to bring that feeling to their business or product. Because they won't see it for what it is: *marketing*.

What was it RuPaul had said? We're all born naked and the rest was drag? Even Facebook posts were drag.

Ashton cleared his throat, gazed out the window at the gray, overcast sky over Gay Street, and called up the campiest, most brilliant part of himself. He pushed aside any lingering darkness and focused on how it felt to smile, to laugh, and how to gift that to others even at his own expense.

He didn't know what he was going to do about the bed bugs, or about Justin's account at Oaks Rehab, or if he'd ever get past his grandmother being a heinous, abusive bitch. But he did know how to move on with his day. And it didn't even take Christmas magic. All it took was him. Just him.

He cued up Mariah and listened to the whole song twice. "Yes, yes, okay, then…all I want for Christmas is youuuuu. Let's do this." Ashton cracked his fingers and wrote a pitch-perfect post.

By the time he hit enter, he was grinning.

# Chapter Two

"S ORRY TO INTERRUPT," Nicole said, poking her head into Walker's office with a small smile. "But, uh, have you seen Ashton's Facebook post?"

"No?" Walker had a Facebook account, of course. It was necessary for business purposes, but he rarely used it. He preferred making face-to-face connections. Previously, he'd done so on the golf course and at the country club. This past year... Well, he'd been lucky enough to work solely from referrals. It was the best kind of feeling to know his clients found him helpful enough to send their friends and clients to him. So he'd always left the social media side of things up to Casey and Ashton. They were both good at it in completely different ways. "Why? What did he say?"

"It's just... Typical Ashton, you know," Nicole said with a fond grimace as she entered and closed the door behind her. Wearing a black sheath dress and sensible heels, she tucked her near-black hair behind her ears before crossing her exposed arms over her chest. She leaned back against the closed door, her expression thoughtful. "But maybe this time it's a little too much?"

"Ashton? Going too far? Who'd have thunk?" Walker smirked. He'd told Casey before they'd created SRS that Ashton was as much of a branding liability as an asset, but Casey had just given him a penetrating look implying he knew far too well what Walker's hang-ups were about Ashton—and Walker had decided not to say anything additionally incriminating.

Besides, after Walker's father refused to back their enterprise in a hissy fit about Walker leaving *his* company, they'd needed the money—and Ashton'd had it. Emphasis on the word *had*, because Ashton certainly didn't have any money now. He'd apparently blown all of his savings to buy into their baby firm. Technically, Walker should have asked to see the financial statement of anyone he was partnering with, but then he'd have had to pony up his own. He wasn't sure he wanted Ashton or anyone else to know just how much he didn't have. Especially given how much he *should* have had.

Amazing what a few months of reckless gambling could do to a guy's trust fund.

"Here, just have a look," Nicole said, passing Walker her phone. "I mean, I get that Ashton's a jokester, and I understand he's out and proud. That's fine. That's what we're all about. Refreshing honesty, etc. But some things *do* reflect back on our company, and I don't know about this post. It's likely to upset some clients, don't you think?"

Walker decided to reserve comment until he'd read it for himself. He skimmed it once and then, blinking away his disbelief, he read it more closely. Why he was surprised, he didn't even know. Everything about the long-winded post was one hundred percent pure Ashton.

*Ho ho! Merry Christmas! Ashton here! As you know, I blew up my homophobic fam three years ago by bringing a muscled, shirtless, Grindr hookup as my date to the family Christmas party. Getting disowned was never so easy! A+ experience! Do recommend!*

*This year, in an effort to spread the holiday joy, I'm making a generous offer. For the low price of a place to stay for three days while they fumigate my entire apartment building, I'll help you turn your seasonal family gathering into a shitshow of epic proportions! If you've got homophobic parents, asshole aunts, ugly uncles, and aggressively insensitive cousins, you too can experience the joy of blowing up their holiday!*

*Hire me as your fake boyfriend and your nosy Aunt Karen won't ask you when you're getting married or if you're ever gonna give your mom some grandkids. She'll be too busy wondering about why you're dating a gay man (if you're a woman), or when you suddenly turned queer (if you're a man). You'll be the talk of the family for months to come!*

*With two years of university theater classes under my belt, I can pretend to love anyone. That's right! Even you. And I can play it however is most likely to cause your family to implode/explode/breakdown. I can do serious and committed, or casual and slutty. I come in two modes: butch and hyper-masc, or glorious femme-queen covered in glitter. Okay, that was a lie. I only come in femme-queen mode. Just call me Mr. Jingle Bells! And for the right price (I honestly need a place to stay for three nights only! I swear!), I'll be at your service!*

*PM for more info!*

*(No, but seriously, help! The hotels near my office are TOO EXPENSIVE! Who said Knoxville could grow up all fancy like this? What marketing whiz branded these places as super posh? Oh, that was me. Anyway, please. Three nights. Save my wallet.)*

Beneath the post, no one seemed to be taking his offer seriously, which was probably the point. Ashton was the king of what Walker was pretty sure the kids called "shitposting," which seemed to consist of making some kind of a useless point in the most absurd and comedic way possible? He wasn't sure that was the definition, but he was *sure* this was a shitpost.

Ashton's friends passed jibes back and forth in the comments with most of them expressing regret that they couldn't offer him a place to stay for various reasons.

"I mean, it makes it sound like he has no money?" Nicole said, leaning her hip against Walker's desk, her brow wrinkled. "Which doesn't reflect well on our company's success or potential longevity. At least in our clients' eyes. Or am I overthinking it?"

Walker read the post again, a small smile fighting its way onto his lips. From a business perspective, it wasn't really funny. But from a personal one, it was hilarious. Only Ashton would even think to post something like this instead of just asking his friends for a place to stay. His post already had over sixty reactions and twenty responses.

This was the sort of absurdity that Casey said made Ashton special—the kind of unexpected behavior that would draw attention to their firm. But was this really the attention they wanted? The replies were getting more and more ludicrous by the second. Someone had only just now commented asking if Ashton charged extra for platonic blow jobs in his Fake Boyfriend package.

"Thanks for bringing this to my attention," Walker said, rising from his desk. "I'll take care of it, Nicole."

She took her phone back. "I'm not trying to cause trouble. I just want what's best for our firm."

"I know you do." Walker gestured toward the door to his small office, and when Nicole left, he texted Casey.

*You available? Need to talk. Now.*

Casey appeared in the doorway a moment later, wearing jeans and a button-up shirt with little ducks printed on it. When Walker had first met him, he wore only solid color button-ups and khakis. He wasn't sure who'd influenced Casey's change in style, but somehow he doubted it was his husband, Joel, because that guy wore T-shirts, jeans, and flannels like he'd just escaped from the slacker nineties. Maybe it was Ashton.

"S'up?" Casey asked, shutting the door behind him. He sat in the leather chair across from Walker's desk and leaned forward, elbows on his knees and his expression all worry. "You okay?"

"Have you seen Ashton's most recent Facebook post?"

Casey's lips quirked. "No?"

Pulling his own phone from his pocket, Casey tapped at the screen. Walker knew when his shoulders started moving with suppressed laughter that he'd found the post. "Holy shit, he's such a brat."

"I know he's young—"

"Not that young."

"Right, but this was one of my concerns when we added him as a partner. You can see how this is problematic, can't you?"

Casey shrugged, his eyes going distant as he stared at the wall just over Walker's head. Walker was familiar with this expression. It meant Casey was running out potential scenarios in his mind and weighing each of them. "It's not entirely off brand."

Walker frowned.

"Look, we've talked about this," Casey said. "You're used to working in a conservative field with your dad's petroleum firm, having to worry about impressing old men in suits with deep pockets. But that's not what we're doing with SRS. That was never the plan."

"We could use some accounts with deep pockets. We can't keep living on chicken feed."

"That's just scarcity mentality talking. There are plenty of accounts out there, people looking for a fresh, salty take to catch the eyes and pockets of the disillusioned Millennials and Gen Zs. That's where Ashton's entire…*everything*…comes in. He's one of them."

"So are we."

Casey shrugged, chuckling softly. "Technically, in terms of age, yeah, but c'mon, you know he's got his finger on the pulse, while we're still trying to figure it out."

Walker groaned and slumped back into his chair. "What if he runs off potential clients? This post is everything we're told to keep quiet about in the South: queerness, sex, money, religion."

"And we're not catering to those folks, remember? We agreed. No homophobes for clients. All three of us are gay!"

"I'm bi."

"Right, of course. Sorry. Didn't mean to erase you." Casey stuck out his tongue playfully. "But even so, why would we want to pretend we aren't queer? And the internet has cracked open the concept of privacy for Millennials and Gen Z. They post their gender identity and sexual preferences at the top of their Twitter feeds! Sex is on full display now."

"I don't know. This post feels reckless."

"To you. Because of your background. But Ashton is smart. He doesn't do anything without thinking it through. Even this. Look," Casey said, passing his phone over to Walker. "His post has more activity on it than you or I have ever generated with anything on our profiles or SRS's main Facebook page."

"But is it *good* activity?"

Casey shrugged. "He's got four of our biggest clients in the comments suggesting that he create a marketing strategy for his new Fake Boyfriend side business, and Aimee from design just posted a mockup ad. You can see that everyone's having fun with it. People like fun, Walker. Laughter. Joy. It engenders good will for us."

Walker scrubbed a hand over his face. He could practically hear his father's voice in his ear telling him what a terrible mistake he'd made throwing his lot in with the likes of Casey and Ashton instead of staying tied to his cushy oil firm job.

"He admits he can't afford to pay for a hotel. How is that going to look to clients? When one of the three main partners of our firm can't cough up the money for three nights in a goddamn hotel?"

"It's gonna look like we're a fledgling business reinvesting everything we make to grow our firm."

"But that's bullshit! Why *can't* he pay for a hotel? Ashton's got some fantastic accounts, and I know the size of his checks. Where's all that money going anyway?"

Casey shrugged. "Isn't that his business?"

Walker blinked. "He's our partner. What he does reflects on us. It could sink us if he's doing something illegal. What if he's doing drugs? That might explain some things about him. Or...or paying for prostitutes, or..."

"Gambling?" Casey threw in. Which was a low blow.

Walker reared back. He should never have told Casey about his past mistakes and why he'd walked away from golfing and the country club.

Not if he was going to use it against him like this.

Casey's gaze went soft and contrite. "Sorry. That was an asshole thing to say." His brow crinkled gently. "But, hey, what if it's none of those things? What if he's aggressively paying down his student loans? Or what if he gives his money to some amazing charity that owns his heart? You won't know unless you ask."

Walker narrowed his eyes. "*You* know."

Casey shrugged again. "Maybe I do. But you need to make more of an effort with Ashton." His lips lifted in a small smirk. "You know what *would* look bad for our firm? If no one here offers the man a place to stay for three nights while his place is fumigated." He lifted a brow pointedly.

"You've got an extra room." Casey and his husband Joel had completed the work on their cabin by the lake a few weeks before their wedding the year before. Walker had been over several times and even spent the night once in their guest room when he'd had too much to drink to safely drive home. "*You* offer."

"No, you offer."

"Why?"

"Because he's our business partner, and you've made next to no effort with him." The stare that followed that statement had all kinds of weight, and Walker wasn't sure how much meaning to assign it. Casey knew him well enough to guess what hang-ups Walker suffered over Ashton, but he hoped Casey wouldn't expect him to admit them out loud.

"Fine."

"Do it now."

Walker glared but picked up his cell phone to find the last text thread he'd started with Ashton. Christ, it'd been over a month ago and brief as hell, just a quick exchange about an ad placement for one of their rare shared clients. "Okay. I'll text him."

"No, do it on Facebook."

"Why?"

"This is a publicity stunt. So be public."

Walker sucked on his teeth. If he commented, then everyone would know he'd seen the post. Plausible deniability would be out the window if his father or anyone else confronted him about the inappropriateness of his business associates. "Fine."

He thumbed in a comment offering his spare room up for Ashton's use and hit return before he could change his mind. "Happy?"

Casey grinned. "I was always happy. You're the one who was stressed." Then he stood up and walked out whistling "Joy to the World."

Bah. What did Casey have to feel so smug about? He acted as if he were Santa Claus and had the perfect gift for Walker in his bag: three nights hosting Ashton Sellers in his home. Ugh.

Talk about a nightmare before Christmas.

ASHTON STARED AT his computer screen.

Had he really thought his day couldn't get worse?

Oh.

Oh *no*.

Had Walker really offered for him to stay with him during the fumigation period? Walker *Ronson*? Someone must have put him up to it. Casey. Probably Casey. And just when Ashton had started to forget his rough morning and really dive into the fun generated by his shitpost, too.

He read Walker's comment again.

*You can stay with me while they fumigate. No need to go to extremes. No fake boyfriend needed.*

"Great. Love it." Ashton groaned and jumped when his phone buzzed. At least this time it was an appointment alarm and not another notification with unwanted news. He checked his face in the small mirror again, added a little moisturizer, some lip balm, and curled his eyelashes. Then he gathered his keys and wallet and waltzed out of his office, calling to Damien, "Off to the barber! You know how to find me!"

Gay Street was glistening with wet, drizzly rain and colorful with Christmas decorations. Red ribbons festooned the streetlamps, the shops had gone all out for their Christmas window displays, and the sounds of the season could be heard through the various open doors. The weather was ugly, but the temperature was warm enough that he didn't need a coat. The sprinkle of rain hadn't been worth an umbrella either. He was used to being lightly misted from above. Typical Tennessee December.

He nodded at familiar faces and strangers alike on the street and smiled at Hank, a homeless man who was huddled in his usual crevice between buildings, looking mild and distant as the misty rain slipped down his face and neck. Ashton pulled his wallet out and added a few dollars to the small pile inside Hank's upside-down ballcap.

"Merry Christmas, Hank," Ashton offered, and that got his attention.

The man looked up, a confused smile on his face, and he whispered, "Happy Holidays."

Ashton continued down two more blocks, and then cut off toward Yeppuda Salon. When he entered the poshly decorated, sweet warmth of the salon, he shook off the wet from his coat onto the rug in the entryway while looking around for his stepsister Angel. She'd been hired on as an assistant at Yeppuda while attending cosmetology school and typically worked on weekdays after noon. After scanning the room, full of chattering women and men, and loud with hair dryers and the sound of snipping scissors, Ashton found her. She stood by some shelves of product helping a woman in yoga pants and a raincoat choose a styling product. Which reminded him, he needed to replenish his styling wax soon.

"Hey, babe." Angel grinned and stepped toward him as she finished with the client. "I meant to text you. Becca said she could fit you in a little later today, if you'd rather see her instead of Kenzie."

"No, it's fine. Kenzie did good work last time."

Ashton followed Angel to Kenzie's empty chair where Angel fitted him with a cape to keep the hair from falling onto his clothing.

"She'll be right out to get started." Angel leaned back against Kenzie's station and briefly studied him. Her dyed black hair made her eyes stand out sharply against her pale skin. "You doing okay? My mom said Bill's upset because you guys are on the outs again."

Ashton winced. It wasn't like he hated his dad or anything. Bill just wanted things from Ashton, now that they'd found each other again, that he could never give. Like, for example, blanket forgiveness for both himself and Ashton's mom. "Bill doesn't like how I deal with things."

"What things?"

Thinking back to his last conversation with his dad, the one that had ended with Ashton yelling and storming out. "My mom." He shrugged. "It's not his business how I handle her."

"Handle her? More like how you don't handle her, right?"

He tightened his jaw and met her gaze steadily.

"I know. I know. Believe me, I get it." Angel reached out and took a pink sharpie off Kenzie's station and uncapped it. She sniffed it before holding it out for Ashton to smell too. He pulled his head away with a frown. Angel shrugged, and then drew a pink heart on the back of her hand as she said, "When your dad married my mom, I was so damaged by what my own dad had done to us that I had a hard time trusting Bill at first. But eventually I realized Bill's a really good guy."

"I know." Or he was *now* anyway, about twenty years too late for it to mean anything good for Ashton's life. He certainly hadn't been a good guy when it'd truly mattered.

"And, well, maybe you don't want to hear this," Angel went on, embellishing the heart on her hand as she talked. "But she's doing better these days, too. *Your* mom, I mean."

"Mn."

"*My* mom says they're considering letting her move in with them until she can get on her feet. But for now she's still living at the women's shelter."

Ashton rolled his eyes. "Generous of Miranda."

"She says Jamie Rae's part of the family."

Ashton bristled. "She's not."

"She's your mother, though. And you're Bill's son."

"No," he said coldly. "She was never my mother in any meaningful way."

Angel shrugged.

"Mark my words: Miranda letting my mom move in with them is and will always be a bad idea."

Angel shifted uncomfortably. "Maybe. But Jamie Rae says she just needs a place to recover."

"Right. That's what she always says. She lies."

"You're still angry."

Ashton huffed. Of *course* he was still angry and he had every right to be.

Angel touched his shoulder. "She's doing better, though, for real."

He gritted his teeth. How many times had he heard that over the years?

"I'm sorry. I know she's a tough topic for you." Angel leaned in and hugged him. He let her, though his hackles were still up. Too many bad memories were seeping into his day. And he'd wanted it to be a good one! Dang it! "She's hurt you too much."

Ashton nodded, his throat going tight.

Angel pulled back and pondered him a moment. "Do you want me to draw a heart on your hand, too?"

He accepted the change in topic as an apology and put his hand in hers. She drew a pink heart with sharp lines radiating out from it just beneath his ring finger's middle knuckle. It almost looked like a child's idea of a ring. The silence between them was comfortable. No matter what Angel said, he knew she got it. Her biological father hadn't been around in years, but he'd been a real asshole and she understood the language of the betrayed child too well.

"Besides, there's Justin," Ashton said as she perfected the starburst heart. "Guess I used up all of my forgiveness on him. My bucket's empty. I'd need a rainstorm of peace and grace to fill it up again, and I don't know when that'll ever come. I'm tired of people lying to me and breaking my heart."

"I get it," Angel agreed, adding a pink star to his other knuckle even though he hadn't asked or requested one. Whatever. Sharpie only lasted a few days, and he didn't have client appointments for the rest of the week. Besides, pink stars and hearts were on brand for him.

Kenzie arrived. She sported punk-short hair and wore a red sweater with a sweetheart neckline, putting tons of bosom on display. Angel departed after pressing a kiss to his cheek.

"Look at these curls," Kenzie said cheerfully. Her fingers shifting through his hair were soothing, and she shot him a grin in the mirror. She grabbed a spray bottle and wet his hair. "Same cut as before?"

"Yes, please."

"Easy-peasy then." She reached for her scissors. "Cute Facebook post earlier. Saw you got a taker."

"Yeah. My business partner."

She caught his eye in the mirror, clearly hearing something in his tone though he didn't quite know what. "Oooh. Office romance?"

"Ha!" Ashton closed his eyes, trying not to laugh too hard since she already had scissors snipping through his hair. "No. It's not like that."

"Ah." She let off a small sigh. "Too bad. I'm curious—would you have really done it? Played a fake boyfriend in exchange for a place to stay? You know, if someone had wanted that?"

"Sure. It'd be fun. Why? You in need of one?" He waggled his brows. "Wanna blow up a family holiday? Or need a date for New Year's Eve?"

Kenzie chuckled. "I'll keep you in mind but I'm good."

"Anytime. But, yeah, I knew no one would really ask me. I just thought it was funny."

"It was." Kenzie caught his eyes again before pulling some finger-lengths of hair to compare length and curl direction before cutting. "So, what's with your vibe about this guy who offered? He hot or something?"

Walker? *Hot?*

Ashton furrowed his brow. He'd never considered it. Walker was so far from his usual type—always wearing boring Polo shirts and, worse, khakis, and never looking at Ashton like he was made of magic. Which was a new rule for any guy Ashton found attractive. Too many men Ashton had dated or hooked up with had failed to look at him like he was special. After some deep exploration of his heart during those too-few therapy sessions his insurance had allowed for, that was his new litmus test for a man's appeal. Thus, he'd never objectively considered Walker's physical merits.

"He's got nice arms." Lots of golfing, Ashton guessed. "He's not especially thin, which is fine. Good for cuddling. He's blond, which isn't something I usually go for. I prefer brunets." He clucked his tongue. "But it's a nice color blond, and his eyes are good. Grayish-blue, but not cold." And Walker had, overall, a nice shape: broad shoulders and narrower hips. Now that Ashton was considering it objectively, Walker wasn't half bad.

"Mm-hmm," Kenzie said, brows furrowed as she worked. "Sounds like he's pretty average. Not bad, but not great."

"Yeah. That's the perfect way to put it." Ashton sniffed. "He's a country clubber. Old money. You know the type."

"Do I ever."

"He doesn't suck as a human, though. I'm not saying that. He just has really different priorities from me."

"Totally."

Ashton's hair was already shaping up nicely. He'd look good for his happy holidays spent *all alone.* Awesome. He loved that. He'd just have to make sure to spend plenty of time admiring himself in the mirror. Maybe do some intensive self-care: face masks, mani-pedis. Buy small, inexpensive presents for himself to put under the tree and unwrap. After three years, he was used to being alone on Christmas now.

"Sometimes the average-looking ones are the best in bed," Kenzie said, winking at him in the mirror.

"Ack! No!" Ashton exclaimed. "We're friends. I don't think of him like that."

He didn't think of Walker as a friend, either, exactly, but that was too awkward to explain. What was he going to say? *"My business partner doesn't seem to want anything to do with me?"* Well, he *could* say that. Maybe Kenzie could help him understand it.

It was just so weird.

It couldn't be homophobia—Walker was queer himself—but something about Ashton clearly made Walker want to stay at arm's length. Probably that Ashton wasn't masc enough or wealthy enough or country club material enough. Or maybe Walker thought Ashton was immature? He didn't know for sure. He supposed he didn't want to. He just wanted to get past it somehow.

Maybe spending three days at Walker's place would be enough for them to get on better footing at least. He'd like for them to be friends eventually. Or at least to hold each other in mutual esteem. That was more important than friendship when it came to business.

"So what are they gonna do about the bed bugs?" Kenzie asked, wrinkling her nose.

Ashton repeated all that he'd learned from the internet, as well as the instructions he'd been given by his building's super. "So, after this appointment, I have to go home and move all the furniture in the bedroom and living room away from the walls, take off the light-switch and plug covers, and put *everything* fabric through the hottest setting on the dryer and then seal it all up in plastic bags—pillows, clothes, everything."

"Oh, hell."

"Yeah. It's gonna be a long night. Everyone in the building will be vying for three dryers."

Kenzie clucked her tongue in sympathy.

"It's not even my apartment that has them—the bugs, I mean. But they found evidence in enough apartments in the building that they want to be prudent and treat every unit."

Finally, he fell quiet, stressing over the amount of work he'd be facing at home just to prepare his apartment for the bed bug treatment. He wished he could just skip out on the responsibility and go to a Christmas movie alone instead. Eat handfuls of buttered popcorn. Lose hours to a story crafted for escapism and entertainment. Avoid it all.

"Fairytale of New York" broke the usual monotony of traditional Christmas music that had been jingling through the speakers of the salon. Oh heck. His stomach flipped. Ashton closed his eyes, wincing against it.

*His mother was lying on the ratty sofa across from him. The needle sat on the coffee table with the spoon, the powder, and the fir-scented candle used to heat it… His mother met his gaze. Her eyes were red and hollow, and he wanted to scream, to kick her teeth in, to beg her to just—*

"Stop!"

"Don't move, babe," Kenzie said when Ashton jerked in the chair. She lifted her scissors away from his head.

"Sorry!" Ashton blurted. The cold sweat in the small of his back felt gross. "I just… I don't know. Sorry."

"It's okay. Let me grab some water for you." Kenzie sounded concerned, and a glance in the mirror told Ashton why. He'd gone white as a sheet with a little green around his mouth. "Feeling all right?" she asked as she passed a plastic cup with chilled water into his hot hands. "Did you get too hot under here?" She lifted the bottom of the cape around his shoulders and fanned air beneath.

"No. I'm okay," he said, taking a sip. "I just..." He waved his free hand around, trying to encompass something indescribable and way too personal to share anyway. "I'm all right. Sorry. Did I mess up the cut?"

"Almost. But I can fix it." She smiled, releasing the cape and letting it settle again. "Your curls are forgiving. Luckily."

The song droned on endlessly it seemed, and he'd never been more relieved to hear Dolly Parton's sweet soprano break in with "Hard Candy Christmas."

The therapist Ashton had been seeing—back before Justin returned to his life and swallowed up all his extra income—had told him triggers were unpredictable. But it was important to remember everything was in the past now: his mom, the overdose, life with his grandmother, the abusive church. It was over. It was done. He didn't have to see or deal with any of them ever again.

*I'm grown. I'm safe.*

"You sure you don't need a fake boyfriend for something?" Ashton asked as Kenzie finished up his cut by blowing the tiny hairs from his cape with a hair dryer. "I'm happy to oblige. I'd even try to play it straight for you." He winked but knew he was too shaken for his playfulness to come across as sincere.

She laughed. "You're sweet. But I'm all good alone. See you in four or five weeks?"

"You bet." He kissed her cheek and pressed an extra-large tip into her hand even though he really couldn't afford it. "Merry Christmas."

"You too, Ashton."

Then he skirted past Angel with just a wave goodbye over his shoulder. She would absolutely notice something was wrong if she even took one look at his still-haunted face, and he didn't have it in him to explain or deflect. Rushing out into the street, he took deep gulps of cold air and headed toward his apartment to start the business of taking everything there apart.

While he'd been inside, the temperature had dipped enough that the drizzle from earlier had turned into fluffy flakes of snow. They drifted in front of him now like traces of memories he didn't want to chase.

# Chapter Three

O N THE FIRST day of fumigation, Ashton rode in Walker's car with three pieces of luggage full of his stuff. They were quiet all the way from their office to Walker's home in Sequoyah Hills. Ashton was quick to notice it wasn't the nicest house on the street by far, but it was still quite luxurious and located in the most prestigious, old money neighborhood in the city.

"Posh," Ashton said. "Love it."

"It belongs to my grandfather," Walker said as Ashton unbuckled his seat belt and leaned forward for a better look at the two-story, Tudor design home. The front garden looked like it had stepped out of a British children's book, a beautiful mix of ivy and winter colors. The grass was neatly mown, and everything looked well-tended. Ashton suspected Walker didn't do all that himself. "Um, I don't actually own it."

"Well, it's beautiful."

Walker grunted softly as they exited the car. There was no built-on garage—the house was that old—but there was a small carport that kept the snowy sleet from falling on their heads.

"I should warn you. The dogs will bark."

Dogs? Ashton hadn't thought of Walker as a pet owner. "Ah, cool! I love dogs!"

"Good. Because I have four."

"*Four?*" Ashton almost choked.

That went beyond being a dog lover and into "maybe this man will one day hoard puppies" territory. It also made Walker suddenly a hell of a lot more interesting.

Ashton searched his memory of Walker's desk and office, trying to think if he'd seen pictures of dogs or even a dog calendar, but came up with nothing. Now that he thought about it, he was pretty sure the only photos in Walker's office were of his sister, Evelyn, and his mother. None of his father.

"Yeah. Two poodles—they were my grandfather's actually, but he abandoned them along with the house when he moved to Florida—and two hound mixes. Evelyn says I should pay to have them trained by a professional so they're better behaved. You know, since I can't seem to manage it myself." He smiled, and something about the way his eyes crinkled at the edges caught Ashton's attention.

Was this the first genuine smile he'd ever gotten from Walker? Score. Too bad the smile was for his dogs and not for Ashton himself but close enough.

"Are you going to take her advice?"

"Nah. They're too cute."

"Too cute to train?" Ashton hoisted a big roller bag out of the trunk of Walker's BMW and watched Walker take the even larger duffle easily.

"Absolutely."

Ashton snorted softly, retrieving his backpack and hefting it over his shoulders.

Walker shrugged. "They're loud when anyone comes in but they're harmless. I promise."

Ashton wasn't afraid of dogs. *Justin*, however, had been deathly terrified of them, and that'd always made Ashton sad. Dogs were such wonderful creatures! To not even be able to enjoy seeing a cute one on the streets or love on one at a friend's house was just too horrible to contemplate.

Walker hadn't been exaggerating. The dogs went wild as soon as he opened the door, almost bowling Ashton over. The barking was so loud that, had Justin been there, Ashton was sure he'd have wet himself in fear. But the happy smiles on the dogs' faces made it clear this was just their way of greeting their human pack member and welcoming him home again.

"This is Bitsy," Walker said, pointing at a brown poodle, barking and twisting around in a frenzy near the back of the pack. "She's the oldest. My grandfather got her when I was thirteen so she's going to be twenty this year."

"Wow."

"Yeah, a real old lady. And that's Marble." He pointed to the other poodle. This one was black with light streaks creeping into her fur. "Grandpa got her when Bitsy was ten, thinking she wasn't long for this world. He didn't want Grandma to be sad, you see, so he got her a puppy in advance of Bitsy's death. Now Grandma is gone, but Bitsy and Marble remain."

The hounds were the more aggressive greeters and Ashton had his hands full trying to pet them while simultaneously warding off being licked and keeping his backpack from falling onto their heads. His roller bag was on the floor of the entryway being trod upon by their paws, and he was glad it wasn't leather like his backpack.

"Who's this with the eyebrows?" Ashton asked, scratching the floppy ear of a soulful-eyed brown and black beagle mix.

"Nina, and the other is Simone."

"Ah, you're a fan?"

Walker smiled. "Of course. Who isn't? Anyway, come on inside, they'll calm down."

The dogs quieted to a joyful trot as they headed through to the kitchen. A set of back stairs led up to the second story, and Walker took Ashton up them to the spare room right away. The hounds and Marble followed at their heels, but Bitsy stayed downstairs.

"Here you go," Walker said, throwing open the guest room door. "Make yourself at home. The bathroom is out in the hall. There's another room up here that my grandfather uses when he comes to town, and the last room down there is my 'office.' Though I don't really ever use it. It's mainly storage, actually. My bedroom's down on the first floor." Nina and Simone jumped up on the guest bed and Walker whistled them off. But no sooner had their paws hit the floor, than Marble hopped up and plopped against the pillows. "Sorry." Walker sighed.

"It's okay. She's cute. Thanks again for doing this," Ashton said, putting his bags on the bed next to Marble as Walker put the duffle he was carrying by the door.

"No problem."

"Evening meal?"

He pointed at Marble, then Nina and Simone. "Can't say the other word."

"Oh! Right. Dogs. Smart, cute things!" Ashton cleared his throat. "How about pizza?" He wiped his palms against his pants, wishing he understood why things between the two of them were always so strained. "On me? Since you're putting me up and all."

Walker consulted his phone for a moment and then nodded. "Okay. Sounds good. I'll get it, though. No big deal." He tapped open an app on his phone. "How do you like it?"

"However you like it is fine," Ashton said brightly. "I'm not picky."

Walker blinked a moment at that like he might scoff or protest the declaration, but instead he said, "Meat lovers okay?"

"Perfect."

He tapped a few more times before running a hand over his hair. "Well, uh, I'm going to go feed these monsters their dinner. And—"

Marble hopped from the bed, and all the dogs raced ahead down the hall to the front stairs, barking and yipping with excitement.

Ashton chuckled.

"Yeah, so you can just make yourself at home," Walker said, following them out the bedroom door. He paused in the hallway. "Oh, be sure to shut your door tightly at night if you don't want them piling in with you." The dogs raced back to him, trying to get him to follow them to the kitchen, making quite a ruckus. "Bitsy sleeps with me. I try to make the others sleep in their beds in the living room. But they'll take a cracked door as an invitation."

Ashton smiled softly at the word "try" in that sentence. He wondered how often Walker ended up with all four dogs in his bed. The way he looked at them, all fond and sweet, and the way his fingers strayed down to touch them even as they scampered demandingly at his side, spoke to a tender heart.

It was odd to think that he'd never considered Walker might have a gentle side to his personality. All he'd ever shown Ashton before now was the tense, frowning man he was at the office.

"They'll take advantage if you let them," Walker said over his shoulder as he headed down the stairs. "Like I said, make yourself comfortable. Closet's all yours."

"Got it," Ashton called weakly.

In the quiet silence, Ashton inventoried the room: queen-sized bed with a comfortable number of pillows, closet along the side of the wall by the hallway, and an antique chest of drawers topped with a big, gilded mirror. All of it was a little fancier than he'd imagined Walker might choose for himself, but he liked it personally. The broad windows looked out on the backyard, which was just as well kept as the front.

He carefully opened the closet and stared at the empty rods. He tried to imagine his clothes filling the space even for a few days, but he wasn't sure he felt welcome just yet. So he simply hung a few of his more precious pieces and sat on the bed, his leg jiggling and his fingers tapping against his knee.

He pulled out his phone and scrolled his Instagram timeline, replying inanely to everyone's various photos, before switching to Twitter for a while. Anything to delay going down to be awkward with Walker.

The doorbell rang. The dogs went wild. Walker's footsteps were discernible beneath his useless shouts for the dogs to calm down.

The pizza was here.

Ashton stood, checked out his reflection in the big mirror, and took a slow breath. It was just three days. He could do this. He'd lived with his grandmother for years and she'd *hated* him. Walker just seemed to find him mildly off-putting. So what? He could cope. He was grown and safe.

After a sufficient amount of time had passed to allow for the dogs to stop barking and for Ashton to calm himself completely, he headed down the front set of stairs Walker had taken earlier. This deposited him in a dim hallway that led out to the living room. The scent of meaty pizza filled the air, and his mouth watered. Spotting the entry to the kitchen and hearing the sounds of Walker setting the table, Ashton paused only to take a moment to look around the living room.

Leather sofas were covered in woven blankets, to protect them from dog nails no doubt. Dark, masculine furniture, outdated by today's standards, stood steady and firm around the room. It was definitely the house of a certain kind of person. Like the guest room, not what Ashton would have guessed for Walker's home. But then Walker had said this was his grandfather's place, hadn't he? That made sense. A lot of the furniture looked quite old, from the nineteen-twenties or even earlier. Antiques.

Ashton also hadn't expected Walker's house to be all done up for Christmas. If questioned in advance about it, he'd probably have said that Walker might have a wreath on the front door, and *maybe* a small table-sized tree.

He'd never expected to find the entire living room festooned with lights and gobs of piney-smelling greenery over the mantel, and a red, cinnamon-scented candle on the coffee table. There were poinsettias and a full-size, real tree decorated with old-fashioned ornaments and with a good number of glittery, wrapped presents beneath it. Unexpected indeed.

"Pizza's here," Walker said from the kitchen doorway with a tight, anxious smile.

"Great! I'm starved!" Ashton wasn't hungry actually, but eating his feelings was something he excelled at. So he was going to eat the pizza like it was the best he'd ever had, express his gratitude for the place to stay again, and go right up to bed to escape Walker and weirdness for the night. He would be fine and dandy, he knew that. He just needed to get through this bit.

They sat at the table in front of plates arranged with napkins, forks, and knives like they were fancy folk. Ashton watched as Walker lifted pieces of pizza from the big box in the center of the table and onto his plate, relaxing as Walker picked up a piece and took a giant bite from it like a normal person. If he'd actually used the fork and knife, Ashton wasn't sure he'd have been able to resist the impulse to laugh. And laughing at your anxious and uncomfortable host seemed inexcusably rude.

"The dogs always beg," Walker said, in needless explanation of the cuties sitting at their feet, shifting restlessly and gazing up with wide eyes. "Sorry about that."

"No worries." Ashton reached down to pat Nina before taking five pieces of pizza for himself. He wasn't sure he could get them all down, but he'd grown up in such a way that he never took free food for granted.

The first bite was better than he expected, and he made a soft noise of pleasure as the flavors of pepperoni, sausage, ham, and beef flooded his mouth.

Walker's eyes darted sharply to his face, and the temperature in the room seemed to go up a little.

Ashton cleared his throat and murmured, "Heavens, this is a good pizza pie. Where'd you order from?"

"Brenz."

"I've heard good things about them. All warranted, I see."

Walker nodded, looking a little confused. Why? Ashton had no idea. Wasn't he supposed to like the pizza?

Silence fell again, aside from the dogs panting their hope in eager gusts between them and the sound of chewing, which was something Ashton hated most of the time. The uncomfortable circumstances didn't improve the experience.

As soon as Ashton swallowed the last of his second piece, he pushed back from the table. "Well, I'm full as a tick, as my horrible grandmother used to say. It was delicious. How much was it? I'll Venmo the money to you. No reason for you to pay when I'm the guest." Ashton picked up his phone and brought up the app before looking at Walker again expectantly.

Walker's brows lowered in the usual frown, and he glanced between the phone in Ashton's hand and his own unfinished pizza on the plate. "Don't worry about it. I was going to order pizza tonight anyway."

Ashton wasn't sure that was true, but he decided not to argue. Any further protest would just make things even more strange between them, so he stood, slipping his phone into his pants pocket. "All right. Well, it's been a long day for me. Hope it's not too rude if I head on up to bed?"

"No, of course not. I'm tired too." Walker stood and carried their plates to the sink. "Go on. I'll put this all away." He put out his hand to stop Ashton when he opened his mouth to offer to help. "Like I said, it's no big deal. Go on up. There are extra blankets in the upstairs hall closet if you think you might be cold and plenty of towels in the bathroom if you want to grab a shower."

Ashton yawned with a little more effort than was probably necessary, spreading his arms wide and leaning back. He hoped it was a convincing show. "All right. Good night puppies," he said to the dogs as they shifted around near Walker's feet, watching hopefully as he put away the leftover pizza and began to clean up. "Thanks again for having me."

"Yup." Walker bent over the dishwasher, taking out clean plates to put in dirty ones. "No problem."

Upstairs, Ashton firmly shut the guest bedroom door behind him and sat on the bed, staring out at the backdoor neighbor's Christmas lights visible through the trees. He wondered why Walker had offered to host him at all.

Despite claiming Ashton was welcome, and his insistence that none of this was a "big deal," it didn't exactly feel that way. The awkward tension between them hadn't dissipated and, truly, if Walker hadn't wanted to host him? Why had he even asked Ashton to stay?

Casey. It had to be Casey.

Ashton went hot all over with a hint of anger. He hadn't done anything wrong. The bed bugs at his apartment building weren't his fault. He deserved to be staying somewhere with someone who made him feel comfortable, and if Walker couldn't manage to do that then…

Then what?

Then he'd have to tough it out and sleep on Angel's miserable couch or cough up money for a hotel room he couldn't afford.

Taking a slow breath, Ashton got his irritation under control. As he brushed his teeth, he stared at himself in the mirror and shook his toothbrush at his reflection muttering, "One awkward evening down, just two more to go." He spit in the sink and rinsed. "Great. Good. Love that for me."

THE NEXT NIGHT didn't start out much better. The ride from the office to Walker's house was laced with silence and that ongoing tension that seemed to swallow all the space between them. Ashton was ready to do anything to dispel it, even open the windows of the car and hope it flew out like an accidental fart. He had his finger on the power window button to try just that when Walker stopped at a traffic light and almost started to talk.

"So, uh…"

Silence again. "Yeah?" Ashton prompted.

Walker chewed on his cheek for a second and leaned forward, looking up at the light like it might have turned green in the few seconds they'd been sitting still and he'd somehow missed it. "Well, so… There was something I wanted to talk to you about, but I…" He cleared his throat and sat back, squirming in his seat. "I don't know. It's not a big deal I guess. Never mind."

Ashton huffed and squeezed his fingers into fists. He couldn't deal with this bullhonky. He'd spent way too much time with people who didn't like him. Dang it, he'd rather sleep on Angel's lumpy couch for the next two nights than put up with tension from Walker. "Clearly it *is* a big deal, so go on and spit it out."

Walker shook his head. "Nah, it's nothing."

"For heaven's sake just tell me. I can't feel comfortable staying with you if it's going to be like this between us." Walker flinched, as any good Southern boy would when being accused of being inhospitable. "So, what is it? Are there house rules or something? Don't spend more than eight minutes in the shower? Clear the hair from the drain? Don't flush at night? What?"

The light turned green. Walker tightened his grip on the steering wheel, pulled through the intersection, and turned into his neighborhood. "I had a question is all, but it's really not my business."

"Look, I'm this close to calling my stepsister to crash on her couch. I need you to be upfront with me. We're business partners if nothing else. Let's just get it out on the table. What's the question?" Ashton's stomach churned with acid, but whatever it was, it really was better to deal with it now.

"It's nothing. I'm being an asshole. Look, I'm sorry. Don't go stay on your sister's couch. Casey would—"

"Stepsister. And I knew Casey set this up."

"He didn't. Not really, but… Look, my house has a whole bedroom that's hurting from disuse. You need a place to stay. Forget I said anything. It's really no big deal."

"Walker?"

"Yeah?"

"Let's get real, okay? We've been walking on tiptoes around each other for nine months now. We're obviously really different people, and maybe we're not sure what to make of each other, but I'd like to think we could be friends. So..." Ashton spread his hands. "What's the question?"

Walker's face pinked up like he was embarrassed at being called out, but he nodded thoughtfully. "Friends, huh?"

"Yeah."

"I guess that would be good." He didn't sound altogether sure of it, but Ashton thought it had to be progress.

"At the very least, it'd be good for our business."

"Right. It probably would. Okay, I'll just ask."

"Please do."

"Why couldn't you afford a hotel?"

"Ah." Ashton's lips quirked up. "I get it. I see. Well, it's a funny story, but I invested every last dime of my savings into an illegal cocaine shipment that got confiscated off the coast of South Carolina by the feds. So that has me kinda financially strapped at the moment."

Walker narrowed his eyes.

"Kidding. It was the strippers. All those dollars tucked into their waistbands add up."

Walker rolled his eyes.

Ashton reached out and took hold of his arm. "No, I'm sorry. It's... Wow, it's a long story." He glanced out the window where night descended. Colored Christmas lights blinked on all the neighbors' houses as they approached Walker's street. He wished one day he'd have a home in a neighborhood like this: normal, suburban, and his free and clear.

He focused his attention back on Walker again. "A story I'd more easily be able to tell over a glass of wine and maybe dinner." He grinned. "Leftover pizza? Or a new delivery? On me for real this time." He pulled out his phone and pulled up the delivery app. "Name your poison."

"Tonight I'm cooking," Walker said firmly, directing the car into his driveway. "But opening up wine? Sure. We can do that once we're inside."

"Great. The story will flow better if I'm a little tipsy for it."

"You don't have to tell me anything. I'm being a jerk."

"Walker, you're curious and I get it. But at least get a guy a drink before he divests himself of, how can I put this? Semi-sordid unmentionables."

Walker snorted, and Ashton's insides untangled a little. At least Walker could take a joke. "Fair enough."

Once they were inside and they'd greeted and fended off the ecstatic dogs, Walker led Ashton into the living room and over to a tall wine rack. He ran his fingers over the bottles. "Red all right?"

"Sure."

Walker motioned toward the sofa. "Have a seat. I'll be back with glasses."

The dogs piled onto red and white checked dog beds, and Bitsy jumped tentatively up onto the sofa to press herself against Ashton's thigh as soon as he got situated.

Patting Bitsy's soft head, Ashton waited, trying to decide how much he wanted to explain to Walker. He wasn't looking forward to talking about hard things with a man who didn't entirely like him, but he did want to be friends with Walker and maybe if he understood…

He heard the pop of the cork coming free, and Bitsy jerked a little, pushing even tighter against his thigh. "It's all right, sweet girl," he murmured. "I've got you."

"Here you go," Walker said, stepping back into the living room and passing a glass of red wine into his hands. The stem was delicate between

Ashton's fingers, and he snorted to himself, imagining hosting Walker at his shabby apartment and serving him wine in a chipped mug.

They might be business partners, but they sure lived in different worlds.

"So, you really love Christmas, huh?" Ashton said, deflecting from the conversation at hand and motioning at the decorations and the big, beautiful tree with his wineglass.

Walker shrugged. "Grandma always had it done up like this every year. Seems disrespectful not to carry on with it."

Ashton pondered that. "You were close with your grandmother?"

Walker nodded, sipping his wine. He eyed Ashton. "I suppose if I'm going to ask nosy questions, it's fair to ask me some too."

"Is that a nosy question?"

"A little. Probably not as nosy as why you can't afford a hotel."

"Why don't we agree to play a questions game then? I ask one and you answer, then you ask one and I answer. In the interests of being friends, of course, for the good of the business." Ashton sipped the wine and found it delicious.

Walker chuckled but nodded. "For the business."

"Right."

"To answer *your* question, Grandma took care of me and my sister Evelyn when we were kids. Mom worked with Dad at the office. She was his assistant for a good number of years and didn't get off until five, so after school Ev and I came on over here."

"Ah." Ashton glanced toward the dark fireplace and the evidence of ashes beneath the grate. "That sounds nice, having a good relationship with your grandparents like that."

"I had a good relationship with my *grandmother*," Walker corrected, sitting down on the hearth with his wine and reaching out his hand to pet Nina, who nuzzled it in return. Simone flopped onto her back at his feet, and Walker kicked off a shoe to rub her tummy with his socked foot. It was sweet. He really was like an entirely different person with his dogs. Ashton wondered who the real Walker might be—and he suspected it was this one.

Ashton sipped his wine again and patted Bitsy at his side. "Go on."

"My grandfather always wanted more out of me, but I don't know what that 'more' was exactly." Walker shrugged. "Obviously, I shouldn't complain. I live here in his home free of rent. I'll likely inherit it when he goes. The fact that he doesn't completely *like* me shouldn't be a problem."

"But we always want people to like us."

Walker nodded thoughtfully, taking another sip of his wine. "Unfortunately."

"It's my turn now, I guess," Ashton said, shivering slightly. He wasn't cold but the idea of sharing the true reason why he was always short on cash was nerve-racking. He took a big gulp of wine and hoped it would warm him from the inside.

"Sure," Walker said, but he seemed embarrassed, like maybe he regretted having asked the question in the first place. Still, Ashton was determined to satisfy his side of the agreement, and as he opened his mouth to do so, Walker abruptly stood up. "First let me start a fire. It's not too cold out yet, but it'll take the dampness out of the air."

"If you want, sure." Ashton couldn't remember the last time he'd had the luxury of sitting in a cozy house in front of a log fire. Try never. It was almost romantic, especially with the Christmas lights turned on and the snoozing dog by his leg. Homey and sweet. Except for the part where he was about to talk about difficult, hurtful things. Ugh.

Plus Ashton didn't want Walker to feel obligated to put in extra work for him. He was already doing enough just by having Ashton here and by agreeing to this little game of quid pro quo.

Walker went to the stack of wood in the brass log holder on the hearth and pulled out three, setting them up inside the fireplace on the grate. As Ashton watched, Walker made sure the flue was open, and then coaxed a flame to life between the logs with a small starter block. The dogs began to pant and moved away over by the door to the hallway. Walker sat on the hearth again, his back to the flames.

"All right, are you ready for the big reveal?" Ashton teased, his throat a little dry. "It's sadly not as exciting as you might be expecting."

Walker straightened up and nodded, his expression serious and a bit grim. He clearly regretted ever asking while still being held by the grip of curiosity. It was understandable. It wasn't as if Walker wasn't perfectly aware of the size of Ashton's paychecks. He must wonder where the money was going.

"Hmm, where should I start?" Ashton took a bigger sip of wine and watched the flames grow in the grate.

"You can start anywhere," Walker said softly.

"Anywhere, huh? I'll start with the fact that my grandmother helped raised me too, and that's part of why I don't have enough money for a hotel room." He smiled at Walker.

"You help her out financially?" Walker asked, his brows scrunching low.

"No." Ashton felt his smile grow sharp. "Never."

Walker blinked at him.

"My grandmother and I aren't close. We'll never be close."

"Oh. I'm sorry."

"Yeah. In that Facebook post I made? I was joking about a lot of things, but I *wasn't* joking about having blown up my family three years ago by inviting a Grindr hookup to the family party. That was my way of ending my relationship with Grandma Hudson. I have no regrets. It was that bad."

Walker straightened, sweat beading on his forehead, probably from being so close to the fire but maybe also at realizing that his question had definitely opened an ugly can of worms. Good. Ashton hoped he squirmed a little. "I'm sorry. That sounds rough."

"It was. I'm sure you're wondering how that's related to the money thing though? Well, my cousin Justin was also raised by Grandma

Hudson. He and I were close when we were kids. More like brothers than anything. I protected him from my grandmother's abuse for as long as I could while I lived there, but eventually I had to go. Being gay in that home wasn't safe, and sticking around, even for someone else's sake, wasn't sane."

"He was younger?"

"By just a year."

"Ah. And was he gay too?"

"No, straight, but he was a troublemaker in other ways, so he felt the brunt of Grandma Hudson's wrath plenty." Bitsy began to snore by Ashton's thigh, and he laughed softly, glancing down at her. "She's completely asleep. I'm not sure how I can ever move again."

"We'll have to start bringing your work to you," Walker said with a fond gaze at the old dog. "You can meet with clients here. We'll fit you with a catheter."

Ashton almost choked on his wine holding back his sudden laugh. It wasn't that Walker's joke had been all that funny but rather that he'd joked at all. Ashton hadn't been sure Walker was *capable* of witty comebacks. "Sexy. Love that future for me," Ashton said.

Walker smiled, and this time it was real and it was *all* for him. Well, damn. That *had* been worth waiting for. Who knew?

Perhaps he'd been wrong to agree with Kenzie that Walker was average. Maybe the guy was just a teeny, tiny bit good-looking after all. Just a little bit. Nothing to write a letter home about. Maybe worth a short text. Nothing more.

"Justin and I had similar experiences growing up." Ashton wrinkled his nose and shook his head. He didn't want to spell out anything. One flashback for the week was enough for him. "Let's just say we lived with our grandmother and not our parents for darn good reasons and leave it at that. Unfortunately, my grandmother's house wasn't much better than the homes we'd been taken from."

Walker nodded, a bead of sweat slipping down the side of his face.

Ashton pondered him a moment, seeing the way Walker was dissolving under the heat. "I don't bite. You can move to the sofa if you're too hot."

"Huh? Oh." Walker wiped the sweat away. "Yeah, I just didn't want to disturb Bitsy."

Ashton pointed at the opposite side of the sofa. "She won't wake up, surely. And I couldn't even *reach* you over there. Even if I tried to bite."

Walker moved to the sofa and Nina got up from where she was sprawled by the hallway door and came to him. She jumped up and rested her head on his thigh. "Now we'll both need catheters," Walker muttered.

"And we'll have to order in after all. Do you have a neighbor with a key that can let the delivery guy in? Someone who might be willing to stay to feed us? And refill our wine glasses?"

Walker laughed. "Don't worry. These two will move soon enough. They'll be wanting their own D-I-N-N-E-R before long and we'll be freed."

"So funny that they know the word. They went absolutely bonkers last night when you said it."

Walker nodded. "I know. They know that one and a few more like T-R-E-A-T and W-A-L-K."

Ashton chuckled.

"Sorry. I didn't mean to interrupt your story. I mean, if you want to tell more? I realize now that I was being insensitive, no, a real jerk, and I'm sorry for—"

Ashton waved the apology away. Not that he didn't deserve one, but because if suspicion and lack of true knowledge of who Ashton was, and who he had been, were all that was standing between him and Walker being on good terms, then he'd rather just get it all out there. He'd like for them to trust each other and be comfortable together from now on.

"Oh, don't apologize. We're in too deep to turn back now. We're just getting to the part that answers your question. So, yeah, Justin's in rehab these days," Ashton said quickly before Walker could try to apologize again or stop him. "I pay for it. It's his third attempt at sobriety, and I hope the last. I don't want to give up on him, but…" He sipped his wine; it was nearly gone. "It's expensive."

"Man, I'm sorry. That sucks."

"It does. Family." Ashton downed the last drops. "Gotta love 'em."

"But you're optimistic? Third time's the charm and all of that?"

"No." Ashton flinched to hear how cold he sounded.

"No? Then why…?"

"Someone has to show him they love him enough to go this far." Ashton focused on patting Bitsy, not looking at Walker. "Everyone deserves that, even if it's not enough. In Justin's life that person is me. Can only be me."

Walker's shoulders rounded, as if Ashton had placed something heavy on them with his words.

"So that's the depressing truth about where all my money goes, which is why I never talk about it." Ashton aimed for a bright smile. Even if Walker had made him uncomfortable the night before, and even if he'd been nosy in the car leading up to all this *chatting* tonight, Ashton still felt like he shouldn't bring his host down.

Walker was doing him a favor by letting him stay in his home, and even if none of this had really been his business, Ashton understood why he'd been concerned. If Ashton thought Casey couldn't afford three nights at a hotel, he'd be worried too. But the last thing he wanted from Walker or anyone else was pity. "Helping Justin is my choice and the burden of that is on me. No one else."

Bitsy stretched in her sleep, and the other dogs took that as a cue or something because they all started barking and jumping. Walker huffed. "Must be six o'clock. Dinner time."

Bitsy leapt up from Ashton's side as if she'd never been even a little drowsy, darting away like a dog half her age.

"You stay here and enjoy the fire," Walker said. "I'll bring the bottle for you to refill your glass, and I'll feed them before I get our meal together. We can eat in here tonight? Watch some television too? It's a little informal, I know, but that's what I usually do."

"Informal sounds great." Ashton put his wine glass on the coffee table and stretched. Informal sounded like they were well on their way to being business-friendly. Nosy questions were good for something after all, even if he *was* feeling a little twitchy after talking about Justin and skirting the subject of the rest of his family. "Do you need help in the kitchen?"

"No, thank you. Just relax. The remote control is there if you want to find something on Netflix."

Then Walker was gone and so were the dogs. Turning to the TV, Ashton cued up a comedy show he'd been enjoying recently but didn't start it. The dogs trotted back in after their own meal had been finished and Bitsy re-joined him on the sofa. Before long the sounds and scents of cooking wafted from the kitchen.

Ashton watched the fire as the flames sank lower and the heat filled the room. He was just starting to get too warm when the air conditioner automatically clicked on, which made him snort.

He wondered how long Walker had been harboring questions about Ashton that had affected their relationship. He wished Walker had simply asked earlier. As awkward as it was to confess to having grown up with a fucked-up family situation, it was better than having his business partner view him with wary suspicion.

He was sure, no matter how bad of a relationship Walker had with his grandfather, the rest of his family must be incredibly boring and normal in comparison to his own. They had to be since Walker still seemed very close with his mom and his sister.

The Christmas tree and its gilded-wrapped presents sat cheerily in the corner, and Ashton couldn't help but ponder the probable normalcy of all the family members those gifts must be for, and what it must be like for a grown man to still have a functioning relationship with his parents. At the very least, it must be pleasant, if not outright wonderful. One thing was for sure: Ashton would never know a family life like that.

Ho, ho, ho for Walker. Boo-hoo-hoo for him.

# Chapter Four

USUALLY CHEERFUL AND chatty, it turned out that morning-Ashton was quiet and disheveled with sleep creases on his cheeks. He came down to the kitchen in his pajamas—a loose pair of sweatpants and an even looser T-shirt that showed off his collarbones in a way that made Walker's throat feel dry and his breathing go wonky—and proceeded to slouch at the table in a daze.

Walker, already wearing his work clothes and feeling guilty as hell for having ever made Ashton feel unwelcome in his home, and for having harbored uncharitable suspicions of him, handed over a mug of freshly brewed coffee. "Do you take anything in it? Cream? Sugar?" He watched as Ashton stroked the dogs, his eyes half-lidded with sleepiness as he shook his head and lapsed into stillness again.

When Walker placed the plate of bacon and eggs in front of him, Ashton gasped and stared at it like he'd never seen breakfast food before.

"This okay?" Walker asked.

"This? This is *amazing*." He took the fork Walker handed to him and dove in.

Walker found himself smiling a little at the pink hearts drawn in Sharpie on Ashton's right hand, glowing bright in the morning sun through the kitchen window. He'd noticed them before, but now he *really* noticed them. They were ridiculous, but somehow so Ashton.

The night before had passed easily enough after the awkwardness of their quid pro quo session. Learning that Ashton wasn't low on cash because of some bad habit like gambling or drugs but because he was an actual hero, doing his best to help a troubled cousin had pricked Walker's conscience badly.

After all, Walker was living in his grandfather's house because he'd savaged his trust fund to pay off reckless gambling debts. It'd been hard to look himself in the eye while brushing his teeth before bed, thinking of all the unkind things he'd accused Ashton of when talking with Casey, while all along *he* was the one who'd been proven untrustworthy with money. It was amazing Casey hadn't been sterner when reminding him of his gambling history. He'd deserved a lot worse than he'd gotten.

Walker also felt like there was a hell of a lot more story behind what Ashton had revealed to him the night before—especially about his family—but he wasn't about to push. He'd already come across like a total jackass, and, truth be told, if they played quid pro quo again? Well…the last thing he wanted was for Ashton to ask more questions about Walker's life and choices. Right now, it seemed like Ashton thought Walker was exactly what he appeared to be: a moderately successful thirty-three-year-old with his life all together, and Walker didn't want Ashton to realize he was actually anything but.

They'd watched three episodes of a comedy series on Netflix, laughed together over the hijinks, and finished off the bottle of wine before turning in early. Walker had slept lightly, overly conscious of the fact that there was a guest in his house who wasn't his grandfather. He woke several times fretting over thoughts that Ashton might be too cold, or too hot, and wondering if Simone had done her trick of using her paw to push open the guest room door, demanding access to Ashton's bed.

So far, Ashton hadn't mentioned any of those possibilities, so Walker just served orange juice alongside the coffee and allowed the silence to extend.

Finally, after his cup and plate were empty, Ashton leaned back from the table and stretched until his back cracked. "Gah," he groaned. "That felt good. And this breakfast was amazing. Thanks for all of this. You didn't need to go all out or anything. I'd planned to have you go to the Starbucks drive-through on the way to work, my treat."

Walker didn't know what to say. He knew he hadn't needed to do this for Ashton, but he'd *wanted* to make breakfast for him. Just like he'd wanted to make dinner the night before—even before he'd heard Ashton's story. It was one of the only ways he'd known to impress him and to make up for having been a bit of a jerk the first night.

Walker might not be as cute as Ashton, or as glossy, and maybe he didn't wear clothes that looked like they'd walked out of a magazine, and *maybe* Ashton made him jumpy with all of his casual shininess and ambitious pursuit of a good laugh, but Walker could make a good dinner, provide a warm bed, and serve a delicious breakfast the next morning.

He didn't know exactly why it was important to him for Ashton to know all that, but it was. He crossed his fingers it was enough to make up for having been such a jerk of a business partner these last many months. Ashton was right: it would be nice if they could be friends. For the business. Hell, for themselves. "I hope this coffee was good enough," he said. "I know it's no Starbucks and you only drink one a day, so…"

Ashton nodded, his hand circling in front of his face. "More dries my skin out."

"Ah."

"Don't worry, this coffee was very good. A-plus, would drink again." The freckles over his nose seemed to glow like amber dots in the light through the kitchen window, and the thick black of his lashes brushed against his high cheekbones. He was even prettier without his makeup, Walker thought. Which seemed nearly impossible, and yet…

Sipping his own coffee and watching Ashton chew on his bacon slice, Walker felt a wave of satisfaction sweep him. Who gave a damn if he was being weird or heteronormative or whatever else? He felt like a *man* taking care of his beautiful business partner, giving him good food, and a soft bed, and seeing him all sleep-rumpled and gorgeous. Making friends with him. For the business.

Fuck it. He needed a therapist because he had no idea what any of that meant. It sounded like nonsense even to him.

Walker cleared his throat. "Got appointments today?"

Ashton shook his head slowly and glanced at his phone, checking the time. "Oh, that's right. You like to get into the office early, don't you? Let me just…" He pushed his plate back and stood up quickly, startling Nina out of her hopeful place at his feet. "I'll skip the makeup today but I have to shower and moisturize. Then I'll get ready super fast."

"Don't rush. There's not much going on at work. It's all right."

Ashton smiled but didn't stop hustling from the kitchen and up the stairs. Simone trailed after him, leaving Walker alone with his other three dogs. Alone to wonder weird things like why the delicate collarbones sticking out of Ashton's T-shirt made him feel so protective, like he wanted to kiss them and cover them at the same time.

So weird. Definitely not friendly thoughts.

Maybe the wine they'd had the night before had muddled his head. Or maybe Santa was bringing him a whole new collarbone kink for Christmas this year. Or was it a coworker kink?

He certainly hoped not.

"WHAT'S HIS PLACE like?" Kayla asked, closing the door to Ashton's office behind her.

Ashton glanced up from some sketches he was doing for the rebranding of Rockstroh Fine Tailoring and shrugged. "It's a normal house. Sequoyah Hills, which I suspect you already knew, and four dogs."

"*Four* dogs?"

"Two hounds and two poodles."

"Really?" Kayla sounded breathless with interest. She wore a red and green sweater with a brown skirt and some golden Christmas bell earrings. Cute as always, but her usual pretty smile was replaced by a round O of surprise. "What are their names?"

Ashton tipped his head to the side. "Why do you care?"

"Maybe I got him for Secret Santa and I'm looking for a clue on what to get him for his gift." She grinned cheekily.

Ashton snorted. "You didn't."

"How do you know?"

He shot her a wide-eyed glance of exasperation. "Because you didn't."

"Ohhhh, so you have him."

"Maybe. But I know for sure *you* don't. So why did you want to know their names?"

"Sheer curiosity. What does a man like Walker name his dogs? Something boring like Rex? Or Buddy?"

"Nope. They're named… None of your business."

"Ha, I'll find out." Kayla grinned and dropped into the chair across from his table-desk. "You obviously have him for Secret Santa, so what are you going to get him?" She waggled her brows.

Ashton had just been pondering that question in the back of his mind, actually. He'd noticed that Walker had a few amazingly soft blankets that he cuddled up in while watching television. He'd insisted on Ashton using one the night before, handing it over in a really sweet way that'd left Ashton feeling cared for and a little flustered.

Which was frustrating, since he'd only ever wanted a smile from Walker, not a whole new set of feelings. But he supposed that's what came of spending time in his house and playing dangerously intimate question games like quid pro quo—an unwarranted sense of intimacy.

The brand on the blankets was something he'd never heard of, and when he'd googled them to investigate getting another in a nice red to match the curtains of the living room, his mind had been blown. To say the blankets were pricey was an understatement. Even just a small throw went far, far above the agreed upon maximum price for Secret Santa.

Maybe Kayla was on to something with the dogs, though.

"Isn't there that new dog boutique over by the bookstore?" he asked.

"Yes! They have the cutest stuff! Like little Christmas cookie chew toys, and Santa hats full of dog treats, and—!"

"Perfect," Ashton interrupted.

She clapped her hands. "Now that's solved, back to the good stuff. What'd y'all do the last two nights?"

"Ate dinner. Watched Netflix."

"What'd he serve for dinner? Takeout? Frozen food?"

"So nosy. The first night we had pizza, but last night he cooked."

Kayla's eyes went wide again like this was exciting news. "A regular old meal, or is he like a secret chef or something?"

"Well—"

A knock sounded and Kayla frowned, obviously annoyed to have her gossip sesh interrupted, but she stood and opened the door to reveal Casey. He wore a green button-up with tiny red bows embroidered on it. Ashton smiled, pleased to see the shirt. He'd helped him choose it and a few others from a sales flier that'd arrived from Rockstroh after they'd secured the account.

"Hey there," Casey said with a smile for Kayla. "Just need to talk with Ashton, but, uh, I can come back later if there's a fire you're putting out?"

"No, you're fine," Ashton said, motioning him into the office.

Kayla backed toward the door, pointing at Ashton with her long, pink nail, and mouthing, *"Later."*

Casey dropped into the seat Kayla had vacated and gazed at Ashton steadily from across the table-desk as the door clicked shut behind her. Ashton closed his laptop and gave Casey his full attention. "What's up?"

"How's it going with Walker?"

Ashton laughed. "You too? I thought Kayla had the title of lead gossip in the office."

Casey leaned back in the chair. "I just want to make sure Walker's been putting in some effort. I know he's been cold to you in the past, and I'm sorry about that. You've deserved better from him, and hopefully he's coming through for you now."

Ashton lifted a brow. "Oh, so you *are* the one who strong-armed him into asking me to stay at his place. Despite his protest to the contrary, I admit, I'd wondered."

Casey frowned, clearly annoyed with himself for having given that much away. "He's been a dick then?"

"Only a small, flaccid one. Not an erect one."

"Ah, damn, I'm sorry again."

"He's come around though. It seems he had a few worries about my financial situation that have been weighing on his mind—"

Casey blew a raspberry and rolled his eyes again.

"But after I explained about Justin, he calmed down."

"That wasn't any of his business."

"As SRS partners, we owe each other the truth about certain aspects of our lives, don't we? If we're going to work together as a team?"

Casey pressed his lips together but nodded in agreement.

"Exactly. So I'm glad I told him, even if it was weird, because it seems to have made all the difference. Last night, well…" A strange flutter started in his belly. "I don't know. How can I put this?"

Casey's brows lifted.

Ashton shrugged. "He was great. I think we can actually be friends." Heat bloomed in Ashton's chest, and he hoped it didn't spread up his neck and into his face. He was wearing his favorite white silk blouse today and had the first two buttons undone revealing his collarbones. It would be incredibly obvious. And also strange, because what in *heavens*?

"Friends, huh?"

"Yeah. I mean it's not like we're going to become besties or some-thing, but he's nice, cute as hell with his dogs, and cooks a mean meal." Ashton cleared his throat. "You know. That's all."

"All right. Glad to hear he's being good to you." Casey narrowed his eyes, casting a glance down to Ashton's neck. Heck, he must be really blushing then. But *why*? Walker had been a good host last night, which was a pleasant change from the first night, but that was all. "Did something happen between you?"

Ashton's laughter burst out wildly. "What? Of course not."

"Huh. All right." Casey tilted his head. "So what'd you do at his place?"

"You and Kayla are actually the same person. Who knew?" He smiled. "The first night we had pizza with a side of awkwardness. But last night, after our little talk about Justin and money, he built a fire, gave me a glass of wine, cooked me a wonderful meal, and we watched Netflix together. Friendly"

"Hella friendly."

"I'm sure he's done the same for you."

Casey blinked at him. "I dunno about that. Sounds real cozy."

Ashton was the one to roll his eyes this time. "What the heck, Casey?"

Casey chuckled.

Ashton sat back in his chair and crossed his arms over his chest. "Why are you in here interrogating me anyway?"

Casey shrugged, but his eyes sparkled oddly. "Walker's just being weird today, that's all. I asked him how it's been, you know, with having you stay over. He got all flustered and strange. I've never seen him do that before. Said something odd about it being *fine* if he wants to make a man breakfast. That it's *normal* to want to take care of people. That it meant he was a *good host*. He sounded super defensive about it, which made me wonder why." His lips quirked and he suppressed another chuckle. "I thought maybe he'd been a jerk and you'd called him out..."

"Well, I *did* do that."

"Good for you."

"But ever since then he's been great."

"So what's his deal?"

"Beats me."

Casey shot Ashton a strange, unreadable look. "Well, like I said, I'm glad he's being good to you."

Ashton shifted through his paperwork, hoping he appeared more dismissive of all that Casey had said and implied than he actually felt. Nothing, absolutely nothing, was happening or going to happen with Walker Ronson. "He's a good guy. Just really different from me."

Casey nodded thoughtfully. "Cool. All right, show me the sketches for Rockstroh?"

They spent some time going over the drawings and agreed on a plan for a new presentation to the tailor after the New Year. As the day passed, a small excitement grew, a sense of anticipation for the night ahead. He told himself he was just curious what Walker might make for dinner if he planned to cook again, but deep down he had to admit it was about a lot more than food.

The night before had turned out so nice. Low-key and easy, but not at all lonely. And lonely was one thing Ashton was still not accustomed to being. Especially during the holidays. Growing up, he'd always been surrounded by family during this time of year. Hateful as they may have been, there had been plenty of them: aunts, uncles, cousins, Justin, and Grandma Hudson.

Speaking of family, Justin must be lonely too. Ashton hadn't called him in over a month. The last time he had, Justin's counselor had asked him not to call again. She said Ashton's voice was a trigger for Justin and had caused a real setback. She'd asked that Ashton wait for Justin to reach out to him instead.

But it was Christmastime. It seemed a shame to think of Justin alone in the rehab facility without even a card from someone who loved him. Ashton decided to walk over to Market Square in the afternoon to see if he could find a suitable Secret Santa gift for Walker in the shops there. If he just happened to find the perfect Christmas card for Justin, so be it.

# Chapter Five

*I'll MEET YOU at your place tonight? I'm running an errand after work, but you don't need to wait for me. I can Uber it. Want me to grab some takeout for dinner?*

After replying to Ashton that grabbing takeout was unnecessary, Walker leaned back in his desk chair with a groan. He'd received the text right as he was wrapping up his final task of the day. He hadn't even realized until that moment how much he'd been looking forward to the car ride home with Ashton.

He didn't know why. It wasn't as if the conversation from yesterday's car ride was one he was hankering to repeat. If anything, he was still embarrassed that he'd so misjudged Ashton and asked him such an intrusive question.

A hollow sensation swelled in his gut.

Why? There was nothing to be disappointed about. He'd still see Ashton at the house later. They'd still have dinner together. Besides, why did he even care at all? He'd enjoyed cooking for Ashton the night before, and making breakfast this morning, and the dogs had liked having him around too, but that was it. They were just being friendly. For the business.

God, he must be really lonely.

Shrugging, Walker got his things together and said goodnight to the rest of the staff on their way out. The car ride was unremarkable. He listened to a Spotify playlist Evelyn had texted him earlier in the week. She'd promised it was full of new holiday music by younger artists, all of which hadn't been worn into the ground by over thirty years of repeated listening. He had to admit it was nice to hear the jangle of sleigh bells and other wintery vibes in songs without knowing exactly what lyric came next.

Walker drove home the long way, passing by neighboring houses decorated for the holidays, delaying his arrival to an empty home. Well, empty of humans. But when he finally pulled into the driveway, he was surprised to find the place might not be so empty after all.

Evelyn's Jeep was parked under the carport, and he found her in the kitchen feeding Bitsy extra dog treats from her palm while the other three dogs looked on with saliva dripping from their lips. The bag of Beefy Bites sat open on the table next to her.

"How do you get them to sit so patiently?" he asked, taking off his coat and hanging it up. The dogs were clearly torn between greeting him and the chance at a treat from Evelyn.

"I'm not a pushover," she said, standing and kissing his cheek as he approached. "Unlike my baby brother."

Walker rolled his eyes but didn't take the bait. "Tom's working tonight?"

"Yeah, he's putting the finishing touches on a woman's back piece."

Walker grabbed a can of soda from the fridge and handed it to her before opening a beer for himself. "Those organic corn chips you like are in the cabinet if you want some."

She grabbed them along with salsa from the fridge. After feeding the dogs their dinner and putting the beef treats out of sight, Walker joined her at the kitchen counter and gave her his full attention. If she was here waiting for him when he got home, there was a reason for it, and it wasn't like his big sister to keep her problems to herself.

"So, the wedding is coming up in two weeks," she said, soaking her chip in the salsa and pulling it out so that only a fine sheen of red remained.

"Yes."

"And I'm already wondering why we didn't just elope."

"You still can."

Evelyn groaned. "Tell that to Daddy and his fifty-thousand-dollar investment into this whole wedding weekend scheme."

"You never wanted that."

"I sure as shit didn't." She sighed as she popped another chip in her mouth and then took a swallow of soda. As she placed the can back on the table, Walker glimpsed a dark spot on her wrist that he hadn't seen before.

"New ink?" he asked, nodding toward it.

Evelyn broke into a grin. "Yes! Let me show you." She shoved her sweater back and presented her forearm for his approval. The new addition was a black sewing needle threaded with a red string that seemed to trail up her arm. He waited for an explanation, but none was forthcoming. "I got it before Thanksgiving, but it needed to heal, so…" She shrugged and covered it up again.

She'd spent Thanksgiving with Tom's hillbilly family out in the sticks, so Walker hadn't had a chance to notice it then. "Cool," was all he offered up.

He didn't have any tattoos himself, but he didn't have a problem with them either. His sister's tattoos weren't his business. No matter how often his mother, father, uncle, and cousins tried to turn them into his business by grilling him about Evelyn's body art and life choices. Including the choice to marry her tattoo artist, Tom.

"You know the wedding's going to be a shitshow, Walker." She turned her big, brown eyes on him. "The entire thing. Top to bottom."

"It is," he agreed.

"Hello!" Ashton's voice came from the direction of the door to the carport. The dogs leapt up from the floor and barreled down the hall barking. "Hey there, hi, hi, hello, hi Simone, hi Bitsy, hi, hi!" His light, lispy voice came chirruping amidst the barks, and Evelyn stared at Walker like he'd suddenly grown two heads.

Wearing his usual fashionable office attire—in this case a red, glittery King of Hearts cardigan over a silk white shirt that opened over his beautiful collarbones, and a pair of black pants that Walker had noted earlier made his ass look amazing—Ashton appeared in the doorway with Bitsy in his arms and the other three dogs dancing around his feet.

"Hope it's okay that I let myself in, I—" he broke off when he saw Evelyn, a smile of surprise blooming on his features. "Oh, hi. I guess that's your Jeep?" He threw his thumb back over his shoulder. "I thought maybe Walker had a friend over. Which I guess he does? I mean, you're probably friends too, right? I hear most siblings are." A flush crept up his neck. He looked adorably flustered. "I mean—"

"Come on in," Walker said, standing up. "You've met Evelyn?"

She rose, putting out her hand, a careful expression on her face. "Yes, we met at the open house to celebrate the new office."

"That's right," Ashton agreed. "I didn't get to talk with you long. It was a hectic night."

"No problem." She looked between them, avid interest in her eyes. "And so… You've got a key and…" She grinned widely. "What's going here?"

"Oh, no, I don't have a key!" Ashton's green eyes went wide, and his cheeks stained red.

"I left the back door open for him," Walker explained.

That didn't seem to dissuade her from her original assumption at all. She blinked wildly beneath her brown fringe and grinned. "Oh, I see. Well, come on and join us." She moved from the counter to the kitchen table. "Grab a beer from the fridge—or a soda, whatever you want."

Walker frowned at her but let her do the directing. She was the big sister after all. She was used to taking charge, and he usually let her.

"Sure, okay," Ashton put Bitsy on the floor, patted the other dogs again, and headed to the sink, where he washed his hands. He grabbed a beer and pulled up a seat at the table, taking a chip from the bag. "I'm staying here with Walker while they fumigate my apartment."

The disappointment in Evelyn's sigh was almost funny except it suddenly hit Walker that tonight was the last night Ashton would be staying. He wished fumigation took a little longer, because, weirdly, he wasn't tired of Ashton's company yet.

"That's a lot less exciting than I'd imagined."

Ashton laughed, his cheeks still pink, though the darkness of his afternoon stubble obscured some of it. "Well, Walker's been a great friend. I really appreciate him letting me—" His phone buzzed, and Ashton's perfectly shaped eyebrows dropped low. "Excuse me, I need to take this." He slipped upstairs.

Evelyn popped her own well-shaped brow at Walker. "He's cute."

"He's my business partner. And he's not my type."

She rolled her eyes. "Whatever. Your type has been consistently lame. Consider changing it up."

Walker rolled his eyes in return. "He's my *business partner*."

Evelyn waved his words away and bit into a chip. "Anyway, so like I was saying, the wedding's going to be a disaster."

Walker sat next to her. "I told you that when you said you were going to marry him."

"It's not Tom's fault."

"No, of course not." Walker rubbed the back of his neck and dove into the breach. "But it's not *not* Tom's fault either."

"What's that supposed to mean?"

"C'mon, Ev, you know as well as I do that Tom loves to push our family's buttons."

"Well, who wouldn't!" She flapped her hand around again. "Everyone makes him out to be a felon when all he ever did was marry the wrong woman."

"And have two kids with her. And leave her when the youngest was only a few years old."

"There were *circumstances*, and you know it." Evelyn gently slapped his arm. "Hey, you love those two kids."

"I do, but they complicate things."

"How? Because they're not my flesh and blood?"

"No because they *are* your flesh and blood." Walker snorted. She was being purposely obtuse tonight. He supposed she needed him to remind her of the cold, hard facts for some reason. "As you're well aware. Morgan is our cousin, and that means her kids are genetically related to us, and that means Tom was married to a *family member*, and that makes everything with the extended family awkward. No one's sure whose side to take on this thing."

"Tom's side!" Evelyn gestured with a salsa-dipped chip.

"But Tom isn't family."

"*I'm* family!"

Walker shook his head. "You're the woman who stole Tom from his wife and kids."

"That's not how it happened and you know it!"

"Yeah, but that's how they see it."

Evelyn bit into her chip angrily. He wasn't telling her anything she didn't already know. Hell, she'd been the one to spell it all out to him the first time. She just didn't want to hear it now. "She was cheating on him! And she was stealing! From Walmart! And selling the stuff on eBay for a profit! She should be in jail!"

Walker nodded at each exclamation.

"Uh…sorry?" Ashton's voice came from the kitchen door. "This sounds private, and I'll leave you alone momentarily, but Walker? That was my landlord… And it turns out the bed bug thing in the building is worse than they thought? And even though they still haven't seen any evidence of them in my unit, I'll need to stay out for another three or four days. I mean, I can technically go back, but I'll have to move all the furniture again for another inspection, and my bathroom and kitchen are full of bagged clothes and stuff." He winced. "That okay? Or should I find another friend to let me crash?"

The prickle of pleasure Walker felt all over was unexpected. "Sure.

No problem. I'm happy to have you here longer."

"Really?"

"Of course. The dogs like having you here. Don't you, Nina?" He patted Nina's head where it rested on his knee, staring up at him, hoping for a chip to drop.

"Thank you. I'll leave you two alone now," Ashton said and turned to go again.

"No, no, go ahead and sit back down," Evelyn said, nodding toward the empty chair at the table. "Nothing I'm saying here is a secret. The whole damn town knows." She frowned. "I mean, unless you don't *want* to hear it."

Ashton laughed. "Oh, pshh, if you're gossiping, I wanna hear it!"

For the next hour and a half, Evelyn entertained Ashton with tales of Ronson family dysfunction. The bitterness between uncles, the political strife between nephews and cousins, the lying aunts, the furious competitiveness between their father and his brother, and the judgmental disinterest of their grandfather. Ashton seemed to eat it up as eagerly as he devoured the chips and salsa. Walker had to get up twice to get more from the cupboard and fridge.

Then Evelyn started to explain about Tom's family.

Ashton's eyes grew wider and wider as she elucidated the tawdry connection between them, what with Tom having been married to their cousin Morgan, and the way the whole family reacted to that marriage and assigned all the blame to Tom for Morgan's descent into whatever that mess was she'd descended into.

"Drugs aren't involved?" Ashton asked hesitantly.

"Not as far as we can tell," Evelyn said. "She's just bent on doing whatever she wants, whenever she wants, kids and whoever else be damned. Tom and I want to try for full custody once things settle. Which is another piece of contention in our family. Some say I'm trying to steal Morgan's husband *and* her kids. Others say that I'm going to regret taking them on. And others say even uglier things. It's true the kids have their troubles." She wrinkled her nose. "My own mom says I won't love them as much once I have kids of my own. Just imagine what she'll say when I tell her that I don't want any of my own! Tom's are enough for me."

"Stability is important for children," Ashton said softly. "But being with people who love them is most important of all."

"I love them very much," Evelyn said. "Enough to put aside my own vain fantasies about what a family looks like and devote my future to them."

Ashton smiled, his lips shiny and swollen from the hot salsa. "It sounds like you know what you want."

"I do."

"And you want this insane over-the-top wedding?" Walker asked, bringing the topic back around to the start again.

Evelyn huffed, rising for a second soda. "I thought I did. But I really wish one of the cousins would show up with a surprise out-of-wedlock baby just to take the pressure off. Is it too much to ask for someone else to be the quote-unquote fuck-up so that I can just be the bride?"

Walker huffed a laugh. "Maybe Sheryl will show up with that butch woman she was dating. That gave all the aunts and girl cousins something to chat about at the last family reunion. Remember?"

"I wish. Or if only Camille could start making porn again. That'd do it. Why'd she have to find Christ and stop having sex on camera before my wedding, huh?"

"Wait, what?" Ashton said, sputtering. "You have someone coming to the wedding who was in porn, but that's not going to be enough to distract the conservative sharks in the family?"

Evelyn blew out an annoyed breath. "She's not coming. Says she's busy with her church's Christmas charity drive and can't make it. For the record, I have no problem with her having made adult films. The fact that *she* has a problem with it now is her own issue. Yadda, whatever. You know what I'm saying." She waved her hand around dismissing it all. "But, man, it would have helped take the focus off me and Tom—and the kids—if Camille had been able to attend. Which is horrible of me to say. I know, I *know*. I probably deserve every ounce of trouble I get just for wishing that hell on her."

"Ev, calm down," Walker said. "No one is going to actually say anything to your face at your own wedding."

She glared at him.

"Probably," Walker amended.

Evelyn rolled her eyes. "You don't know, Walker. You have no idea."

A beat of silence lapsed, broken by Ashton's low chuckle. "Wow, rich people are fucked up too." His eyes creased adorably with his grin.

"Of course," Evelyn agreed. Her phone beeped and she glanced down at it. "Speak of the devil, it's Morgan. She wants me to come get the kids because she has a date tonight. Last minute much? But *she's* a responsible mother who puts her kids first, and I'm the conniving bitch trying to steal them from her loving arms, right? Whatever."

Goodbyes were exchanged and Walker wasn't exactly sad to see her go. While Evelyn was his best friend as well as his sister, and always entertaining, he'd felt an odd flare of envy watching Ashton interacting with her.

How Ashton had responded so easily to her every word and gesture, how he'd come to life with each horrifying revelation about their messed-up family... What could Walker ever do or say to be on the receiving end of that light and interest?

Ashton had so much *life* in him, and seeing it playing off Evelyn's own ready light, Walker realized he hadn't had that kind of spirit in his own heart in years. Maybe ever.

Which was why he'd been so easily enticed by the thrill of a heart-poundingly large bet on the outcome of a single hole.

Shoving the shameful memories away, he returned from walking Evelyn out and found Ashton still seated at the table with Bitsy curled in his lap.

"Will I sound like a total jerk if I say that I'm glad she's gone so we can have dinner?" Ashton's long lashes lay against his cheek and the look he raised up through them was nearly coy. "And can I ask what you're planning to make?" He grinned again, the shine of his teeth and scrunch of his nose doing funny things to Walker's heart. "I've been thinking about it all day. You're a really good cook. Did you know?"

Walker smiled, warmth in his belly. A strange satisfaction that Ashton was also relieved Evelyn had left bloomed. He ignored the compliment. "Dolsot bibimbap."

"More Korean food?"

Walker nodded, moving to the refrigerator and pulling out the ingredients. He turned to a cabinet to gather the soy sauce, Korean chili paste, and other items before he grabbed his favorite cast iron skillet from the pan hanger over the stove. The site where he'd found the recipe said it would work as a suitable replacement for a Korean stone bowl.

"I'm working my way through foods of various countries. It's sort of a project I've been doing for a few months now. I've done Italy. Norway. Mexico. Now I'm on Korea."

Ashton's eyes lit up just like they had when Evelyn had been gossiping. God, what *was* that feeling in his chest? It was like a hot lamp had flicked on inside his heart. It warmed him all over.

"Really?" Ashton asked. "That's amazing! Where did you get the idea? How do you choose your next country? How many foods do you make per country? Most importantly, why are you doing this? Tell me *everything*!"

Walker laughed. "I'm not sure there's that much to say. I was bored, so I started it as a game for myself."

"Bored with your usual meals, or bored-bored?" Ashton asked.

"Both."

Ashton followed him around the kitchen as Walker worked, watching eagerly and getting in his way a bit, but it was nice. Friendly. Casey hadn't been wrong to suggest that Walker really needed to make more of an effort with Ashton. Being friends like this was great and would only strengthen their work together in the office.

If Walker enjoyed the flash of delight in Ashton's green eyes or his teasing smile as he stole a bite of this and that, if he had loved seeing him in the morning without makeup—freckles on display—or now got goosebumps all over when Ashton left briefly and returned wearing just sweatpants and a collarbone-revealing T-shirt, then so what? Walker could keep things professional.

It was better to feel these shivery things than all the frustration and aggravation Ashton had always engendered in him before. So much better. Yes, Casey had definitely been on to something.

Even if it meant nothing at all.

As he worked, Walker told Ashton about how he came upon the idea to do a food tour of the world in his own kitchen via a random YouTube video he found while down a rabbit hole one lonely night. He explained the process for choosing a country—closing his eyes and spinning the globe—and that alone got the best reaction from Ashton yet. Eyes scrunched, lips stretched into a giddy smile, Ashton clutched his heart and fake-swooned. "Oh, Walker, that's the sexiest thing I've ever heard anyone say outside the bedroom. That's flat-out *dreamy*!"

Walker sputtered. "Sexy? Why?"

"It's so random! And whimsical! I love it! Who knew?"

"Who knew what?"

"That Walker Ronson could be so fun."

His ears burned, and he knew Ashton had to be joking about the sexy thing, but he still felt *so* pleased. Like when he'd achieved a miraculous hole in one—and weren't they all miraculous? Or taken home a thick stack of winnings won by the skin of his teeth. Or, more innocently, when he'd been a kid and the biggest present beneath the tree had been passed into his lap to unwrap.

Somehow Ashton's sweet laughter and thrilled smiles felt better than all of those things combined. They felt like the purest gift he'd ever received. And Walker didn't want to think too closely about that.

He just wanted to enjoy the unexpected present.

THAT NIGHT, AFTER they'd eaten and watched Netflix, Walker cleaned up in the kitchen while Ashton sprawled on the sofa with Nina and Bitsy, sipping a bourbon and poking around on his phone. He'd offered to help of course, but Walker had waved him off. He preferred to do it himself. Besides, he liked looking out into the living room to see Ashton smiling or laughing over something on the small screen. It was gratifying somehow.

Plus he had a great view of Ashton's collarbones poking out of his loose T-shirt neck, all sweet and sharp-looking. Grrr, what *was* his deal with those? They were entirely too delicately shaped and far too enticing for Ashton's own good. He was smart to keep them hidden by his more typical fashion choices. The unbuttoned silk blouse earlier had been an anomaly, thank God, or Walker would have even more trouble at the office dealing with Ashton's clothing. If those collarbones were on display all the time, Ashton would be in danger. People would be trying to lick them on the street if they could see them.

Walker finished up the dishes, poured himself a bourbon, and squeezed onto the opposite side of the sofa from Ashton. He barely had room with the sprawl of the dogs, but Nina moved her feet a little to give him space.

"I can't believe this Facebook post is still getting traction," Ashton laughed, typing in a response with his thumbs. "I just got a request from a local reporter to do an interview about it."

"And you're going to?"

"Maybe." Ashton grinned. "Listen to his pitch: 'I'm writing an article about the concept of bringing fake boyfriends to family holiday events and weddings, but your offer with the focus on stirring trouble is a unique take.' That's right. Murdering people with my annoyingly inappropriate comments and charming smile is uniquely me."

Walker frowned, sipping his bourbon. He imagined inviting Ashton to a big family event. It was strange to consider. The shock Ashton would generate with just his effeminacy alone would be substantial. Homophobia ran deep in many of his cousins and uncles, not to mention his father in his own way. Ashton's uncensored thoughts, which so often seemed to simply burst out of his mouth, would definitely grab everyone's attention…

Walker sat up a little straighter. Tilted his head. Considered.

"What?" Ashton asked, looking up from where he was thumbing in some sort of message on his phone.

"Do you…" Walker cleared his throat. "I mean, have you ever done it? The fake boyfriend thing? Or was it just a joke?"

Ashton put his phone aside and leaned forward, a smile already teasing his lips. "Why? Are you in need of—" His green eyes took on a gleam and his gaze darted toward the wall by the Christmas tree where a photograph of young Evelyn in her prom dress was next to one of Walker in a tux, exactly where his grandmother had hung them ages ago. "Oh, oh…ohhhh!" He leaned over the dozing dogs, eyes sparkling wildly, and he grabbed hold of Walker's hands with surprisingly cold fingers. "Oh, yes. Walker, yes, *yes*. This could be *so fun!*"

How had Ashton known what he was thinking? Was he a mind reader on top of being a shimmery, shiny, silky, sexy man? Wait, what? *Sexy?*

Walker focused. "Have you done it before? Ever?"

Ashton flapped his hand. "Sure, sure. How do you think I paid for college? Playing a fake boyfriend was totally my meal ticket."

"Really?"

Ashton half fell over laughing. Simone moaned grumpily at the interruption to her evening doze. "No! Of course not! I mean, who really *does* that? Outside of Hallmark movies, I mean?"

Walker shrugged. "I guess it's called being an escort."

Ashton laughed again. "Exactly! No, I've never been an escort. Though I feel stupid now that I didn't think of it back then. Just imagine how much money I could have charged to just be seen in public with lonely widows! I mean, with this face!" He gestured at it, laughing, but somehow, he didn't sound egotistical at all. Just amused.

Besides, he had a point. Ashton's face was the definition of dreamy.

Ashton pulled himself upright again, still laughing, but he seemed to want to wipe the grin away. "No, seriously. *Seriously*, don't look like that! Stop frowning! Who does this kind of thing, you ask? I'll tell you who does this kind of thing. *You*! You do! And now me! And I will for real be your fake date to this wedding, and we'll solve all of Evelyn's problems in one dramatic, ridiculous swoop, and it will be amazing!"

Walker shook his head. It was too absurd. How had he even let himself think of it to begin with? There was no way, even if this ruse succeeded, to truly solve Evelyn's problems. Though, he supposed, all she really wanted right now was the space in which she could simply be the bride… Still, it was just too much. "No, this is dumb."

"And that's why it's a *great* idea," Ashton said. "Fortune favors the brave, and the brave are idiots. Don't talk yourself out of it. Look, of course, we'll get Evelyn and Tom's buy-in first, right? We wouldn't throw a wrench into the works of their wedding without their permission, but you saw her earlier. She was basically begging for a drama bomb to hit so she and Tom wouldn't be the focus of all that family animosity anymore." He grinned. "You'd be a hero younger brother taking all the family's knives in your back for her!" He clutched his chest again. "*Dreamy*."

Walker startled to realize that Ashton looking at him like he really did find Walker dreamy was what tipped him over into pulling out his phone and texting Evelyn.

*Meet at Peter Kern tomorrow for drinks? I have a solution to the family-at-the-wedding problem.*

He was sweating when he pressed send, but he did it anyway. Heat poured through his veins like liquor, and he let out a long push of breath. Wow, he hadn't felt so dizzy with adrenaline since his last big bet. Fuck. What a rush. Ashton smiled at him with glowing eyes, and another pulse of heat went through him. Walker's chest felt tight. It was hard to breath, even harder to swallow, and he gulped embarrassingly when he tried.

Ding.

He glanced down at his phone to see Evelyn's reply.

*5:30? And if this is for real, you'll be my hero forever.*

Hero. He looked up at Ashton and wondered what it took to impress a guy like him enough to be considered a hero. Ashton was so shameless and over the top, it probably required something terrifying like cliff jumping or sky diving.

Well, Walker wasn't always averse to taking risks. His bank account reflected that didn't it?

He wanted to shake out his sweaty hands but instead calmly put the phone aside and rubbed his palms on his jeans. His voice wavered a little. "We'll meet Evelyn for drinks at Peter Kern tomorrow. Explain it to her then. If she's in, then…" He swallowed again, this time without an audible gulp. "Then I'm in too. With you, I mean. For the, uh, the fake boyfriend plan."

Ashton nodded eagerly, his white teeth biting into his pink, plump bottom lip. "This is going to be so fun. Just wait and see. A fun time for me, and an easy win for you."

Walker ignored the sudden flash of memory from the last time someone had told him that. "So long as the wedding is a win for Evelyn," he said. "That's all that matters to me."

*And that smile*, he thought, when Ashton flashed it at him again. Holy hell, how was being given that smile more rewarding than any bet he'd ever won? And what the hell was wrong with him that he was thinking that way now? Ashton had always gotten under his skin. But not like this.

Not like…*this.*

Walker didn't want to analyze his sweaty hands and pounding heart too closely. Instead, he lolled his head against the back of the sofa and turned to gaze at Ashton's profile. He was busy typing into his phone again. He looked so beautiful, delicately pretty both with and without makeup. What would it mean if Walker actually felt something for a man like Ashton? What would people think? His father? His grandfather? Himself?

"There," Ashton said. "I declined the interview. Wouldn't want to give away the game before the wedding, now would we?"

"What about the post itself?"

He shrugged. "If we really sell it, the post won't matter. People will believe it."

"Sell it?"

"Yeah. I'm a good kisser. Don't worry." He winked and Walker's heart pumped so hard he felt like he might pass out.

"*What?*"

"I'm kidding. I mean, we'll need to do some PDA at the wedding for sure, but nothing big. Don't panic." Ashton reached over and patted Walker's thigh. He set his phone aside and turned his body to plop his socked feet into Walker's lap like that was normal.

Like they'd sat on the sofa like that ever before. Like it was easy. The dogs even shifted to make room for him. With shaking hands and a weird feeling like he might start to laugh or levitate or do something else wholly unexpected, Walker took up Ashton's feet and began to rub them.

"Oh! You didn't have to… I didn't mean for you to…" He giggled a little nervously. "I was just stretching out and being a brat."

"Good practice." Walker rubbed. "It's not a big deal."

Ashton groaned softly and melted against the sofa. "That feels so good. Wow. Thank you."

"Mm," Walker murmured, his blood racing.

What would it mean to want a man like Ashton? How would it feel to let himself admit to such a thing? And to acknowledge that he wanted Ashton to want him back?

He swallowed hard and massaged Ashton's feet longer, confused and relieved when Ashton reached for the remote and turned on Netflix, starting a new episode of the show they'd been watching together. He didn't know what exactly they were doing, but he supposed there was no harm in doing this.

His stomach swooped and lifted until he finally calmed down enough to focus on the TV. Still, every once in a while, when Ashton laughed or giggled at Walker's touch on a ticklish place on his foot, Walker's pulse soared again.

*What would it mean if...?*

The Christmas tree glittered in the corner like a silent, amused observer of Walker's sleigh ride of emotions.

# Chapter Six

PETER KERN LIBRARY was a modern speakeasy dressed up to look like a library and accessed by a hidden door in the lobby of the posh downtown boutique Hotel Oliver. The pale leather sofas, low tables, and the soft lighting leant a romantic air to the place, though it also held a serious enough vibe to bring clients for celebratory drinks after a particularly successful meeting. Tonight, it twinkled with added white Christmas lights and gilded decorations, and Walker admired them silently.

Ashton sat with his arm outstretched behind Walker on the sofa, and Evelyn sat across from them in a leather chair. Tom was at the bar collecting their drinks since the waitress was busy and they all wanted to get liquor into their bellies for this conversation. Walker did especially.

"So, you know how I posted on Facebook proposing to be a fake boyfriend for the holiday?" Ashton started when Tom returned, because, of course, the post had become such a viral sensation that nearly everyone they knew in Knoxville was at least a little aware of it.

Tom chuckled. "Hysterical, bro. Reminds me—I've been meaning to ask you for an appointment to consult about rebranding my business. Never got around to it, what with the crazy family goings-on, the kids, and the wedding plans, plus my business has been booming out of the blue for some reason. Can't complain about that. But, as Evelyn is always pointing out, my tattoo shop really needs a reboot in branding, and I think you could help." He shot Walker an apologetic glance before rapidly adding, "Uh, you and Walker both, of course."

"I'll have my assistant Damien call you," Ashton said, smiling with a cute, but somehow professional, wink. How did he do that? "Sound good?"

"Yup." Tom grinned and slipped a hand over his long, auburn beard, pulling it taut and then releasing it again. Walker knew from the hugs they'd exchanged since things got serious with Evelyn that it was incredibly soft—much softer than it looked. "So, yeah," Tom went on, getting them back on track. "That fake boyfriend post. What's that got to do with our wedding problem?"

"I think the boys have a plan, honey," Evelyn said, her eyes already sparkling. She was wearing a business-sensible navy dress, having left her office at their father's petroleum company to come here directly. She still looked glamorous in the low lights.

"Involving a fake boyfriend?" Tom asked, confusion crossing his face.

"I believe so." Evelyn laughed and lifted her drink, tilting it toward Walker and Ashton. "And I imagine you two would be the ones faking being boyfriends?"

Tom blinked. "*Oh!* But how would that work?" He looked between Walker and Ashton.

"Well…" Ashton took hold of Walker's hand on the table. His slim fingers fit perfectly between Walker's own, and his buffed nails gleamed in the candlelight.

Walker looked at their joined hands. Was that really necessary? Wasn't this selling the concept a little earlier than necessary? Ashton didn't have to hold Walker's hand just yet did he? That was the kind of thing they'd eventually need to do at the wedding, but…

Ashton's fingers squeezed Walker's lightly. A shiver slipped through Walker's body, and he couldn't tear his eyes away from where Ashton held on to him, not even to look up and see his sister's reaction to the plan as Ashton outlined it.

"Walker and I would pretend to be dating. Seriously dating. Like, so in love we're in the running to be the next wedding in the family kind of dating. And, to really pull focus from any gossip about you two, I'll play the part of the absolute worst choice for him ever of all time."

Ashton laughed. It sounded like a series of low and high bells that fluttered out of his throat like magic. Why had Walker never noticed how beautiful his laugh was? "All four of us can make a plan around that—outline what's the most scandalous thing I could do or say in any given situation. Or I can just keep them guessing, saying the absolute worst thing as it occurs to me? I'd be amazing at that."

Walker's heart thumped, and he listened hard for some sound that might indicate what his sister and Tom were thinking about this scheme since he still couldn't stop looking at the way the rings on Ashton's hand glittered and how his pale skin contrasted with Walker's slightly darker tone. When he did drag his eyes up, he saw his sister staring at him with intense eyes, but Tom spoke first.

"Guys, Evelyn and I totally appreciate this sweet gesture, but there are a few really obvious problems with this plan."

Ashton smiled again, and his fingers tightened around Walker's. "I'm sure we can deal with them all."

"I don't know. I mean, you posted about an idea like this on social media and everyone who's anyone knows the gist of the scheme, right? So, half the family would just think you were faking it, wouldn't they?"

Ashton shrugged and took a sip from his cocktail. "I could delete the post and make a brand new one all about how my new, *very* serious, and already incredibly committed *lover*," he snorted, and Walker swallowed hard, "doesn't want anyone to think I was being for real with the offer, and thus he's asked me to eighty-six the post."

He shot his shiny smile at Tom again, and Walker's fingers clenched in his reflexively. No one should light up like that. A little lip gloss shouldn't add that much to a smile, should it? "A post like that alone will get more attention than it deserves, but that's the point, right? Pulling attention from you two onto us."

"Okay, but what about Mom and Dad?" Evelyn asked, sipping her own pink drink and smirking. "What are they going to think?"

Walker grew hot all over imagining his father's reaction to the idea of him dating someone like Ashton. But...well... "Dad brought it on himself by insisting on this giant wedding, didn't he? And we'd be careful in how scandalous we are at the event itself. We'd only target family gossipmongers, not Dad's clients or friends."

"That's why a plan will be essential," Ashton said. "I'll need to know who to avoid. But everyone's on Facebook or Insta or TikTok these days, so I can totally scope out the folks to scandalize and those to schmooze. I'm good at schmoozing. I promise." He blinked with faux flirtation, and Evelyn laughed.

"I'm sure you are." She cleared her throat. "Will you tell Mom and Dad about this plan beforehand? Or let them believe you're dating him too?"

Walker's stomach clenched. "You know we can't tell Dad."

Evelyn glanced over at Ashton and raised a brow at Walker. "Why not?"

"He'd put his foot down to stop it."

"Mm." Evelyn sipped her drink again and caught Tom's eye. "That he would. He's never been one for these kinds of shenanigans, but then again, he's no fun, and he's not the one who has to deal with all the jerks in our family. They're too afraid to be assholes to his face."

"Right."

"And can you imagine telling Mom that you're bringing a fake boy-friend so that you can dodge backstabbing family at the wedding?"

Walker shook his head.

Evelyn bit into her lower lip thoughtfully, tilting her head and gaz-ing up at the tin ceiling. "It's a tough choice, but I think if we're going to do this then she'd have to believe you two are really dating. Otherwise she'd blow it or give away the game or talk you out of it. And that means lying to Mom. You're willing to do that?"

"She wouldn't understand?" Ashton asked.

"Mom's too nice," Walker explained.

"No, she's too *kind*," Evelyn elaborated. "She'll be worried that we'll *embarrass* people by fooling them, and she won't want that. Better to be kind than right, she'd say."

"At what expense, though? At the expense of you enjoying your day as a bride? A—hopefully—once in a lifetime event?" Ashton asked.

"She'd say there's a better way."

"Like not inviting these assholes," Tom grumbled.

Evelyn laughed. "No, not that. Alas."

"What way, then?" Ashton implored, his hand still tight on Walker's. He seemed invested in the idea of faking being boyfriends, but also in protecting Evelyn from having her special day ruined.

"By growing a thicker skin."

"I'm sorry to say this, because I'm sure your mom is a lovely person, but *that* doesn't seem very kind."

"I agree," Evelyn said, lifting her glass to cheers at Ashton before taking another sip and smiling. "So, tell me more about this plan."

"Babe," Tom interrupted before Ashton could get going again. "I still don't think it will work."

"Why?" she asked.

"Yes, why, Tom?" Ashton piped up.

"Well, don't take this the wrong way, but what about the fact that Ashton's…"

"Ashton's what?" Walker asked, bristling.

"He's not exactly…" Tom shrugged a little uncomfortably.

"Go on," Ashton said.

"No offense, but you're not Walker's type."

Ashton sat up a little straighter, and Walker clung to his hand even harder. He suspected his squeeze might even hurt a little, but no way was he letting go now. Ashton's voice tipped higher. "Are you saying no one would believe Walker would be into me?"

"No, I mean, well, yes, I guess that's what I'm saying." Tom winced. "It's just that he's only ever dated guys who, you know, look like *him*." He gestured Walker's way. "All those Polo shirts and country-club memberships." His lip curled a little, and Walker tried not to be offended. "That sort of guy."

*Hey,* I'm *that sort of guy,* Walker wanted to say, but Ashton was already talking.

"Oh, I'm well aware." Ashton drew himself up even more. "But maybe that's why those relationships never worked out." His smile cut like a glittering knife. "Ever consider that?" He pulled Walker's hand up to his mouth and kissed the back of it, leaving a soft, sticky residue behind. And, hell, Walker…liked it. Really liked it. "He needs someone like me."

Evelyn cleared her throat, and Walker realized that while he'd been watching Ashton, Evelyn had been watching him. Her lips tilted in a small, familiar smirk, like the time when he was sixteen and she'd found his secret stash of computer-printed pornographic photos beneath his bed. "Walker, was this your idea?"

Walker realized that he'd let Ashton take control of the presentation, and he lifted his chin confidently. "It was. I thought of it last night, and I think we can pull it off. And even if we can't, even if people suspect that it's all for show and that I'm paying him to escort me, or even just pretending to be dating him like his post suggested, that'll be fuel enough for gossip, right? Like why would I do that? People will have a lot to say either way. And none of it about you, Tom, Morgan, or the kids."

"And Mom and Dad?"

"There should be nothing shameful in their son bringing a beautiful man to your wedding."

Evelyn looked between him and Ashton and then down at their joined hands. Her mouth twitched up at the corner again, and she turned to Tom. "Let's talk in private for a minute? In the hotel lobby?

We'll be right back."

Walker thought Ashton would let go of his hand as soon as Evelyn and Tom left, but he didn't. Instead he traced Walker's knuckles with his thumb, saying, "I can't believe they think I can't do this. I mean, I could absolutely make anyone believe I'm in love with you. It wouldn't even be hard."

"But what about me?" Walker asked gruffly. "Maybe I'm not as great an actor."

Ashton looked up at him, his green eyes shining in the candlelight. He searched Walker's face and grinned. "Ah, no, just look at me like that! And everyone will believe we're madly in love! That's perfect, Walker. You're a really good actor already, see?"

Walker almost gaped. He wasn't *acting* right now? And he wasn't *in love*? He was just…impressed by how much he'd missed about Ashton before. By focusing on all the ways Ashton was different from him, by feeling uncomfortable with Ashton's dissimilarities instead of appreciating them, he'd almost missed out on a really cool person.

Ashton sighed happily, gazing up at him. "Man, the person you look at like that for *real*? They're gonna be so lucky." Then he released Walker's hand and took up his drink.

Walker's skin tingled where Ashton had been touching him, and he wanted to wrap their fingers together again. But he lifted his bourbon and sipped it instead. Weird how lines got so easily blurred when a person was lonely. He needed to keep that in mind.

Tom and Evelyn returned from the lobby, Evelyn with a grin spread across her face like Christmas-come-early, and Tom with a smirk directed at Walker that he didn't quite know how to interpret.

"We're in," Evelyn said. "Right, Tom?"

Tom nodded, his eyes on Walker. "Yup. We're good to go with this plan. Initiate Operation Fake Boyfriend."

Ashton squirmed with excitement next to Walker. "Fantastic! Now we just need to decide on the details."

Immediately, Ashton and Evelyn began to plot. Tom kept sneaking indecipherable looks at Walker but saying nothing. It wasn't long before they all needed another round of drinks.

"Okay, so like how crazy can I go?" Ashton asked, leaning forward over the table toward Evelyn, hand to his chest. "I assure you I don't ever want to take attention away from you as the bride—"

"No, please do!"

"Okay, I could wear this for example? To the wedding?" Ashton flipped his phone around and displayed a picture of himself in the most flamboyant suit Walker had ever seen. It was a sky-blue skinny tuxedo with orange and white koi fish printed all over it. Why did Ashton even own this atrocity? And why did Walker suspect that Ashton would actually look smoking hot in it?

"God, that's perfect. Perfect," Evelyn cooed. "Oh, Tom, just think of everyone's faces. Your Uncle Dave will shit a brick."

"Or maybe this one?" Ashton turned the phone around again, flipped through some of his photos, and then found what he was looking for. "Too much? Or just right?"

"Oh God, it's great, but almost not enough."

How could it not be enough? In the photo, Ashton wore a fitted, burgundy suit that was so tight through the legs and ass that it made Walker feel a little…well, a little aroused and tingly, and he wasn't sure that was what he wanted to feel on his sister's wedding day.

Nor did he think he wanted to feel that way about Ashton at all. Though it seemed to keep happening. Like the other night when he'd been unable to tear his eyes away from Ashton's collarbones, or when he'd had to shift around as he'd massaged his feet to keep from getting hard.

"I have another more exciting option," Ashton said. When he presented the next photo, Walker's legs went numb and a cold sweat broke out in the small of his back. Fuck. That suit was some kind of high-fashion bondage gear combination. How had Ashton even afforded these pieces? They all looked like they were incredibly pricey. Plus, was Ashton into that? Bondage and all that went with it? Because Walker absolutely wasn't.

Why did it matter? They were just friends! *What* was going on in his head?

"Okay, that's too far." Evelyn laughed. "Maybe can you add that chain to the other suit and sort of imply that you and Walker are into playful BDSM?"

"Sure," Ashton agreed. "I'll add a love bite too. On my neck? I'm good with stage makeup like that."

"Yes!"

"Evelyn…" Tom warned gently. "Let's not go too far. We have to live the rest of our lives with these people when it's over."

Walker licked his lips. He'd wanted to do this for his sister's sake and to fuck with his extended family, but implying that he's into BDSM with Ashton? That seemed a little far. And a fake love bite? He studied Ashton's long, white throat, gritting his teeth. He'd give him one for real if he didn't stop lifting his jaw in that casual way that made his Adam's apple stick out, all suckable and sexy.

*Ridiculous.*

He was being ridiculous. He was a man's man—he played golf and drank beer with the men he screwed. He didn't have any interest in a boyfriend who put on makeup and wanted to look pretty before heading out to the grocery store, or before hitting the links—if Ashton even knew golf at all! Plus, Walker felt sure that at the country club, Ashton would want to eat upstairs in the nice luncheon rooms with the chattering women and grannies, not hang out below with the sweaty men in the pro shop café.

Not that Walker was going to be going golfing or dining at the country club again any time soon. He wasn't going back to that life. But that wasn't the point. The point was they had nothing in common.

Not that you could convince Walker's dick of that. That traitorous appendage seemed to suddenly think he and Ashton could very well have a *lot* in common. A naked lot. Complete with blow jobs and orgasms galore.

But dicks weren't very good judges of men. Nor were they helpful in any other way. They weren't even capable of buying Secret Santa gifts for gorgeous men who wore more mascara than Walker's mother—or were those false eyelashes? How could he even tell?

He was really hating his dick right now. Better to ignore it, have another drink, and help plan Operation Fake Boyfriend. He was probably just horny and needed to hook up with someone, though he hated those apps and didn't really do one-night stands. It wasn't his style.

Clearly, he was just lonely. Much too lonely.

But tonight he didn't need to be lonely; he was with his sister, her fiancé, and his *friend*. Got that, dick? Friend. No, *coworker*! God, get it right!

After they left Peter Kern Library, laughing and flushed with a rushing giddiness, Walker decided to just let himself enjoy the moment. He walked arm-in-arm with Evelyn through Market Square while Ashton and Tom discussed various potential branding concepts for Tom's tattoo parlor. Ashton promised to draw up some sketches and send them after the New Year.

The twinkle lights in every shop window, the triangular-shaped trees made from strings of light perched on the top of every store-front's roof, and the carols from the outdoor ice-skating rink (set up, as always, for the holidays in the middle of the square) leant an even more festive air to the already enjoyable night. Walker noticed a new store had just opened on the Market Square, a Christmas-themed shop called Winter Wonderland. He'd try stopping in there the next day to look for a Secret Santa gift for Ashton.

When Tom and Ashton paused to give money to a violinist busking by the Tennessee Woman's Suffrage Memorial, Evelyn spoke quietly in

Walker's ear. "Are you really up for this, Walker? All the attention? All the negativity and gossip? It's not like you to want to bring any of that onto yourself. You've always tried to keep your problems and foibles private."

Walker stopped walking, looking back to where Ashton was now dancing with Tom to the fiddler's tune. "I know, but some things are worth it."

She watched him in the darkness. "You really like him."

Walker scoffed. "He's my business partner."

"Seems like he's more than that."

"Well, he's becoming a friend." He realized he might not have said that only a few days ago. "And he's a nice guy. Fun. Makes me laugh. But when I said some things are worth it, I was talking about you." Walker smiled down at her. "You protected and took care of me my whole life. Let me do that for you for a change. Besides, this plan is…" He coughed slightly. "To be honest, I haven't felt this excited by anything since…" He cleared his throat and changed direction. "Since I left Dad's office to start SRS with Casey. It feels fun."

"I hate to say it but I can't remember the last time I saw you having fun," Evelyn murmured.

Neither could he. Not since he'd stopped gambling. Not that it had been exactly *fun* near the end. Or maybe ever? It'd been a rush, and that had broken up the monotony of his life, sure, but was that the same thing as fun? He liked to think it wasn't.

This wedding plan was risky, a gamble of its own kind, but hopefully with no real victims and Evelyn and Tom as the sole winners. It felt like the kind of fun he used to have when he was still a kid. If he now felt a certain underlying wild excitement at the thought of doing this with Ashton in particular, he wasn't going to admit that to Evelyn. At least whatever thrill this was, it wouldn't eat through his trust fund. After all, he'd already accomplished that.

"Golfing used to be fun," he said.

"No. Golfing used to be safe." Evelyn tsked. "And that was the whole problem, wasn't it? That's how it went so wrong for you. How golfing became 'golfing,' right? No matter how boring you seem on the surface—"

"Hey!"

"You need a little danger, Walker. You want to touch the flame."

He opened his mouth to ask what she meant by that but Tom and Ashton had finished dancing. They approached huffing and laughing. "That fiddler's damn good," Tom said. "We should have *him* at the wedding."

"Sure, sure, we'll just tell Daddy the string quartet he hired isn't good enough and we've hired a street busker instead."

"A string quartet?" Tom asked with a groan. "Babe, why?"

"I let my mom decide on the music. It was better than disappointing her."

Tom sighed and wrapped his arm around Evelyn's shoulders. "When this wedding is over, we're taking charge of our own lives, understand? No more letting them run the show."

Evelyn shrugged. "You say that now. But why don't we see what kind of show they want to run first? You never know. We might like it."

Tom rolled his eyes and kissed her forehead.

After Walker gave Tom and Evelyn hugs goodbye, they split off toward the parking garage while Ashton and Walker strolled toward Gay Street. Ashton hummed under his breath and danced a few steps as the Christmas music from the ice rink—"Joy to the World" currently—faded out behind them. The sidewalks were busy with people carrying Christmas shopping bags, and they turned left heading toward Jackson Avenue and the apartment that Ashton apparently rented there.

"It won't take long," Ashton said. "I just need to grab a few more days' worth of clothes and then we can go. Thanks for saying I can cook them in your dryer. I promise they didn't find any bed bugs in my unit."

"I know. It's okay."

"And thanks again for letting me stay with you."

"It's not a problem. I'm…" Walker cleared his throat. "The dogs are enjoying it."

Ashton caught his eye with a grin. "Simone grabbed my underwear from the bathroom floor while I was showering and holed up under my bed with it."

"She did?" Walker laughed. "Guess she really likes you."

"She's silly," Ashton said with a giggle. "I love her. But I guess that'll teach me to lock the door, huh? I had no idea she could use her paw to push the knob."

"I meant to warn you."

Ashton bumped his shoulder and gave him a sweet smile. "It's okay."

A woman with blond hair was sitting on the front steps of Ashton's apartment building when they arrived, looking a little lost and frustrated. She had her phone out, punching at something on the screen, but her face brightened when she looked up and saw them approaching.

Ashton came to an abrupt standstill. "Oh, hell no." He turned on his heel, catching Walker by the arm. "Let's go."

"Why? Your clothes?"

"Nah. Forget 'em. Who needs more clothes? No one needs more clothes. I could just be naked. I've got a great body. It'd be fine," Ashton babbled as he tugged on Walker's arm. "Besides, I can use your washing machine, right? Right. And there's always the dry cleaners, too, though their bills are whew!" At the quick sound of the woman's feet as she ran up behind them, Ashton walked even faster.

"Ashton Hudson, stop right there!"

*Hudson?* Ashton's last name was Sellers.

The woman's voice was sharp, commanding, and it made Walker freeze but not Ashton. He just put on even more speed until he realized Walker wasn't budging.

Turning around, Ashton sighed and met Walker's gaze with an expression of miserable regret. Walker's stomach sank at the dark look in his eyes. Somehow, just by stopping he felt like he'd truly let Ashton down. Walker had just been a hero, and now he was a disappointment.

"Mom," Ashton said, turning his attention to the woman who was breathlessly approaching. Walker had never heard him sound so witheringly hostile before.

The woman drew closer, and Walker got a good look at her dirty jeans, stained sweatshirt, and the worn jacket tied around her waist. Her blond hair looked unwashed. Walker studied her sunken, tired face, looking for a hint of Ashton's beauty in it, but found nothing.

"Ashton, you haven't returned my texts."

"Lies already? You don't even have my number," Ashton said blandly. "There's a reason for that. How'd you get my address? Dad? Angel?"

"It doesn't matter, does it?"

"Of course it does."

"Don't you worry your head about that." She smiled, showing gaps in her teeth. "I just need a place to stay tonight, baby. You can put your poor mama up, can't you?"

"No."

"His apartment's dealing with bed bugs. But you're welcome to stay with—" He hesitated. Before he could finish the sentence, Ashton put a hand on his arm.

"Walker, stop." He turned his attention back to his mother. "Just no, Mom. No. *Forever* no."

Ashton's mom put her hands out. The nails were gnawed and there were sores around the knuckles. Walker's heart twisted but something kept him silent. She peered up at Ashton pleadingly. "Don't be like that."

Ashton started to turn away, but she grabbed hold of his coat. He shook her off. "Don't touch me."

"Fine," she muttered, eyes darkening. "If I can't stay with you, then I just need a few dollars to get through the night, baby. Enough for a hotel room and some dinner, and a little more so I can get some food for my dog."

Walker turned to Ashton, brows raised; worry at the thought of the woman and her dog suffering filled him. The night was expected to grow quite cold in the wee hours. Did she and the dog really not have a place to sleep? Christmas was drawing near, and Christian charity called for some kind of generosity here surely. Did he even have more than a few dollars in his wallet? He'd paid for their drinks with a card earlier. Should he offer up his home for the night despite Ashton's protest, or…?

"You don't have a dog," Ashton said coldly, his back straight and stiff.

"I do!"

Ashton rolled his eyes. Walker had never seen him so disdainful, never imagined Ashton's beautiful mouth could curl into such a hateful sneer. "I gave you all the money I will *ever* give you four years ago, and I'm not giving you another dime. I told you to never come around me again."

"But—"

"Not ever, ever, *ever.*"

"Ashton Christopher Hudson, I am your mother."

He hissed through his teeth. "I'm *not* your son."

"It's Christmas!" Her eyes grew feverish as she spread her hands wide, imploring. "If I can look past your," here she shot Walker a significant look, "filthy sins of nature, then you should look past me and mine."

Ashton's already hostile expression grew cold as ice. "I don't need you to look past anything about me."

Instantly, the woman changed tacks. "I'm sorry, baby. I really am. I know I hurt you before, but I've changed. You have to believe me."

Ashton's jaw tensed and released. "I've heard every apology and every excuse from you a million times. They're always lies. Go. Get out of here."

She crossed her arms over her chest and snarled, "Where am I supposed to go exactly?"

"Angel said you were at the women's shelter. Did you already blow it with them there? Let me guess: they caught you using and kicked you out?"

"It was just once."

"Right, and I also heard you were trying to con Bill and his wife into taking you in."

"Sounds like you do care about your old mama, keeping tabs on me like that."

Ashton huffed. "Leave Bill alone. He owes you nothing."

"Owes me nothing? I raised you without his help—"

"You did *not* raise me. Neither of you did."

She again switched her tone, becoming gentle once more, as if she thought she might be able to reach Ashton if she implored him just the right way. "Your father and I have become friendly again, that's all. He mentioned I might be able to move in with him once I leave the shelter, but—"

"But you got kicked out for using, and he's rescinded the offer, right?"

"It's your responsibility to take care of me. I'm your mother."

Ashton's eyes blazed. Though Walker didn't fully understand what was happening, he was gleaning that Ashton's childhood had been raw and painful, and this woman wasn't just homeless but an active addict.

"So there. You have to take care of me," she said smugly, as if she'd played a winning hand of some kind.

"I owe you nothing, Mom. Go to Grandma's if you're so desperate."

Ashton's mother scoffed. "You wouldn't wish that woman on anyone. Even me."

Ashton took a long, slow breath. "Listen carefully: I'm not giving you anything. No money, no energy, no time."

"But my dog!" she cried, darting a glance at Walker as if she suspected his weakness.

"You don't have a dog."

"I do!"

"Where is it then?" Ashton put up his hand. "Never mind, stop. I'm not arguing with you."

His mother narrowed her eyes and took Ashton's measure. Walker felt sweaty despite the cold air, worried and uncertain, but he stood firm beside Ashton. "Fine," she snapped bitterly. "I'll see if your *sister* will help me since you won't. She doesn't live too far from here. Why is it that she's nicer to me than you are?"

"First off, Angel's not my sister." Ashton sounded dead and dull, like he'd turned into someone Walker had never met before.

"Stepsister then."

"Secondly, Angel's nice to you because she doesn't know what I know about you. And it looks like I'll have to explain it to her more clearly. She shouldn't be throwing her money away on you."

She flipped the sad, hurt expression back onto her hollow face. "But, Ashton, baby, I'm better now."

Ashton just snorted. "If you ever come back here to bother me again, I swear I will have you arrested for stalking."

Walker was pretty sure he couldn't do that, but it sounded like a good threat all the same.

"I just want to make it all up to you, baby. Just give me a chance to prove—"

Ashton brushed past her, moving back toward his apartment building, and Walker followed. He glanced over his shoulder to find her trudging back toward the lights of Gay Street. Despite all Ashton had said, Walker wondered if he should have given her the few bills he had. Would she be all right out there on her own in the night? What if she really had a dog?

"That was my mom," Ashton said needlessly as he keyed into his apartment building with shaking fingers. He didn't sound worried about the woman's prospects or how she would spend her night. If anything he sounded numb and, underneath it all, hurt. "Jamie Rae Hudson." He spat her name like it tasted bad. "I took back my father's surname when I turned eighteen. Not that she respects that I've changed it." He blew out a hard breath. "Don't worry. She doesn't have a dog."

"Are you sure?"

"Pretty sure." Ashton winced. "Look, please don't hate me, okay? I know I sounded cruel back there, but… I tried. For years I tried. I studied addiction, and I supported her attempts at recovery. But now? Now I really don't care. There's nothing she can say to me, nothing she can do…" He trailed off, shaking his head. "Please forget you ever saw her. That's what I'll try to do."

Walker wondered about just how bad things must have been for Ashton—sweet, funny, charming Ashton—to cut off his own mother. He turned the thoughts around over and over in his head as he followed Ashton up a flight of stairs and down a dark hall to an apartment that, when Ashton opened it up, was in a state of utter disarray.

Every piece of (rather shabby) furniture was pulled away from the walls, framed pictures were stacked in a corner, and plastic bags were stacked in the kitchen and bathroom from what Walker could glimpse.

Ashton returned with a sealed black plastic bag in each hand. Seeing Walker standing there in the middle of the mess, no doubt looking shell-shocked, Ashton blushed. "It's not normally like this, obviously."

"I figured."

Ashton gestured toward a half-open door that clearly led to his bedroom. "If you think this is a mess, you should see in there."

Walker noticed white powder all around the baseboards of the walls and around the ugly brown sofa's legs. "That's to kill the bugs?"

"Yup." Ashton glanced around the apartment and grimaced. "One day, I'll move somewhere better than this. But…" He let out a slow breath and gave a shaky smile that didn't touch his eyes. "Anyway, let's go."

He paused, looking shy all of a sudden and even a little ashamed. "I mean, if I'm still…if you still…" His eyes locked on the floor, his breaths coming in small shudders. "My life isn't what you probably thought when you invited me. You were suspicious of me before, and now you know…well, what you didn't know… What I didn't quite tell you." His usual eloquence and chattiness seemed to have fled, leaving behind only broken sentences that went nowhere good.

"C'mon," Walker said, stepping forward and grabbing one of the plastic bags from Ashton's hands. "Let's go home. The dogs'll be worried and hungry. They're not used to being left alone at night."

Ashton's relief was palpable, and Walker slung an arm over his shoulder to shake him a little, surreptitiously scenting his cologne. It smelled like paper and tobacco. More masculine than Walker would have imagined Ashton would prefer, but he liked it. It stirred his blood and he wanted to sniff it again.

Pulling away, Ashton laughed softly, but it didn't sound quite as bell-like as it had before they'd run into his mother or stepped into this shabby apartment. "Thanks. Yeah, let's go. I could use some dog cuddles right about now." He glanced at Walker. "And I promise my mom doesn't have a hungry dog, or any dog at all. Don't worry."

Walker let Ashton guide him out of the apartment building and back out to the street. There was no sign of his mother. As if he expected her to jump out, Ashton looked around every corner as they headed back to the parking garage and Walker's car.

Jamie Rae had seemed small, fragile, and harmless enough to Walker, but it was clear that to Ashton she was dangerous. Walker didn't ask questions. As they walked, each of them held their tongues and a plastic bag of clothing apiece.

Walker hoped Ashton was right about Jamie Rae not having a dog. If she did, he hoped the dog would be all right. No animal should be cold or hungry. And no human should be either.

Despite everything Ashton must have gone through as a kid to warrant that kind of treatment of his mother, Walker truly wished she would be okay. Christmas was the time for miracles, right? For her sake, he hoped Jamie Rae got one.

# Chapter Seven

DURING THE DRIVE back to Walker's house, Ashton stared out the window at the Christmas lights strung on every building and house and tried to decide if he felt more mortified or terrified.

When he'd asked Walker if they could drop by his apartment to pick up more clothes, he'd anticipated the embarrassment of Walker—Sequoyah Hills-dwelling, trust-fund recipient—seeing the seediness of his current home. But that idea hadn't bothered him too much. Walker already knew Justin's rehab was the reason Ashton was so strapped for cash and surely wouldn't judge him too harshly for his living situation.

But meeting his junkie mother? The woman who'd abandoned her responsibility to Ashton in favor of deep, endless dives into heroin or meth? The woman who'd been in and out of prison twice for drug use? The woman he'd given all his savings to four years ago for a stint in rehab? The woman who'd never even checked herself in, instead blowing the money on drugs and an extended trip to Florida with her then-dealer? The woman who'd left Tennessee state authorities with no choice but to send Ashton off at a tender age to be sheltered in his grandmother's hateful arms?

Ugh. No. It was all such nasty stuff. Jamie Rae Hudson wasn't anyone Ashton had wanted Walker—or frankly anyone from his new life—to ever meet.

Nor had Ashton wanted Walker to get a glimpse of his other nemesis: the sick, haunted feeling that swamped him whenever he came too close to memories of his past. The feeling that had grabbed him with such sharp claws at the hair salon the other day. And the one that threatened to snatch him up again now.

He took a slow, steady breath, allowing the Christmas songs from Walker's playlist to wash over him. The awful feeling remained, pressing in around him with images and feelings he couldn't seem to fight. All that hot, suffocating horror.

Carrying the plastic bag of his clothes had been too evocative too. Viscerally reminding him of the day when the social worker had come to take him away from his mother for good. Stuffing the few things he owned back then into a big, black trash bag and carrying it in his scrawny arms out to the social worker's car. The one that had taken him to Grandma Hudson's house. Back then he'd done it with his chin held high. Just like he had tonight. Pretending that he was all right. Pretending that everything was fine.

*For heaven's sake, get a grip.*

*Everything's fine.*

*You're grown. You're safe.*

"You okay?" Walker asked quietly after what must have been a very long, awkward silence. But given that the parking garage was only a ten-minute car ride from Walker's house at this time of evening, it probably hadn't been all that long. It just felt that way. Like Ashton was stuck in time. Stuck in a bad memory.

"I'm great."

Walker stayed silent, not refuting the obvious lie, but something about his body language told Ashton he hadn't accepted it either. It hung between them, obvious and strange.

"What do you want me to say?" Ashton asked after a few beats, irrational irritation rising beneath his fear. "I'm sorry you saw all that, okay? Can you just try to unsee it?"

"Unsee what?"

"Her. My place. Everything."

Walker frowned. His confusion irritated Ashton even further. He didn't have space for any of this right now. He couldn't breathe. He was about to drown. He snapped, "I had a rough childhood, all right?"

"Understood."

"Understood? Ha. As if you could *ever* understand." Hot shame followed his words. Why was he acting like this? Walker was becoming a friend now. He shouldn't ruin all the progress they'd made with a tantrum. He whispered, "I'm sorry. That was out of line."

"Rough childhoods come in different shapes and sizes," Walker said steadily. "But I won't pretend to know what you went through with her. You're doing so much for your cousin. Hell, you're doing so much for me and my sister, faking a relationship with me for Evelyn's sake. You're a good guy. Anyone can see that. If you don't have the space in your heart for your mom anymore, then I figure she did something truly awful, and I trust you on that."

Ashton blinked tearfully at the houses passing outside the car windows. They were bright and shining with colored lights and decked out with wreathes and garlands. The entire neighborhood looked like a Christmas miracle to the kid who'd grown up first with Jamie Rae's addiction and then with Grandma Hudson's abuse. He wished for an absolutely ludicrous moment that Walker was truly taking him home—that Walker's house was his own, that they were a real couple, not about to be a fake one, and that they'd live happily ever after together.

Most of all he wished he could believe in Walker's beautiful world of peaceful, comfortable things—warm houses, soft dogs, good meals—and believe that he had a place in it.

"Thank you," he whispered instead.

"Sure thing."

Christmas music continued to play lightly from the car speakers but oddly none of the songs were familiar at all. Which was a relief. It helped Ashton to firmly ground himself in the present moment, leaving behind the memories of carrying all his little-boy things in a plastic bag, of Grandma Hudson giving him nothing but a spanking for Christmas, of his mother ODing on the ratty couch as "Fairytale of New York" played through a set of dented Goodwill speakers.

"I'm sorry I brought down the mood," he said as they turned onto the riverside road that would ultimately culminate in Walker's driveway. "We were having such a fun night." He smiled, or tried to, but it felt plastic and strange on his lips. "I'm still excited about the wedding plans and Operation Fake Boyfriend."

Would Walker truly want to play pretend like that with a junkie's son? With a cold-hearted man who'd rejected his mother's pleas for help near Christmas? There'd been so much ugliness in that quick interaction with his mom. Ugliness that might bring to light for Walker alarming things about Ashton that he didn't want to be associated with—especially not as a fake lover anyway. Not in public.

"Are your suits in these bags?" Walker asked suddenly. "The ones from the pictures you showed Evelyn?"

Ashton shook his head. "No. They're at the dry cleaners. Expensive, I know. I could have stayed at a hotel for the cost of having them cleaned. But if there were any bed bugs in them, the cleaning process will take care of them without damaging the material. I've invested too much in those pieces to let them get ruined. Why?"

"I was just wondering," Walker said. "Didn't want to think of them all wadded up and wrinkled."

Ashton's heart eased slightly. Walker was being so kind. Maybe the thing to do was get everything about his mom and his life out in the open. Tear the Band-Aid off, and just let the chips fall where they may. Mixed metaphors be danged. He cleared his throat. "So, do you have any questions for me? About anything?" His heart hammered, and his palms grew even more sweaty.

"Questions?"

"Sure. I don't want any more weirdness between us. May as well just get it all out there."

Walker's neck turned red, then his cheeks. "I don't know."

"C'mon. I'm an open book." Ugh. But he felt sick to his stomach at what he was offering to reveal.

"So that one suit. The BDSM-y one. That's something you wear a lot?"

Ashton sat in silence for a moment, surprised. He'd expected questions about his mother, his childhood, or his reasons for turning her away. This was…unexpected. Then he spent a few frantic heartbeats trying to decide if Walker was asking about the suit, truly, or if he was asking about BDSM.

"It was a gift from a guy I dated for about three months last year." Careful to make sure he was being as clear as possible, though he didn't know why, he said, "It didn't work out with him because…" He huffed. "Well, I don't like those kinds of games. Who knew, right? Me? Not liking games?" Ashton laughed, and he was pleased it didn't sound too forced to his own ears. "But it turns out pain isn't my cup of tea."

"Oh."

"Yeah, and giving pain was one hundred percent his." Ashton shivered. "I, uh, tried, though. He was handsome and made me feel special. I liked that. So I thought maybe I could get past it, but I couldn't. All the pain stuff… It just brought up bad memories, and…" He stopped himself from saying much more. "But hey, I got that great suit out of it, and now we can scandalize your entire family on Evelyn's big day with the chain. So it was worth it!"

"Was it?"

"Of course!" Ashton lied.

"He hurt you?" Walker said it quietly, like he was trying to figure something out, but Ashton didn't know just what. The mechanics of that kind of play were pretty straightforward in his mind. And he'd already specified it was pain he didn't like, *and* that it was pain the guy was into dispensing.

"Yeah. A lot." Ashton tried laughing again, but it sounded even weirder this time. His blood pulsed in his ears. "I hated it."

"Did you have a word? You know…a, um, safe word."

"Yeah. Of course. He wasn't an abuser."

"Oh, okay. That's good."

"I didn't use it, though," Ashton said softly. "I wanted to like it? I really tried to like it."

"Why?"

*I really wanted him to like me.*

"I don't know." Ashton shuddered. "Anyway, I faked it until I couldn't anymore."

"Christ."

"Yeah." He licked his lips. "I went through the wringer with him four different times. I guess you could say I'm a good sport."

Walker's knuckles were white on the steering wheel. "You shouldn't have to be. No one should feel like they have to be a 'good sport' to be cared for in the way they want."

And just like that Ashton *broke.*

Hard.

When the world had righted itself again, they were pulled over in the greenway by the river. Walker was crouched on the pavement outside the passenger door, holding on to Ashton's hands and saying his name.

"Ashton? You with me?"

"I'm sorry," he whispered, tasting vomit in his mouth. Had he thrown up? He hoped not. Fuck, he *really* hoped not. "Just, uh, PTSD. It's a thing. I'm sorry." He blinked and was relieved to see there was no puke in the car. No vomit on his clothes either. He must have swallowed it back down. "I'm sorry," he said again.

"No, no, I'm the one who should be sorry. I didn't realize…" Walker reached out and stopped short of touching Ashton's hair. "Is it okay if I touch you? I don't know what's right for me to do."

"Yeah, it's fine. I'm fine." He took a haggard breath. "I'm grown, and I'm safe, and I'm fine," he said aloud. "I'm *safe.*"

"You're safe," Walker repeated, this time stroking a hand through

Ashton's hair soothingly. "You're safe."

"I'm grown, and I get to choose now. I'm fine. I'm safe."

"Yes. You're safe."

Ashton let out a long breath, feeling nauseous, clammy, and supremely embarrassed. *This* was what he'd been terrified of as he'd climbed into the car with Walker tonight after running into his mother. This exposure of his darkest underbelly. Walker could gut him now if he wanted to. It'd be easy.

"I'm so sorry," Walker said, his voice hoarse with feeling. "I had no idea asking about that stuff would…" He gestured at Ashton.

"Who would? I didn't either. Another night, it wouldn't have bothered me at all. Joking about Gerald and his need to hurt people so he could get off can actually be healing for me." And it was—usually. "But after seeing my mom…"

And seeing his apartment torn apart like that, reminding him of the topsy-turvy life he'd lived with her. And after carrying his stuff in a plastic bag, reminding him of that day he'd been forced into his grandmother's hands. And remembering the way he'd screamed when Gerald had hit him with his shiny, leather belt, the fire from it so like his grandmother's switch. And even remembering the way Gerald had been nice enough to hold him when he'd utterly flipped out after their last time.

All of it had just been a little too much. Walker didn't even know how dark the hole in Ashton could be. Oh, heck, what had he said to Walker while freaking out? What had he done to make Walker pull the car over?

"Uh, hey, really, I'm so sorry?"

"No, like I said, it's fine." Walker touched Ashton's cheek gently. "You're fine, and grown and safe," Walker said, like he was hoping that would fix everything, like he'd learned Ashton's mantra already and wanted it to work like a magic spell.

"Did I…" Ashton touched his face. It wasn't wet, so he hadn't been crying. There was no puke anywhere, so he hadn't thrown up. "Did I scream?"

Walker nodded.

"Wow, I'm so *sorry*." He covered his face, wishing he could blot out the last however many minutes. Had he also lost time? "How long did it last?"

"Not long. Once I pulled over, you stopped."

"Okay, yeah." He met Walker's eye and tried for levity. "Well, hi! I've got PTSD just so you know!" He attempted a cheeky grin but it was useless. "Great, wonderful, love that for me." He gripped Walker's forearm. "Please don't tell Casey. Don't tell anyone?"

"Of course not. I wouldn't." Walker sounded so gruff. "I'm sorry. I messed up by asking about…and now… Listen, you're safe with me. I would *never* hurt you—" He broke off, his eyes growing wide and panicked. "I mean, not that you'd want to be with me like that, but if you did, I would never, and that's not the point." His face went splotchy. "I just want you to know that I would never hurt you, and I believe you. About your mom. About whatever it is you experienced with her. And I believe you about what happened with him."

"Okay. Thank you." Ashton didn't know what Walker meant with his babble about "not that you'd want to be with me like that" but the rest of what he said mostly made sense. "I don't normally lose my shit like this. I really do have it together. I swear. I saw a therapist until I couldn't afford her, so I have some good coping skills usually, and I'm fine. We're fine. Everything's fine."

Walker studied him.

"Really. You can get back in the car now. I promise. No more screaming. Not tonight."

"Are you sure? We can take a walk. Or sit here. Just look at the lights. Whatever you want." He motioned at the greenway by the river full of brightly lit Christmas trees and Ashton wondered that he hadn't even noticed them before now.

"No. I'm good. Let's head back. The dogs are waiting. They'll want their dinner."

Walker nodded and got up from his crouch, squeezing Ashton's hand one last time before closing the door and starting around to his side of the car.

Ashton pulled the vanity mirror down and took a fast look at himself: sweaty, a little green around his mouth, mascara smeared, and hair a mess. Nice. Great. Gorgeous.

He rolled his eyes and tried not to feel like he'd just split himself open in front of a near stranger and then scooped his guts out like a madman. But he kind of had, hadn't he?

"Um, let's pretend this didn't happen," he said as Walker shut the driver's side door and started the engine again.

"Which part?"

"All of it?"

Walker frowned. "Is that healthy?"

"No?"

Walker nodded and stayed silent, pulling out of the park onto the road and then directing the car toward his house again. "I'm not going to pry. You don't have to worry. But I don't think we need to forget it either. It's nothing to be ashamed of."

"Easy for you to say. You weren't the one who lost his everloving…" Ashton trailed off before the curse left his lips.

"No, but I'm also not as strong as you. And maybe I don't want to forget that. Seeing you just now was a good reminder of how strong I should aim to be."

"Strong?" Ashton huffed. What was strong about screaming in a car until the person driving had to pull over and talk you down?

"Whatever you've been through? You came out of it one of the most optimistic people I've ever met, and I think that's something worth aiming for. I've been less of a man than you have and with much smaller problems." He shot Ashton a reassuring look as they pulled into the driveway. "Don't be embarrassed. I'm not judging you, and I won't tell anyone either. But pretending it didn't happen won't help me or you. Instead, why don't we just agree that we're definitely friends? That we trust each other now."

Ashton nodded. "All right."

"Good. Let's go inside. The dogs will be thrilled to see you again."

ASHTON SAT CURLED on the sofa with Nina on one side and Bitsy on the other. The Christmas tree glittered beautifully and the fire roared. He was warm and tired as he sipped at the Sleepytime tea that Walker had brought in after they'd devoured their pizza from Brenz.

Apparently, even Walker wasn't up for cooking after the events in the car, but he'd still insisted on doing the clean-up in the kitchen while Ashton cuddled with the dogs. He used the excuse that Ashton was his guest, and Ashton couldn't help but feel surprised at how much he liked being cared for in these small ways.

Walker, as it turned out, was a caring and generous friend. Ashton understood now why Casey liked him so much. Now, if only he could get another one of Walker's gorgeous and sweet smiles before bed, he'd feel like they really had moved on from that ugly breakdown in the car.

"So," Walker said as he came into the den with a mug of his own. "Tomorrow is grocery day. Want to help me out with something?"

Ashton sat up a little more fully, disturbing Bitsy, who huffed and then put her head down harder on his thigh as if she could hold him in place that way. "Sure! Just name it! Want me to pick up a few things? Pitch in for the cost? Whatever you need!"

Walker smiled, and Ashton's heart kicked. *There!* That was what he'd wanted.

"Nothing like that. It's been my pleasure to host you. No, it's time to pick a new country." Walker put his mug aside and strode out of the room. He returned a few seconds later with a globe like the kind Ashton had seen in his classrooms at school. Walker held it aloft. "I thought maybe you'd want to do the honors?"

"Me? Really?"

Walker smiled and sat on the edge of the coffee table, holding the globe toward Ashton. "Go on. Spin it."

He hesitated, peering into Walker's gray-blue eyes, feeling warm to his toes at the play of humor and kindness he found there.

"Go ahead," Walker urged again.

Ashton spun the globe and watched the colors whirl. The globe came to a halt, and Walker nodded. "Great. Now close your eyes and do it again. Put your finger down whenever you're ready."

Ashton hesitated. "Are you sure—"

"Hurry up. I'm ready to see what I'll be eating next."

Laughing, Ashton leaned forward, closed his eyes, and spun the globe. He heard the whir of it, and Walker's snorted tease that he was stronger than he looked. Putting his finger out tentatively, he waited until the sound of the spinning slowed and dropped his finger down. "What'd I get?" he asked before he'd even opened his eyes.

Walker laughed, a rasp that made Ashton's skin tingle.

"What?" Ashton exclaimed, opening his eyes and giggling. "The Pacific Ocean!" He shook his head. "What's that mean? Fish and more fish? Saltwater stew?"

"No, it means you spin again," Walker said with such a fond smile that Ashton couldn't help but answer it whole-heartedly with his own.

"Okay, I'll do it more seriously this time," he said, laughing. Ashton closed his eyes, whirled the globe, and waited. He could hear Walker's chuckling breaths and then a strange hitch as though Walker had suddenly stopped breathing for a moment. Ashton put his finger down.

"Scotland," Walker said softly just before Ashton opened his eyes.

"Haggis? Oh no! Please tell me the Scottish have other famous dishes!"

Walker grinned, putting the globe aside on the coffee table and pulling his phone from his pocket. "Let's google. Hopefully there's something."

"Because I'm not eating sheep offal served in stomach!"

Walker glanced up at him, eyes glowing warmly. "No, of course you're not." He said it so tenderly that Ashton felt the words like a touch. "I would never ask you to." Walker turned his attention back to his phone. "Now, let's see. There's something called Cullen skink—a fish chowder of some sort—and black pudding, though that's made with blood and oatmeal?"

Ashton shuddered, putting his hand on Walker's wrist to turn the phone results his way so they could look at them together.

"Kedgeree," Walker read aloud softly. "Spiced rice, flaked fish, hard-boiled egg…"

"Mmm, could be gross, could be yum," Ashton said, a wave of heat washing over him along with exhaustion. He was always tired after a PTSD episode, but now, in the warmth of Walker's living room with the dogs, the fire, and the tea, he was almost liquid with exhaustion. He leaned back again, releasing Walker's wrist.

Walker looked up at him and put his phone away. "Tired?"

"Yeah."

"We could call it a night."

"We could, but…" Ashton glanced toward the television screen. He didn't want to be alone. Not just yet. "Do you want to watch some more of our show?"

Walker's mouth turned up at the corners. "All right."

"I mean, it doesn't have to be *our* show. You can watch it without me. I guess you will, right? When I go back to my apartment in a few days? I just meant…"

"It can be our show," Walker said quietly, shifting to sit on the other side of the sofa and moving Simone and Marble aside, pointing them toward their dog beds. They went willingly. "I don't plan to watch it with anyone but you."

"Really?"

"Sure."

"Um, so, like you'll still want me to come around? When this is all over? With the fumigation?"

"Why wouldn't I? I thought we agreed we're friends."

Ashton gazed at Walker in the low light from the fire and Christmas tree lights and wondered how it was only a few days ago he'd told Kenzie that Walker was nothing special to look at, because right now he was incredibly handsome. The fire in his golden hair, the softness of his gray-blue eyes, and the way his smile crinkled the edges of them.

Friends? Maybe Ashton didn't want to be friends anymore? Maybe, in this exact moment, he wanted a little more?

*Such a greedy child. That's the devil blood in ya.* Ashton blinked his grandmother's voice out of his mind. "Yeah, we're friends."

"Friends get together for TV nights, I've heard."

"What do your friends watch together?"

"Ha. Well, most of my friends just get together to play golf. Sometimes we'll watch a tournament or football game together." Walker's voice went soft. "But I'm trying to branch out from that set."

"Yeah?"

He nodded, picked up the remote, and turned on the TV. As the show went on, Ashton found his eyelids growing heavy, and eventually he felt Walker pick up his feet and move them up into his lap. "Go on and sleep then," Walker said softly. He moved his fingers over Ashton's feet gently, rubbing the tender spots and relaxing him further.

*Safe. He was grown and safe.*

Ashton couldn't fight the warm comfort, and before he knew it dreams had pulled him under.

Waking hours later on the sofa, he found himself tucked in with two blankets and a lingering sense that Walker hadn't been gone very long. The lights on the Christmas tree were turned off. The fire was banked, the ashes still glowed, and the windows out to the backyard were foggy with the difference in humidity between the inside and out. But Ashton was snug and comfortable, and the bed upstairs seemed a long way away.

Marble, Nina, and Simone drowsed on their beds across from the sofa, and he heard the sound of a shower running somewhere down the hall that led to Walker's bedroom. The white noise and warmth tugged Ashton back to a peaceful land of no-dreams.

As he drifted under, a comforting thought occurred: for the first time ever Santa had brought him a gift. Walker's friendship.

Ashton smiled. He'd take it.

# Chapter Eight

WALKER STOOD BENEATH the hot water of his shower having turned the nozzle to the most forceful setting to let the water pummel against his back, trying to lean into the powerful sensation as a distraction from his painfully hard dick.

He wasn't sure why watching Ashton sleep had brought this on in him. Ashton had looked so peaceful and innocent lying there with his eyes closed. His lashes had swept beautifully over his freckled cheekbones, exposed ever since he'd washed off his makeup upon returning home.

*Home.*

Wow, how long had it been since Walker had felt like this house was a home? Not since Grandma had died. There hadn't been a single day he'd lived there when he'd considered the house his own. It'd always been his grandfather's. But something about the gentle act of holding Ashton's feet on his lap, a mundane television show running in the background, and the dogs sleeping in their beds had felt so pleasant, so persistently right, that he had, for a moment, allowed himself to fantasize that this house was his true home and this man his true lover.

And *that* had prompted him to really look at Ashton. To see him fully.

He was gorgeous. And yeah, not his type. But he'd known that before. There was nothing new in that observation. Except that somehow everything had changed. Ashton was sweetly vulnerable when he was asleep, and his collarbones were once again wickedly on display—had

Ashton bought those shirts just to make men suffer?—and when his lips fell open slightly, they looked like plump candies begging to be tasted.

Maybe Walker's type was changing.

It could happen. Evelyn used to date a much older nerdy professor before meeting and falling in love with Tom. Not that Walker was going to fall for Ashton. No, nothing like that. But given the fact that his dick was hard just from looking at him sleep, there was no way to deny that Ashton appealed to him sexually.

And as a friend.

The vulnerability he'd entrusted Walker with earlier had been unprecedented in his experience. No lover or boyfriend—or girlfriend for that matter—had ever given him so much of themselves like that. And he didn't mean the surprise revelations about Ashton's mother, his PTSD issues, or the shabbiness of where he lived.

But rather the intimacy that came with the realization that Ashton wasn't going to run after being forced to reveal those things to Walker. He wasn't going to shut Walker down—or out—and was sleeping there on his sofa, having trusted Walker to hold all of that information in his heart.

Who did that? What man had Walker ever touched or fucked who'd let him see them laid so bare and then sat on his sofa to watch a TV show together? None of them. Hell, most of them didn't stick around to cuddle for that matter.

Not that sex with most men was anywhere near as vulnerable or intimate as every single moment had been since the scream had first ripped from Ashton in the car. Hell, eating pizza together had felt different. Special, like Walker had finally met someone who would let him be a human being and not just a very perfect show-and-tell. Ashton was vulnerable, and that meant that maybe Walker could be too. Sex wasn't even as intimate as that with most guys.

Fuck.

What was he going to do now? He wanted Ashton. He liked Ashton.

And the idea that such a great guy was going to head back to live alone in that dingy apartment in just a few days' time was…

He didn't like that idea at all.

Walker touched his cock, pulling the foreskin back to expose the head, watching water cascade around his pubes and thighs. He closed his eyes, thinking of Ashton's mouth, his lips so pink and plump, and his delicate collarbones just begging to be licked and kissed. Walker barely needed to stroke himself before he came.

The orgasm wasn't explosive, but it was like scratching an itch: necessary if he planned to interact with Ashton the next day like nothing at all had changed. Like he hadn't shot his wad down the bathroom drain just from imagining his mouth against Ashton's collarbones.

Christ, how much harder would he have come if he'd let himself think about—

No!

No, he wasn't going to lust over his soft, troubled, beautiful, brilliant, optimistic, strong business partner and now friend. He wasn't. He *wasn't*!

Walker gazed down at his cock, still standing out proud from his body.

Oh, fuck. He was.

ASHTON SIPPED THE orange juice Walker had placed in front of his omelet and sausage breakfast. He absently patted Simone as he took a bite and chewed the warm meat. The greasy flavor spread over his tongue, and he groaned softly.

Walker looked up, his cheeks flushing. "Everything okay?"

"Mm, good. I never thought I was a breakfast person, but you've proven me wrong with your skills." He smiled at Walker, who flushed a little bit more. Ashton hoped he hadn't made everything awkward by…

Well, everything the night before. "Your sofa is super comfortable. Sorry if it was weird that I fell asleep there."

"No, it's fine. It *is* comfortable. I stay out there when one of the dogs is sick, and I often slept on it when my grandma wasn't doing well before she passed on. Grandpa stayed upstairs. He wasn't strong enough to deal with the situation."

Ashton caught the tone there, and he thought Walker meant that in more than one way, actually. "Ah, so you like taking care of people?"

"I don't know if I like it. I just know it's the right thing to do. When someone needs you, you take care of them. Help them out." He looked up at Ashton. "I mean, I like it enough. Don't get me wrong."

"You don't have to take care of me so much while I'm here. I wouldn't want to burden you."

"You're no burden. In fact..." Walker trailed off, glancing toward the hallway leading to the carport. "Uh, I was thinking..."

"Yeah?"

"We're getting along well now, aren't we?"

"I mean, it's only been a couple of days, but sure. I think so."

"Better than most roommate situations."

"I haven't had a roommate in years but given that my last one was Justin, and he was stealing my stuff and sneaking off to sell it and then shoot up, okay, I'll agree to that. Yeah."

"Why not consider..." Walker cleared his throat again. "I mean, would it be weird? If you just...stayed?"

"Stayed?"

"Here."

"Stayed *here*? Like, for good? Walker Ronson? Are you asking me to move in with you?" Ashton blinked wildly, hysteria rising in him so hard and fast that he laughed. "You haven't even kissed me yet!"

*Yet?* What was he *saying*? Walker would never kiss him at all. Not in a million years.

Walker flushed harder and waved his fork around. "No, no, not like that. I meant, we're friends, right? And you like it here, and the dogs like you, and that place you've been living is…" He frowned, frustration in his tone. "Hell, you deserve better than that place, Ashton. And I'm lonely." He choked a little, like maybe he hadn't intended to say *that*. "And we have this Operation Fake Boyfriend to pull off, right? If you stayed here, it'd be more convincing, don't you think? And you'd be safer. And I'd be…happier. With you here."

Ashton blinked, putting his fork down. "You'd be happier? Really?"

Walker looked like he wanted to eat his own tongue, but he turned his attention to his silverware, straightening the fork into a line beside the knife and then adjusting his napkin in his lap, all fidgets and embarrassment. "Of course. You're easy to live with and fun. You're great."

"I'm great?" Ashton laughed. "Can I get you to record that so I can send it to my grandmother as proof that not everyone thinks I'm the spawn of the devil?"

Walker snorted.

"Seriously though, you think I'm great? And fun?"

"You know you're fun. Everyone thinks you're fun."

"But I didn't know you thought so."

Walker shrugged.

"Let me think about it. It's not a bad idea. For Operation Fake Boyfriend. But I don't know about anything more than that."

"Of course not," Walker said, eyes flying wide in a good impression of panic. "We're friends. I meant this offer as roommates. Friends. Just friends."

"I know," Ashton said, a cool disappointment descending on him like a blanket of snow. "I wasn't confused about that."

"Think it over." Walker stood with his breakfast mostly uneaten. "I have to head out. Can you catch an Uber to the office? Uh, I have to run an errand."

"Sure. No problem. Don't forget the office Christmas luncheon is at noon. Secret Santa time!" Ashton said with a waggle of his eyebrows, hoping to obscure his nerves about his choice of present.

Walker ran a hand over his hair and nodded. "Wouldn't miss it for the world."

Ashton laughed. "Of course you wouldn't. I used to think you were a grinch, acting like you're all anti-Secret Santa and stuff. But now I know you're a huge Christmas fan." Ashton pointed toward the decorations in the living room. "Can't fool me, Walker Ronson."

"I wasn't trying to."

Ashton's heart skipped a beat, and he took a sharp breath. "No, you'd never try to fool me, would you?"

Walker smiled, and Ashton swallowed hard.

After Walker left, Ashton headed upstairs, the dogs trailing at his heels—except for Bitsy who'd returned to snoozing in her bed. He made a mental list of Walker's newly discovered attributes and pondered his own reaction to all of them as he picked out his outfit and did his makeup. Tugging on a cream-colored sweater with a gold-threaded reindeer embroidered on it, perfect for an ugly-but-not-too-ugly Christmas sweater party, he asked himself a vital question: Could he be developing a crush?

He peered at himself in the bathroom mirror, adding a little more glitter lip gloss before feeling satisfied.

Yes, a crush seemed likely. Ugh. Stupid really, since Walker would never return feelings for him. Tom himself had said that Ashton wasn't Walker's type, and neither Evelyn nor Walker had disputed it.

He reached for gold eye makeup and added some beneath his lower lashes to make his eyes look even bigger.

"So, hooray! Good going, Ashton," he said to his reflection. "Somehow you look this gorgeous and still have no chance with the man you like. Merry Christmas! You've got yourself a big ol' dumb crush with no hope of it being mutual. Great. Good. Love that for me."

He blew himself a kiss, caught it, and pressed his fingers against his own cheek.

"That's the only kiss you're going to get this Christmas and you'll just have to be satisfied with it."

His phone dinged, announcing his Uber driver's arrival. Ashton collected his bags, including one carefully hidden in his closet containing the wrapped Secret Santa gift, patted each dog on the head, and steeled himself with positive thoughts.

It was going to be a good day. A holiday party kind of day. And he'd get a gift. Hopefully a good one. He took a slow breath.

*Yes, great, good. Love that.*

His phone dinged again. "All right, all right. I'm coming."

And he went.

WALKER STRODE INTO Earth to Old City as soon as the boutique gift store opened. Nestled comfortably in Market Square, it was one of the most beloved gift stores in downtown Knoxville, full of eclectic and fascinating items. Surely he could find *something* in here for Ashton's Secret Santa gift. Plus, he was pretty sure they gift wrapped.

It wasn't that he hadn't given any thought to what to get Ashton before now. He had! He'd gone into multiple stores over lunch during the last week. The day before, he'd gone into the new Winter Wonderland shop in hopes of finding something, and while it was full of beautiful and very Christmas-y things, none of them had seemed right for Ashton.

The truth was, he was entirely out of his depth. He understood more about Ashton every day but that didn't mean he knew how to choose a gift for his new friend. He hoped inspiration would strike amidst the international and artistic hodge-podge of Earth to Old City—otherwise he was going to have to give in and buy expensive chocolates from the shop around the corner and call it a day.

As he trailed through the store, fingering scarves and pondering tea sets, he thought maybe he should have just gone that route. But something about buying chocolates felt far too *romantic*, almost like some kind of declaration of intent. The thought of romance and intent together with Ashton made him squirmy and hot and reminded him of the time he'd spent in the shower thinking of his friend and business partner. *Inappropriate* time.

No chocolates. It would make his confused libido think it stood a chance or something. He would find something in this store, so help him baby Jesus.

There was a lot to choose from—everything from handwoven scarves, soaps, scented candles, gag gifts, elaborate Japanese tea sets, shoes from Italy, and shawls from Brazil. But nothing in the place really screamed *Ashton* to him, and certainly nothing that cost less than twenty-five dollars.

Dammit, it wasn't as though he had a ton of time. He needed to get back to the office to wrap up a few work-related things before the party. So he really needed to find something quickly.

After pacing several times past various gag gifts—would Ashton like some Jesus bandages proclaiming His Healing Power?—fingering through the multicolored scarves that were more boho than Ashton's typical glitter-and-shine style, and studiously sniffing his way through their selection of scented, handmade soaps, he finally stopped in front of a sample box of six organic bath bombs.

Evelyn liked those, he remembered from high school. They fizzed and smelled good and were usually considered an extravagance, one that those on a budget didn't always indulge in. He pondered and picked up the set. It could be the perfect gift for someone who enjoyed pampering themselves but didn't always have the funds for it.

Opening the package carefully, he sniffed the chalky bombs one by one and found they were all fairly pleasantly scented. Best of all the price tag read only seventeen dollars and ninety-nine cents. He could just imagine Ashton stretched out in a warm tub, relaxing with his beautiful collarbones on display, his sexy shoulders above the water as scented, fizzing color swirled around him. He'd look so beautiful with his curly hair dewed from the steam and pale cheeks flushed from the heat.

Oh, Lord, the vision was delicious.

Walker's gut curled warmly, and he jerked his thoughts from Ashton in the bath and instead tried to remember if the apartment where Ashton lived even looked likely to have a tub. What if he only had a shower there? Walker's guest bathroom had a nice tub, and surely Ashton could be convinced to use the bath bombs at his place. Hopefully he'd be staying longer than just the next few days like they'd discussed, if only for Operation Fake Boyfriend.

Walker chose a box of the bombs from the bottom of the stack, one that hadn't been handled by who knew how many people, and carried it to the register. Vada, one of the owners, was chatting happily with a new customer, her silver hair gleaming beneath a jolly, red Santa hat, but she smiled at him as he approached and took the box to ring it up.

"Do I remember correctly that you gift wrap?" Walker asked. "I have to give it to my colleague at noon. Secret Santa."

"Secret Santa! Ah, that sounds like a fun time!" Vada laughed. "Of course! No problem!" She took the box of bath bombs to the opposite side of the glass counter where a bunch of bohemian-patterned wrapping paper waited with multi-colored strings.

As Walker waited, his gaze fell to the jewelry in the glass case beneath the cash register. He ran his eyes over garish rings, chunky bracelets, and gaudy necklaces before catching on something delicate and lovely. The ring featured a thin band and a small flower shaped from slivers of opal placed carefully between sculpted rose gold leaves.

The flashes of green in the opals brought to mind Ashton's eyes, and Walker stared at it for a long, strange moment, almost suspended in time. His heart thumped. He glanced at the price tag. Too much. Far, far too much for a Secret Santa gift. Far too much for any kind of gift between friends, really.

Still…

The ring was beautiful, unique, tantalizing, and sparkling. Like Ashton. Like his clothes, and lip gloss, and his eyelids when he'd trailed gold dust over them. Walker had always been bad at giving gifts on demand, but he was a big believer that when you found the perfect gift for a person at any time, you should buy it for them immediately.

And he *did* have an excuse to give a gift like this to Ashton, didn't he?

Christmas was coming up soon. And everyone deserved to unwrap a special present on Christmas Day. Especially Ashton.

"Excuse me, Vada? I'd like to get this too."

"Gift wrapped also?"

"Yes, but separately, please."

"Of course, darlin'!"

Walker's pulse tripped wildly, and he noticed his fingers shook as he passed his credit card over to Vada. He couldn't wait to see the ring on Ashton's finger, or the look on his face when he unwrapped it.

Ashton deserved a beautiful Christmas.

# Chapter Nine

ASHTON BALANCED A paper plate on his knees. He'd stacked it with pretzels, two different kinds of Christmas cake, baked beans, three sausage balls, and a wedge of gelled cranberry sauce. His can of Coke rested on the conference room table, squeezed in between all the other soft drinks and steaming cups of coffee.

Someone had set up a Bluetooth speaker on the conference room's casserole-strewn table, and familiar carols jingled and jangled from it, all of them tinny and bright. Satisfaction seeped into Ashton's soul as he looked around the room at his co-owners and employees.

Their smiles seemed genuine as they laughed, teased, and joked about the Secret Santa gifts being passed around and opened. These were his people, his firm, and his life. He'd built all this for himself with hard work and determination, and yes, some hard-won luck. He was safe and grown. This was all his.

Nicole had placed Kayla in charge of distributing the pile of gifts stacked beneath the glittering tree. In honor of the party, Kayla wore a straight, red skirt with a decorated Christmas tree embossed on it. The green of the tree wrapped around her hips and stretched all the way down her side, and she'd completed the ensemble with a star-strewn black sweater with a big star front and center in gold thread. It was over the top but festive as heck, and Ashton loved it. It definitely made his shiny reindeer sweater look tame in comparison.

Kayla made a show of rattling each bag and box, guessing at the contents, before passing it on to the intended recipient. "This is clearly a potato," she joked, as she tossed a big, egg-shaped, oddly wrapped gift to Damien, Ashton's assistant.

Everyone laughed when it turned out to be a candle scented with eucalyptus and lime.

"I'll cherish it forever," Damien said with a smirk. He tossed it in the air and caught it easily, tucking it beneath his arm and pretending to run with it like the former football player he was.

Kayla passed on another gift after guessing it to be a partridge in a pear tree, and Ashton stuffed his face with cake as he watched Aimee from design open a set of six plastic tumblers, each imprinted with a cat wearing a different kind of wreath around its neck.

"I love them," Aimee squealed. Everyone knew she fostered cats for a hobby, so her Secret Santa remained a mystery.

"And now we have…" Kayla lifted a box that had obviously come from Earth to Old City. Ashton recognized the wrapping paper. "Ashton." She shook the box. It rattled a little, but not a lot. "It's obviously pencils."

Everyone giggled.

Ashton put aside his half-full plate and shook the box himself, delighting in the heaviness. Good presents were often heavy, weren't they? He didn't have a ton of experience with gifts, but he remembered a friend telling him that once back in high school. He caught a whiff of a beautiful scent before slowly unwrapping the paper, enjoying taking his time as everyone ordered him to hurry up.

Inside was a pink box of bath bombs. Ashton bit into his lower lip, a weird flutter in his belly as he contemplated the gift. Was it a joke? Pink because he was gay? Bath bombs for the same reason? An instinct toward offense rose and fell away as he opened the box and sniffed the bombs more closely.

"I love them," he declared with a big smile, because he truly did, and if someone was trying to embarrass him, he knew if he leaned into it, that would foil the plan.

Aimee rolled her chair over and grabbed the box from him. "Bath bombs! Lucky! Someone likes you, Ashton."

"Yup," Nicole agreed. "That's a nice set too. No gag gifts for you."

Ashton shrugged and preened slightly. "Well, I deserve it."

"You do!" Kayla agreed. She took the box from Aimee and studied it more closely. She lifted the lid and took out the paper on top which named and described each bomb, her eyes growing larger and larger as she read. "What on earth?" she giggled.

"What?" Aimee asked.

"The titles of these bombs! 'Let's Get it On'? 'You Are *the* Best Thing'? Ashton, I think you may have a secret admirer!"

"Ah, so it's a gag gift after all," he said, laughing, determined not to feel hurt. These people were his friends, his employees, and yet someone was teasing him for being gay. Great, love it. "Ha-ha, very funny. I get it."

"Let me see," Aimee said, pulling the box toward her again.

Ashton rolled his chair back and let them go at it over his present. Kayla and Aimee started tugging the bombs out of their slots in the box and sniffing them.

"'Let's Get it On' smells like my dad's cologne!" Kayla squealed with a horrified expression. "Oh God! There's one called 'Be My Girl'? Ashton! What on earth!?"

Ashton took the "You Are *the* Best Thing" bomb from Aimee's hand and raised it to his nose. He smiled. It smelled like roses and oranges with a hint of spice. He put it back and took "Be My Girl" from Kayla. It was a little too floral for his liking but he'd still use it.

A bath bomb was a bath bomb after all. And he didn't feel as offended as he probably should at the thought of being some man's "girl," not if it meant that he was also that man's "Best Thing."

Besides he had no doubt this gag gift *was* from a man.

He skimmed the room looking for a telltale sign of the gift giver. If he discovered who was trying to embarrass him, he could use that information to his advantage later.

In the corner by the tinsel-strewn office Christmas tree, Casey chuckled at the titles of the bombs, but he didn't seem to hold any particular attachment to Ashton's reaction to his gift, at least not that Ashton could see.

Joe was holding in guffaws, clearly in fear of jeopardizing his job. Ashton got it. Laughing at the most obviously gay partner as he contemplated his very pink gift of inappropriately named bath bombs ranked pretty high in terms of potentially offensive behaviors. Ashton didn't care if Joe was laughing at him, though. The bath bombs were pretty funny. And pretty great. And Ashton loved them.

But Joe wasn't laughing at *him*. It was more like he knew more than he should about the present, or like he knew who *had* given it to Ashton and that added to the humor of it.

Ashton followed Joe's darting gaze to Walker, and his heart stopped.

Walker's cheeks were fire red, and he didn't look up from where he was shoveling fruitcake into his mouth like it actually tasted good. Ashton knew for a fact that cake tasted like fruit-flavored plastic. Heat rushed through Ashton's own body, his chest and cheeks getting hot, and he pulled his gaze from Walker back down to the box of bath bombs in his lap.

Wait.

Would Walker look so embarrassed if the gift was meant as a gag? No way. And he wasn't the kind of guy to give gag gifts anyway. But, still… Surely Walker wouldn't have bought something so suggestive, especially knowing it would be unwrapped in front of the group, unless he meant it as a joke? But it didn't *matter* if he meant it as a joke or not, because one thing was clear: There was no doubt Walker was Ashton's Secret Santa. He looked like he wanted to sink through the floor all the way down to the pits of hell.

"Gag gift or not, they're perfect!" Ashton declared, smiling hugely. "I love baths and these scents are one hundred percent me! Whoever bought this? Thank you! I love them! You must know me very well!"

Walker looked up, and Ashton caught his eye. He tried to search out the intention behind the bath bombs, but Walker turned away quickly, standing to throw away the remainder of his plate of food, which was still quite full. He found an empty spot along the wall, leaned back against it, crossed his arms over his chest, and tilted his head up to the ceiling, pretending to study the paneling there. Ashton almost laughed. Walker would be a terrible poker player. If he ever tried, he'd lose like crazy.

"Who's next?" Ashton asked. "Kayla? Pass the next gift out, please!"

The girls in design were happy with their gifts of lip gloss and cheap eyeshadow pallets, but Ruby lucked out and got the Fenty gloss that Ashton had been hoping for. He glanced toward his bath bomb box and grinned. He supposed he'd take these and Walker's ridiculous blush over a vial of Fenty lip gloss any day. Some things in life were priceless.

"And Walker? This is for you." Kayla shook it and tilted her head. "Sounds like a red-nosed reindeer."

Ashton lounged back in his chair, affecting an air of bored disinterest. Walker wiped his palms against his pant legs and took the package from Nicole. Ashton admired his own wrapping work. He'd gone down to Mast General Store to grab some wrapping paper and extras for pizzazz and was pleased with the way the package jangled with the sleigh bells he'd added when Walker gamely lifted the package and shook it.

"Kayla's right! Sounds like reindeer!" Aimee said.

"Or Santa's sleigh!" Ruby called out.

"Pulled by reindeer," Joe added.

"Go on, open it!" Casey called. "Stop stalling."

Walker worked open the wrapping paper with more care than Ashton would have expected and used a pocketknife to break the tape. Of course he had a pocket knife, Ashton thought. *Of course* he did.

Ashton snorted softly, watching as Walker opened the cardboard box and stared at the gifts inside.

"What is it?"

Walker lifted up a very boring navy-blue Polo golf shirt that Ashton had bought at Planet Xchange for a couple of dollars, and then his lips curled into a satisfied grin as he glimpsed the presents that had been packed beneath the shirt.

One by one, Walker lifted up red and green tennis balls, chew toys for the dogs in the shape of Christmas lights and candy canes, and soft lumps of "coal" and balls of "snow" also meant to be thrown for fetch. The last thing he held up was a stuffed Grinch dog toy that Ashton had picked up for Bitsy since she was too old for the more active stuff. She'd be able to cuddle and chew it in her bed at least.

All told, the gift had come in way over the budget, but Ashton hadn't been able to stop himself. Nina, Simone, Bitsy, and Marble deserved the fun, and he knew Walker would love playing with them.

Walker snorted again before meeting Ashton's eye. "Thank you, Ashton," he said with a gruff laugh. "They'll appreciate it. And so do I."

Ashton grinned. He hadn't intended to keep his identity secret. No one else in the office had known about Walker's dogs so it was always going to be obvious. But he wasn't going to be a fool who bought his Secret Santa recipient something that would go right to the landfill. These at least would be played with first.

"Dog toys?" Joe asked, looking baffled.

"He has four!" Kayla exclaimed. "Ashton told me."

"Four!" Ruby exclaimed. "Why four?"

"It's a strong, even number," Walker said with a straight face. "Only a psychopath would have an odd number of dogs."

"How did Ashton know?" Ruby asked.

"He's been staying with him," Aimee said.

Ruby met Kayla's eyes, and Ashton could easily see what they were thinking. He'd have to set them both straight later.

"Walker, dude, why are you hoarding dogs, buddy?" Joe asked with a grin "And why didn't you tell us?"

Walker rolled his eyes.

Ribbing went on for some time over Walker's secret stash of dogs, but Walker didn't seem to mind. He told everyone a little about Bitsy, Marble, Nina, and Simone, even showing Kayla and Nicole some pictures on his phone.

Annoyance prickled Ashton when Nicole looked at Walker with something new in her expression—interest perhaps. Ashton blinked and looked away from where she was pressed against Walker's side, looking at the photos on his phone and holding on to his arm like she had a right to do that.

Because she did.

Walker wasn't Ashton's…well, anything. He was a friend. Business partner. And maybe a roommate? He was a co-conspirator for Operation Fake Boyfriend, but he wasn't Ashton's to feel all proprietary over. He wasn't *that* at all. Even if Ashton maybe wanted him to be? Ugh. Which was just great. Ashton loved that for himself.

"So," Casey said, dropping into the empty seat next to Ashton. "Things are going well."

"Hmm?"

"Staying with Walker? It's going well, I see."

"Oh, sure." Ashton shrugged. "He's great."

"I know." Casey smiled smugly.

"What?"

"Nothing."

Ashton narrowed his eyes at Casey, a strange suspicion coming to him that Casey was up to something but he didn't know what exactly. "How's Joel?" he asked instead.

Ashton typically tried not to remember the time he'd hit Joel up to be the plus one at his final Christmas with his grandmother. That had been before Joel and Casey were an item. Angel had arranged for Ashton to approach Joel with his plan, and… Well, it'd been embarrassing.

Joel had been kind when he'd rejected him of course. In the end, it'd probably been better that Ashton had chosen an anonymous Grindr hookup anyway. It was so much more *appalling* that he'd brought a stranger. It really had made it all the more unforgivable. Perfect for being disowned. He was a genius really.

"Joel's good. Sales are up again this year."

"Is he thinking of expanding? A second location maybe?"

"No, we're happy with the business we have. At most, he might hire more help for next year so that he has more time for his books, but something tells me he won't do it. He likes being hands-on at Christmas with the store. The rest of the year, he's less invested and more willing to hand the reins over to someone else." Casey sighed. "Too bad Angel left. She'd be a shoo-in for manager by now."

Ashton smiled. "Had to follow her dreams."

Casey grinned. "Yeah, Becca says she's doing well at the salon. Happy to hear it."

"Thanks for setting her up there. I know I've said it before, but it really means a lot."

"Of course. We're business partners. Friends. Right?"

Ashton's throat grew a little tight, and he looked toward his new friend Walker before he nodded.

"What?"

"I just… Yeah, of course we're friends."

"Not used to having friends or something?" Casey teased.

"Not used to a lot of things like that." Ashton smiled sadly. "Most of my 'friends' are really clients, contacts for business, co-workers, or yoga studio acquaintances back when I was doing that…" He trailed off and looked toward Walker again.

It was possible Walker was becoming his first friend of a more intimate nature. The kind of friend who really meant something more than just a few laughs over drinks. Very few people knew the real Ashton. And *no one* knew the Ashton that Walker had glimpsed the other night.

"But it turns out I like having friends." Ashton turned his attention back to Casey. "Thanks. I probably sound like a twelve-year-old girl or something. Not that twelve-year-old girls aren't great. I love them, actually. Big fan."

"Hey, don't sweat it." Casey patted Ashton's thigh and stood up. "Talking about it will just make it awkward." He winked and headed over to Walker wearing a grin. He immediately delivered a big shoulder punch.

How masc. How cool. How good for them.

Ashton fought a small but fond eye roll and turned back to the gift he'd been given. From Walker at that. He opened the box of bath bombs, and the scents puffed up into the air around him. In the end, after much sniffing, he decided that he liked "You're *the* Best Thing" above all the others. He'd use it tonight. Assuming Walker didn't mind him using the guest room bathtub and not just the shower. But he'd assume it wasn't a problem since Walker had given the bombs to him.

When he looked up, Walker was watching him, and Ashton gave him a wide smile. Walker turned red again, but he didn't look away or scurry down the hall to his office the way he used to. Instead, he gave Ashton a smile of his own.

*Oh*, Ashton thought. *Oh, no.* His gut curled in tight on itself.

*He's gorgeous.*

Ugh. Why did he feel like he'd simultaneously received the best Christmas present ever *and* a big, black lump of coal?

WALKER THREW THE green and red ball over the gray grass of the sloping backyard and watched Nina and Simone barrel after it. Their hound dog ears flapped, and their tails wagged wildly. Ashton had stayed late at the office to handle a call from a frustrated client, telling Walker he'd grab an Uber back to the house and not to wait or hold dinner for him.

It'd seemed lonely putting together his first Scottish meal without Ashton there to try it with him. Walker had gone with the traditional Scottish stovies because the prep time was low, and because it seemed like one of the less interesting dishes he'd researched. He couldn't explain it, but he really wanted to share the more adventurous food with Ashton.

Though he'd enjoyed the thick, stew-like stovies, he'd have relished them more if Ashton had been there to gasp and exclaim and laugh his way through the process of making and eating them. Or, even if Ashton had stayed out of the kitchen, as he often did, Walker would have felt the satisfaction of preparing something for his beautiful friend.

There was something so rewarding about making food while Ashton sipped wine and petted the dogs in the living room, reading on his phone or texting with clients. It was strange how much Walker enjoyed that.

The sound of a car door slamming was enough to alert Walker to Ashton's return, and he whistled, summoning the dogs back toward the house. They flew to the back door, tongues out and happy whimpers escaping, apparently just as eager to see Ashton as Walker was.

But when Walker got inside, he found Ashton in the kitchen, staring down at the remains of the stovies with a peculiar expression. He only absently greeted the dogs as they leapt and twisted for his attention.

When he turned to face Walker, his troubled eyes were more gray than green, and his skin was so pale it nearly shone against the darkness of his hair. He hadn't looked this distraught since he'd screamed in the car and Walker's heart had nearly stopped in sheer terror.

"What's wrong?" Walker asked, feeling woozy at Ashton's drawn expression. "Another PTSD episode?"

"No," Ashton said, but he sounded shaky and unsure. "Look, I don't mean to be—" he waved a hand around, his usual sweet lisp dulled by whatever was haunting him. "A mess. But I kind of am right now. To be honest, I just want to take a bath with one of these bombs you got me and call it a day, you know?"

"You know I got them for you?" Walker winced. What a ridiculous thing to ask, especially when Ashton was clearly upset about something serious.

"Of course. And thank you. I do love them."

"Ashton, you can talk to me. You're grown and safe," he said, remembering the words Ashton had used that evening in the car. "You're safe here with me."

Ashton's shoulders collapsed, and he groaned, rubbing his face. "I know." He sighed heavily. "Look, just before I left, I got a call from Oaks Rehab. Justin's gone AWOL. Just poof. They aren't sure where he went."

Walker stepped forward, hands out, offering what exactly, he didn't know, but he wanted to touch Ashton and make this better for him. "I'm sorry. That sucks."

"Plus I still owe them six grand." Ashton winced, his eyes going haunted again. "Merry Christmas to me. Love it."

"Oh," Walker said, stopping short of putting his hands on Ashton's shoulders. "That's…"

"Don't." Ashton waved away whatever Walker was going to say, moving out of range of his touch. Frankly, Walker didn't even know what had been about to come out of his mouth, so he was relieved for the interruption—though a little disappointed by the way Ashton had evaded his comfort. "He's made his choice. I did what I could." Ashton's shoulders fell again. "Now, I'd just like to be alone for a little while. Is that rude? I'm sorry."

"No, do what's right for you. I'll make a fire so it's warm in the living room for you later. And…" His mind scrambled trying to think of something to ease Ashton's heart and mind. "I could make tea? Would you like that?"

"Wine," Ashton said. "That is, if you don't mind opening a bottle?"

"I'll bring a glass up to you. You can drink it in the bath."

Ashton nodded. "Thanks."

Walker took his time choosing the wine, going with an Italian 2015 Planeta Santa Cecilia Nero d'Avola he'd noticed Ashton had particularly enjoyed with dinner a few nights before. Distantly, he heard the upstairs bathwater running. The dogs milled around his feet as Walker uncorked the wine and poured out a glass, swirling the contents and smelling it. His mouth watered. It truly was a delicious wine. He'd have his own glass later.

Carefully, he carried the wine upstairs, avoiding tripping over the dogs who still trailed him through the house. He stopped outside the bathroom and knocked, smelling the warm rose and citrus bath bomb wafting from under the door.

"Come in," Ashton called.

Walker froze. Had he heard right? Was Ashton telling him to come in? He'd imagined Ashton's wet hand sticking out and taking the glass from him, not this. Perhaps Ashton was still dressed. Walker hesitated, his heart speeding up as he turned the knob to let himself inside.

Ashton was *not* still dressed. Not at all.

He sat in the old-fashioned bathtub, complete with claw feet, with his knees up against his chest. The steam had risen to fog the mirror and make the sink and toilet glisten with moisture. His cheeks were pink, and his curls were tighter from the humidity, and his collarbones were still so damn lickable.

Walker felt a little lightheaded. It was just as good a scene as he'd imagined when he bought the bath bombs. Better even, because Ashton gave him a wry, grateful smile as he reached out for the wine.

Walker was rooted to the floor. He stared dumbly as water dripped from Ashton's fingers and wrist to the bath rug, raking his gaze up that gleaming arm to Ashton's chest where a patch of dark hair showed over where his knobby knees hid his nipples. Walker's heart skipped a beat as he took in how flushed Ashton's pale skin was from the heat. The scent of the bath bomb was dizzying, it was so strong.

He flashed back to when Ashton had unwrapped the gift earlier, how the women had teased him over the names of each, and he had to know. "Which one did you choose?" Walker broke free of his paralysis and handed over the wine before gesturing at the water, which swirled and fizzed pinkly as more water cascaded into the tub from the running faucet.

"Hmm?" Ashton asked, sipping the wine as his green eyes slipped half-closed. "Mm," he moaned. Walker's dick took notice of that noise. "Delicious. Where do you find this?"

"Italy."

"Hmm?"

"I bought it in Italy."

Ashton snorted softly, shaking his head. "Of course you did. Love that for you." Then he sighed, opened his eyes, and refocused on Walker. "What were you asking?"

"Which bath bomb did you choose?"

"Oh?" His cheeks seemed to grow even rosier as he replied, "You're *the* Best Thing."

Walker nodded, swallowing thickly. His eyes traced over the trimness of Ashton's pale arms and the way the knobs of his spine showed down his back in between lithe muscles and stark ribs. Ashton wasn't too skinny, but he didn't hold an ounce of extra fat either. He noted the way Ashton clenched his knees to his chest, tight and tense.

"You're safe," Walker said suddenly. He didn't even know why, but the gratification that washed over him when Ashton's body immediately released all his remaining tautness, relaxing his shoulders and softening his eyes, was like the best rush off the largest bet he'd ever won. Ashton's expression gentled as he gave Walker a close-lipped smile that made Walker's heart clench.

"Thanks." Ashton raised the glass, taking another sip. "I just wish Justin were safe too, you know? But there's only so much I can do for him." He met Walker's eyes and then looked away. "You don't even know. We were so damaged…" This last was said so quietly that Walker almost didn't make it out over the rush of the water filling the tub.

"I'm sorry."

Ashton shrugged, sipped more wine, and gradually loosened his hold on his knees.

"I should go."

"No," Ashton said, reaching out toward him. "Stay."

Walker could fully make out the dark hair on his chest now, tufts around his nipples and a tangle of it between his pecs. He steadfastly kept his eyes from falling lower to see just how far down that hair went and how trim Ashton's stomach might be. "Stay?"

"Yes. Stay. I need to… I need to tell you. About it. About me."

"You don't have to."

"I do. It'll help if I say it out loud."

"If you're sure?"

"I am."

"All right." Walker took a deep, steamy breath and let it out. He hoped his dick didn't betray him further. Not now when Ashton was trying to be open and earnest, not sexy. Walker leaned against the sink and nodded. "I'm willing to listen."

Ashton relaxed again. He sipped the wine and started to talk. "Justin's mom was an addict. Just like mine. How Grandma Hudson managed to raise three addicts…" He shook his head. "It's not like I don't know, actually. She made living so hard and ugly that escape felt like the only option. I ran. Mom, Aunt Coral, and Justin chose another way out."

Ashton looked up at Walker, eyes less harrowed than before. Maybe talking about it really did help, like he said. "Do you know anything about that? About wanting to escape?"

Walker nodded. His throat went dry, and his heart pounded. Now wasn't the time to share his own stupid choices with Ashton. Besides, what had been his reason for it all? *I hated my job, my life was empty, and*

*I wanted to feel something, **anything**, aside from low-boiling rage so much that I got in too deep?* No. Ashton would have so much disdain for that. And why shouldn't he after what he'd been through?

Walker shrugged. "I guess."

Ashton gazed at him narrowly. "Yes, poor little rich boys do want to escape too, don't they?" He didn't sound mean or angry about it. Walker felt like he should be insulted but somehow he just wasn't. "Life's not easy for anyone, huh? Money seems like it will fix things. It seems like it *should* fix things. Like, that's what money is for, isn't it? But it doesn't always help. Evelyn's situation for example. Money couldn't prevent that."

"No. It doesn't solve everything."

"Neither does talk, though I do feel a little better. Thanks for listening."

"No problem."

Ashton suddenly leaned back in the tub, exposing his entire front and stretching his legs out straight. Using his foot, he turned off the faucet. Walker's heart fluttered, and he tried to look anywhere else but didn't know where to focus his gaze. Like his eyes had minds of their own, they raked over Ashton's whole body, and his mouth went dry at the view before him.

Long and lean, with dark hair that trailed from his chest down to his crotch, where it fanned out again around a perfectly respectable-sized dick, Ashton was gorgeous everywhere. Walker felt heat flood his face, and he turned. "I'll, uh, leave you to—"

"Wait, don't go."

"Um? Is there more you wanted to tell me?"

"Not about that, no. I think I'm done talking about Justin now. It won't change anything. I just needed to say aloud that I'd done the best I could by him, to remind myself how we got where we are, and I needed someone else to hear it."

"I heard it and I believe you."

"Thanks. It seems small, I'm sure, but I feel like I can breathe again. Thanks to you and the wine and this bath bomb." Ashton suddenly grinned. "*Am* I the best thing?"

Walker's pulse thudded. He swallowed. "Uh—"

"Just kidding. But seriously, don't go?" He swished the water around, swirling pink over his body. "We should talk over the plan. For Operation Fake Boyfriend."

Ashton wanted him to hang out and chat? While he bathed?

What? The? Hell?

Walker was pretty sure his nether region was going to expose him and all of his filthy-minded desires if he stayed much longer. "Yeah. When you get out. Sure. Enjoy your bath."

Ashton laughed. "Oh, sorry. I didn't know you were a prude."

"I just…" Walker cleared his throat, keeping his eyes averted. For fuck's sake he was seriously going to spring a boner like some high schooler. "I, uh, wasn't, um…"

Water splashed again. "Walker, please don't go. Seriously, I'll cover myself. Just sit and talk to me a minute."

"I thought you wanted to be alone."

"I changed my mind."

Walker huffed another soft laugh but sat down on the closed toilet seat, keeping his eyes focused on the painting across from it. A landscape of a lake in Italy where his grandparents had gone for their honeymoon. Lake Bolsena, he thought it was called. He prayed it would give him something else to focus on and save him from any obvious arousal.

"I'm thinking we may need to come out as 'dating' at the office before the wedding or it won't be believable," Ashton said. "Casey, Joel, and Nicole will be there for sure, won't they? And either we need to let them in on the plan, or we need to make them think we're really dating. I'm willing to play it either way."

"Hmm, I don't like lying to friends. So I think we should just tell them the truth. Only Casey and Joel will be there. So I think we can leave Nicole out of it. I'm sure those two will play along if they understand this is what Evelyn wants."

"Oh? Nicole isn't invited?"

"She didn't make my dad's list of important people to impress."

Ashton snorted. "I see. All right. That's fine. So, we tell Casey about our fake dating plans?"

"Sometime before the wedding, sure."

"Great. We're agreed there. I was also thinking we should discuss Christmas plans." Ashton splashed around a little more, but Walker refused to look at him. He did *not* need to see those glistening collarbones again. He *did not.* "I don't know what you typically do for the holidays," Ashton said, "but if you're going to make your family—aside from Evelyn—think that you're really in love with me, at a minimum you're going to have to talk about me during your Christmas events. Like, do you have an aunt who's always asking about your love life or when you'll be giving your parents grandbabies? If so, you'll need to wax poetical to her over me. How I'm gorgeous and stunning and the best man you've ever known and how you feel like you're going to pass out when you look at me."

Walker felt like he'd pass out if he looked at Ashton *right now*, that was for sure. He stared at the blue water of the painting and tried to imagine that he was at Lake Bolsena sometime in the mid-nineteen-fifties instead of in this bathroom right now having this conversation while Ashton was beautifully naked just a few feet away.

"Um, yeah. My Aunt Harriet. She's my grandmother's sister. Wanted me to marry her best friend's granddaughter, Rachel. She's relentless."

"Perfect! Tell her I make you swoon."

"Mn." Walker felt a bit swoony. Probably the humidity in the bathroom and the fact that Ashton kept on being naked and chatty and *naked.* Again, Walker willed his dick to stay flaccid. "She won't be at Christmas this year, though."

"Why's that?"

"It's her year to be with her son's family."

"Oh. Well, too bad. It would be fun to mess with her, don't you think?"

Walker garbled a response.

*Focus! Blue water. Bolsena. Italy.*

"And your folks? Are you still committed to keeping them unaware of the plan, or…?"

"Definitely. If they knew, it would defeat the entire purpose."

"Right." Ashton sounded thoughtful. "So you really don't mind lying to your mom and dad?"

Walker shrugged. He'd lied to his parents about a lot worse things than having feelings for Ashton. And fuck, maybe having feelings for Ashton was starting to not be so much of a lie after all. "It'll be fine."

"When we 'break up' after the wedding, they'll probably be relieved, right?"

"I don't know." His father would be relieved for sure, and Walker hated that.

"Yeah." Ashton sounded quiet and a little small. "I'm certainly not the type any parent wants to see their son with."

Walker furrowed his brows, gazing fiercely at the white-capped waves on the painted blue lake. "Why the hell not?"

"Uh…" Ashton sounded taken aback. "Um, because—"

Walker spoke to the painted water fiercely. "You can't pretend you don't know how handsome you are. You're smart, charming, funny, and passionate about your career. You're a partner in a reputable firm—or a soon-to-be reputable firm, anyway. You've got a lot to offer, Ashton. Any parent should be thrilled for their son to be dating you."

But Walker's parents wouldn't be. Not his dad, anyway. Not at all. *Fuck that.*

Ashton splashed around, and Walker couldn't help but dart a look his direction. True to his word to cover himself, he had a washcloth draped over his crotch, and the pink water obscured most of the rest of him, but he looked so startled and pleased by Walker's words that Walker felt a sudden swell of pride. He'd put that look on Ashton's face. He'd made him momentarily happy. He owned this moment and that feeling in Ashton.

What was wrong with him? Why did it feel so right to make Ashton feel good? What would it mean if…?

"Really? You really think so?" Ashton sounded skeptical. "I don't know."

"Of course. You're so handsome it hurts. You have to know that. I'll be proud to be seen with you. Anyone would be." He chanced another look at Ashton.

"Wow." Ashton smiled, and his entire face was just so beautiful that Walker's heart ached, and his fingers shook with a desire to touch his mouth, smooth over his cheeks, and brush back his disorderly hair. "You know, you don't have to go so hard on this."

"What?"

"This whole pretend boyfriend thing. You don't have to go so hard. You're so darn good at it, I might start to believe you care." Ashton laughed and slipped down beneath the pink water, the upper half of him disappearing entirely, including his head, so that just his knees stuck up and out. Walker quickly looked away as the washcloth floated off.

Lake Bolsena shimmered in the painting before him. He stared at it and waited for the sloshing splash that meant Ashton had come up for air. "I do care," he muttered, but Ashton was still beneath the water and couldn't hear him.

A massive whoosh accompanied Ashton's surfacing.

"All right, well, I'm going to quickly rinse all this off and wash my hair. Meet you downstairs?"

Walker rose, careful not to look Ashton's way again, ridiculously glad his dick had cooperated. "Yeah. Yeah, sure."

"Thanks, Walker. For the bath bombs, and for being my friend."

"Anytime." Did he sound husky? He thought he sounded kind of husky.

The dogs were waiting on the sofa when he stepped into the living room. They followed him to the kitchen as he poured himself a glass of wine and sipped it slowly, trying to calm his racing pulse and get a grasp on his unruly mind.

Ashton Sellers was everything amazing.

Wow. How had he not known?

Walker was starting to think Casey forcing him to put Ashton up for a few nights might be the best Christmas gift he'd never known to ask for.

Or the worst.

Because, right or wrong, likely or unlikely, naughty or nice, Walker was pretty sure he was falling for Ashton.

Hard.

# Chapter Ten

THE OLD HOUSE in the Fourth and Gill neighborhood was the same as it ever was. Built in the early nineteen-hundreds, it had been Grandpa Hudson's before he'd died way too young and left it to Grandma and their kids.

Ashton stood on the sidewalk, wishing he had a car at his back that he could hop into to drive away any time he wanted. Alas, he'd spent any funds he could have used on a vehicle sending a certain runaway cousin to rehab. As a poor substitute, he clutched his phone and told himself that Uber had dropped him off, and Uber could pick him up again. He wasn't trapped here. He'd be allowed to leave any time he wanted. He was grown, and he was safe.

Ashton took the stairs up to the wraparound front porch and hesitated. From inside he could hear the sound of the television tuned to a preacher giving a sermon. The sound was dampened enough that he couldn't make out just what the man was railing on about, but there was no mistaking the cadence and passion of a Southern Baptist preacher in the midst of making his point.

After a deep, careful breath, Ashton raised his fist and knocked.

"Hold on! I'm comin'! Just a minute now! Be right with ya!"

Grandma Hudson sounded the same as ever. Cheerful as could be. Ashton remembered wondering how it was she could put on such a pleasant show for everyone in the world but him and Justin. And Aunt Coral and his mother, he supposed. He always tried to remember they'd gone through the same nasty stuff he had. It was all the generosity he had to spare for them anymore.

The door swung open and the tall, stern lady in front of him looked almost exactly the same as she had three years ago when he'd shown up on this very porch with a stranger from Grindr. He'd fucked the guy after the screaming and yelling and Bible shaking was done. After they'd run from Grandma Hudson's house, laughing, and shouting, and angry as sin. It'd been too heady of a rush to resist the physical release after it was all over. But following that quick collision of bodies in the back of the guy's van, Ashton had never wanted to see him again. And he hadn't.

Same for the woman in front of him.

Grandma Hudson wore a pair of loose jeans, a T-shirt proclaiming Jesus as the Reason for the Season, and her big, round glasses, the frames of which she hadn't changed since before he was born. That was just like Grandma Hudson: decide on something and stick with it, no matter what.

"Hi," Ashton said.

Her lips firmed into a straight, angry line.

"I'm looking for Justin. Is he here?"

Grandma Hudson didn't move a muscle. Then she looked around him, over him, and through him. Like he wasn't even there. "Must have been a prankster knocking. There ain't no one here."

She shut the door in his face.

Ashton blew out a long breath, closed his eyes, and lifted his hand to knock again.

"She ain't gonna answer." Justin's voice was quiet and rough. The scent of cigarette drifted on the breeze, and Ashton turned to where the porch wrapped around the corner of the house and led to a shaded area with a swing.

He followed the scent around that corner and took in Justin smoking as he kicked off against the porch, swinging back and forth. His eyes were red as he raked a dark glance up Ashton's body. "She's done with you, remember? 'Til you turn straight." Justin huffed a laugh. "Such a bitch." He smirked. "Like that's how it works. Like you could ever be different."

Ashton swallowed thickly. He hadn't seen Justin in what felt like forever, even though he'd been footing the bill for his treatment. He didn't look good: scrawny and gray. He was all angles and sharpness, even his eyes were sharp like knives.

"It's good she's done with me, because I'm done with her too," Ashton said. "I'm just here for you."

Justin took a long draw off his cigarette, his eyes roaming over Ashton with a hateful gleam that made Ashton's heart hurt. "You're looking good. Fancy."

Ashton glanced down at his crisp brown pants, falling perfectly over a shined pair of leather shoes. His russet sweater was plain, and his leather jacket was soft, obviously expensive, but not anything that would have infuriated his grandmother on sight. Which is why he'd worn this ensemble. It was far from his most fancy or flashy. Far from the real *him*, in fact. It was the worst kind of drag. The kind he used to wear all the time.

"On the other hand, *you* look like hell. What's going on, Justin? You were doing so well."

"What do you know about it?" Justin asked, his eyes flashing angrily. "You know nothing about what it's like in there. Or in here." He jabbed his index finger at his temple. "You got off easy."

Ashton held back a disbelieving laugh. Between the two of them, he'd been beaten more often for who he was, while Justin had been beaten for what he'd done. Ashton had a lot of thoughts on who'd really had it harder back then. But now wasn't the time for any of that. "Let me take you back to Oaks so you can finish out your treatment. Being here? Listening to her hatefulness? Living with her abuse? It's not going to do you any good, Jus. You know it won't. In the end, being near her will just make you want to use again."

Ashton really hoped Justin wasn't using now. His eyes looked clear at least. He didn't seem high. He still seemed possibly sober.

Justin shrugged. "At least we know what happens after that."

Ashton frowned. "Meaning?"

"Meaning, this whole 'sober' thing is for the fucking fantasy dwellers of this world, the people who ain't never seen or felt nothing real in their whole fucking boring lives. Sober is for people who ain't got pain, ain't got what I got up here, and in here." He tapped between his head and his heart again. "Sober is for people who've never truly hurt a day in their privileged pretty lives."

"I'm sober and you know all that doesn't apply to me. I've been hurt."

"Maybe, but you're a pervert. So there's that."

"Excuse me?" Ashton stepped back, feeling slapped. It wasn't as though Justin had never said mean things to him before, but never anything about his sexuality and never when he was sober.

"You act all high and mighty, but you're addicted to your perversion and you know it. Give up suckin' dick and we'll talk." Justin sucked suggestively on his cigarette. "Bet you can't give that shit up if you tried."

"Being gay isn't the same as—"

"Ain't it? It's sick and sinful and it relieves your pain. It's the same damn thing."

"Justin, why are you saying this? You've never said these kinds of things to me before." Was Justin high? Ashton thought he could always tell, but maybe he couldn't anymore. "You always supported me. Loved me."

Justin huffed. "Loved you? Sure. But not what you do. I can't believe you call that sick shit you do love."

Pain sliced over him, hard like Gerald's shiny belts. He gasped, tears coming to his eyes. Then a terrible thought came to him. "Did something happen to you? In rehab? Did someone make you do something you didn't want to do?"

"As if. You and Grandma Hudson are so much the same. All judgment and suspicious thoughts. You hate her but you're just like her, you know."

"I'm not."

"You are. She thinks it's your fault I use, did you know that? Yup, Grandma keeps wanting to know if you ever *touched me*. Asks me all the damn time. Did you know?"

"Fuck her."

Justin laughed then. "Oh, look at you! Got a rude ass mouth on ya now, huh? I remember when you was so prissy. Heaven this and heaven that. Too afraid to say fuck or shit or damn or Jesus H Christ Almighty."

Ashton shoved his hands into his pockets and he fought tears. The cold wind whipped around the edge of the house and stung his wet eyes. "Grandma lets you stay here talking like that?"

Justin huffed. "She don't got no choice. I'm here unless she wants to call the police on me and she ain't gonna do that. The preacher maybe but not the police."

"Justin…" Ashton's voice broke. "You don't have to—"

"I know damn well I don't *have* to." He pointed his cigarette at Ashton, the end burning as red as his eyes. "But I am. I'm doing what I want for a change, got it? What I need to do. For me! For my future!"

"What future if you're not sober? Prison? Death?"

"Sure! If it means I get to feel good one more time, sure I'll fucking die for it." Justin's eyes burned hotly. "Just like you'd die for dick."

"Justin—" His breath came in shallow gasps, sobs balling up beneath his ribs, aching hard and struggling to burst out.

"If I die, I die, Ashton." He threw his hands up, eyes wide and challenging. "I ain't no pussy willing to live in this fucked-up world. I ain't like you. I'm a real man."

"A real man doesn't kill himself with drugs and—"

Justin sneered. "A real man doesn't suck cock."

"Get off my porch." Grandma Hudson's voice was soft and low behind him. When Ashton turned his breath caught. She held a pistol. An honest to heaven pistol. And she was aiming it at his heart. "Go on. Get. You ain't welcome here, sinner. Repent and then we'll talk. Until then, you're just a demon who looks like my grandson."

"Better go, pansy," Justin said. "She ain't joking about shootin' ya." He winked and rubbed his ass where Grandma Hudson had hit him with a BB gun pellet when they were still just teens. "I'd hate to see you die when you're so damn keen on livin'."

"Language," Grandma Hudson said sharply.

"Justin, please go back to Oaks. I'll go with you. Take you there." His throat burned and hot tears escaped. "We can still make this right."

"Oh, big whoop. You'll go with me? You'll take a car ride with me and then leave me there alone. Fuck you. You go on with your life, why dontcha? Suck a bunch of dicks and roll around in *your* addiction. Leave me and mine alone. I'm fine."

The sound of the pistol cocking was enough warning for Ashton. He stalked off his grandmother's porch and half a block away before stopping to punch in instructions for an Uber to pick him up.

His chest felt like someone had kicked him with a boot. His throat was mercilessly tight and painful, tears streamed down his face, and those sobs that he held back fought to break loose. But he couldn't let them. He had to hold it together. Get home before he lost his shit. Get somewhere safe. Get back to Walker.

He wiped at his eyes with the palms of his hands as he waited. He'd tried. He'd done all he could for Justin. Once he'd had hope for him. Once they'd been close like brothers. What had happened?

He hadn't ever truly believed Justin would get and stay sober, but he'd never thought he'd turn on him this way either. Those slurs. Those hateful comments. Where had his sweet-but-rowdy cousin gone? Who was this monster in his place?

Fuck addiction. It destroyed everything good.

By the time the Uber arrived, Ashton had managed to stop his tears, though the unreleased sobs stayed hard and painful beneath his ribs, pressing and hurting there. As he rode with the thankfully silent driver back to Sequoyah Hills, he told himself that his cousin was a lost cause, and his grandmother was a demented bitch, but at least he had Walker to go home to tonight. At least he had the comfort of Walker's home and the dogs. He was grown and safe. There was no addiction in his life. He was free from that now.

"Love that for me," he murmured sincerely.

His throat loosened. His chest eased.

He could breathe.

Snowflakes fell in aimless circles from dark clouds above, and Ashton hummed "I'll Be Home For Christmas" under his breath until the Uber pulled up outside Walker's house. Would it be too much to ask Walker for a hug? Did friends do that kind of thing? Maybe he could just request it, like as a present?

Merry Christmas—can I have a hug?

Merry Christmas—hold me, please?

The outdoor Christmas lights clicked on as he strode toward Walker's house, bathing his misery in the glitter of the season. He snorted. "Get real, Ashton. Walker Ronson will never hold you."

*Not even for Christmas.*

"YOU'RE NOT INVITING him?" Evelyn asked, popping a chip into her mouth and staring at Walker like he was possibly the stupidest human being she'd ever met. She'd stopped in earlier with a box of Christmas fudge and some presents for beneath his tree. Most of them were for Layla and Brody. She'd asked him to keep them at his place because those two kids couldn't be counted on not to open them, take a peek, and then rewrap them with Evelyn and Tom none the wiser.

"Me? Invite Ashton?" Walker asked, though he knew exactly who she meant.

"Yeah." She crunched into her chip pointedly.

"Why?" Playing dumb had worked for him a lot growing up, but these days Evelyn didn't usually let him get away with it. Still, it was worth a shot.

"Because it's Christmas?"

"So?" Next stop, faked obtuseness.

"Sooo, where's he going to spend his day?" Evelyn asked, brows at her hairline. "My understanding is he has no family of his own anymore. Or am I mistaken?"

"I don't know what his plans are." Walker squirmed a little to admit the truth. "I didn't think about it." Mostly what he'd thought about for the last few days was every last detail of how Ashton had looked all naked in the bathtub. It'd been pretty distracting.

"You didn't even ask?"

"Don't scold me. I just assumed he probably has something to do."

She shook a salsa-slick chip at him.

Walker groaned. He didn't want this. And he knew exactly why, but he couldn't admit it to Evelyn. Not when he hadn't fully admitted it to himself. "So you're saying I should bring him? To Mom and Dad's? For our family *Christmas?*"

"Yes. That's what people in serious relationships do, Walker." Evelyn rolled her eyes. "And that's what you're pretending to be in right? For my wedding?"

"Right."

"That's why I have to drive up to Johnson City on Christmas Day to do the rounds with Tom's family, because he's going to be at our family event on Christmas Eve this year. Working things like this out is normal for a couple. It's what people do when they're in love."

"Oh." Walker felt a little dizzy. The idea of introducing Ashton to his parents as his lover had been so easy before he'd realized he actually felt anything for the guy. Now, the thought of his father's cold disdain raining down like slush on Ashton's beautiful head? It made him want to be sick. "I don't know."

"You're not really in love. I get it."

Walker winced.

"But if you want people to think you are, then you have to act like someone who *is* in love. Remember how excited I was for Tom to meet the family?"

"No?"

"Well, that's because he already knew them. But I was still excited to introduce him as *mine*. My man. Deep down. I wanted everyone to see the man I love and think he was as amazing as I did. And I wanted him to see our Christmas traditions, the things we do that are special to our family. I wanted *him* to see me with *them*, to know that part of me that I am only when I'm with you all. Get it?"

Walker once again imagined taking Ashton into the Ronson family house and introducing him around. He fidgeted. Sweat trickled down from his temple.

"You're not wimping out on me, are you?" Evelyn sighed. "I mean it's fine if you are. Embarrassing yourself on my behalf was always more than I expected from you. I was shocked that you wanted to do it. But it really was such a good plan." She reached out and patted his hand gently. "I get it. You've always hated being judged by anyone, and I know you'd be embarrassed for people to think you're with him."

"I'm not embarrassed to be seen with him! I'd be *proud* for people to think he's my—my boyfriend!"

"You would?"

"Of course."

Evelyn's brows quirked a little, but her eyes glittered dangerously. "Even though he doesn't golf? Or slam empty beer cans against his head?"

"No one I know has done *that* since college."

"Even though he'd want to sit with the lovely old ladies in the dining area upstairs instead of in the golfer's cafe at the club?"

"I don't care about any of those things. And who says he wouldn't want to eat in the golfer's cafe with the men? He's gay for God's sake."

Evelyn sat back, satisfied. "Then what's the holdup on the Christmas Eve invite? You know it would strengthen our Operation Fake Boyfriend scheme for the wedding. You're worried about what Mom will think of him?"

"No."

"But you do care what Dad thinks."

Walker grimaced. "I shouldn't, but I guess I do."

"Mm-hmm. So you were hoping to get away with, what? Not telling anyone about Ashton until the wedding weekend and then avoiding Dad for the entirety of that? If you can't commit to the ruse, baby brother, then you should back out now."

"I can commit." Walker sat up straight. He could. He would.

"It's all right. You've never liked the idea of people thinking poorly of you. You always wanted to impress everyone you met. And you've really always wanted Dad's approval."

Walker scoffed. "I left the firm. How's that asking for his approval? He was furious with me."

"But that proved your masculinity in that you didn't need him. Dating a man like Ashton, bringing him home. Now that plays into Dad's hang-ups about you being queer. You know, I think he's the real reason you've never admitted that you prefer men."

"Evelyn, for fuck's sake, you know I'm bisexual. Everyone knows I'm bisexual."

"I'm not saying you're not." She lifted her hands in surrender before dropping them and leaning forward. "I'm saying you *prefer* men."

"And that's not news, Evelyn," Walker said. "Hell, even Mom got the message. Remember? She tried to set me up with Casey. She wanted me to marry him and merge the Stevens and Ronson families." He rolled his eyes. "Big, soapy, oil dynasty vibes."

"That was Dad, actually. And Casey's Mom. Our mother couldn't care less."

"Regardless, no one thinks I prefer women anymore."

Evelyn chose another chip carefully, taking her time to get the most triangular one, before asking, "When's the last time you even slept with a woman?"

Walker frowned. "There's no time limit on bisexuality. It's not a 'use it or lose it' identity."

"Still, when?"

"I don't know. Eighteen months ago? She was..." Walker waved a hand around. "There. And I was drunk. And I'd just won a big jackpot on the ninth hole."

He'd actually fucked her up against a wall in a private room at the country club, flushed with success and high off the rush of winning a round of golf that had landed him with fifteen thousand dollars' worth of checks clutched in his hand. He couldn't remember her name. She'd been the niece of one of his dad's country club friends. She'd had red hair.

"It was..." He wrinkled his nose. "A bad choice all around."

"Do you ever miss it?"

"What?" Surely his sister wasn't asking him if he missed pussy?

"Gambling."

Walker gritted his teeth. "I guess."

"You guess or you do?"

"I miss golfing," he hedged. "It was my safe place." Until he'd made it a living hell.

"And there's no way you could just, you know, golf?"

"Maybe? But not there." Not at the country club where he'd been a member for his entire life. Not with those friends. Or "friends," he supposed.

None of them had been very supportive of him walking away from the game and their ever-increasing bets. Several of them had even claimed it was un-sportsman-like of him to not allow them the opportunity to break even with him and win back their prior losses.

How well he remembered that thought process. Just one more bet would fix it all. Just a streak of good luck would replenish his accounts. Until there was no way he could ever win enough back to replenish his trust fund or his grandfather's respect for him. Those were both gone for good.

At least his father didn't know what he'd done. His grandfather and mother had kept that secret for him. Evelyn too.

"Why not?"

"Too many triggers."

"Mm," Evelyn hummed, considering. "There's always the other country clubs in town. There are plenty of other courses in the area. You could even drive to Crossville sometimes."

"I don't want to risk it." Walker said it in his most "butt out of my business" tone, and she shrugged, clearly getting the message.

"All right. Back to Ashton and Christmas. You have to at least ask him."

"Fine." Walker wiped a hand over his face. "But what if he's a dick to him?"

"Who? Dad? A dick to Ashton?"

"Yeah. At the wedding, Dad'll have to play nice or risk a scene in front of everyone he wants to impress. At a family Christmas, though…" Walker let the point linger.

"True. But Ashton's no weakling. He's tough. I saw that right away. There are iron studs inside that man. Don't worry so much, Walker. He can handle Dad. I have no doubt about that."

It was true that Ashton was strong, but Evelyn hadn't seen him the night after they'd run into Ashton's mother or two days ago when he'd come home looking so defeated about his cousin leaving rehab. Walker didn't want Ashton to have to be strong again. Not on *Christmas*.

"I don't know. I'll have to think about it."

"Ask him. What else is he going to do? Sit here at your house with the dogs waiting for you to come home? How pathetic."

Walker bristled. "How pathetic that you think he doesn't have friends."

Evelyn rolled her eyes. "It's not that I think he doesn't have friends, baby brother. I just think he doesn't have *friends*."

"What's the difference?"

She shot him another glance that told him she was questioning his intelligence. "Look, I'm friends with Sadie, the girl who cuts my hair, right? But I wouldn't ask if I could spend Christmas with her and her family. I think Ashton is like that. A friend to many but a *friend* to none." She gave him a cheeky grin. "Except maybe now to you."

Walker didn't like that description of Ashton's situation. Ashton was bright, bubbly, beautiful. Of course he had *friends*. Except it was pretty clear he didn't. What was wrong with people?

"Hey! Sorry I'm so late!"

Ashton's voice came from the carport door, and he sounded a little tired. Walker hoped he still had it in him to help with stringing the new Christmas lights along the carport's gutter, because it was a two-person job for sure, especially in the newly fallen dark.

When Ashton walked into the kitchen, his eyes were downcast and there were dark circles beneath his eyes like maybe he'd been crying and his mascara had smeared before being wiped away. Walker's heart twisted. Who'd made Ashton look like that?

But when Ashton looked up and saw Evelyn at the table, he instantly smiled.

It was remarkable how good he was at faking it. A week ago Walker would have assumed the smile was genuine and that he was truly as happy-go-lucky as he appeared. But now, after just days in Ashton's presence, watching him, listening to him, and really seeing him, Walker recognized the difference between Ashton's real smile and this brittle one on display.

"Oh! Evelyn! I didn't see your car?" Ashton said, coming over to hug Evelyn and kiss her cheek.

"Layla has figure skating lessons at the Ice Chalet on Tuesdays, so I had Tom drop me off here to chat with my brother about Operation Fake Boyfriend, amongst other things. I say let Tom hang out in the rink's lobby. It always smells weird. Like stale hot chocolate and piss."

Ashton laughed, and Walker was glad to hear that it at least didn't sound forced. "What a description!" He met Walker's gaze and in the depths of his green eyes, Walker saw a sadness, despite Ashton's best efforts to project to Evelyn that all was well. "And where's Brody?"

"Boy Scouts. One of the other moms is going to drive him home."

"Ah." Ashton crossed to the stove, lifting the lid on the pot and taking a deep sniff. "Mm. As much as I want to know what's been decided about Operation Fake Boyfriend in my absence, I'm also starving. How long until this… What is this? How long until it's ready?"

"Cock-a-leekie soup," Walker said.

"Ha!" Evelyn exclaimed. "Are you serious? Cock-leaking soup? Is it made of piss or something?"

"What's with you and piss tonight?" Walker asked, rolling his eyes. "It's Scottish."

"Hmm." Evelyn sounded skeptical still. "I don't know. Scottish piss. What else do you have for dinner?"

"For you? Nothing. You're not invited."

She rolled her eyes but gave him a wink and smiled. "I see how it is."

"You see how what is?"

She crunched another chip. "Nothing. Anyway, are you going to eat cock-leaking soup, Ashton? Or are you smart?"

"Walker's a great cook and it smells amazing," Ashton said, leaning over the pot again to take another sniff. His stomach growled, and he gave Walker a plaintive look as he asked again, "How long?"

Walker checked his watch. "Now is fine. It's been almost thirty minutes since I put it on."

"What's in it?" Evelyn asked as Ashton helped himself to a bowl from the cupboard and grabbed a ladle from the drawer over the junk drawer. Walker was pleased to see that he was making himself at home. Maybe he really would stay.

"Chicken, leeks, rice, carrots, salt, pepper."

"Hm, maybe I will have some then," she said, as Ashton sat next to her with his bowl and spoon.

"No. It's not for you," Walker insisted.

"So mean! After all the times I made you soup growing up."

"From a can."

"But you couldn't make it!"

"Because I was a child!"

"Wow, guys, it's just soup," Ashton said, laughing. "No reason to start the next sibling world war over it."

"I made you *so much* soup," Evelyn said, crossing her arms over her chest.

"You just compared mine to urine."

"I didn't know you'd get so butthurt over a joke!"

"Fine." Walker pulled two more bowls down and prepared them for Evelyn and himself. Ashton watched with tired but twinkling eyes, as if he'd found the exchange more amusing than he'd let on.

Walker didn't know why he was being a jerk about the soup. There was more than enough for Evelyn, Tom, and even Layla if the kid wanted some. It was just that when he'd started cutting the carrots, before Evelyn had arrived, he'd imagined eating it with Ashton alone. Watching him enjoy it or hate it or tolerate it with his usual happy commentary. Along with the—

Oh shit.

He jumped up and pulled open the oven. The bread was a bit darker than he wanted it to be, but it wasn't burned at least. "Here," he said after dumping the rolls into a breadbasket and placing it on the table.

Ashton grabbed one immediately and tore bits of it into his stew. Evelyn watched in confusion. "Is that how the Scots eat it?"

"No," Ashton said with a smile. "Just me."

Walker dipped some of his bread into the stew and tasted it. It was good. The soggy, chewy texture was pleasant, and he followed Ashton's lead. Evelyn watched him, her eyes taking on a strange gleam. She shrugged and followed suit too.

"What are your plans for Christmas?" Evelyn asked, and Walker kicked her beneath the table. She shot him a look, but then smiled at Ashton like nothing had happened.

"Oh, uh, yeah. Well, Bill and Miranda—my father and his wife—and my stepsister Angel invite me every other season, and sometimes I do go. But this year Bill and I are struggling to see eye to eye on a few things…"

"Like?"

Ashton laughed. "Ah, I see, you're like Kayla at the office. Reeled in by the gossip."

"You have to admit your vagueness makes it sound juicy."

"Well, it is, but it's also a long story."

"Oh? I've got time for a long story."

"Eh…"

"You don't have to tell me, but you know all of my family's mess, so obviously you know there's no judgment from me."

Ashton sighed. "Yeah. I'll try to sum it up because it truly is quite long. We aren't close. We never were. He didn't participate in raising me. When I was older, he came through when it counted. Paid for my college, for example. And his wife has always been nice to me, so I can't turn my back on him completely. But we have different, uh, priorities when it comes to a few important things, so… Yeah. That's that."

"Oh," Evelyn said, looking even more confused, which was how Walker felt as well, but he wasn't about to pry. He'd learned his lesson on that front.

"Yeah." Ashton took his time eating several spoonfuls of stew before he said, "It's complicated. You get it. Your family's complicated too."

"Of course," Evelyn said, but Walker could tell she was dying to dig into it more.

"What do you usually do for Christmas Eve when you're not spending it with your dad?" Walker asked, hoping to steer Evelyn away from what was a more painful topic than she realized.

Ashton sat back and gave another one of those fake, brittle smiles that didn't quite get into the depths of his eyes. "Oh, I usually just watch a marathon of Christmas episodes from favorite TV shows: *Friends*, *Chuck*, *Veronica Mars*, *Supernatural*."

"You watch TV? Alone?" Evelyn said, and Walker recognized that tone. She was about to meddle whether he liked it or not. "Well, not this year! This year, as part of Operation Fake Boyfriend, you'll be coming to the Ronson Family Christmas."

"Oh?" Ashton glanced between them. When Walker nodded, his smile flashed again, but this time it looked slightly more genuine.

"It's on Christmas Eve this year, since I'll be spending Christmas Day with Tom's family."

"Exciting. Can't wait. Who will I mess with first?" He rubbed his palms together gleefully. "You know what we need? A spreadsheet! One for Christmas and one for the wedding! You know, featuring every important family member and what exactly gets under their skin, but won't cause a fist fight. What do you think? And you'd note anyone that I shouldn't mess with. I don't want to upset some sweet old lady unless you really want me to!"

"Yes! I knew you'd see it my way," Evelyn said. "But you won't need to mess with anyone on Christmas."

"Oh?"

"Christmas Eve will be a small affair this year," Walker said. "Just immediate family."

"Oh." Ashton deflated a little. "I don't know. Is it necessary?"

"For you to be there? Absolutely!" Evelyn enthused. "And don't worry, just Walker turning up with a man like you… Well, with a man *at all* will be unsettling enough to my parents to throw them off. Don't get us wrong! He's out, but they'll be confused by the suddenness of it all, which is perfect. It'll get their minds off me, Tom, and the wedding. No need for any extreme shenanigans, of course. Just a little light teasing about the seriousness of your relationship will do."

Ashton's shine faltered.

"Don't look so glum," she said, patting his hand. "We can still plan some over-the-top stuff for the wedding. There'll be plenty of people to torment and tease there. Where's your laptop, Walker? We can start a shared document."

Ashton still seemed fairly low energy, but he didn't argue. As he and Evelyn created notes about the family and friends attending the wedding, marking the ones most likely to cause problems to Evelyn or Tom, the heaviness around Ashton gradually lifted and dissipated into the air.

Walker felt a stab of envy that his sister had been the one to distract Ashton from his emotional burden, whatever it was today. He wished *he'd* been the one to ease Ashton back to this giggling, smiling self.

But Walker had always been a more solid person, lacking in effervescence and fun. It was part of how he'd ended up sucked into gambling. Winning made him feel special, notable, and alive. Now he was back to being ordinary. Maybe even less than ordinary. It was for his own good, but he wondered if he even had it in him to ignite that light in Ashton.

At least he could still turn on the lights for the Christmas tree.

WHILE WALKER WENT out to the carport to see his sister off, Ashton waited inside with the dogs and a second glass of wine. The peace of Walker's home had wrapped around him like a blanket, and he'd almost teared up again when he sat on the sofa and Nina jumped up next to him for a cuddle.

"You won't think I'm an asshole if I say that I'm so glad she's finally gone?" Ashton asked with a sigh as soon as Walker returned.

"Not at all," Walker said with a small laugh, leaning against the doorjamb from the kitchen into the living room. "I was ready for her to be gone as soon as you came in."

Ashton's heart fluttered. "Oh? Why's that?"

Walker's neck and cheeks flushed, and he bent his neck to rub at the back of his head. "I don't know." He stood up straight and looked at Ashton. "Well, partially it's because you looked like you'd had a bad day, and I wanted to make it easier on you. But I guess she cheered you up? You seemed happier by the time she left."

Ashton picked up his wine glass and patted the sofa. "Grab a glass. Sit down." Then he seemed to check himself. "I mean, if you want to."

Walker skipped getting his own glass of wine and sat next to Ashton wordlessly. He crossed his leg at the ankle and rubbed his hands over his thighs, gazing at the tree instead of looking at Ashton. His nerves were cute, though Ashton wasn't sure why he was anxious. Maybe he thought Ashton was about to have another breakdown on him?

"I've been thinking about your offer for me to stay," Ashton said slowly.

Walker shrank slightly. "Oh, yeah?"

Heat flushed over Ashton, and embarrassment crept through him again. Okay, so maybe Walker regretted his impulsive invitation. "Do you still want me here?"

Walker cleared his throat. "Sure."

"Really? It's okay if you don't." Ashton furrowed his brow, studying Walker's expression, looking for the truth. "You don't sound as certain as you did when you asked."

"I'm sure." Walker turned to him, meeting his gaze, and though his cheeks remained flushed his gaze was steady. "I'm enjoying having you here. I'm not ready for it to be over."

"Yeah? Me either."

"So you'll stay?" Walker bit into his lower lip, and Ashton's gut coiled with interest.

He sipped his wine to focus again before saying, "I had a message from my landlord today. The tenants can all move back in now. But he's upping the rent of everyone who has their lease renewal coming up in the new year. Apparently, the bed bugs incident reminded him of some updates he wants to make. I'm included in that group."

"Can he do that?"

"I don't know. I think so. Whatever the case, I don't have the money to fight him on it. Or the desire. For better or worse, with Justin having left Oaks, I'll have more money going forward, and I wouldn't want to renew there anyway. So I think I'll look for a new place. You're truly okay with me staying here with you until I find one?"

"Of course."

Ashton nodded. "All right. I like being here, and if you like having me, then I want to stay."

"Yes, great. Because I want you here."

Ashton smiled, but his soul ached painfully. Memories of the hurtful words Justin had slung at him still pierced his heart. "You might be the first person to ever want me in my whole life."

Walker's eyes grew soft and worried again. His voice was low as he murmured, "No."

"Yeah." Resignation flooded him, and Ashton went limp on the sofa, exhausted by the truth of it.

Walker whispered, "That's not possible."

Ashton turned his head, looking at Walker's firm profile, his steady jaw and slight Adam's apple. "Walker?"

"Yeah?"

"Shut up? Please?"

Walker obediently closed his mouth and sat with Ashton in silence.

The dogs moved around, exchanging beds and positions. Nina got down from the sofa and went to cuddle Bitsy, and Marble hopped up next to Ashton until he petted her gently.

The evening descended around them, and eventually Walker got up to get a fire going before turning on the television and starting an episode of their show.

Ashton put his feet in Walker's lap as was becoming a habit and groaned lightly when Walker started to rub. He wished with his whole heart that he could stay here with Walker for a long time. Maybe he'd drag out the process of finding a new apartment. Maybe nowhere would be as pleasant as here.

Maybe, just maybe, there would be a Christmas miracle, and he'd never have to leave.

*Am I delusional now? Great, good. Love that for me.*

ASHTON WOKE IN the night with a sharp cry. His breath came in harsh pants, and he sat up in bed, sweaty and hot. Heaven help him, why had he dreamed of that day again?

"Fairytale of New York" was still rattling around in his mind like someone had been playing it by his bed as he slept. He could still see the needle in his mother's arm. He was still standing there helplessly watching as she went under. He was still on that 911 call.

It was still happening, and it was years ago.

Pounding steps on the stairs were the only warning Ashton had before his bedroom door burst open and Walker appeared, outlined by the hallway nightlight left on to illuminate trips to the bathroom. "What's wrong? Are you okay?"

Ashton rubbed his face. "I'm fine. I'm sorry. Go back to bed."

Walker flipped the light on, revealing that he wore only a white T-shirt and a pair of black sweatpants. Ashton winced under the brightness. "Bad dream?"

"Yeah."

Walker turned the light back off and hovered in the doorway.

"I'm good now. Seriously, sorry. You can go."

"Are you sure?"

Ashton laughed. It sounded bitter. "Yes."

Still Walker didn't move.

"Really, I'm okay."

When Walker did speak, his voice was quiet and yet sure. "When I was little and I had nightmares, my mom would get me out of bed, take me outside, and we'd look at the moon together."

Ashton blinked. What different worlds they'd lived in. "When *I* was little and had nightmares, my mother would be too high to care. When I was older, my grandmother would pray over me. Believe me when I say that wasn't comforting."

"Come on," Walker said, holding out a hand barely visible in the darkness. "Come with me."

Ashton thought about arguing but instead swung his legs over the bed and stood. He still felt hot and horrified, like if he closed his eyes, he'd be right back in the dream again, right back with his mother falling away in front of him.

Wearing just flannel pajama bottoms and an oversized T-shirt, he followed Walker downstairs, where only Simone waited, pacing and worrying. Still barefoot, he let Walker tug him out the back door to the patio. The wintery, cool air greeted him, pricking his exposed skin and stinging his face, fully waking him and instantly making him shiver. He smelled woodsmoke either from their chimney or possibly a neighbor's, and the wind creaked in the trees.

"Holy crap it's cold," Walker said, laughing and slinging an arm around Ashton's shoulder and tugging him close to his side. "This will wake you up."

Ashton grunted, wrapping his arms tightly around himself, trying to hold in some of the warmth from his bed. He sucked in a stinging breath, eyeing the gray world around him dizzily. The gloom of night was broken only by the glow of various Christmas lights and decorations twinkling in the surrounding yards.

"There," Walker said, pointing up when silver light expanded over the yard. "She's waxing gibbous tonight."

Ashton looked up at the moon as it came out from behind a dark cloud. Shadows and scars showed dark against the gleaming surface. Like me, he thought. Shiny but battered as hell.

"Take some deep breaths," Walker instructed, his hand chafing up and down Ashton's arm, trying to rub warmth into his chilled skin. "Let that dream go."

Ashton did as he was instructed, staring at the face of the moon and thinking of mothers. "What's she like?" He asked after a few moments. "Your mom?"

For some reason, Ashton had always thought of Walker and Evelyn's mom as a probable prig. Bringing her son out to look at the moon after a nightmare seemed more whimsical than he'd imagined her to be. It was too easy for him to believe in terrible mothers. Perhaps he was wrong about this one.

"She's a good person," Walker said. "She's gentle and funny. Loving. She worked a lot when we were growing up, but I always knew she wanted the best for Evelyn and me."

Silence rose up for several shivering moments, until Ashton whispered, "My mom wasn't like that. I'm glad you had a mom who loved you."

Walker stepped behind Ashton, rubbing both of his goose-bumped arms now. "Still cold?"

He nodded. Walker wrapped his arms around Ashton's chest, pulling him close. Ashton let his back rest against the front of Walker's body, the warmth of him seeping into his chilled skin. Walker's chin fit against his shoulder, and Ashton stood very still, wondering how the nightmare had turned into this sweet dream of connection and friendship and maybe something more.

Suddenly, Walker pulled away and Ashton shivered as the cold air replaced the heat at his back.

"Is the dream washed away?" Walker asked.

Ashton nodded, his throat growing tight at the fanciful question.

"Good. Let's go back inside."

He followed him in, his body trembling from both the cold and the tumble of emotions elicited by Walker's touch. His heart twisted in his chest. It used to be that all he wanted from Walker Ronson was a smile, but now he wanted so much more.

He wanted bath bombs, homemade dinners, puppy cuddles, unqualified affection, and a home. Was that all he wanted from Walker for Christmas? Heaven knew that was already way too much to ask.

As they walked through the living room, Ashton caught a glimpse of the star atop the darkened Christmas tree. On impulse he closed his eyes and made a wordless wish—he didn't do prayers anymore—one that held all his yearning and hope.

"Are you all right?" Walker asked when they came to the bottom of the staircase. "Want me to come up with you?"

"I'm pretty sure the nightmare isn't hiding out under the bed waiting for me," Ashton said, but his eyes pricked with tears at Walker's caring.

"I could check and see. Just to make sure."

Ashton laughed. "No, I'm fine. Thank you…" His throat went dry. "For taking me outside. For showing me the moon."

Walker's lips opened slightly, and Ashton felt like he could just lean in a little and Walker would simply take him into his arms. Maybe kiss him. What would it be like to be held by Walker? To be loved by him?

"My pleasure," Walker said, and his voice sounded gruff.

"Good night." Ashton turned, heading up the stairs with his heart pounding, his head whirring, and a powerful desire flooding his body.

He longed to know whether Walker Ronson kissed as sweetly as he'd hugged from behind while pointing out the moon.

In his room, Ashton found Nina passed out in the middle of his bed. She'd taken the opportunity of the open door to make herself at home. Ashton scooted in beside her, curling his cold body up against her warm, steadily snoring form. Like all sleeping dogs, she smelled like popcorn, and she was warmer than his blankets. Ashton kissed her by her ear, pulled the covers around himself, and snuggled close to her.

She wasn't Walker, but she would have to do.

# Chapter Eleven

Angel's tiny Ft. Sanders-area apartment, consisting of two rooms carved from the back of an old Victorian house, was decked out for the season in her usual goth style. Ashton pondered the jarring profusion of hot-pink-on-black decorations as he untied his boots, worked them off, and hung up his coat, wondering where she'd managed to find a black Christmas tree.

"Wow, you're in the holiday spirit! Look at all this *festive* décor!" Ashton generously didn't mention that it looked like a Monster High doll from the mid-2000s had thrown up all over Angel's living room. "Thanks for having me over."

Angel, barefoot and wearing a black shirt and black jeans to match her freshly re-dyed black hair, gave him a one-armed hug before going up on her tip-toes to plant a kiss on his cheek. "Glad you approve."

"Well, I didn't say *that*."

She laughed. "Come on in, the pizza's already here. Dig in while it's warm."

There wasn't a ton of space in her living room between the black Christmas tree, the too-large hand-me-down sectional sofa, and a La-Z Boy recliner that looked like she'd possibly hauled it in from the sidewalk when another tenant had tried to discard it.

She still had room for a big screen against one wall. They'd watched many a movie on it happily huddled on that giant, lumpy sofa together with a bowl of popcorn between them. One of the best things about locating Bill when he'd turned eighteen was meeting Angel. He'd never had a sister before.

Angel plopped into the La-Z Boy, and he took a corner of the sofa before grabbing a piece of pizza. He felt a stab of regret to be missing out on Walker's latest Scottish dish—Cullen skink soup—but when Angel had invited him over, he'd figured he should take her up on her offer or risk alienating her since he'd declined Bill's invitation to Christmas.

"So, what's the deal?" Angel asked, shoving her dark bangs away from her forehead and peering at him with that intense expression that implied she knew him inside and out, even though he knew good and well that she didn't. No one did. Though Walker was starting to come terrifyingly close enough.

"What do you mean?"

"Bill said you're going to some guy's house for Christmas this year. I didn't know you were dating anyone."

"I'm not."

Angel snorted. "Bill says you are. You're many things, Ashton Sellers, but you are not a good liar."

"I didn't lie. I'm spending Christmas with my business partner, Walker."

Angel reached for a piece of pizza and took a big bite before wiping the grease from her lips with the back of her hand.

"Use a napkin," Ashton said, picking up some of the rough, brown ones the pizza place had supplied in their delivery bag and tossing them at her.

She caught one, and the other two fluttered to the carpet. "What kind of business partner invites you to spend Christmas with his family?"

"The kind that wants you to pretend to be his boyfriend later in the month at his sister's wedding."

Angel almost choked. "What?" she sputtered, grabbing her cola and taking a gulp to clear the food from her throat. "Are you serious?"

"Deadly."

"But why?"

Ashton laughed. "Okay, but this is just between us, all right?"

"Of course. Hand to God." She put her hand in the air and then over her chest.

Ashton didn't want to think about how Grandma Hudson would have felt about that gesture. As they ate the two pizza pies Angel had ordered, Ashton shared with her the general idea around Operation Fake Boyfriend and then some of their specific plans.

Angel clearly found the whole concept entertaining, but when it was over, she came back to her first question. "I get that this is a great prank and all—"

"More than a prank," Ashton corrected.

"Fine, maybe so, but what about *your* family? Mom and Bill were really hoping you'd come this year. They really wanted you there."

Ashton frowned. He didn't think his father disliked him, and he knew Angel's mother wasn't against his presence in their lives, but he'd never thought they especially cared one way or another about his rare visits. They always seemed to invite him more out of obligation than actual enjoyment.

"Why, though?" he asked. "What's so important about having me there?"

Angel shifted a little in the chair, her eyes dropping to the floor. She shrugged. "Bill hates being on the outs with you."

"Does he?" Ashton blinked. "Could have fooled me. We had that last argument about my mom in August. He texted me on my birthday, but I hadn't heard from him since then. I was the one to message him to let him know I wouldn't be there for Christmas after he hadn't even sent a message specifically inviting me. So I don't see any evidence that he's particularly upset about me not coming around."

"Well, he is."

Ashton cocked his head. "What? No, he's not. He can't be."

"He just wants to make up with you and for you to make things right with him."

Ashton put his unfinished piece of pizza down. "Me? Make things right with *him*? Do you even know what we fought about?"

"Your mom—"

"My mom and my cousin, yeah. He told me…" Ashton waved his hand around. "Never mind what he said. I'm not mad about it now, and I doubt he is either. I told him why I wasn't going to be there, and it's the truth. It's not about him."

"Not even a little?"

"No, of course not. Look, if I'm avoiding him for any reason, it's not about that last fight. It's about everything else that ever happened in my whole life. But the truth is I have this obligation to my business partner. Otherwise…" he gestured as if things might have been different this Christmas, though he doubted he would have gone to Bill's anyway.

Angel and Bill were right—he wasn't really interested in trying to have a relationship with Bill right now. Not after the things he'd said about Justin or what he'd said about Ashton's responsibility to his mother.

"I get it. Bill wasn't there for you," Angel said, nodding in understanding. "But he wants to be there for you now. I know you don't want to talk about it, but tell me from your perspective, what did you fight about?"

Ashton sighed. He didn't want to get into any of this tonight or ever. Especially since he'd already had two PTSD episodes lately.

"He told me I had the wrong priorities. He said I needed to ditch helping Justin, to cut him off and focus on helping my mother instead." Ashton shook his head.

"What did you say?"

"I told him I didn't have my priorities wrong, thank you very much. Justin never got the chances my mom has had. I said he deserved another shot."

"How is that going?" Angel asked.

Ashton's stomach twisted. "Horribly. He ditched rehab."

"I'm sorry."

Ashton saw the sincerity in her expression. She was truly sorry. Still, why was she interrogating him like this? What was she trying to do? Why was she taking Bill's side? "I know you are, but you and Bill need to understand something."

"What?"

"My mom is a nonstarter for me." Ashton gazed at her a moment and felt a little sick when she looked away from him, guilt flashing over her features. "Hey, did you know I ran into her?"

"Oh? You saw her?" Angel looked even more uncomfortable, picking at the toppings of her pizza.

"She found my apartment. Please tell me you didn't give her my address."

"I didn't. I swear." She looked up at him, panicked.

"Okay, I believe you. She told me you help her out with money sometimes, so I had to ask." He put down his pizza slice. "You don't do you? Give her money, I mean."

"I don't! Much. Okay, I've given her a little cash for her dog, but otherwise…"

"She doesn't have a dog!"

"Well, she sure doesn't now!" Angel cried, throwing her pizza crust into the box. "Bill's keeping it for her until she gets a job and finds her own place to live. It's a little mutt she found on the street. So sweet."

"Bill's keeping her dog?" Ashton blinked, his stomach aching. "He's keeping her *dog*? Are you for real right now, Angel? Bill…he… He wouldn't even keep *me*!"

Angel swallowed hard, her cheeks glowing with heat and color creeping up her neck. He couldn't tell if she was angry or ashamed or both. "Ashton, things are different for him now. When you were a kid, he didn't have a job or any stability at all."

"Angel!" He shouted, pizza coming up his throat. She wasn't about to… She couldn't be about to try to justify… Not Angel. Her dad had abandoned her too. She understood. She'd always understood.

She gazed at him earnestly. "He's just trying to be a good person. And a dog isn't a kid, and—"

"Stop!"

"I'm sorry."

He breathed in and out through his mouth, trying to catch his breath. What was happening? Angel was supposed to be like a sister, the one who never questioned his pain, the one who'd had her own horrible childhood wounds, the one who got this part of him without the need of explanation.

"Listen," she said, getting down on her knees at his feet and taking hold of his hand. "You know what a piece of crap my dad is—what a piece of crap he will always be, and that's why I have to say all this. Even though Bill hurt you growing up, he's changed. Bill is a *good guy*. He might not have been the dad you needed when you were young, but he's in a better place now."

Ashton rasped, "I don't care what kind of place he's in. I can't have anything to do with him now. Not if my mom is in his life." And if Bill was taking care of his mom's dog—and holy heavens she actually *had* a dog? that she cared enough about to find a *good* home? unlike him?— just how far had she wormed into his father's life? How long until he was giving her money? Hell, he probably already was.

How long until she stole from Bill? Or worse?

"I know you think it's black and white like that, but is that really fair?"

"Fair to who?" Ashton's scalp began to prickle with heat. No one ever thought about what was fair to him, did they? No one. "If he's going to support her, then I'm out of his life. It's the way it has to be. I can't be near her."

"Ashton…"

"What?" He gripped her hand back, almost too hard. "What's going on, Angel? Why are you being like this?" He felt a tear slide down his cheek, hot and surprising.

Angel reached up and wiped the tear away, keeping her voice soft. "I promised not to tell you, but I really think you ought to know so you'll understand why it's so important to him that you come for Christmas this year."

Ashton's blood ran cold. "What?"

"Jamie Rae's actually staying there right now. With Mom and Bill. Bill had hoped you'd come for Christmas so you could make up with her over, I dunno, an overly well-done roast beef and some candy canes, I guess." She winced. "I, uh, I think he was hoping that if that happened, you'd… Well, you'd take her in."

Ashton stared at her.

"I shouldn't have told you," she whispered, her eyes welling with tears.

Ashton could barely breathe. "Holy heck. You were just going to let them ambush me?"

"No?" Angel said in a small voice. She dropped her head to his knee and pressed it hard there. "Maybe?" She peered up with wet eyes. "I always thought it was a bad idea, Ashton. I swear I told them so. I did. I really did."

"You. Were. Going. To. Let. Them. Ambush. Me." Each word felt like it was a final breath sucked out of him by pain and betrayal.

"Ashton, please don't go!" she called from where she knelt on the floor. "I'm sorry."

He hadn't even realized he'd stood up until she said the words, but hell yeah, he was going now. Angel probably hadn't meant any harm, and she was the only family he felt close to in any way, but this cut deep. He couldn't breathe.

Ashton grabbed his shoes by the door and pulled on his coat. He struggled with the stupid lace-ups of his mid-calf boots and finally just wrapped them around and tied them at the ankles. Angel hovered behind him. The garish pink-on-black Christmas mess behind her seemed to dare him to vomit.

"I'm sorry," Angel said, grabbing hold of his arm. "I know how you feel about her, but Bill says—"

"He left me with her!" Ashton shouted, turning to Angel with tears stinging his eyes. "I thought you understood."

"I do."

Ashton shook his head. "No, I guess you don't. Bill *left me* with my mom. He knew what she was doing, what dangers I was living with, and he didn't *care.*"

"Ash—"

"And when the state stepped in? He left me with my *grandmother.* She was another kind of hell. And now you're telling me that he wants me to *forgive him* for that and forgive my *mother* for all the times she rolled into my life saying she was better only to steal from me— financially! Emotionally! Spiritually! She broke my heart!"

"I know, Ash, I know."

"You know? And yet you want me to forgive *you* for going along with these schemes of inserting her into my *finally safe* life because 'Bill is a good guy'? Does a good guy let people neglect and abuse his son? Does a good guy try to ambush this son with the one person he never, ever, ever wants to see again?"

"Please—"

"But okay, he took in her dog! Great! Good for him! Good for the fucking dog! I mean, fuck, Angel! *Fuck!*" Ashton's voice broke, and he yanked the apartment door open, shrugging off her attempts to hold him back.

He stomped down the stairs and out onto the street. His phone vibrated in his pocket. It was a message from Angel starting with: *I'm so so so so so so sorry.* She should be, but that wasn't enough, was it?

Was there anyone in this world that was trustworthy? Anyone who he could count on not to pull the wool over his eyes in some hideous way in order to inject addiction and horror back into his life again?

Ashton's fingers shook as he opened the Uber app and ordered a car to take him to Walker's. At least he'd be safe there.

He found his way down to busy Cumberland Avenue, where he'd asked the driver to meet him. The winter holiday sidewalk traffic was heavy near the university, and students dodged left and right but he didn't move. Carols and cheerful holiday music drifted in and out of the restaurants and bars as the doors opened and closed, releasing handfuls of happy, laughing kids not that much younger than himself, all having a merry old time, while he waited for a ride from a stranger to take him to a home that wasn't his, to a man who wasn't his, and to some dogs who weren't his.

Everything that *was* his? Trash. Pure trash.

Ashton wiped his eyes with the palms of his hands, startling as a man walked up next to him. It was Hank. He was further away from Gay Street than was his norm, but drunk college kids could be generous with their cash. Hank was dirty and a little stinky as he leaned in and whispered, "You all right?"

Ashton nodded, his throat too tight for words.

"It's a tough time of the year, ain't it?"

Ashton nodded again.

Hank patted him on the shoulder. "Could you spare a little change for an old man to buy himself a bottle?"

He shook his head, the words opening him up like a wound again. "A bottle's not going to help you."

"Ah, I see." Hank's eyes narrowed. "Some change for a warm meal then? I'm awfully hungry. It's been a long, cold day."

Ashton sighed and pulled out his wallet, handing over a ten-dollar bill. It was all he had on him.

Hank took it. "Thank you, friend. Happy New Year. Seasons greetings. Blessed be the baby Jesus and all that."

He nodded, his stomach aching and his eyes still burning. As the Uber pulled up to collect him, Ashton watched as Hank crossed the street and went into the liquor store. Because of course he did. Ashton had known he would.

Because addicts lie.

"MOM, HEY," WALKER said into the phone as he paced back and forth in the living room, the glittering Christmas tree shining in the corner of his eye.

"Walker! Bless my soul, is it really you? Have you truly called your own mother using this magical device called a phone? It's only been, what? Two months?"

"We've texted! We had brunch last month!"

"I know, I know. I just like to give you a hard time, sweetie." She laughed and Walker's heart warmed. "But seriously, honey, is everything all right? You wouldn't call without a good reason."

"It's about Christmas."

"Oh? Hold on a minute." He heard her cup her hand over her phone. "It's Walker, honey. I'm going to take this call in the bedroom. No, no, he's fine. Keep on watching your game. You can catch me up on it later." Her feet clacked against the marble tile floors of his parents' house. "All right now, what's this about Christmas? Are you still having trouble finding a gift for Brody? I can give you one of mine to give to him if you want. We can just replace the tag with your name. It's not a problem."

"No, no, that's not it." Walker cleared his throat and ignored the weird rush that came with his next words. "I wanted to ask if... Well, actually not ask, but tell you that—" He felt a little lightheaded. Were they really doing this? Wow. All right. For Evelyn. It was for Evelyn. "I'm bringing someone special with me to Christmas dinner. A man."

"Oh?" Her voice perked up with excitement. "Someone *special*? Honey, I didn't know you were even dating anyone!"

"I've been…" He made a choked noise that he didn't fully recognize and finally strangled out, "It's an unexpected situation. It's been fast and slow all at the same time. See, I've known him a good while now, but it's only recently that I felt… That I realized… That we both realized…"

"Oh, honey, please don't tell me it's that idiot from the country club. What's his name? Harding Howard?"

"What?" Walker blinked rapidly. "*Harding Howard?* Really, Mom? He's twenty years older than me. He's almost your age."

"Well, that doesn't signify anything. He's been interested in you for years now."

"That doesn't make it better! I think he started coming on to me when I was sixteen!"

"I didn't know that." She sniffed. "I suppose I'll have to give him a piece of my mind over that next time I see him."

"Leave it, Mom. Nothing came of it. Please have some faith in me that I have better taste in men than that." He rubbed a hand over his hair, annoyed and confused about how he'd gone from preparing to tell his mom about Ashton to talking about Harding fucking Howard of all people.

"All right, don't keep me in suspense," she said with laughter in her voice. "Who is this special man you want to bring home with you?"

"It's Ashton." He heard the quiet pleasure in his voice as he said the name and wondered if she heard it too. Wondered if he could stop having all these weird feelings sometime soon or if he was going to continue to suffer with them all the way through to the end of their arrangement. "My business partner, Ashton Sellers."

There was a long silence before his mother said softly, "The pretty one? With the, uh, oh goodness, all the makeup?"

"Yes."

"Oh, gracious." She was silent again. "He's not your usual type."

"No, he's not." Walker's stomach flipped anxiously. "But I guess that's how I missed out on what a great guy he is for such a long time. I wasn't looking for anything with him because of…" He cleared his throat, trying to think of how to encompass all that'd once made him irrationally irritated over Ashton but now got under his skin in a different way. "Because of all *that*."

"I see." She sounded as if she did see, actually, but was also worried about what it was that she saw. "Well, if he makes you happy…"

"He does."

"I'm sure your father will get over it eventually."

Walker swallowed hard. "Hopefully."

She huffed. "You can't date or marry people just to please him anyway. Evelyn surely hasn't."

Walker snorted. "No, she's dated a lot of men that Dad despised."

"Like that pompous, odious, middle-aged professor." She sniffed.

"Dad likes Tom, at least. For the most part." When Tom wasn't pushing his buttons, which he'd been trying very hard not to do lately for the sake of Evelyn's sanity.

"Tom is a good person, and your father recognizes that. Now anyway. It took some time. But you know, and I know, he would rather have seen her marry someone from a better background."

Walker rolled his eyes. "What does that mean anyway? Better background? Who really has a good background these days? I sure as hell don't."

"It's not as though you come from a *bad* background," she said, sounding a little affronted.

"No, of course not. I'm just saying that there are suitable people from all walks of life, and after all the mistakes I've made, how can I judge anyone for something as innocent as the family situation they were born into?" He swallowed, hoping his mother and father never got a whiff of Ashton's mother's history. Not if they were going to judge Tom for being from the sticks.

"Well, I won't deny you've made some mistakes in these past years, but you're coming out on top, just like I knew you would."

And he never would have made those mistakes if he hadn't been trying to be the person his father wanted him to be instead of the man he really was. He'd never have started gambling at such high stakes if living that lie hadn't stoked a rage in him that only self-sabotage and poisonous rushes dampened.

"But me 'coming out on top' isn't because I'm from a good background. It's because I decided to change my life."

"With the help of your family."

He gritted his teeth. He really did not want to argue with his mother. He loved her, and hell, she was right. He did have the help of his family. He was living in his grandfather's house after all. "But you're right, Tom's a good man," he said instead.

"He is. And I'm sure your Ashton is a good man too. Tell me more about him."

"He's funny. And smart. He's unique. I don't think I've ever known anyone like him. He's so creative and intuitive, and I... I really care about him," Walker said, the truth of his words making his heart beat fast. He tried to focus on Operation Fake Boyfriend and not his all-too-real feelings. "I guess that's obvious since I wouldn't bring him home with me if I didn't."

"What about his family? Won't they miss him at Christmas?"

"It's a long story, but he doesn't really have anywhere to be."

"I see."

"You should know I intend to have him with me at Evelyn's wedding. As my date." He licked his dry lips, feeling like he was confessing so much more than he intended with every word. "I hope you and Dad can like him. He's special."

"He certainly must be if you care for him. I just want you to be happy, and if that means dating this... This fancy boy, then I'm glad of it."

"Thank you, Mom."

"Of course."

He wanted his mother to like Ashton. Even if a relationship was all pretend between them, he was still Ashton's friend no matter what, and he wanted his mom to see the magic in the man. Maybe he'd been stupidly slow to discover it but it was possible his mother wouldn't be.

"And I'll prepare your father."

Walker cringed. Ah, yes, his father. *He* would definitely see the magic in Ashton and call it something hateful. Walker disliked that he was putting his mother in the position of mediator even in advance of Christmas, but that was half the reason for this call.

He couldn't turn up to the family holiday with Ashton in tow without giving his parents some kind of advance warning. That would have been rude in so many ways. But had that not been the case, it still wouldn't have been a smart move. Walker needed his father to be prepared for the man his son was bringing home. Otherwise, things might get ugly, and no one needed that on any day, much less Christmas.

After listening to his mother talk about her most recent trip to the salon and the candy cane-themed fingernail designs she'd had done there, he got off the phone. It was time to feed Bitsy, Marble, Simone, and Nina. They'd been very patient throughout his phone call, and they deserved a little more in their bowls for that, so he opened an extra can while they danced at his feet.

He let the dogs out back to roam the perimeter of the yard after they'd gobbled down their dinner and returned to load the dishwasher, his heart skipping happily when he heard the sound of the door to the carport opening.

Walker quickly closed the door to the dishwasher and turned it on, smiling to greet Ashton as he entered the kitchen wearing a pair of tight jeans that somehow looked expensive, a candy-cane-striped sweater with silver filigree around the neck and wrists, and bright red mid-calf boots that were not entirely tied. He hadn't been wearing that outfit at work earlier, so Walker took it all in for a breathless moment, shocked as always at how beautiful Ashton truly was. His heart soared with pleasure.

Until he saw Ashton's red-rimmed eyes and the tell-tale smears of mascara.

"Are you okay?" Walker wiped his wet hands on a towel and tossed it aside, striding toward Ashton with his arms open.

Ashton's green eyes shone with tears, his lips trembled, and as Walker drew near, he collapsed against him, shaking all over.

Walker hooked his chin over Ashton's shoulder and rubbed his hands up and down his back. "Are you all right? What happened? Tell me."

The cold of the winter day—the day before Christmas Eve—seemed to have seeped into Ashton's body. He felt like ice as he shivered in Walker's arms, and he smelled like winter, along with that tobacco and paper cologne he used.

A noise that started deep in Ashton's throat turned into a small wail, and Walker hugged him tighter, whispering, "You're grown and safe, baby. You're grown and safe," until the horrible grief-sound abated.

Still he held Ashton close, breathing in his scent, keeping him tight in his arms. He didn't know what had gone wrong, but he could do this for Ashton. He could help hold him together while he gathered his strength.

"I'm sorry," Ashton said finally, but he didn't pull away. "I'm so sorry, Walker. I'm so, so sorry."

"Hey, it's okay. You're with me now, and you're safe."

"I'm safe?"

"You're safe."

And then Ashton did tug free of Walker's embrace, leaving him both relieved and a little bereft.

Ashton wiped at his eyes with his palms. Mascara smeared even further down his tear-wet cheeks. "It's been a hard few weeks."

"I know." Walker wanted to kick in the face of whoever had made Ashton feel like this tonight. Ashton who had already confronted *so much* recently: possible bed bugs, his mother, and his cousin going AWOL from rehab. He'd deserved a good night out with his stepsister. What could possibly have happened? "Oh, baby, I wish I could have made this week easier for you somehow."

Ashton stopped rubbing his face and stared at him with wide eyes.

Walker swallowed hard. Ashton was a pretty crier. God, everything the man did was gorgeous. Hell, what was wrong with him? Why was he fighting this? He could do so much worse than fall in love with a good-hearted man who was also so incredibly beautiful.

"But you did make it easier for me," Ashton whispered. "You've been the only thing that hasn't hurt this week." He touched Walker's cheek with two trembling fingers and then let his hand drop, but not his eyes. "You've been a good friend to me. Please don't doubt that. I'm just sorry you have to see me this way." His breath hitched. "I'm not always such a mess. I promise."

"It's the holidays," Walker said with a shaking voice. Ashton's mouth was right there. And he looked like he could really use a kiss.

*No.*

Not when he didn't know if Ashton wanted one. Not when Ashton didn't feel safe. He stumbled doggedly on. "Holidays are hard enough without all you've been dealing with too."

Ashton's plump lips tilted at the edges into a tiny smile. Then his eyes filled again, and he shook his head as if trying to toss the memories or thoughts out. "Ugh." He pushed back against Walker's chest, putting space between them. "I need to shower. Wash this day off me."

"Of course." Walker wanted to gather him close again, but he took a step back.

"And I'm starving."

"You are?"

"I ate so much pizza there, but I could really go for some of that soup you mentioned. The Scottish soup?"

"You can eat when you're upset?"

"Always," Ashton said, wiping his hands over his face again, smearing even more mascara. "Eating my feelings is something I've excelled at my whole life."

Walker didn't point out that Ashton's physique didn't indicate any such thing. Instead he simply said, "There's plenty left. I'll warm it up if you truly feel like you can stomach it."

"I can. Let me just go shower." Ashton waved toward the hall leading upstairs. "I need to get all of this off me. I promise I'll be calmer then."

"Take your time." Walker watched as he walked with jerky, unsteady steps toward the stairs. Just as his foot hit the first riser, Walker said, "Hey, it's okay if you're not calmer after the shower, or at all tonight. I can handle it. You're safe here."

Ashton paused and turned back around, licking his lips tentatively. "Walker?"

"Yeah?"

He swallowed and whispered, "Thank you."

Walker waved it off.

Ashton's eyes filled with tears again. "You give good hugs, by the way. The best hug I've ever had and right when I needed it."

"Anytime."

"And you…"

"Yeah?"

"You called me baby."

"Oh." Walker's stomach flipped.

"I liked that." He disappeared up the stairs.

The dogs started to bark outside, demanding to be let in. Walker waited until he heard the water running upstairs before going to the door and allowing them to charge inside. He watched with a pounding heart as all four of them sniffed around looking for Ashton.

"I know. He's pretty great," he said. Nina looked up the stairs and whimpered, turning in a stressed circle of fretting. "I know. I'm worried about him too."

And he was worried about himself. How far gone must he be to have called Ashton baby without realizing it? His heart fluttered.

He was worried about Christmas Eve. Ashton had already gone through so much this week. Walker didn't want him to have to face Walker's father's disdain now. He wanted to keep him home, wrap him up in a cozy blanket, and give him hot cocoa as they watched snowy Christmas movies on TV. Then summon the nerve to kiss him. Truly kiss him. Long and slow, in front of the fire.

Oh, wow. He was falling in love.

"MY DAD LEFT me with my mom when I was three. He says he's not sure how he made it that far with us," Ashton confessed as he spooned another delicious hunk of haddock and chowder into his mouth.

The shower had worked wonders on calming his nerves, and when he'd come downstairs to find the dogs waiting for him, he'd felt comforted and truly safe. Which was why he was carefully telling Walker about his childhood now. He felt strong enough with the dogs at their feet, the warm stew in his belly, and Walker's steady gaze on him.

"That's a horrible thing for him to say, but surely it was about her, not you."

"I don't know. It doesn't matter whether he was running from her more than me. The end result of him leaving was that I was a small child left alone with an actively using addict. The things I saw…" Ashton squeezed his eyes shut.

"You don't have to tell me."

"I don't think I can yet."

Walker took Ashton's free hand into his own and squeezed. "That's okay."

Ashton ate more stew, gathering fortitude along with all the nutrition in his belly. "The point is, when the opportunity came for Bill—my father—to make things right? When she overdosed and I had to go *somewhere*, he said no."

Walker's hand flinched in Ashton's fingers.

"He said not him. Not his house. So I ended up living with my grandmother. A woman who saw only sin and Satan in me, the barely twelve-year-old entrusted to her care." Ashton shoveled in more stew, swallowed, and confessed, "To say I blame him is an understatement."

Walker nodded. "I get that. But you've tried to have a relationship with him anyway?"

"Yeah, of course. He's my father." Ashton shook his head. "But he won't take responsibility for any of it. I swear, I've tried to accept that—accept *him*. For the most part I've managed to do it. He did help me, you know. After I left Grandma Hudson's. He helped me through college. Helped me so I didn't live on the street."

"That's good?"

"Of course. But it was a little late!"

"Yeah." Walker scowled.

"I'm grateful too. Don't get me wrong. But it's a mess. *I'm* a mess about it."

"Anyone would be."

"Now that I'm an adult, I can usually put aside the past and try to embrace whatever relationship Bill and I can have. Because I do want a father in my life. I do want to know him." Ashton felt his throat grow too tight to swallow, so he put his spoon down and wiped at his eyes again. When would the tears stop? "But now that he's actively interacting with my mom? Now that he wants me to 'make up' with her? Wants *me* to take responsibility for her?" He gasped, his throat feeling raw. "What does that even mean? Invite her into my home? To live with me?" Ashton trembled at the very thought. "No. Just no. I won't bring her toxicity and addiction back into my life. I can't do that. I won't."

"Of course not." Walker's brow furrowed.

Ashton picked up his spoon and pointed it at Walker. "Addicts—it doesn't matter what they're addicted to—drugs, alcohol, gambling, whatever it is—they can't be helped. They'll never change."

Walker went very still. "But you were willing to help Justin. Three times even. You believed he could change."

"I've learned my lesson now. If he's changed, it's only for the worst." Ashton spooned more soup into his mouth, chewed, and swallowed, trying not to remember his last conversation with Justin. The verbal arrows and dirty shots were more than he could stomach. "Addicts and bingers and me? We can't mix."

Walker's golden lashes touched his cheekbones, and he seemed to ponder for a long moment before he whispered, "Bingers?"

"People who just lose control over something. I can't be around that ever again. I won't." Ashton put his shoulders back, pulling his hand from Walker's. "That's my boundary and I think it's a fair one after all I've been through."

"It is," Walker agreed, his voice trembling slightly. "It's entirely fair."

Ashton studied him a moment. "Do you know much about addiction?"

"Some."

"It's an evil thing."

Walker's lips thinned, and he nodded slowly. "It's destructive. What counts as addiction to you?"

Ashton frowned. "What do you mean?"

"Like, are all bingers addicts? Say… Say someone had a history of letting something get out of hand—drinking, drugs, or maybe gambling—but they'd gotten themselves back together again. It was a one-time thing, a rough patch, but it's over now. It hasn't been a problem for them for a long time. What about them?"

Ashton considered carefully. He realized he'd been a little strident in his commentary tonight, but after all he'd seen, all he'd been through, he had a right to be pessimistic, didn't he? Still…

"I do think some people recover, but when it comes to addicts, I don't know if I'd ever be able to trust that they'd stay sober. As far as bingers go, I guess they'd have to prove it to me."

Walker's eyes grew avid. "Oh? And how would they do that?"

"By living the life." Ashton shrugged. It seemed obvious enough to him. "Letting me see that they aren't ruled by the substance or behavior anymore." He put up a hand. "But when it comes to my mother and now Justin, I'm just done. They'll never have the opportunity to show me anything. Because they won't be allowed in my life again. Never again. It's not safe for me."

Walker swallowed and pressed his hands together in his lap. "That makes sense."

"So that's that," Ashton said, shoving the now empty bowl away. "I guess I have to be wary with Angel now too. I wish I didn't, but if she's letting Bill and my mom use her like that, getting dragged into these schemes of theirs…"

"Maybe Angel just wants you to have the option of having your mother in your life if you decide you want that," Walker said softly. "Maybe she isn't clear on the reasons why—"

"I don't *care*," Ashton snapped, cutting him off with a sharp gesture. Walker recoiled, and Ashton felt momentarily guilty for yelling, but he couldn't hear any more excuses from anyone tonight. Not over this. "I forgave and forgave and *forgave* my mother. I can't tell you how many times. And every single time she chose the drugs over me. Every time, Walker. *Every* time. I know her. I don't care how 'sober' she is right now. She'll go back to it. That's what addicts do."

Walker cleared his throat. "But you agree that some don't?"

"They're few and far between." Ashton smiled bitterly. "Trust me, addicts break hearts. Don't get involved with one. Ever."

After a long moment, Walker nodded.

In silence, they washed out their empty bowls of Cullen skink and then Walker rubbed a hand over his eyes. "I'm really tired. I think I'm going to let the dogs out and head on to bed. I'll finish up the dishes tomorrow."

"Don't worry about it," Ashton said, a gentle ache starting in his heart. He'd taken a lot from Walker tonight. He should give back something, even if only this. "I'll do them now. It's not a problem. And I'll take care of the dogs too. I'll let them out and get them settled in their beds and all that."

"All right," Walker agreed. He looked exhausted. "I'll be back for Bitsy after I shower."

"Sounds good. Hey, I'm sorry for being such a downer tonight." Ashton took hold of Walker's wrist, rubbing his thumb up and down against the soft skin there. "It's a crap hand I've been dealt as far as my family goes—" He huffed a bitter laugh. "I know, gotta love that for me. But I don't need to bring you down with me. I'm sorry."

"No, please, don't apologize." Walker pulled his wrist free with a sad smile. "You didn't do anything wrong. I'm just tired. You really don't mind the dishes?"

"Of course not. After all you've done for me?" Ashton wished he could make Walker understand just how much he appreciated him. "It'll feel good to pay you back even just a little."

"All right."

Ashton moved to the dishwasher and started to unload the clean glasses to put them away in the cupboard over the sink.

"Hey, Ashton," Walker said from the doorway.

Ashton glanced over his shoulder. "Yeah?"

"I'm sorry. About your mom, and your cousin, and how your dad abandoned you, and that you feel like your stepsister betrayed you."

Ashton put the glass in his hand down, feeling a "but" coming. His stomach twisted at the thought.

"But I have to have faith that some addicts and bingers can recover." Walker rubbed the back of his neck. "I'm not saying you need to interact with your family ever again, because that's your call, and it's a fair one. But... Yeah. I have to believe that some bingers can stop binging and some addicts can quit their addiction. That's all."

Ashton frowned, resting his hip against the counter, his heart trembling. Had he hurt Walker with what he'd said tonight? In some unknown and unknowable way? He didn't want that. He never wanted that. "Okay. I get it." He pitched his voice lower, trying to sound tender and understanding, hoping he didn't let his doubt seep in. "Someone you care about has problems?"

"You could say that."

"Ah." Ashton fought for a hint of encouragement, a note of kindness. Everyone deserved to have some optimism about addiction before having their hopes dashed. "I'll wish for their full recovery. I'll wish really hard."

"Thanks. I appreciate that." Walker disappeared, leaving Ashton with the dishes and the dogs, and a glimmering Christmas tree shining alone in the living room.

# Chapter Twelve

"T HIS IS IT!" Ashton grinned cheerfully as he spoke, and Walker's heart clenched with fondness at that beautiful smile. "Phase one of Operation Fake Boyfriend." He made a trumpeting sound with his fist to his mouth. "Christmas Eve at your folks' place!"

"Yup," Walker said, shifting down a gear to get up the slope ahead.

After their conversation the night before, he'd gone to bed conflicted and twisted up inside about Ashton's insistence that addicts never heal. But the morning light had brought Walker some peace of mind. He wasn't an *addict*, per se, and never had been.

He'd been a binger. He'd made bad choices with gambling and gotten hooked in for a period of time. But he had stopped completely and didn't feel too worried about being drawn back in. Truthfully, despite how much power gambling had had over him when he'd been in the thrall of it, it hadn't been that hard to walk away. He knew others struggled more than he had, finding it a true hardship to put an end to their habit, but Walker didn't yearn for gambling. He yearned for golfing, for the camaraderie of his old friends, and for the way it'd felt to win, but he didn't miss at all how it felt to lose.

So, it'd been a rough patch for him—a really damn expensive rough patch—and he'd been lucky to come out of it without a daily struggle against temptation. So, when it came to Ashton's requirements for having a binger in his life, Walker felt he was fulfilling them already: living his life successfully, free of his previous problem. He was living proof that bingers could and did stop binging.

Oblivious to Walker's thoughts, Ashton went on jabbering. "I've never been taken to anyone's parents' house before. Gerald wasn't interested in that kind of thing, and he's the man I dated the longest."

"Oh?"

"Yeah." He twisted suddenly in his seat, excitement on his face. "Any chance I'll get to see little Walker's bedroom? Let me guess, your folks are so proud of you they've still got all your pee-wee golfing trophies on display in your old room, right?"

Walker laughed. "I didn't play golf until high school, and alas, little Walker's been erased."

Ashton's expression softened to empathy as he patted Walker's hand on the gear shift. "Oh no. Let me guess, they cleared it all out when you went to college to make way for something else?"

"No. Well, yeah," Walker said calmly. He hadn't minded at the time and he didn't mind now either. "But it's not what you think."

"It's not a crafting room?"

Walker grinned. "No. I grew up in Sequoyah Hills, just a few streets over from my grandparents' place."

"Where we're living now?"

"Yup." Walker repressed a pleased smile at the use of "we," unsure what it even meant that he wanted Ashton to consider the house his home as well. It was all moving so fast. His heart had skipped blithely ahead of common sense and logic, but he didn't even want to call it back.

"My folks built the house they live in now, where we're headed to-night, back when Evelyn and I were in college. I don't have a room in it. In fact, as far as I know, neither of us have ever even spent the night here. It's not the kind of place I'd call home, but they love it."

"That's all that matters."

"Yup."

"You nervous?"

"A little."

Ashton patted his hand on the gear shift again. "It'll be all right."

He, Ashton, and Evelyn had agreed to let Christmas Eve pass by as easily as possible for everyone. There would be no real mischief tonight. But there was no way Walker's father wasn't going to have some *opinions* about Ashton in general. What with Ashton's hair styled meticulously, his satiny green blouse shining beneath his silver cardigan, and the tight red pants he'd pulled out of one of those not entirely emptied plastic bags. As always, Ashton looked gorgeous and over the top. Which was, Walker supposed, exactly what Ashton was. And *that* was exactly what his father would hate.

He shifted gears again as they came to the top of the ridge.

Ashton sucked in a breath. "They live *there*? In that…box?"

"Yup."

Ashton gaped as they mounted the top of the hill and pulled down into his parents' driveway, which fed directly onto their lakefront property. "It's just windows and more windows."

"Pretty much."

"Aren't they worried about people seeing in at night? What's wrong with them? Do they hate the concept of privacy or something?"

Walker laughed again. Ashton's big-eyed outrage made his heart feel lighter. "There's really no one around to see inside. Their closest neighbor is a good half mile away through the trees, and the developer had it built at an angle so the lake is visible from the house, but the house isn't visible from the lake."

"Wow, it's…" Ashton hesitated. "Different."

"It's all right if you think it's ugly."

Ashton frowned, his carefully shaped brows coming together in the middle. "I wouldn't say that. It's just… It's so *stark*." He perked up. "But surely the inside is homier?"

Walker laughed. "Don't count on it. C'mon."

He led Ashton to the front door, his stomach twisting in knots. He wanted to pull off Operation Fake Boyfriend for Evelyn's sake and tonight with his parents was part of that, but if his father reacted the way Walker knew he would, it was going to hit in a different way than he'd planned. It was going to hurt for real.

The front door slid open like a wall parting, and Ashton shrank a little behind Walker as Walker's mom stepped out onto the carefully lit sidewalk. She smiled at him, hands on her hips. Her bobbed and styled dark blond hair glinted in the flood lights from the side of the house.

"Why Walker Alan Ronson, look at you all dolled up."

She went up on tiptoe to touch the front of his hair, specifically the piece Ashton had carefully styled with some kind of product before they'd left the house. "*You'll look so much more dashing,*" he'd declared, and Walker had caved immediately.

"It's…different." She turned her attention to where Ashton was hiding behind him. "And who is this handsome young man you've brought with you?"

"Mom," Walker said, kissing her cheek and motioning for Ashton to hand over the Scottish shortbread cookies they'd made together earlier in the day. She took them with grace and a polite smile. "You remember my business partner, and, uh…" His heart sped up. "Well, my uh—" Holy shit, what was he supposed to call him? How big of a lie was he going to tell?

Ashton chuckled and actually blushed. Walker felt that in his gut.

"Um, this is my boyfriend, Ashton Sellers."

Ashton tensed next to him, looking at him with big eyes.

So he hadn't anticipated being called "boyfriend" tonight. Great. Maybe Walker should have gone with "date," but who brings just a date to their parents' house for Christmas? He was supposed to be selling them as passionately in love for their plan! He was probably overthinking this. He had to be.

"Of course," his mom said. "It's so good to see you again, Ashton. Walker has told me so much about you." She looked to Walker with assessing eyes and then back to Ashton again. Her smile was a little cooler than Walker would have liked, but she wasn't being rude, thank God. "We're happy to have you with us for Christmas."

Ashton's beautiful green eyes were earnest as he replied, "I'm happy to be here, Mrs. Ronson."

Walker cleared his throat anxiously. He felt lightheaded.

His mom's expression lightened, tension battling beneath her skin before she smiled again. It wasn't quite as warm as Walker wished it might be, but it wasn't cold either. It was definitely tainted with apprehension and maybe a little dread. No doubt she'd already had to face some of his father's ire over his choice. And for what? They weren't really dating, even if Walker wished they were.

Maybe they were assholes—he, Evelyn, Ashton, and Tom—for doing this at all. They probably were. Still, he was here, and he couldn't back out now.

"Your home is so unique," Ashton said, indicating the outside of the house. "I've never seen any place like it. Did you design it yourselves, you and Mr. Ronson?"

"Oh, goodness, no!" Walker's mother said, laughing. "We hired a ridiculously expensive architect with a 'unique vision,' as Evelyn would say. Please, come in. You can toe your shoes off there and hang your coat just so. Oh, and Ashton, please don't call me Mrs. Ronson like I'm a schoolteacher or my own mother-in-law." She smiled again and this time her eyes were genuinely warm. "You'll have to call me Mindy."

Walker's heart squeezed. Wow. He wished this moment was really real.

"All right, Mindy. Thank you."

"Come along, both of you. Evelyn and Tom arrived a few hours ago with the kids." She started down the gleaming, white hallway, calling over her shoulder, "Did you hear? They're predicting snow for her wedding day. Can you even imagine? A white wedding!"

"Go on," Walker said, his hand resting lightly on Ashton's lower back. "She won't bite."

"Great, good, love that for me," Ashton murmured, but he followed. Walker stayed at his heels, sweat pooling in the small of his back and a giddy, almost-nausea starting up in his stomach.

Walker hoped Evelyn was right and that his father wouldn't be unkind to Ashton tonight. No one deserved that kind of treatment at any time but especially on Christmas Eve, and Walker wouldn't stand for it if his father tried. But there was no telling what his dad might say to Walker if he got him alone. Whatever it might be, he wasn't looking forward to it.

It surely wouldn't be a warm seasons' greetings.

ASHTON WAS ASTONISHED by the streamlined, aggressively white interior of the box of glass and concrete Walker's parents called their home. After dropping the shortbread cookies off in the kitchen, Mindy showed him through to the living area, explaining that her husband— "You can call him Nate!"—was out back at the charcoal grill, getting the flame going for the meat.

The house was one long space that linked from room to room, with the kitchen connecting to the entryway and the entryway connecting to the dining room, and so on. It felt more like a spaceship than a home in his estimation. But if the elder Ronsons liked it, he guessed that was all that mattered.

Ashton spotted Evelyn and the kids at the far end of the living area just as Mindy stopped next to the Christmas tree, exclaiming, "Oh! That was the oven dinging! Make yourself at home, Ashton. Walker, take care of your guest."

"Of course, Mom."

Ashton smiled at Mindy, and she left with a kind twinkle. Even so, his palms felt sweaty and his stomach ached. He didn't quite know why. All he had to do was be charming and not make waves. Mindy had even said she was glad he was here and she hoped he'd enjoy himself. That was his only responsibility for the evening. This should be easy-peasy. It was all fake, for heaven's sake. So why did he feel like he really was meeting his boyfriend's parents for the first time?

In the ultra-modern interior, the Christmas tree looked out of place with colored lights and handmade decorations from Walker's and Evelyn's childhood. On closer inspection, it looked like there were some new handmade ones from Layla and Brody too. Piled beneath it were loads of presents. Many of them looked familiar, having been previously stowed beneath Walker's tree and transported over earlier in the day by Evelyn and Tom.

Ashton had never seen so many gifts all in one place. He could count ten without even having to look around or beneath others. He'd always known that most families made a big deal over Christmas presents, but he'd never received more than three and usually one of those was a gag gift from Angel and another was something he'd bought for himself. Gerald's gift, bestowed during the holiday season during which they'd been dating, was a studded cock cage and, overall that experience had been unbearably disappointing.

Which reminded him: He hadn't bought anything to unwrap this year. It'd be a present-less Christmas for him. Oh well, it wasn't his first and probably wouldn't be his last.

"There you two are!" Evelyn said, rising from where she sat with the kids on the shiny, marble floor by one of three big, equally shiny black coffee tables, surrounded on all sides by a massive, white leather sectional sofa. She wore a simple green and red plaid skirt and a red, short-sleeved sweater. Her long dark hair was loose around her face, and she looked happy and beautiful.

Evelyn sidled up to Ashton and Walker with a wine glass in one hand and a big grin on her face. "Daddy stepped out to the grill. We're having steak this year," she said to Ashton specifically, "and he's making sure the grill's hot enough to get them well done. Also known as tough as shoe soles. Mom's worried about the children getting food poisoning." She elbowed Ashton fondly. "I hope you enjoy a little jaw exercise with your meat."

"Oh God, please don't say it," Walker muttered. "The joke is too obvious. Plus there are children present."

Ashton giggled and held up his hands innocently.

"I'm serious, though," Evelyn said quietly. "The steaks will be rough going. Daddy isn't the grill man he thinks he is."

"Didn't he just buy this Big Green Egg Grill last week?" Walker asked.

"Because charcoal tastes better, yep," Evelyn agreed with a sad smile.

"I suppose now isn't the time to claim I'm a vegan," Ashton said.

Evelyn smirked. "Not unless you want to offend Daddy even more than just being here with Walker will offend him."

Ashton tilted his head curiously. Just being here would offend Walker's father? That tidbit hadn't been offered up before. A quick glance up at Walker's face proved that he wasn't pleased at Evelyn for letting that small cat out of the bag. "Ah, well, good thing I'm not a fan of a bloody steak then."

Evelyn scooted closer. "I know we're clear on this, but I just wanted to repeat that there's no need to sweat tonight too much. We'll just enjoy Christmas Eve and not worry ourselves about Operation FB." She winked. "We'll save the best for the wedding."

"Where's Tom?" Walker asked, clearly wanting to change the subject.

"Out back with Daddy. No doubt being instructed on the finer points of grilling and of keeping me happy—or else." She mimed cutting a throat.

"Walker!" Mindy called from the direction of the kitchen. "Can you come help me, please?"

Walker squeezed Ashton's arm. "You okay if I…?" He jerked his thumb toward the sound of his mother's voice.

"Of course. Evelyn's got me. She'll keep me safe from harm," Ashton said with a wink and a laugh. He pushed Walker lightly. "Go on. Help your mother."

Walker lingered. "She's going to interrogate me about how we started dating, probably."

"For sure," Evelyn agreed.

"But we didn't make a plan for that yet," Walker said with wide eyes.

"Wing it," Ashton encouraged. "Just say we started getting closer at work."

"That's what I told her on the phone."

"Then stick with it."

Evelyn shoved his arm. "Go on. Get it over with!"

She guided Ashton over toward the children playing UNO on the floor by the tree. "Ashton, meet Layla and Brody. Kids, this is your Uncle Walker's friend. You can call him Mr. Ashton." She glanced to Ashton for his approval, and he nodded.

Ashton had to smile at the way Layla looked exactly like a miniature Tom wearing a Christmas dress, sans tattoos and beard of course. Light brown hair, sparkling blue eyes, pink cheeks, and a rounded jawline. She was definitely her father's girl.

Brody, on the other hand, looked like a little woodland creature, with fawn-shaped chocolate eyes and pointy ears. His chin was sharp and his skin was incredibly pale over a soft-brown sweatshirt with a snowman design on the front. He frowned a little and then waved hello before returning to his cards and laying down a draw four.

Layla groaned, gave him a sharp glare, and pulled new cards from the stack. Once she had added them to the fan of cards in her hand, she turned her attention back on Ashton, curiosity enlivening her small, pug-nosed face. "You're Walker's friend?"

"Yes," he agreed. Why did that feel like a lie? He *was* Walker's friend. Never mind that lately it seemed like he wanted to be more.

"*Uncle* Walker," Evelyn reminded Layla.

Layla narrowed her eyes. "All right. Why does *Uncle* Walker get to invite friends? I wanted to invite Kristina but you said Christmas Eve is for family!"

"Darling, don't be rude."

"But you said!"

Evelyn crouched next to Layla, putting her drink aside and pushing the hair back from Layla's flushed face. "Usually it is for family, but Mr. Ashton didn't have anywhere else to go tonight. It's different, you see? Even if Christmas Eve *can* sometimes include friends, Kristina had her own family activities tonight."

"But she's my *best* friend and we could have at least asked! Dad's always saying there's no harm in asking." She pointed at Ashton. "Uncle Walker asked, and his friend came."

"Well, uh…" Evelyn glanced up at Ashton desperately, but he was out of his depths. He could mess with grown-ups' minds all day long, but when it came to little kids, he was at a loss. "If you must know, Walker's friend is special."

"Special? How?" Layla gave Ashton a very thorough once-over and clearly found him lacking.

"He's a…well, a special friend," Evelyn hedged.

Layla's expression grew rebellious at that proclamation.

"Don't be homophobic, Evelyn, darling," Mindy's voice came suddenly from behind Ashton.

He turned to find her carrying a plate of sliced vegetables and other appetizers. Walker was with her, holding two glasses of red wine in each hand. His eyes opened wider at his mother's words.

"You'll confuse the children," Mindy added. "In PFLAG I learned it's better to just be upfront and forthright with children. They'll understand." Mindy placed the plates on one of the empty coffee tables, knelt down by the kids, and gestured up at Ashton. "Layla, Brody, this young man is Walker's boyfriend. Do you understand?"

Evelyn met Ashton's and Walker's gazes over the kids' heads, and they shared a quick "oh-shit" moment as Walker passed a glass of red into Ashton's hand. It was clear none of them had considered the fact that there was a chance they'd also end up lying to Evelyn's soon-to-be stepkids. Lying to children just seemed extra wrong.

"Because Walker's gay?" Brody said, tossing down a yellow six.

"He's bisexual," Mindy said.

"That means he likes boys and girls," Layla whispered, like she was reminding him of a conversation they'd previously had, probably with Evelyn. She put down a blue six. "We support all kinds of love in our family, remember?"

"Oh, okay." Brody met Ashton's eyes and smiled. "Hi."

Ashton lifted his glass toward Brody and then sipped the wine. It was delicious, and he quickly took a bigger gulp to see if it was really as tasty as it seemed *and* in hopes of it going straight to his head. He could only surmise it was expensive.

Mindy stood up, patting the children's heads and smiling. "See? That's what they said to do in PFLAG, and it worked."

"Mom," Evelyn said, rolling her eyes. "They already knew he's gay."

"Bisexual," Walker, Mindy, and Layla corrected at the same time.

"God, fine, bisexual." Evelyn rolled her eyes.

"There will be no bisexual erasure in this house, young lady," Mindy said with a wink to take the sting out of her scolding.

"I know, I know," Evelyn said from where she sat next to Layla. She took a big swallow of her wine before pointing her glass at her mother. "They probably taught you that at PFLAG."

"So what if they did?" Mindy sniffed. "And if you already know, and if they already knew, then why did you try to introduce this lovely young man as just a friend?"

"I didn't want to overwhelm them," Evelyn said with a hint of embarrassment.

"They're fine with it," Mindy pointed out.

Brody and Layla continued with their game as if they weren't being talked about right in front of their little faces.

"I meant Ashton and Walker, Mom. Maybe they wanted to ease into this whole thing tonight? Not dive in with love declarations in front of the children and all that?"

Love declarations? Oh, wow.

Ashton's head swam at the idea. Would Walker go that far? Tell him he loved him as part of the show? He felt shivery inside imagining it and then hollow knowing it would all be pretend. It wasn't a good sign that he *wanted* Walker to look him in the eye and declare his affection, even if he didn't really meant it.

Ashton wanted to smack himself. How pathetic to be so hungry for love.

*Great, good, love that for me.*

Mindy's expression turned momentarily worried, but Walker stepped in. "No, it's fine. I'm proud to be here tonight with Ashton as my date. Isn't he handsome, Layla?"

"I guess," Layla said, rolling her eyes and placing a red six onto the pile of cards.

"Yes," Brody said. "He's the most handsome man I've ever seen."

The adults all chuckled, and Walker's smile made Ashton's heart sing, especially when Walker met his gaze and said, "Me too, buddy."

Mindy's smile glimmered with a hint of tears, and guilt hit Ashton in the heart. He hoped Walker wasn't going overboard. He didn't want Mindy to be actually hurt when they "broke up" after the wedding.

Mindy patted Walker's arm. "I'm going to check on the casseroles and finish up the salad. You five need to make a dent in those veggies by the time I get back. Evelyn, go get your father and Tom if they dawdle much more. They're probably arguing about football again."

"Ugh, veggies," Brody said, but he reached out and took a carrot stick, crunching it as he tossed down a red four.

Mindy patted his head before she left the room, and Brody smiled.

Ashton's heart softened even more toward Walker's mother. She obviously loved these two kids no matter what unfortunate things she'd said to Evelyn in the past about them.

Not long after, Tom joined them in the living room, smelling of smoke and charcoal. He gave Ashton a welcoming hug and Walker a punch on the shoulder. So masc, so silly. Ashton almost laughed at them.

"I'm trying to talk your father into getting a gas grill. He insists he likes the taste of charcoal, and I get that, but he's the pits at getting the charcoal lit for some reason. How's the game kids?" Tom asked, squatting down next to his daughter to examine her hand. They both ignored his question as he took the cards from Layla to rearrange them in a different order.

"Dad, did you know it's okay to ask boyfriends and girlfriends to Christmas Eve, but not best friends?" Layla flopped back onto the hard floor mournfully, before sitting up again with mussed hair.

"I…did know that?" Tom asked looking toward Evelyn to see if that was the correct answer to this question.

Layla moaned. "And Kristina is *not* my girlfriend."

"It's okay if she is," Tom said, handing the cards back to his daughter.

"But she's not," Layla muttered darkly. She then pinned Ashton with her eyes again as if studying him.

"Hi," Ashton offered, waving a little and giving his best smile. It usually worked on kids but who knew this time? What if Layla, like so many children, had a built-in lie detector and saw right through their story?

As she considered him, Ashton's heart pounded, and he felt weirdly dizzy. He'd been less nervous when he'd brought the Grindr hookup to his grandmother's house on Christmas but then he'd been flying high on adrenaline and had known exactly what he'd wanted the outcome to be.

In Walker's family home with the kids on the floor playing UNO and breathing in the scent of whatever side dishes Walker's mom planned to serve with the steak, he didn't know what he really wanted anymore.

He'd signed on to be nothing more than a charming, wicked distraction from Evelyn and Tom's family drama at their wedding, and supposedly he was here tonight to further that plan. But in this moment, he wanted Walker's mom to like him *so much*, he wanted the kids to accept him, and he wanted to fit into this family. He wanted to feel like this was real.

"You're not handsome," Layla proclaimed finally. "You're pretty. Prettier than a boy should be."

"Layla," Tom said in a low voice.

"What? He *is* pretty. And what's wrong with calling a man pretty? Don't we support all kinds of men in this family?" She raised an impertinent little brow at Evelyn.

Evelyn cleared her throat. "Yes, Ashton is pretty, but he's not prettier than he *should* be. He's exactly the right amount of pretty for him."

"I don't know. I think God may have gone overboard with it," Layla said. "Like, just look at him. He's gorgeous. It doesn't seem necessary."

Ashton's cheeks burned, and he caught Walker's eyes over the kids' heads. Walker stared at him with his mouth partially open and his eyes a little dark. Did he think Ashton was too pretty too? Not masculine enough? Or… What *was* that look about anyway?

"Sorry I was outside so long, kids. Got a business phone call and had to take it. Can't get away from it all even at Christmas."

Walker's father's voice was higher pitched than Ashton had imagined when seeing his face on the billboards advertising the local oil firm. But when Ashton turned around to see the man standing there, barbeque tongs in hand and a blue button-up worn over expensive jeans, the steel in the man's eyes was undeniable.

"And who's this you've brought, son? Your business partner?"

The adults in the room went tense. Tom glanced toward Evelyn, and

Evelyn looked at Walker, and Ashton's stomach felt a bit tight, so he took another big sip of wine.

"Dad, you remember Ashton Sellers, uh—"

Ashton didn't think they'd ever met. He'd met Walker's mother at the opening of their firm but his father hadn't come. At the time, the man had still been angry Walker had left his position at the oil company to work with Casey—and Ashton.

"Sir, it's nice to meet you," Ashton said formally, putting out his hand to shake. In a quick sweep, he took in that Walker was a little taller than his father, but otherwise they looked very much alike save for the gray creeping into Walker's father's sideburns and the wrinkles around his eyes and in his forehead.

Walker's dad darted a glance down to Ashton's hand before he grasped it and shook politely. "Call me Nate," he said with a smile. "'Sir' is a bit too formal for Christmas, don't you think?" He gazed between Walker and Ashton. "So you've brought your business partner to Christmas? We're happy to have you here, Ashton."

"Ashton is Walker's *boyfriend*," Brody said helpfully, slapping down another draw four as Layla whimpered. "Walker's *bisexual*. He likes *boys and girls*."

"I see," Nate said, his mouth clamping into a tight line, quite like Walker's did when he was displeased. "Well, make yourself at home. Would you like a drink?" Then seeing the glass of wine in Ashton's hand, he backpedaled. "Ah, I see. You've been taken care of. Dinner will be ready soon. The steaks are nearly done."

Mindy returned from the kitchen at that moment, and he smiled at her. "Babe, how's it going in there?"

"The casseroles are finished and warming. The salad is ready. I think we can start whenever the steaks are finished."

"It won't be long now."

He shot her a strange look, but Mindy just smiled more forcefully and asked, "You met Ashton?"

"I did."

"Good, good. Anyway, yes, let's all go into the dining room now. We can pick out where we're going to sit. How does that sound?"

The kids grumbled about leaving their game but stood up anyway and each took one of Mindy's hands as she led the way.

Mindy kept talking, presumably to them all but somehow pointedly at Nate. "We'll eat and then the kids will open their gifts. That'll be fun, won't it, my sweet darlings?" She glanced back over her shoulder at Ashton. "Oh, Ashton, the cookies you made are delicious, sweetheart! The butter to sugar ratio is perfect. They'll be a wonderful addition tonight. Everyone should try one." She smiled and tugged the children toward the dining room. "All I made for dessert were pies."

"Apple pie?" Layla asked.

"No, pecan this time, darling."

She wrinkled her little nose. "No apple?"

"I'm sorry, sweetie. I'll make sure I have it for you next Christmas."

"Really?" Layla sounded surprised by that. "Thank you, Mindy."

"You can call me Grandma, remember?"

Layla squeezed her hand, but didn't say anything, and Ashton wondered if she wanted to call Mindy "grandma" or not. He remembered having all kinds of mixed-up feelings about seemingly innocuous or even sweetly intended things when he was a child. It was hard to undergo so much tumultuous change with ease. Mindy at least seemed like a grandmother who would truly love her new step-grandchildren no matter what they did or who they were, unlike his own. Ashton hoped so anyway.

"I've put your cookies in a place of pride," Mindy said to him, waving toward the long sideboard as they all closed in around the very wide and very white table.

Ashton didn't bother correcting her assumption that he'd made the cookies. Instead he turned his attention to Walker, who was staring at his father—who was staring right back across the dining table, both of them engaged in a tense conversation with just their eyes and clenched jaws.

Ashton took hold of Walker's arm. "I'd love another glass of wine." Somehow, he'd downed the entirety of his first one already and didn't even feel buzzed. His nerves must have burned the alcohol off.

Walker's eyes left his father's face and met Ashton's gaze, and Ashton felt the questions in them down to his bones: Was he okay? Was he intimidated by Walker's father? Was he still good to go?

Ashton smiled reassuringly, radiating his answer: *Yes, I'm fine. I'm with you, aren't I? Your father could chew me up like one of his tough steaks, but I know I'm safe.*

"More wine?" Walker repeated.

"Yes."

Walker smiled, relieved Ashton of his empty glass, and kissed Ashton's cheek, a simple brush of lips that took Ashton's breath away and made his knees weak. "I'll be right back with that, baby."

Ashton almost swallowed his tongue but managed to call out, "Thank you, sweetheart," before turning his attention back to his hosts. "Is this spot taken? Across from Layla and Brody? I'd like to get better acquainted."

"Oh no, dear, sit across from me," Mindy insisted. "I want to know everything there is to know about you." She smiled with such warmth that Ashton's own smile crept up in response.

Ashton sat, preparing himself for interrogation. So, this was what Christmas with the in-laws was like. Wanting them to like him made everything so much harder.

"Thank you again for having me for Christmas Eve. I'm honored to be here with your family."

"It's our pleasure, isn't it Nate?"

"Of course," Nate said, but he lied less well than Mindy.

Wine appeared at Ashton's right hand just as Nate went to bring in the steaks. "Walker, come help me, please."

"I'll come too," Tom said, starting to rise.

"No, no, stay and enjoy yourself. Walker can help me."

Walker tensed all over but followed his father from the room. Alone with the rest of the family, Ashton kept his chin up.

The first act of Operation Fake Boyfriend had commenced.

# Chapter Thirteen

"I THINK YOUR mother has fallen in love with me already," Ashton said as they finally, finally, *finally* (thank fucking God) climbed back into Walker's car and escaped.

"Mm," Walker replied, his mind a weird, roaring blank after the "success" of the evening. He almost couldn't believe how they'd pulled it off, and yet his father's clear and barely constrained annoyance was evidence enough that they had.

"She was practically begging me to have lunch with her the week following the wedding. I almost couldn't find a way to say no!"

Walker nodded. He'd seen the way his mother and Ashton had hit it off and watched as Ashton had squirmed with clear desire to accept the invitation, eventually begging off with an excuse about work appointments. He'd felt strange about the whole thing. Part of him loved the way his mother clearly adored Ashton, and part of him hated it because it was all fake.

"And when she got out your baby book to show me pictures of your chubby cuteness? Oh!" Ashton pressed a hand to his chest. "My soul almost left my body. Why did your father have to take it away from us?" Ashton sighed a little miserably. "You know, I may never forgive him for that."

Walker snorted. "He was trying to prevent her from embarrassing me further." As well as trying to put an end to his wife's coziness with the flaming queer in the room.

"Embarrassed? About what? How could you be embarrassed at being the cutest, chubbiest, most adorable baby that ever lived?"

"I wasn't adorable at all, according to my father."

"Lies."

"I was colicky and cried a lot."

"Ah, poor baby Walker." Ashton patted his arm and slipped his hand down to squeeze and knead Walker's thigh for a moment.

Walker blinked, and his throat went dry.

Ashton pulled his hand back after a few more tantalizing strokes and babbled on, "But seriously, she adored me. And the kids liked me too. Brody's hilarious and so flipping cute. With his little elf-face? Ah-*dor*-able." He snorted. "And that Layla's cute too. She's going to give Evelyn so much grief when she's a teenager. I can see it now. That child has flair." He paused in his cheerful report and lost some of his enthusiasm. "But your dad… No. He didn't like me much." He chewed his lower lip. "Yeah, I dunno. He doesn't like gay men in general, does he?"

Walker cleared his throat. "I'd hoped he'd be more welcoming."

"Oh, he was polite enough. He just wasn't warm." Ashton shivered.

"I'm sorry. I never meant for you to feel that way."

Ashton waved off the apology. "Homophobic men of his age are nothing new. I'm just sad you've had to live with that."

Walker didn't say anything else. How was he supposed to explain to Ashton that the problem wasn't the man-on-man sex his father imagined they were having but that he didn't think Ashton was "masculine enough" to warrant being attracted to in that way? He could barely wrap his mind around his father's internalized misogyny and homophobia himself. There was no way he could explain it properly.

"The few minutes when I was left alone with him, short though they were by his own design—thank heavens—well, I don't think it could have gotten more awkward than that."

Walker begged to differ. Things *definitely* could have gotten more awkward. For example, had Ashton seen the text messages his father had surreptitiously sent throughout the evening or overheard the conversation out by the grill when they'd gone out to gather the meat for dinner.

And when his father had summoned him out back to clean the grill with him after desserts. Tom, bless him, had tried to come with them again to head off the inevitable, but a single, cold glare from Walker's father had shut down that attempt as well, and he'd sat right back down again next to Evelyn and taken refuge in his drink.

As Ashton breathed next to Walker in the car, thinking he'd endured the worst Nate Ronson had to offer, Walker's mind cast back over that second horrible conversation by the grill:

*"What's gotten into you? That man's a pansy. He might as well be a woman." His father scrubbed at the messy grill grate and sprayed it again with cleanser, like if he could make the metal shine again, he could erase Ashton's presence too.*

*"Dad, that's uncalled for and rude. Ashton is a man."*

*"Hmmph." He scrubbed harder.*

*"And even if he wasn't—which he is—I like women. So do you."*

*"I like women who are women and men who are men. All that lisping! And his limp-wristed hand gestures—" His father had snarled at that, tossing aside the metal scrubber and grabbing the hose to wash it off. He paused first and glared at Walker. "Look me in the eye and tell me you're not embarrassed by his behavior."*

*"I'm not embarrassed by—"*

*"Bullshit." He shook the hose nozzle at Walker like it was a gun. "That's why you've sprung him on us like this, isn't it? Why you never mentioned him before last week? You're ashamed to be seen in public with him."*

*"I'm not."*

*"Then why is this the first we're hearing about your relationship?"*

*Walker looked pointedly at his father, still gesturing with the hose nozzle angrily, and crossed his arms over his chest.*

*"What? You're saying I'm the reason?" He tossed the nozzle aside and banged his chest with a fist. "Spit it out then, Walker. Be a man."*

*Walker's gut was writhing but he held firm. "All right. I'm saying that Evelyn's known about Ashton from the start of it all because she's always been supportive of me."*

*"Ha! What nonsense. I've been supportive of you for your entire life. Even when you came out to us, I supported you."*

*Walker's eyebrow twitched involuntarily, and he swore his dad saw it. "You've been supportive," he agreed.*

*"I was always proud that at least you dated men like us." His father's lip curled. "So why are you bringing home someone like this now?"*

*Walker's fists tightened, but he kept his arms crossed firmly over his chest, trying to keep his voice even. "Because he's a good man. I care about him. I want you to give him a chance."*

*His father glared down at the nozzle on the ground. Walker bent to pick it up and started spraying off the grate. Bubbles foamed white like snow and dripped to the patio.*

*"What about your grandfather?" His father asked, his breath puffing out in front of him. "What's he going to say about all this? You'll be willing to face him with this…this person on your arm?"*

*"Grandpa's not flying in until the morning of the wedding and then he'll be flying right back out again. He's probably not even staying to see the dogs."*

*"So? What's that got to do with him seeing you at the wedding with that man by your side? You think he'll let you stay in his house after he sees you with someone who behaves like that?"*

*Walker kept his voice steady by some miracle. "Given that he'd have to pay someone to take care of the house and rehome the dogs if he didn't, I think so, yeah."*

*His father harrumphed. "Clearly quitting golfing has left you without good examples of raw masculinity. Or is* he *the reason behind that choice too? You've never been entirely open with me about why you quit going to the club."*

*Walker finished washing off the grate and tossed the nozzle and hose aside.*

*"Has this pansy convinced you to walk away from the game you love? Did he feel threatened by the real men you met there?"*

*"Don't call him a pansy, and don't insult him again," Walker said, stepping forward into his father's space. "I didn't bring him here to be disrespected, and I also didn't bring him here to upset you."*

*Hadn't he though? Hadn't he, Ashton, Tom, and Evelyn kind of done exactly that? He felt sick to his stomach.*

*"I brought him here, to our family's house, because I care about him and I wanted him to share in our family's day. To experience Christmas with us."*

*"What about his own family? Let me guess. They want nothing to do with him. Who would?"*

*Walker stared at the man who'd raised him. He'd expected his father to be rattled by Ashton's effeminate manner, but he hadn't expected this outright cruelty. Walker's right fist clenched. He breathed in and out a few times, matching his father's stare. Then Walker turned and walked back inside, grateful to find Ashton none the wiser to the ugly interaction he'd endured outside.*

Just remembering the conversation, Walker's heart began pounding again. He'd never come so close to hitting his father before. *Why* was he so angry? Yes, his father was being a jerk—an absolute asshole really— but what did it matter? This thing with Ashton would end after the wedding, and his father would feel reassured by that. He'd think Walker had come to his senses, and they'd never have to fight over it again.

But what about the fact that Walker didn't want his father to be reassured? What about the fact that he *cared* about Ashton now? Cared about him more than he'd ever intended or thought himself capable of?

And what was caring about Ashton doing to him? It was changing him, that's what. It was changing everything.

"It shouldn't bother me," Ashton said, as though he'd been thinking of Walker's father during the prolonged silence too. "He's not supposed to like me. That's the whole point. So, success!"

"Yes, success."

"Ah, so you agree he doesn't like me?" Ashton sounded a little wounded.

Walker glanced his way, watching the conflicted emotions play over his face. "He doesn't know you. He's a bigoted jerk sometimes. I'm sorry."

"It's all right. Really. I'm used to it. Like I said before, most parents wouldn't want their kids to date me. I get it."

"Well, I don't get it. I think any parent should be glad to have you as their son-in-law."

Ashton smiled and squeezed Walker's thigh again. "Thank you. That's sweet."

"I mean it." His tongue felt thick as Ashton kept his hand on his thigh for another long moment, squeezed it again, then pulled it away.

"I know you do. Anyway, the steak was terrible, but your mother is a wonderful cook. She must be who you get it from."

Ashton babbled on about the dinner, the presents the kids had received, and the way Evelyn and Tom were so happy together. "They just sparkle with it. Like sugarplums and candy canes and effervescent lights in their eyes when they look at each other. It's adorable. I wish someone would look at me like that."

Walker glanced toward Ashton, who happened to be looking back at him. Ashton slapped his arm. "Stop teasing me. Why are you such a good actor?"

"I'm not doing anything."

"Sure." He shook his finger at Walker. "Whatever you say. Heavens."

Walker smiled fondly, catching Ashton's eye again briefly before turning his attention back to the road. "Why do you say that? Heavens, or some variation of that word? You know, when you could just curse."

Ashton laughed. "I guess old habits die hard. When I was little…" Ashton shook his head. "Let's just say Bad Things—capitalized—happened if you cursed. Saying heavens was an okay substitute. Grandma said it was like calling on heaven to help you without taking the Lord's name in vain."

"Ah." Walker dropped the subject. He didn't want to bring up bad memories for Ashton. Not tonight. The poor guy had already dealt with all the Ronson Family Christmas drama, especially his father's cold homophobia, and Ashton deserved for the rest of the night to be peaceful and pleasant. Walker had a plan for that.

The rest of the way home, Ashton chatted. Walker listened, chiming in with his thoughts now and again but mainly just enjoying the magical warmth of the man beside him. How had he ever thought Ashton was too much? He was exactly the right amount of wonderful.

"Wait here," Walker said as they pulled underneath the carport.

"Why?"

"I want to check on something really fast."

"What?"

"A surprise."

Ashton cocked his head. "What kind of surprise?"

"If I told you, it wouldn't be a surprise."

Ashton got out of the car and leaned back against the passenger side, hands stuffed into his coat pockets. "All right. I'll wait."

Walker headed inside, greeted the dogs, and let them out back to do their business before heading into the kitchen to check the slow cooker. The length of time it took Ashton to get entirely ready—makeup and outfit and all—came in handy for some things, like creating a surprise dessert for just the two of them.

He checked the contents, making sure it wasn't a disaster, and opened a cupboard he'd never disturbed before to pull out a few pieces of his grandmother's Christmas china. He wanted to make the surprise special.

In the living room, he quickly prepared the coffee table and fireplace. After everything was set, he returned to the carport. It was lightly snowing, and Ashton stood in a ring of light from the floods with his gloveless hands up, catching the flakes on his fingertips. He wore a sweet, special grin that made Walker want to press the memory of it into his heart forever.

Ashton caught his gaze. "Ready?"

"Yeah."

Ashton skipped giddily ahead of Walker into the house. The dogs started barking as soon as they were inside, and Walker didn't blame them. It was cold out. "Can you let them in and take a seat in the living room? I'll bring the surprise to you."

"Sure," Ashton said. His voice was quiet and a little tremulous. He touched Walker's arm. "You didn't have to—"

"I wanted to."

"I know you did." He smiled again. Walker almost gasped it was so heartstoppingly sweet. "I've never felt so lucky as I do right now."

"But you don't even know if you'll like the surprise."

Ashton laughed. "I like that you wanted to surprise me more than I could ever dislike whatever it is you've planned." He sniffed the air and winked. "Besides, it smells amazing."

"Meet me in the living room," Walker repeated.

Ashton hustled off, and Walker's heart thrilled to hear him chatting at the dogs, all high pitched and honeyed, as soon as he'd let them in. He knew what this rising feeling was, and he couldn't help but embrace it.

Love was unexpected, but it wasn't unwelcome.

"WALKER RONSON, WHAT are you doing?" Ashton whispered as he took in the sight of the coffee table. It was covered in a red tablecloth, and two candles burned in the center of it. The fire in the hearth was small but growing and above it on the mantle were two full stockings.

Ashton sat on the sofa with Bitsy at his side. Nina flopped over his legs, demanding to have her ears scratched. He waited with a strange tingle in his veins, a giddy sort of feeling he couldn't quite place. It wasn't as though he'd never had a surprise before. It was just that typically they weren't very good ones.

This surprise smelled nutty and cinnamon-y and appley and delicious. That couldn't be bad. Could it? He shouldn't jinx things by asking, not even in his mind.

Right now, his life felt perfect. He was surrounded by cold dogs still shivering from being outside, the seeping warmth and woodsy heat of a new fire, and the cozy, comfortable scent he associated with being in Walker's house.

Safe. He was grown and safe here.

And moreover, he was cared for here. Walker had taken the time to create this surprise as a way to please Ashton, to show him he cared. Wow, just imagining that Walker cared for him was too much. It made Ashton want to squeal or shout. How was this happening? Did it mean what he hoped it might?

It couldn't.

*But what if it did?*

He patted Nina, his heart thumping as he considered the Christmas tree with two packages remaining underneath. One was from him to Walker, the other from Walker to him. He'd looked at them earlier before they'd left for the Ronsons', making sure that no presents had been left behind for the kids. He'd even picked up the small box from Walker and stared at it, wondering what could be inside. What could Walker give Ashton that would warrant a box that small and that square?

It couldn't be…

"Here you go," Walker said as he stepped into Ashton's view carrying two plates with carefully balanced forks on the edges. "Dogs, bed."

They all ignored him, and Ashton just laughed. He shoved a little at Nina to get her off the sofa and took the proffered plate from Walker. It was an adorable, old-fashioned pattern with Christmas holly and cardinals along the edges. And in the middle was a scoop of ice cream? No. A softened and stuffed apple? Yes.

"Cranberry-walnut stuffed apple," Walker pronounced. "It's not Scottish. But it's good. My grandma made it every year for me and Evelyn. But Evelyn never liked the flavor, so I always ate hers too." Ashton watched as Walker used his butt to get Simone off his side of the sofa. Walker rested his plate on the coffee table and tugged it forward, careful not to disturb the candles. "There," he pronounced. "The candles make it nice, don't they?"

Ashton's heart ached. "Yes."

Walker smiled. "I'm glad you're here. You make me want to…" He stopped, swallowed, and went on. "You make me want to do things like this. Turn things into a nice memory, you know? When you leave—uh, if you leave—" He turned red and seemed confused by his own words, but he valiantly pressed on. "I want you to think back on this time…" He paused like he was searching for the right word. "Fondly."

"I will."

"I hope you do."

Walker picked up his plate and motioned at Ashton with his fork. "Go on, try it."

The apple was tender, having been cooked slowly in something that made it meltingly smooth in Ashton's mouth. The cinnamon, cranberries, and nuts added texture and flavor, and he moaned softly. "So good."

Walker smiled. "Isn't it? I love it." He took a few more bites and stood. "Let me get your gift."

"Grab mine too?"

Walker nodded, bending down beneath the tree and warding off Nina's inquisitive sniffing to pick up the bigger package and the small box that had pricked Ashton's brain with a strange hope earlier. Now that hope seemed to flow through him relentlessly. Stupid, really. Heartbreak was around the corner for sure.

*Good. Great. Love that for me.*

Walker returned to the sofa and put the presents in the middle of the coffee table. "Let's finish our apples first." He sounded a little nervous. "Want me to put on some music?"

"Sure."

Ashton's heart beat faster and faster as Walker fiddled with the Bluetooth speakers and his playlists until finally he settled on one of the odd, new Christmas songs that Ashton had never heard until he'd started riding in Walker's car with him. "More Sufjan Stevens?" he asked.

"Mm," Walker agreed, taking a bite of his apple and relaxing back on the sofa. "He's strange. I mean, the music is strange. Part of me doesn't like it, or a better way to put it might be that some of his music makes me uncomfortable. But then another part of me always wants to hear it again once it's over. I don't get it."

"Yeah?"

"Yeah. But it turns out that maybe when I feel that way about something…" Walker trailed off and cast a long look at Ashton. "You know, when I feel conflicted? Maybe it means that thing is good for me, and it'll make me grow in ways I didn't expect."

"That's a playlist title for you: Weird Christmas Music For Personal Growth. A whole new genre of Christmas feeling," Ashton said, taking the last bite of his apple at the same time. "Brand it. Sell it. Make a million."

Walker chuckled and dug into his own dessert. They listened in silence as the dogs snuffled, the fire roared, and the music jangled out into the room. The lights on the Christmas tree shimmered in Ashton's peripheral vision, and he tried very hard not to think about the small box on the table. Instead, he focused on the stockings.

"What did you put in those?"

"Who, me? I did nothing. Santa brings stockings, don't you know?"

"Oh? And Santa visited while we were at your parents' house?"

"Of course. He has to hit all the houses with kids in them tonight, so he stops by the grown-ups' places first."

Ashton put his empty plate on the coffee table, obscuring his smile, mostly because his eyes were also a little wet. He remembered standing outside with Walker after his nightmare and how Walker had kept him warm with his body before tenderly asking if the moonlight had washed the dream away. These fanciful turns were so unexpected in the man Ashton had thought Walker to be—the blue Polo golf-shirted, boring, country club, yawn-worthy, so-so looking business partner. How wrong he'd been.

Walker was beautiful, funny, warm, generous, loving, and staring at Ashton with a look in his eyes that made Ashton's entire body ache with the desire to grab his jaw and kiss him.

Kiss him like his life depended on it.

Oh, heavens above, he felt dizzy just thinking about it. He waved a hand at his face.

"The fire too warm?" Walker asked.

"No, I'm just... It's fine. Here." He reached out for the gift he'd made for Walker and pushed it across the sofa between them. "Open yours first."

Walker looked oddly relieved and didn't fight him at all, putting his own empty plate on the coffee table and taking up the rectangular package. He shook it, closed his eyes, and sniffed it.

Ashton laughed. "What are you doing?"

"Testing it."

"For what?"

Walker carefully opened the package, making sure to slide his finger beneath the tape so the paper didn't rip.

Ashton sat with his hands curled in his lap, trying to keep himself from reaching out and ripping the paper away and flipping through the pages for Walker. He kept himself in check and watched Walker's face carefully instead.

"It's...a book," Walker said. He tilted his head, reading the front cover. "*Around the World with Walker?*" He opened it and smiled. "Recipes."

"Not just any recipes," Ashton said, unable to resist any longer. He scooted over and pointed at the first page. "This is the recipe you used the first night I came. And this one is from the second night. I skipped the recipes we didn't enjoy that much, but anything we liked I added." He grinned. "Along with the date we first tried it and our thoughts on the dish. I wasn't around when you started your project, but there are lots of pages, so you can fill in going back if you want. Or you can just keep going forward with it."

Ashton felt suddenly shy. He wanted Walker to like it so badly that he felt a little faint. "I hope it's okay. I didn't know what else to get. You have everything you really need, and, well, I wanted it to mean something."

"I love it," Walker said gruffly. He touched Ashton's handwriting in the book and said it again, "I love it."

"Good." Ashton heaved a sigh of relief, and started to move away, but Walker caught his wrist.

"Wait."

Walker put the book down on the coffee table and took up the small box. "Here."

Ashton blinked rapidly, his heartrate skyrocketing and a strange laugh trying to break free. It was panic. Sheer panic. And yet it had to be for nothing. His fingers trembled as he ripped into the wrapping paper, revealing a small jewelry box. His blood pounded. His ears rang. Slowly he opened it.

His breath caught.

The ring was beautiful. Completely unusual and like nothing he'd ever seen before. He took it out of the box, almost fumbling it in his shaking hands, and slipped it onto his ring finger on his left hand without thinking. It fit perfectly.

"What do you think?" Walker asked, and his voice sounded far away.

"I think..." Ashton's voice cracked. "Wow."

"Wow?" Walker sounded unsure, and Ashton didn't know what to do with that.

What did this ring mean? What did it *mean*?

"Wow. I mean, what did you get for Casey?" Ashton breathed, trying to distract Walker from noticing the complete tumult of his emotions and mind. "If you got this for me... You must have gotten him a diamond-studded watchband."

*Please say you didn't.*

"No," Walker said. "I didn't get him anything. I never do."

Ashton saw spots, his breath coming in shakily. "Then...why?"

*Please say you care for me. Please say you want me. Please.*

"I saw it, and I thought of you."

That wasn't the only reason, was it? It couldn't be. There had to be more. A man didn't buy another man a ring like this unless...

Unless they were a dumbass, bro-dude golfer with no idea how badly Ashton wanted there to be something more between them. Walker wasn't a liar. He was a simple kind of guy. If he said he saw the ring and thought of Ashton, that was all there was to it.

"Oh." Ashton's cheeks flushed as he stared at the ring on his finger. It looked perfect there. And yet... "This is too much."

"Why? I want you to have it."

Walker sounded so frustrated that Ashton's hope revived for a moment. Could he really want Ashton?

Ashton spoke slowly, hoping Walker would hear him. "You've already given me a lot—a place to stay, somewhere to go for Christmas, your friendship, dinners every night. Do you really want to give me more than that?"

Walker cleared his throat. "I mean, the ring…" He waved his hand. "It's nothing."

"Nothing?" Ashton swallowed his hurt. His heart cracked, but he didn't know if it was with disappointment or shame. How could he have let himself dream for even a minute? "Oh, okay."

"What?"

"Nothing."

"What's wrong?"

"*Nothing.*" His eyes stung with tears.

"Ashton…"

He took the ring off, put it back in the box, and returned it to Walker. "I can't accept this. I'm sorry."

Walker stared at the box in his hand like it was the most confusing puzzle he'd ever seen. He shook his head and caught Ashton's wrist as he tried to stand. "Wait. Why not? If you want a different stone or color, I'm sure the jeweler can make—"

"No. It's not that." Ashton pulled his wrist free.

"Then what is it?"

His throat was so tight, and he felt like a fool even saying it, but he had to or risk being poisoned by his disappointment. "If you're going to give me a ring, Walker," he said shakily, "the last thing I want is for it to be *nothing* to you."

Walker's eyes went wide.

"I mean, it doesn't have to be a love confession or anything, but I'm more than nothing." A hot, humiliating tear slipped down his cheek. "I have to be more than nothing to someone."

Walker stared up at Ashton in confused shock. "I don't understand."

"Of course you don't." Ashton backed away from the sofa, the beautiful coffee table, and the scent of all the fondness he'd imagined. "Oh, heavens, I'm going to bed. I'm sorry." He turned his back on Walker's wide, blue eyes and open mouth, calling out over his shoulder as he rushed from the room, "I'm sure everything will make more sense in the morning."

# Chapter Fourteen

Walker stared after Ashton, his blood thrumming in confusion, before turning to the dogs. "What in the hell is going on?" he asked them.

Marble paced between the door to the hallway where Ashton had exited and the sofa where Walker sat stunned while the other three flicked their heads back and forth between the door and Walker.

Walker rose from the sofa. In a daze, he blew out the candles and took the dishes into the kitchen. He washed them while his mind howled.

How could Ashton think Walker saying the ring was "nothing" meant that *Ashton* was nothing? That was absurd. Of course Walker thought Ashton was "something." They were business partners! And fake boyfriends!

More importantly they were friends, weren't they? Real friends. True friends.

Fact: Ashton's smile was the best thing in his entire life. Fact: he'd wanted to give Ashton the ring in hopes of making that smile even brighter and seeing him laugh with sheer happiness.

Fact: Dammit, Walker *had* wanted the ring to mean something. But in the exact moment when Ashton had asked, Walker hadn't known how to explain what that "something" was. Then Ashton had just left.

Upstairs, Walker heard water running. Through the vents, the scent of a bath bomb came spilling out. Walker remembered the last time Ashton had taken a bath. How he'd insisted Walker come in to talk with him. The way he'd looked beneath the pink water, all flushed and dewy, and the way Walker's body had responded to him then. And earlier...

God, he'd wanted to kiss Ashton, to show him how confused and aroused Ashton made him feel—had *always* made him feel, even back before he fully understood why.

After putting the china back in his grandmother's cupboard, he dampened the fire. He stared out the window at the new snow falling in clumps and starting to stick to the blades of gray grass in the yard.

Christmas snow. A kind of miracle.

The dogs paced behind him, and his heart grew heavy.

Miracle snow and no one to share it with because he'd said the wrong thing. Stupid, Walker. Stupid.

He felt like he might cry or throw up, but after a few minutes, he made up his mind. He knew what he needed to do. It was a risk, a huge gamble in so many ways, but he had no other choice. He needed to risk it all or risk losing it all. Adrenaline pumped into his veins, making him shaky and a little dizzy. A sensation he was sickeningly familiar with.

Walker sent the dogs out to do their business one last time and then pointed them to their beds. In their confusion and worry, they actually obeyed. His pulse thudding hard, he picked up the ring box from the coffee table, closed his palm around it, and headed up the stairs toward Ashton's bedroom. The scent of the bath bomb lingered in the air.

Walker's stomach twisted, and his limbs trembled. He had to make this right. He had to make Ashton understand.

There was only one way to make things clear.

He knocked on the bedroom door, and it only took a few moments for Ashton to open it. He wore a pink, silky-looking bathrobe, his pale chest and neck flushed above it. His hair was damp and his eyes were red as if he'd been crying. Walker's heart felt like it might burst.

"I'm sorry," Ashton said, his voice low and raspy. "I don't know why I got so upset. It's a beautiful ring. You're a beautiful man, a generous friend and I—"

Walker held the ring box out. "Take it."

Ashton blinked fast. "But—"

"Ashton, you mean a lot," Walker said roughly. "To me, I mean." He cleared his throat and pressed the ring box against Ashton's warm chest. "This ring means… It means…a lot to me."

Why wouldn't his words work right? Why couldn't he express himself?

Ashton took the box and opened it. With trembling fingers, he took the ring out and slid it on. He looked up at Walker through the black fringe of his lashes and shrugged a little sadly. "All right," he whispered. He slouched against the doorjamb, looking confused and tired.

Walker felt like he might come out of his body. He took a slow breath. "Ashton, I need you to understand. I feel things for you." Reaching out, he cupped Ashton's jaw, letting his thumb brush over the redness of his lower lip.

Ashton's eyes went wide and turned a darker shade of green, almost like moss.

"It's true the ring made me think of you. Of how you are." Walker's throat threatened to close. "How you're so…glowing. Beautiful."

He started to pull his hand away, but Ashton gripped his wrist and held it in place. "Go on."

"I've started to care for you. I…" He cleared his throat. "I want you—" He felt heat rush through him so fast and hard that he started to sweat. "I want you to be happy." He needed to be honest. No gaps between truths. "I *want* you."

Ashton's eyes filled with tears, and he kissed Walker's thumb as it stroked over that plush lip. "You want me?"

"I do."

Ashton's body trembled as he leaned forward into Walker's arms and tucked his face against his neck. Walker wrapped his arms around Ashton's back and tugged him close, shocked at how well their bodies fit together. The empty ring box fell to the floor, and neither of them bent to retrieve it.

Ashton's mouth moved against Walker's neck as he whispered, "You want me?"

"Yes."

He pulled back to search Walker's eyes. "Kiss me, then." His voice rose in pitch. "If you want to, I mean. Heavens! You don't have to—of course you don't *have* to." Ashton tensed up in his arms. "I'm not saying I'll only take the ring if you kiss me, or even that you *should* kiss me—"

Walker cut off the babble by tucking his fingers beneath Ashton's chin and tilting his head, capturing his lips.

Stubble grazed stubble, and the deep groan that left Ashton's throat made Walker's dick throb. Lust ignited in him as Ashton's soft tongue touched Walker's own, and the heat of his mouth turned Walker's kiss from sweet to passionate in the space of a heartbeat.

Ashton sagged against him, pushing his silk-covered cock against the front of Walker's jeans. Walker moved his hands down Ashton's lean back to his waist, and then down further to hold on to his sweet ass as he ground against Walker. His blood rushed hard, and he crumpled the fabric of Ashton's robe in his fists as he lifted it, trying to find purchase against skin.

"Wait, wait," Ashton panted, his breath stuttering as he pulled back from the kiss.

Walker blinked, dazed, and released his hold on Ashton's robe and ass. Every cell in his body screamed at him not to let go and every ounce of decency made him let go anyway. "You okay?" he asked.

Breathing heavily, Ashton got some space between them, his hands against Walker's chest and hips no longer flush with Walker's own. His eyes were hazy with passion, and his lips were already a bruised-looking red with the heat of their kiss. Beneath his pink robe, his chest was flushed, his pulse throbbing in his long throat. Walker wanted to bend his head and suck on the pulse point, but he held back.

"Yeah, uh..." Ashton's eyes dropped to Walker's mouth again, his lashes fluttering. "Are we… Where are we going with this?"

"Anywhere you want to go. I want you," Walker said gruffly. He swallowed hard and held back from shoving forward again to win some friction against Ashton's hip. "Do you want me?"

Relief washed over Ashton's features as he laughed wildly and indicated his dick protruding from the opening in his robe. Walker's mouth watered as he reached out, barely stopping himself before touching. It was a beautiful cock—cut, pink, long, and would fit so well against his tongue. Down his throat. Fuck. Walker wanted to drop to his knees and suck Ashton before he said another word, but he waited, heart pounding.

"Do you want me, Ashton?"

Ashton's gaze was on Walker's outstretched hand, and he licked his lips before tilting his hips forward enough for the soft head of his cock to graze Walker's palm. "I want you so much," he breathed, shuddering as Walker took hold of him. "So much."

His cock felt perfect in Walker's palm. He started to drop to his knees, but Ashton stopped him. Lifting his eyes to Walker, he looked almost like an angel as he begged, "Wait…please…"

"Please what, baby?"

"Can you please fuck me?"

He made the request sound so sweet that Walker went a little weak all over—except for his dick straining with hot blood. He wanted to hear Ashton say it again just like that, but Ashton dropped his gaze to Walker's lips and stuttered, "I don't know if you'd like that, but it's been such a long time—almost a year—since I trusted anyone enough to let them—"

"I'd love to," Walker gritted out and kissed Ashton again. Ashton's soft mouth moved beautifully against Walker's own, and his hips twitched as Walker loosely stroked his velvety cock. "How do you want it?" He could feel Ashton's heartbeat through his silk-covered back.

"Hard. I want it hard."

Walker groaned again as Ashton walked backward, pulling him along via his grip on Ashton's cock and his tongue in Ashton's mouth. It was only as the back of Ashton's knees hit the mattress that Walker's head cleared enough to ask, "Do you have supplies? We need supplies."

Ashton looked as if he might cry when he whispered, "No. I didn't bring anything."

Walker nuzzled his cheek, Ashton's cock leaking against his palm. "Downstairs. In my room."

Ashton stared at him, red-mouthed and with a look of eager uncertainty in his eyes. "Oh. Yeah, okay."

Walker traded his hold on Ashton's cock for his hand and led him from the guest room. The dogs skittered around at the bottom of the stairs, curious and worried still, but Walker ignored them entirely, pulling Ashton past them and down the hall.

Inside his bedroom, he shut and locked the door. Ashton stood awkwardly for a moment before leaning back against it as if he needed help standing. He was gorgeous with his dark hair, pale, flushed skin, and hard dick—still jutting out from his pink robe, the tip glistening invitingly with pre-cum. Walker's mouth watered.

"Let me just make sure I have what we need." His voice was so throaty he barely recognized it. He strode to the bedside table, opening the drawer and taking out the unopened box of condoms and bottle of lube he kept there, placing them on top.

"Thank heavens," Ashton breathed.

A halo of silver light poured in from the windows and was echoed in Ashton's pale nakedness as he dropped the silky, pink robe to the floor. His pink nipples rose to hard buds and his cock stood tall from a thick bush of black curls that crawled in a sweet line up to his belly button. His chest had that small patch of dark hair, and his body was beautiful, as gorgeous as his face, all long lines and curved muscle.

Walker's dick throbbed. Saliva welled in his mouth. He thought he might pass out.

Ashton lifted his arms out to the side with a timid smile. "Merry Christmas. Hope you like it."

Walker crossed the hardwood floor in two strides. He stopped in front of Ashton, hesitated, then ran his fingertips up and down Ashton's shoulders, down his arms, across his chest, and finally followed the trail of hair down to his groin before taking hold of Ashton's sharp hips and bringing him flush against his own still-clothed body.

Ashton moaned, hips twitching, pressing his cock against Walker's jeans as he kissed him hard enough that Walker had to dig in with his feet to keep from being knocked backward with the force of it. Ashton moved against him, rubbing his nakedness all over Walker until he couldn't take it any longer. He gripped Ashton's hips, stilling him, and panted in his ear, "Do you want me to fuck you, baby? Is that what you need?"

Ashton shuddered. "*Yes*. That's what I need. Please don't make me wait."

ASHTON'S BLOOD RUSHED wildly. He couldn't believe he was naked in Walker's arms, in his bedroom—which, for what it was worth, was exactly the way he'd always pictured it, complete with a sturdy wooden bedhead and soft, fluffy blankets—begging to be fucked while his favorite pink robe lay pooled at his feet.

Walker clutched his hips hungrily, his breath coming in short, sharp gasps and the front of his jeans distended with the evidence of his lust. Ashton's nipples tingled as they rubbed against Walker's shirt, and his dick chafed against denim. Walker kissed Ashton's neck and collar bones, dedicating a special interest to them, licking along their length while holding Ashton against the door with his body weight and the strength of his hands.

"I want you," Walker muttered. "Your collarbones have been making me crazy."

"What?" Ashton gasped, writhing lightly as Walker hit a ticklish spot on his neck.

"They're so fucking sexy."

Ashton blinked in confusion, trying to get his mind to surface out of the haze of lust so he could understand, but Walker had moved on, kissing his nipples, his stomach, and coming back up again to suck on his earlobe before saying, "I want you every way I can have you. On your knees. On your back. I want you against this door. I want your mouth and ass, and..." Walker paused, flushed uncertainty crossing his face.

"What?" Ashton asked, willing to offer anything to get that look out of Walker's eyes.

"I want you to say you want all that too."

"I want it," Ashton answered breathlessly. "All that and more."

"You want more?"

He nodded.

Walker slipped down to his knees, and before Ashton could comprehend what was going to happen, he'd opened his mouth and taken Ashton deep inside. The sensation was exquisite: hot suction, slick cheek, and a tongue that rubbed along the underside of his cock as Walker bobbed up and down Ashton's length.

He tossed his head back against the door, a wordless cry escaping his lips. Walker was good at this. He'd clearly had a lot of practice, and Ashton's body came alive under the attention. His knees buckled and Walker's hands moved to Ashton's hips, holding him in place as he worked his mouth up and down, gulping and sometimes even gagging, making all kinds of wet, hungry sounds that had Ashton's balls drawing up fast.

"Fuck!" Ashton cried as his orgasm began to crest.

Walker pulled off, wiping the back of his hand over his lips as he sat back on his heels, leaving Ashton humping at air and his cock trembling with denied relief.

"That's cruel," Ashton whimpered.

The blue-gray in Walker's eyes was nearly eclipsed by his wide pupils as he gazed up at Ashton with awe and lust. Ashton wanted to drown in that look.

"Come here," Walker said, rising to his feet. "I want you in my bed."

Ashton took Walker's hand, being led to the mattress to climb onto the soft, thick comforter as Walker hung back to quickly divest himself of his clothes. Ashton watched, aching with the longing to touch as Walker revealed his body. He wasn't cut or wiry like Ashton was, but he was handsome and sturdy, with a cock that made Ashton breathless with desire to taste the thick pre-cum at the half-exposed tip and lick the hairy balls below.

He had some chest hair, a bit more than Ashton's small, black strands, but only a thin treasure trail of blond between his belly button and his fan of dark golden pubes. His ass was firm and juicy, and his thighs were strong and also sprinkled with fine, blond hair. Ashton reached out his hands, trembling for a touch, and Walker moved into his arms as easily as that.

They kissed, this time with less heat and more tenderness. Ashton's heart clenched as Walker tugged his fingers through Ashton's curls and nuzzled his throat before moving down to kiss his collarbones again. Then Walker moved lower to Ashton's nipples. Ashton reveled in the sensation of being so wanted and so desired that Walker shook over him, strained against him, and seemed to want to taste him everywhere.

Once he'd only wanted Walker to smile at him. Now he had all this quivering, desperate *need* moving against him, and he felt so lucky. When had he, Ashton Sellers, ever been this lucky? Just now. Only now.

Ashton gripped a handful of Walker's soft, straight hair, pulling until Walker was face-to-face with him again. They kissed greedily until Ashton broke free to trail his mouth over Walker's neck and earlobes, noting which spots made him shake and whimper. They rutted against each other, groaning, whimpering, and cursing as they grappled.

"Fuck me," Ashton whispered. "I need it. Please."

Walker sat back on his heels between Ashton's splayed legs. His chest heaved with his breaths, and he stared down at where his cock jutted up with a slick thread of pre-cum—Ashton wasn't sure whose—connecting it to Ashton's own aching dick. Walker slipped his hands beneath Ashton's knees, moving his gaze up to Ashton's face as he did.

"This okay?" he asked as he pushed Ashton's legs up and apart. "Do you like to be rimmed?"

Ashton's eyes rolled up as his cock flexed. He squirmed against the mattress in anticipation. "Yes," he whispered, clenching his fist in the comforter. "Please. *Please.*"

Walker nodded, licked his lips, and ducked down.

Ashton shouted.

Walker's way of rimming was like his way of giving a blow job. All at once, and intense as fuck. Ashton struggled, overcome with pleasure, as Walker gripped the back of his knees to hold him down and drove his tongue inside his trembling asshole. First narrow and drilling, then flat, wide, and shocking. Ashton whimpered and cried out again as Walker added his fingers to the mix, giving pleasure and a hint of tugging discomfort as he worked Ashton's asshole open.

"That's… Oh, Walker, oh, *fuck*," Ashton crooned. "It's so good. It's *so good*, don't stop, don't…!" He gripped Walker's hair and convulsed with pleasure and joy. He choked out the next words, but he had to say them, or Walker would stop, and he needed him to not stop, never stop. "I'm, oh fuck, I'm going to cry." Walker started to lift his head, but Ashton shoved him back in place. "Don't stop what you're doing. I'm going to cry, but I love it, don't stop, *don't*…stop…"

Walker obeyed so well, keeping his mouth going hard against Ashton's hole even as Ashton began to gasp and sob. He jerked with some kind of harsh, breaking hurt that had nothing to do with how good it felt to be touched and wanted and everything to do with finally having what he'd been denied for too long: a man who cared for him, a man who took care of him, a man who didn't stop when Ashton grew frenzied but just held on tighter and worked him through it, higher, and higher, and *higher*.

High enough that Ashton's nipples ached, his cock thudded, and he shouted with shocked joy as Walker worked a spit-slicked finger into his ass and pressed against his prostate.

"Oh, *fuck!*"

"You sound so sweet when you say that," Walker said wetly against Ashton's thigh before going back to work with his fingers.

Ashton's ass cheeks were scraped by Walker's scratchy chin and cheeks where his beard had started to grow back, a ticklish, burning sensation that he ached to have back against his hole. But Walker fingered him, hitting his prostate with perfect aim so that Ashton couldn't catch his breath, much less ask for anything else, or beg for more, or do much more than tremble and grunt as he wondered if Walker was going to make him come like this.

"You're so beautiful," Walker murmured. "I can't believe I…" He broke off, shaking his head. "I'm so grateful you're here." He kissed Ashton's trembling thigh. "You're so much better than I ever knew. The way you sound. Oh, Christ, look at you shaking for me."

Ashton moaned, his cock flexing against his stomach, dribbling hot pre-cum onto his tummy. He reached to stroke it, but Walker shook his head.

"Don't come yet. I want to be inside you."

"Oh, please," Ashton got out, strangled and helpless. He knotted his fingers back into the comforter, clenching it with all his might as Walker lowered his head and started a slow, delicious sucking of Ashton's cockhead.

"I'll come," he warned. "I'm so close." He barely recognized his own voice it was so tremulous.

"Then let me just—" Walker pulled his fingers free and Ashton sobbed in frustration.

He let go of the sheets to touch his own hot cheeks and felt the dampness where he'd cried during the rimming. Walker reached for the condom box, ripped it open without any of the care he'd shown for unwrapping his Christmas present earlier, and pulled a foil packet out. He rolled the condom on with practiced ease. Ashton reached for him, ready to drag him into his body immediately.

"Wait," Walker said, turning back to the night table for the lube. "I don't want it to be rough for either of us. I want it to feel good."

Ashton touched his own nipples, toying with them as Walker lubed himself, sighing as Walker lifted his legs onto his shoulders and aimed himself at Ashton's still tingling, wet hole.

"I'm sorry," Walker murmured as he pushed in and Ashton hissed. "I'll make it good for you, so this part is worth it," he whispered.

"This part is good," Ashton said, gritting his teeth. His thighs jumped and jittered as Walker opened him more fully with each hesitant press against his tight entrance.

"Open your mouth," Walker instructed gently. "Loosen your jaw. It'll be easier."

"Sorry. I didn't know I'd be so tight."

"Baby, this is nothing." Walker momentarily froze. "I mean, this is everything, Ashton. Being with you is *everything*, and I don't mind being patient while you open up for me."

Ashton flexed his feet and tried to relax, and just as the pain at his hole grew to be too much and he almost asked for a break, the muscle fluttered and released. With a gasp-inducing slide, Walker was *there*, flush against him, his wiry pubic hair scratching against Ashton's lube-wet ass.

"Holy fuck," Walker groaned, his head tilting down and his body convulsing as he dug deeper inside. "Holy, holy, *holy*."

Ashton clenched his eyes shut, trying to breathe. As a tear slipped out, he reached for Walker and whispered, "Yes, holy fuck, Walker."

Walker nodded and kissed him again, rocking in and out gently, almost without any force until Ashton was loose beneath him, his body warm and relaxed and his asshole stretched comfortably around Walker's thick shaft.

"You feel so big," Ashton whispered in Walker's ear, his arms wrapped around Walker's neck, knees tight against his sides.

"Bigger than I look," Walker said roughly. "Thick at the base. You okay?"

Ashton nodded, tears still prickling his eyes. He thought he might cry again like before, but he didn't know exactly why. His cock had gone a little soft during Walker's push inside, but now it ached as much as it had when he'd nearly come in Walker's mouth or when Walker had rimmed him with so much determined joy.

Walker pulled back enough to get on his knees for leverage. Dick still deep inside, he took hold of Ashton's right hand, bringing it up to his mouth. He kissed the tips of each finger, the knuckles, and then, finally, the ring he'd given Ashton that night. "This means…" he rolled his hips. "Everything."

Ashton moaned.

"Understand?"

"No. Tell me again. What does it mean?"

Walker groaned. "It means I want you, baby. It means I want to fuck you like this."

"Like this?" Ashton twisted his hips, fucking himself a little on Walker's cock.

"Yes," Walker hissed. "Do that again."

Ashton obeyed, moving his hips until he got Walker's cock where he needed it, rubbing against his prostate. Fire licked up and down his spine with every squirming move he made. When he touched his own nipples, his eyes rolled up again.

Walker moaned over him. "Look at you, baby. Fuck, you're gorgeous." Ashton shivered as Walker stroked his collarbones and slid his hands over his neck and up to his jaw to cup his face. "How did I ever not know I wanted this?" he sounded lost to wonder, lust, and need.

Ashton felt the same. His cock leaked in spurts against his stomach as he twisted on Walker's dick with abandon.

"Stop," Walker said, grabbing hold of Ashton's hips and holding him still. "You are the sexiest man I've ever seen in my life. Do you know that?"

Ashton shook his head.

"Tell me you know how hot you're making me."

"I feel it," Ashton gasped, squeezing his asshole around Walker's thudding, rock-hard dick. "You're close."

"You're going to make me come." Walker's gray eyes were glossy with need and avid with lust. "Looking like that." He slid his hands down Ashton's neck again, over his Adam's apple and collarbones, knocking Ashton's fingers away from his nipples and taking hold of them himself.

"Do you like this?" He pinched lightly, and Ashton convulsed around his dick. Walker's breathing hitched. "Oh hell yeah you do."

Ashton tossed his head back and gripped Walker's wrists, clinging tight, riding his cock as his own dick grew rigid and hot with blood, his balls aching and taut, begging for release.

"I'm so close," Ashton moaned. "I'm going to come if you don't stop."

"Do you want to come? I can fuck you all night."

"All night?" He whimpered.

"Until your legs are shaking."

"They already are," Ashton pointed out.

"Until you're crying."

"I already have."

"Oh, baby, I want to make you remember this fuck forever."

"I won't forget." Ashton gasped. "Fuck me harder. Please, I want to come. Show me how you'll make me come."

Walker released Ashton's nipples to grip his shoulders and thrust in hard.

Ashton lifted his ass up taking Walker's plunging dick easily. "Fuck me! Please! I need it! I need *you*."

Walker growled softly and fucked Ashton hard, until the sound of their skin slapping together was almost as loud as their shouts and cries. Walker reached between them, taking Ashton's cock in hand, jerking it in time to his thrusts. Ashton met each one with a cry of pleasure.

"Come for me," Walker whispered. "I want to see it."

Ashton shook his head, feeling sweat sliding between their bodies. He gritted his teeth, trying to hold out, to endure that edge of pleasure for a little longer before tumbling into bliss. And it was only when he felt Walker shuddering that he let go too.

His legs convulsed and his heels pounded against Walker's heaving back as his orgasm gripped him. His cock pumped with pleasure and cum shot out in huge jets that took his breath away. He strained with tingling, jolting ecstasy.

"Fuck!" Walker shouted, his cock thudding hard in Ashton's body. Goosebumps broke out over him, rough under Ashton's palms as he shook, his hips rutting into Ashton as he came, jerking with pleasure.

When it was over, Ashton held him there, wanting to stay impaled on the thickness of Walker's dick as long as possible. They breathed together in a wet, sticky heap. Their skin cooled as the intensity of the moment waned and the night began to seep in, breaking through their lust-dream.

"Holy fuck," Walker whispered again.

Ashton clung to him tighter, a sudden wave of fear and shame swamping him. What were they doing? Oh, heavens, what had they *done*?

"You're the best thing that's ever happened to me," Walker slurred, damp against Ashton's neck. "Best fuck of my life."

Ashton squeezed his eyes shut, his mind whirring, a creeping terror grabbing him by the throat. Best fuck of his life? Was this just about sex for Walker? Was it all about having his lusts satisfied and not about that beautiful sense of comfort and home that Ashton had dreamed of earlier? Was Ashton about to get his heart broken?

No! Walker cared about him. This was real. He knew it was.

Still, he wished the sex had never ended so he didn't have to feel scared about what came next between them, or worry that he wanted too much.

"Ashton?"

"Mm?"

"What are you thinking?"

He stroked a hand over Walker's back and whispered, "I'm thinking how much I wish you could just fuck me forever."

Walker groaned, his dick twitching inside. He kissed Ashton's collarbones and pulled free with a hiss from them both. "If only I could. Who needs food or water if we have this?" Ashton's asshole flexed and released achily as he watched Walker pull the condom off and toss it aside. He blinked, anxious and empty, as Walker lay down and pulled him into a cuddle.

*Don't ruin this. Stay cool. Don't panic.*

Apparently, his mind had no intention of taking orders from him. *But what if he likes you but can't love you? What if in the end he doesn't feel the same way? What if this crashes and burns? What if—?*

"Next time, I'm going to fuck you on your hands and knees. So I can watch me going into you," Walker said, like it was as easy as that. Ashton shivered, thinking of how Walker's cock was shaped and how that angle would massage his prostate. His own dick grew half hard again.

"All right," he agreed through his mild panic. *What are we doing? What does this* **mean?**

Walker moaned and kissed Ashton's cheek. "Fucking hell, you're so sexy," he whispered, gesturing at his dick, which *was* somehow hard again already. "I feel like I'm sixteen."

Desperate to stop his mind's anxious spiral, Ashton reached toward the bedside table and took another foil package out of the box. He handed it to Walker. "Stop talking," he ordered, eager to get all his annoying fears fucked out of his mind. "Start fucking."

Walker didn't hesitate to obey.

"WE SHOULD FORGET we did that," Ashton said, still breathing heavily as he lay curled up, sweaty and beautiful by Walker's side.

Walker's heart just about stopped, the hazy afterglow vanishing. Ashton had come so hard while they'd fucked that Walker had been shocked. He'd broken apart with pleasure again, sobbing and convulsing with ecstasy. It'd been the headiest, most intense thing Walker had ever done with anyone in his life. He felt manly, strong, and satisfied. How could Ashton want to forget it?

"Why?" he asked tentatively.

Ashton twisted his fingers into the comforter that was now wrapped snuggly over them both. He sighed and seemed to fight something inside but finally said, "Because I feel vulnerable."

Walker touched Ashton's hair gently. "Me too." Okay. This he could deal with.

"Yeah?"

"Of course." He pulled Ashton closer and nuzzled the back of his neck.

"More than that, though… I'm scared," Ashton said, his voice trembling.

"I know but acting like this didn't happen?" Walker's stomach tightened at the thought that Ashton might have given him *all that* to just turn around and *walk away*. "Would that be healthy?"

"No?" Ashton asked, sounding so much like he had the day in the car when he'd been triggered into a panic attack. "But it might be smart."

"How?" Walker tried to keep his tone gentle despite his own anxiety so he didn't scare Ashton any further. Wait… Had he been too rough? Was that the problem? "Holy shit, did I hurt you?"

"What? No!"

"Did you not enjoy it?"

"You know I did."

"It seemed like it, but…"

"It was the best sex of my life, too," Ashton said with a small shivery after-shock. "That's why it'd be smarter to forget about it."

"Baby, listen." Walker kissed Ashton's curls desperately. He had to keep him here. Had to keep this man tight in his arms and not running scared. "It was the same for me. Being with you was so good. I've never come so hard."

Ashton moaned. "Don't get me going again. My balls hurt."

"Don't you see? Smart could never be pretending this didn't happen or walking away because it's scary. Smart would be sticking around to see if I can make you come like that again."

Ashton huffed a laugh, but the tension didn't entirely leave his body.

Walker nuzzled Ashton's neck again, his own dick throbbing lightly. He *wanted* to get hard again, fuck Ashton until he sobbed one more time, but he was too wrung out; his cock actually felt tender. "First you try to give the ring back to me, then you tell me that we should forget this happened. Are you going to fight me every step of the way?"

"Every step of what way?" Ashton sounded so small and still too anxious for Walker's liking.

"Look, I've never been that self-aware of a person, but even I can see where we're headed. Can't you?"

"Tell me." It was barely a whisper.

"I bought a ring for you before I even kissed you. That's how much I care about you."

Ashton turned in Walker's arms and sat up to face him fully. He twisted the ring on his finger and met Walker's gaze. "You really care about me?"

Walker blinked. "Yes. It should be obvious. I bought you a ring. We made love—"

"Love?" Ashton's eyes flashed.

"Yeah? What do you think all that was about?"

"Sex?"

Walker's heart thumped hard. "Oh, baby."

Ashton flushed before toppling over on top of Walker, burying his face against Walker's chest and then pushing it into his arm pit. Walker barked a laugh and rolled Ashton onto his back, pressing a kiss to his lips and chin and the tip of his nose. "I care about you. This isn't just sex."

Ashton relaxed against him.

*Ahh, so that was the problem.*

He took hold of Ashton's hand and brought it up so they could both see the ring. "I bought you a ring because I'm an idiot for you already, got it? Don't forget that just because I've fucked you silly."

Ashton blushed again. "All right."

"Speaking of fucking..." He rubbed his thumb against Ashton's bottom lip. It was so plush and firm. He wanted to kiss it again. "Do you want to switch out next time?"

Ashton frowned, taking hold of Walker's hand and moving it away from his mouth. "I don't top."

"Never?"

Ashton's eyes darted away. "I understand if that's a deal-breaker for you."

"A deal-break—" Walker blinked in confusion. "No, it's not. Sure, I like being topped, but if you don't like to do it..." He shrugged. "We won't do it."

"I know it's...it's..." Ashton seemed to struggle for words. "I just need to be the one who's penetrated. I *need* that."

Being penetrated clearly meant something to Ashton, and whatever it was, it was important. Walker wouldn't deny him that, and he wasn't going to ask his lover to do something he didn't want to do.

"If you need it, then I want you to have it. I like it, but I don't need it." Ashton was tense again, and Walker rubbed a hand down his back. "Do you want to tell me why?"

Ashton shrugged.

"You're safe with me."

"I know. I feel that." Ashton shivered. "I trust you."

"Good. I want to make you so sure of me. That's my new goal, to convince you of how safe you are with me."

Ashton kissed Walker's chest and said, almost shyly, "All right. I'll try to explain." His cheeks grew pink again. "Being the one who's taking a man's cock like that? It makes me feel…beautiful." He sighed. "More than that. It makes me feel adored. When a man wants to be inside me, to pleasure me with his dick?" Somehow Ashton made all of this sound so sweet that Walker's heart throbbed with affection. "I know it doesn't make sense, because it isn't *true* that every man who's fucked me has adored me, but…" He broke off. "But even when it's not true, I feel closer to that ideal somehow. Closer to truly being loved. I don't know another way to explain." He met Walker's gaze. "When I'm being fucked, I feel precious and almost…" He winced. "*Almost* loved."

"I want you to feel precious. Loved."

Ashton's eyes widened at that word and then he went on carefully. "But when I think about topping, and when I've done it, it feels like I'm *not* loved anymore. Like I'm being used somehow. I don't know. It doesn't make sense." He tensed even more. "It's not because of Gerald or anyone I've ever been with, I promise. I've always felt this way."

"It's all right."

"You really don't mind that I don't want to switch next time?"

"How could I ever mind being inside your tight, hot body?" Walker whispered, holding Ashton against him even closer. "How could I mind fucking you and watching you come so hard you cry?"

Ashton buried his face in Walker's chest, the heat of his cheeks palpable against Walker's skin. "You are so dirty. I had no idea you'd be this way. It makes me…"

"What?"

"Hard."

He felt the heat of Ashton's erection growing along his thigh. "Do you want me to get you off again?"

Ashton shook his head. "Just hold me for now."

"You sure?"

He nodded.

Walker rubbed his back and kissed his hair, letting him relax. Time passed, warm and peaceful in the room. He gazed at the smooth ceiling and enjoyed Ashton's slow, deep breathing.

Walker had grown a little sleepy when Ashton asked, "Who was the last man you dated?"

"Sebastian. A golf pro I met at the club. It's been over a year."

"Was it serious?"

Walker snorted lightly. "Not even close."

"Ah. Have you ever dated anyone seriously?"

He rubbed Ashton's back some more, marveling at the texture of his soft skin. "I guess that depends on what you mean. When I was younger, I dated some women who wanted to marry me, but I didn't want more than sex with them. I never do."

"I forget that you're bisexual."

"Emphasis on sexual, I think. Evelyn thinks I'm homoromantic." He sighed. "And there've been a few guys I've had longer-term relationships with, but none of them felt right. It was more for convenience."

"Sexual convenience?"

"Sometimes, but sometimes it was just for the ease of having a guy in my life who was my boyfriend. It meant I didn't have to keep looking."

"Mm." Ashton sounded distant, and Walker thought maybe he'd talked too much about himself.

"What about you?"

"Same. There's been no one. I've never had sex with anyone I cared about before. Ever."

"What about the guy who…" Walker trailed off, afraid to bring up the BDSM stuff again. He didn't know if he wanted to be reminded of it either. But Ashton knew what he meant.

"Oh, you mean Gerald? I just wanted *him* to care about *me*. There's a difference."

"Oh."

Ashton squeezed Walker close and turned his face into Walker's chest, his body shaking and breath coming in odd huffs.

"What's wrong?"

"This is so scary."

Walker thought he knew what Ashton meant, but he asked anyway. "What is?"

"Caring, I guess? It's really, really scary."

"I know." Walker rubbed his hands down Ashton's back. It was terrifying to think the sex had been so good between them, to think he liked Ashton and cared about him, to think he could fall head over heels in love with him.

To think he probably already was.

Christ! There was so much at stake. They worked together! They were business partners!

Walker tugged Ashton on top of him, trailing his hand lower, his fingers sliding between Ashton's ass cheeks to touch where he'd had his dick not long before. Ashton's hole was still slightly open and slippery from the lube. Walker slid the tip of his middle finger inside, and Ashton relaxed against him, gusting a sigh against his neck.

"Oh, heaven help me," Ashton whispered. "How did you know?"

"Mm?"

"I needed that. I felt so empty."

Walker's cock, so recently spent, filled rapidly again. Was he really going to fuck Ashton three times in one night? Like some hormone-crazed teenager?

Yes.

Yes, he was going to at least try.

"Let me fill you up."

Ashton rubbed his thickening cock against Walker's new erection. "Please."

Walker rolled Ashton onto his back before grabbing another condom and the lube. He positioned himself quickly and kept his eyes on Ashton's flushed face as he slid in. He worked himself into Ashton's burning heat slowly, carefully, and when he was fully inside, he lay on Ashton completely, blanketing him.

Ashton pulled his legs up on either side of Walker's body, panting, face grimacing with a pleasure-pain that Walker was familiar with. Ashton's body pulsed around Walker's hard, sensitive dick with each rough beat of his pounding heart.

"I shouldn't get used to this," Ashton whispered, clutching at Walker's back, his nails scratching lightly as Walker shifted in and out slowly. "It's too good. Shouldn't trust it."

And yet Walker sensed how much Ashton did trust him. In the way his body relaxed beneath him, the way he moaned and whimpered as Walker moved inside him. But more than that—in the way he'd dared to mutter this insecurity aloud, letting Walker hear it, letting him know that he was still scared. So much vulnerability. So much trust.

"I'm going to make you come again," Walker whispered.

"Oh, heaven help me, I think you will," Ashton said, thighs shaking against Walker's sides.

Fucking him harder, Walker said firmly, "You're safe, Ashton. I've got you. You're safe."

Ashton *moaned.* Like a wounded animal.

His entire body racked with a shudder that seemed to come from his soul. He tugged Walker down for a kiss that went on and on. Walker's hips snapped faster, and they kissed while Ashton sobbed with pleasure and Walker fell even harder.

# Chapter Fifteen

ASHTON WOKE THE next morning to a big, wide, empty bed. The morning light shone brightly through the open curtains in Walker's bedroom, and from his warm, cozy place beneath the comforter he could see Nina and Simone scampering through a layer of snow outside. It couldn't have been more than a few inches deep but the dogs rolled in it madly. Ashton smiled, imagining Walker's fond irritation at having to clean up muddy paws and dry their wet fur.

Ashton sat up fully, blinking. The scent of cinnamon, gingerbread, and bacon drifted into the bedroom from the kitchen, luring him fully awake. Stretching, he noted the various aches and pains related to the prior night's activities and grinned even wider.

He didn't know what was going to happen now and that was incredibly terrifying, but last night had been like something out of his most secret dreams. He'd never let himself go like that with any other man. He hadn't thought Walker had that kind of passion in him, but now he was entirely happy to be wrong.

He'd just decided to find his pink robe and head upstairs to shower when the door to the bedroom creaked open slightly, and a scuffle ensued outside the door. "No, he's sleeping," Walker whispered. "You can see him later. Nina, calm down. Simone, you're getting mud on me. Marble, you're going to hurt yourself jumping like that."

Ashton smothered a laugh.

When Walker had finally managed to get himself into the bedroom while keeping the dogs out, Ashton saw he carried a very wet and miserable-looking Bitsy in his arms. He stopped mid-tiptoe when he saw Ashton was awake.

"Wow. Hot damn. You look good in my bed," he said with a smile. "Promise me you'll make a habit of it."

"If you want," Ashton said coyly with a little laugh.

"I do want." Walker lifted Bitsy up a little higher. "I didn't mean to disturb you. I was just going to grab my hair dryer so I can dry her off before she gets too cold."

"Ah, Bitsy, getting all the special treatment." Ashton pushed back the covers. "Do you know where my robe is?"

Walker crouched to get it from the floor and held it out. "Here." Ashton reached for it, but Walker smirked. "Come and get it."

Ashton snorted. "But I'm naked."

"I know. I want to see." His eyes were hot now, and he licked his lips. "A little show, just for me."

"A show for you and Bitsy, you mean."

Walker wrinkled his nose. "Don't make it weird."

Still laughing, Ashton popped a brow but rose from the bed, walking a little slowly toward Walker, who gobbled him up with his eyes. He'd wanted a man who looked at him like he was magic, and somehow Walker managed to look at him like he was both magic and delicious.

*Like Lucky Charms*, his brain helpfully supplied. *Sugary sweet, empty calories. Meaningless.* Ashton shoved the thought away as he reached out his hand for the robe.

Bitsy shook in Walker's arms, and he sighed. "I need to warm her up." He passed Ashton the robe with so much reluctance that Ashton had to laugh. "I'd like to warm you up instead."

"These are absolutely *terrible* pick-up lines," Ashton giggled, sliding on his robe and crossing it closed over his chest. "How have you ever gotten laid in your life?"

Walker laughed. "I'm usually smoother, I swear. You just make me stupid."

Ashton rolled his eyes, kissed Walker's stubbled cheek, and patted Bitsy's trembling head. "Warm this baby up before she gets sick. I'm going upstairs to shower and shave."

"Don't take too long. Cinnamon rolls, gingerbread, and bacon will be waiting in the kitchen."

"Decadent."

"Christmas morning. I wanted to make something yummy. Like you."

"Oh, heavens," Ashton laughed. "More bad pick-up lines. Help." He headed out the door and was immediately set upon by three dogs, jumping, yipping, and greeting him like they hadn't seen him in a year. "Oh, babies," he murmured, trying to pet them all at once. "You're just as bad as he is, aren't you?"

The shower was fortifying, and as Ashton washed away the dried remnants of their sweet debauchery from the night before, he decided that this was already shaping up to be the best Christmas Day of his entire life. Which wasn't that hard given that for his entire childhood Christmases had mostly been a horror show.

But somehow he'd woken up on this particular Christmas morning with a glittery ring on his finger, a sore asshole from some wildly amazing sex, and a caring man who kept giving him beautiful things— like reassurance, kisses, safety, and laughter. Like time spent quietly together in a cozy, safe house. Like the knowledge that said caring man was probably even now plating homemade cinnamon rolls and cutting fresh gingerbread to eat with butter and frying up crispy bacon for Ashton.

Speaking of, he should hurry up and wash so he could enjoy all these seasonal indulgences.

Quickly he washed his hair and soaped his body, the shimmer from the ring on his finger catching his eye as he rinsed the soap from it. The milky stone slivers were veined with fiery red, orange, and blue, and he brought it up to his lips to kiss it.

Just for today, he was going to banish his doubts and fears and embrace this with Walker for all it was worth and call it a miracle. A holy *miracle* of miracles. No matter what came next? He loved this for himself right now.

For him and Walker both.

Wow.

FRESH SNOW FLOATED down outside covering the footprints the dogs had left behind earlier. As far as Walker was concerned, Christmas Day had never felt this magical, not since he was a kid and still believed in Santa. So far, he and Ashton had gorged on breakfast, napped entwined on the sofa, made out, gotten off, and they were now standing by the living room window, sipping hot cocoa and watching the new snow come down.

Magic.

"Want to build a snowman?" Ashton asked eagerly, peering out at the half inch of fresh accumulation. "A small one, at least?"

"Yeah, okay." Walker would make anything with Ashton. He'd make a snowman, or Christmas cookies, or desperate love for hours. He'd make whatever Ashton wanted any time, day or night, so long as he stayed by his side, shining like a Christmas star forever. "We'll need to put on real clothes." No matter how dreamy he felt right now, how in love, there were practical considerations for going out in the snow.

"Do we?" Ashton set down his coffee mug with an elfin grin and turned on his heel.

Walker followed him through the kitchen and into the hallway that led out to the carport.

"Are you serious?" They were wearing nothing but sweatpants, T-shirts, and socks currently—the better to slip down and access tender body parts that neither of them could seem to get enough of touching and sucking right now.

Grinning, Ashton pulled on a scarf from the coat rack and grabbed a pair of Walker's boots and crammed his socked feet into them. He didn't bother lacing them entirely. Pulling a beanie over his head, he grabbed his own coat from the rack.

He laughed at whatever expression he saw on Walker's face as he pulled it on. "C'mon! It's not that cold!"

Before Walker could protest to point out the obvious—snow! sticking! freezing!—Ashton opened the carport door and the three younger dogs dashed out into the bright morning snow with him.

At first, Walker simply leaned against the doorjamb watching. Ashton zipped up his puffy coat, the snow lighting in his dark curls, before gleefully packing a few small snowballs to toss into the air. They both laughed as Simone leapt up to try to catch them in her mouth.

Giving in, Walker chuckled and put his coffee down on the bench just inside the door. He pulled on his better pair of boots and laced them, grabbed his own scarf and another beanie, and headed out after Ashton.

It wasn't *that* cold, Ashton was right. The snow wasn't going to last long, but there were kids up and down the street rolling big balls out of the meager accumulation in their yards, revealing the graying grass beneath.

Ashton called out, "Heads up!" just before a wet, sloppy handful of cold slush hit the side of Walker's face.

"Argh!" he cried, wiping it away.

Ashton laughed and threw another. It went wide and splattered the car instead.

Walker grabbed a handful of slush from the bush next to the carport and started out into the yard at a run. "You'll pay for that!"

"I hope so!" Ashton shouted back, laughing, and darting across the yard, leaving dark footprints in the crust of white.

Walker pursued him, fingers aching from the handful of slush, and grabbed him around the waist. He kissed his neck before sticking his handful of nearly melted snow down Ashton's collar.

Ashton screamed and shoved Walker down onto the ground, crawling on top of him. They laughed and wrestled, wet snow soaking their sweatpants thoroughly. Walker grunted when Ashton kissed him, and for a moment he remembered all the neighbors out in the yard with their kids building snowmen. A shot of worry pierced his happiness.

But that was soon soothed by Ashton's joyful laugh against his mouth and the dogs pawing and nuzzling their way between them. The three of them pranced and yipped, ducking into playful bows, trying to get in on the action.

When Ashton rolled off Walker, he was instantly attacked by a happy Nina and Simone shoving him back into the snow again.

"I'm being licked to death!" Ashton cried, but his laughter rang out over his faux despair. "Save me!"

Walker rolled up onto his knees, packed a handful of snow, and threw it across the yard. Nina, Simone, and Marble darted after it.

In the reprieve that afforded, Walker stumbled to his feet and reached a hand down to help Ashton up. They were both muddy and soaked, shaking from the chill. The snow had been thin enough that rolling around in it just left them filthy and wet.

Still, the sun clung to Ashton's lashes making them glisten, and flakes of snow shimmered in his dark hair. His cheeks glowed with cold and laughter, and his smile was bright and wide. Walker had never felt anything like the wild burst of joy that vision set off in him.

"Okay, never mind. Forget the snowman," Ashton said through chattering teeth, squeezing Walker's hand. "Let's grab a shower and more hot cocoa instead."

"Good plan. Then we'll open the stockings."

Ashton's eyes lit up even more and Walker whistled for the dogs. They all came scampering, and the sound of kids laughing and playing followed them back inside the warm house like a Christmas morning blessing.

"STOCKINGS! STOCKINGS! STOCKINGS!" Ashton chanted, holding a fork in one hand and a knife in the other and banging his fists on the table. He was full of another wonderful meal after a day of sex, cuddles, and playing with the dogs, and he wanted to move on to the next portion of the most magical day in his entire memory.

"You act like you've never had stockings before," Walker said, standing to clear away the dishes before caving to Ashton's eager demands.

"I haven't."

Walker did a double take, almost dropping the plates. "You're kidding."

"Nope. My mother was a mess and my grandmother thought a commercialized Christmas was from Satan. So I can say with absolute honesty I've never had a stocking."

"Well, in that case," Walker said, abandoning his clean-up ambitions. "Let's go open them now. Sorry, we should have done it this morning."

Ashton's stomach had been full of butterflies all day. "I'm going to wake up soon, aren't I? And this will have all been a dream."

"No, but I'm flattered that I'm dream worthy." Walker steered him into the living room and plopped him down on the sofa. Bitsy had to scoot aside to avoid being crushed.

"You *are* a dream come true." Ashton's cheeks went hot, and he hoped that he hadn't said too much. He didn't want Walker to think he expected them to get married or something just because of some amazing sex and a really wonderful Christmas Day.

"You are too." Walker reached to pull the stockings off the wall above the fireplace, but he wasn't looking at Ashton as he said it. He brought the red and green knit socks over. "I hope it's not too big of a disappointment. If I'd known I was making a stocking for a guy who'd always dreamed of having one, I'd have tried a little harder."

"Oh, it could be full of coal and I'd be happy. As you know quite intimately now, I am very, very, *very* naughty."

"I don't know about that. Pretty sure you're very nice. Very, very, very nice." He lowered his voice suggestively. "Inside and out."

Ashton flushed. "How did you make that sound so dirty?"

"Because I meant it in a very dirty way."

Ashton laughed. "Can I open it now?"

"Go for it."

Walker sat back, his own stocking on his lap, and sipped wine as Ashton pulled the stocking apart. Inside he found peppermints, Starbursts, a Life Savers book, and pens shaped like candy canes like he'd seen kids use at school after the holidays when he was a kid. That was it, but that was enough.

"These pens are perfect! I can't wait to take these to work and sign contracts with them."

Walker laughed. "They're actually kind of crummy pens, but I saw them at the checkout when I was getting the candy and couldn't resist."

"Just imagine me next Christmas in a Santa hat, jingle bells on my toes, signing contracts with these candy cane pens." Ashton sighed, delighted in his fantasy. "The clients will love it. It'll be added value."

"The added value of a six-foot elf?"

"Of a good laugh." Ashton giggled. "What's in yours?"

"The same stuff. I just grabbed a bunch of things at the drugstore while I was picking up that box of condoms."

Ashton lifted a brow. "You…planned for all of this?" He motioned between them.

"What? No!" Walker blushed. "I, uh, was buying those for some-thing else."

"For what?"

"For use with some toys." Walker's ears were adorably red. "I'd used the last one a month ago, so I grabbed a box the other day because I'd been feeling a little, uh, pent up."

"Ahh. Not so pent up now, huh?" Ashton said, leaning forward with a smile. He bit into his lower lip. "So you have toys you like to use?"

Walker shrugged. "Doesn't everyone?"

"Uh-huh. And do you want to use them while you're fucking me?"

Walker swallowed audibly. "Yeah. Sure."

Ashton grinned wickedly, pushed the contents of his stocking back inside the sock, and stood. "Let's go see what you have to play with."

"Right now?"

Ashton nodded.

Walker's neck and ears were red, but he didn't argue. Setting aside the wine, he stood and let Ashton take his hand. Ashton's heart galloped as Walker led him to the master bedroom again.

Walker pointed at the bigger drawer in his bedside table, and Ashton slid it open with gleeful joy as he took in the various dildos and prostate massagers. "Oh, wow. This all looks very fun."

"This is my favorite," Walker said, lifting a prostate massager with a hands-free design. "I put a condom on it for easier cleaning." He picked up a silver remote control. "It vibrates. Gets me off hard." He flicked it on, and it started to buzz in his hand.

"Ahhh, that's perfect." Ashton took it from him and examined the length, thickness, texture, and most of all the strength of the buzz. Deliciously intense. "Want to use this while I ride you?"

"Oh, Christ."

"Ah, ah, ah," Ashton scolded lightly. "Only naughty boys take the Lord's name in vain."

Walker's brows lifted. "You can play that game? Without it upsetting you?"

"I love to play with butts. I just don't want to top. It's different."

"I mean the religious stuff. Teasing about the Lord and naughty boys. That kind of thing."

Ashton's face warmed. "What if I told you my favorite role play is dirty preacher?" His pulse tripped wildly. "Is that bad?"

"If you like it, I think it's good."

"I do like it. But only if I always get to be the preacher."

"I'm game."

Ashton licked his lips, pondering the heft of the buzzing toy in his hand. He raised his eyes and said firmly, "Get out of your clothes, Walker."

They were both just wearing sweats again, so it didn't take long.

"Now, get on the bed." Ashton's heart thumped as Walker obeyed without a word. "All right. Can you be good and show Preacher what a bad boy you are?" Ashton smeared the toy with lube.

Naked and on his back in the center of the big, carefully made bed, Walker lifted his legs, displaying his asshole. "Is butt play supposed to be a punishment or a reward?"

"You decide," Ashton said, crawling fully clothed over the mattress toward Walker, toy at the ready. "I'm going to have fun either way."

POST-COITAL ASHTON WAS probably Walker's favorite Ashton. He was clingy, soft, and quiet, but most importantly, he was entirely and completely Walker's in those moments. It was beautiful.

"That was fun," Ashton murmured with a yawn.

"You're evil," Walker muttered. "The way you kept me on edge so long."

"It was only because you were so spent from all the other sex we've had," Ashton said. "You'd have shot off in the first few minutes if not for that."

Walker grinned. It was true. Watching Ashton ride him with that wicked smile as he'd operated the silver remote, amping up and slowing down the buzz, killing it several times right before Walker could reach orgasm, had been glorious. The way Ashton had left him shaking with need had been *wow*. And when Walker *had* finally come, he'd actually shot more than he expected to produce. Prostate massage for the win, as Ashton had proclaimed.

"I loved watching you," Walker said. "You're so sexy."

Ashton smiled, and if he could have preened without moving a muscle, he would have. "Thank you."

"Was it good for you too?"

"I know I didn't lose my mind like before, but I can't take that kind of intensity every time. That's part of why I wanted to ride and control it." He nuzzled Walker's hair and groaned. "It was good. And I liked not going out of my head. Staying present with you, watching you watch me, seeing how much you want me. I loved that."

"You say that kind of thing a lot."

"What?"

Walker hated to bring up Gerald, but he couldn't help it if he wanted clarity. "That you wanted Gerald to want you; that you like to be the object of adoration and love. I just need to make sure you know that you're not just an object to me."

"I know," Ashton said quietly. "I just need it. Not the objectification but the adoration. I know it's not real love. You're so good at looking at me like you mean it…" He winced.

"I do mean it. When I look at you, whatever you see, I mean it."

Ashton rolled onto his elbow and looked down at Walker's face. "I wish I could believe that."

"I'll make you believe," Walker said fiercely. "I'll make you believe in everything about me."

"Okay, Santa," Ashton deflected. "I believe in you."

Walker dropped the subject because it was too potentially contentious for post-sex cuddles. He went back to stroking Ashton's skin and adoring him, whether Ashton believed in it or not.

WALKER WASHED HIS hands and dick in the bathroom before putting on yet another clean pair of sweats and a T-shirt. He hadn't had this much sex in his entire life. In fact, the number of times he'd come or made Ashton come in the last day probably totaled more than the number of times he'd come with men in the last two years.

It wasn't that he was a prude—it was just that he'd never wanted anyone like this before. This onslaught of insatiable horniness was a shock. How was he supposed to go to work tomorrow and pretend he didn't want to bend Ashton over the conference table, their desks, and the office kitchen counter and fuck him until they both ascended out of this reality and into another realm?

Wow, wow. Was he really thinking things like that? He was mad. This was madness.

He needed to call Evelyn.

But what would she say? What was he supposed to tell her? That he was hornier than he should be after coming his brains out multiple, multiple times? That he was having the best sex of his life? His sister didn't want to hear that. He needed a friend, someone he could ask to make sure this was normal and not some crazed binge. Like gambling had been.

All Walker knew was he wanted to keep Ashton. Forever. Naked in his bed. Coming on his couch. Laughing at his kitchen table. Giggling in his car. Twitching on his fingers. Bathing in his tub. Singing in his guest room.

No, in his bedroom. Because he'd moved in.

Oh, fuck, he was such a goner.

Maybe he could talk to Casey about it? No, not Casey. Not on Christmas Day anyway. And not until he'd gotten permission from Ashton to tell their business partner they were fucking now. Man, what was Casey going to think? After all the times Walker had subtly dissed

Ashton to him. He was going to think he was a chump.

So what. It was true. He *was* a chump.

And now he was the luckiest chump in the world.

It was absurd, but being with Ashton made him feel like a man. He'd never even realized until Ashton moved in how much he'd still felt like a boy sometimes—always under his father's thumb, living in his grandfather's house like some spoiled brat, and rebelling against the family system by creating SRS with Casey and Ashton.

But with Ashton, in his arms, he was different. He felt right, fully grown, like he could happily take care of every single one of Ashton's needs until his dying day. Like he had the ability to solve all of Ashton's problems, and the ones he couldn't solve, he'd support him through the fallout. And he'd do it with carefully cooked meals, reassurances of safety, and shaking orgasms wrung out of his gorgeous body.

God, Walker wanted to beat his chest and shout that Ashton was his man.

His phone rang. Glancing at his caller ID, his stomach flipped. He made sure his bedroom door was locked and tapped the call back option on his screen.

"Walker?"

"Hey, Dad. Merry Christmas."

"Yes, yes, Merry Christmas." His father sounded distracted. "It sure feels different without you and Evelyn here to celebrate."

"We celebrated last night," Walker reminded him.

"Right, so we did." He sounded so uncomfortable that Walker flashed through a dozen reasons for worry: his father was sick or his mother was sick or Evelyn… "Your mother said I had to call and apologize to you."

"Oh." Walker's brain tripped on itself in a weird combination of relief and annoyance. It was one thing for his father to apologize (unprecedented, unheard of) and another for his mother to *make* him apologize. It certainly took away the relief of it. A forced apology was no apology at all.

"She said if you want to date that man—"

"Ashton."

"Yes, Ashton. She said we need to support you." He sounded like there were very few things he'd rather do less. "She said if he's making you happy," and here he sounded a little ill, "then we should be happy for you." He sighed heavily. "She said I should tell you I love you and I'm willing to accept him in your life."

"*She* said?"

"Yes."

"But what do you say, Dad?"

His father hesitated before clearing his throat. "I say she's right. I was wrong. I…" He stopped short of actually apologizing, which was no real surprise, but his voice became less constricted. "I want you to be happy, Walker. I admit I didn't understand when you came out to me as bisexual. I thought you'd find a pretty girl. But then you started up with men mostly, and I found my own way to make peace with it. I've always felt uncomfortable around pansies, and I was proud my son wasn't like that, but if your…" He stumbled briefly. "If your tastes have changed, and something about this young man makes you happy, then I'll have to accept it. Though, is it possibly a phase? A kink of some kind? I told your mother that maybe once you've satisfied this—"

"Dad, stop," Walker said, shutting off that line of thought. "Ashton is a person—a good one. I understand that something about effeminate men has always gotten under your skin, and for a long time I let that dictate who I let myself feel attraction for, but with Ashton—"

"I don't need to hear the details, son. I just need to make your mother happy."

"Oh."

"So, now that I've done that, let's go about our day. I'll be open-minded at the wedding with regards to this young man, and that will have to be enough for you."

"Okay." Walker's heart ached. "Have a good rest of Christmas, Dad. What are you and Mom going to do?"

"Head over to the country club for dinner. Then tomorrow your mother wants to drive to Kentucky to go see Nana in the nursing home. Do you want to come?"

"Ah —"

"Without Ashton of course."

"I have to work."

"Right. Makes sense. You're taking a few days off for the wedding. Real proud of your work ethic even if it would have been better applied at the firm with me."

"I know you think so, Dad."

"I'm going to go before we get into an argument about that and your mom makes me call to apologize for something else I didn't do wrong."

"Sure, Dad."

"Merry Christmas, Walker. We love you."

"I love you too," he said faintly, watching as frost formed at the edges of the windows, the temperature dropping as the sun started to go down.

The call ended and Walker texted his mother some cheerful Christmas wishes since he realized he'd been too caught up in Ashton to do it earlier. He received an enthusiastic reply back and placed the phone on the bedside table while he stared at the twisted-up sheets and blankets on his bed.

He carefully stripped them. He didn't want to wash away the scent of him and Ashton together, but as he spread fresh sheets and blankets on the bed, he knew he and Ashton would lie on them together again tonight.

Nothing his father said would stop him from caring for Ashton. The only relationship his father's opinion damaged was the one between the two of them. Walker and Ashton might fall apart—only time would tell—but it wouldn't be because of anything his father had to say.

# Chapter Sixteen

"WHAT'S GOING ON between you and Walker?" Kayla asked the day after Christmas, sitting in one of the chairs across from Ashton's table-desk and crossing her legs prettily. Her post-holiday outfit of a blue sweater over a navy skirt was less festive but still fashionable.

Ashton focused on his computer screen, hoping his face gave nothing away. "What do you mean?"

"I mean, you're still staying at his place, right? And it's been a lot longer than your original post claimed was necessary." She leaned in. "Then you posted that retraction? Saying your *boyfriend* wanted you to let everyone know that you were no longer available for hire. Since when do you even have a boyfriend?"

"Since I do." Ashton kept his tone level, continuing to type words into his open document though he no longer had any clue what he was writing.

"Right." Kayla rolled her eyes. "Are the rumors true? Are you and Walker together or what?"

"Rumors?" Ashton stopped typing and looked up, careful to keep his face neutral. "Who's been spreading rumors?"

"Oh, just everyone." Kayla grinned.

"More like just you."

"C'mon, Ashton! The way he looked at you today in our morning staff meeting?" She leaned in even closer. "Like he's going to burn the place down with his eyes if he can't get to you? And how he practically chased you out of the room and into your office afterward? Are you actually denying it?"

Walker *had* followed Ashton into his office after the meeting, but they hadn't even kissed. They'd just…stared for a while. And then talked about dinner. And just *yearned* at each other.

"Oh my God, the way you flirted with him!"

Ashton scoffed, pushing his laptop away. "Flirt? With Walker? I have done no such thing! Or rather, I have, but I flirt with everyone. It's my trademark."

"That's not true." She shook her finger at him. "You're *charming* to everyone. But you have only ever flirted with Walker. And that's new. Believe me, if you really flirted with everyone, you'd be in trouble super fast. Sexual harassment isn't a joke." She sniffed.

"Of course not. You're right." Ashton charged ahead. "But this is a tomato-tomahto situation. Truth: I'm charming to everyone, and I'm charming to Walker too. That's all. You're reading into things."

"You literally preened for half the meeting this morning."

"Preened? Again, that's nothing new. I always preen." In demonstration, Ashton ran his hand over his hair and smacked his lips together to make sure his gloss hadn't grown tacky.

Kayla rolled her eyes. "Today you touched your neck, and bit your lip, then touched your neck *while* biting your lip *while looking at Walker*. I mean, come on, Ashton! While Nicole was reviewing the schedule for January, you stared at Walker like he was water and you were dying of thirst. It was like she didn't exist. Give it up. You're sleeping with him, aren't you?"

"I…uh…" They hadn't agreed on how to handle any of this. They'd originally planned to just tell Casey about Operation Fake Boyfriend, since he was the only person from their office coming to Evelyn's wedding. But now that they were actually having sex and sleeping together, Operation Fake Boyfriend itself seemed like a big, confusing ball of knotted yarn they hadn't bothered to unravel.

Mainly because they'd been too busy.

Making out.

And screwing.

And *having feelings* together.

And all that went along with that.

Ashton leaned back in his chair, steepled his fingers like businessmen did on TV, and tried to look blasé. "I don't know what to tell you."

"You are totally sleeping with him!" Kayla squealed, her eyes lighting up. "When? How? Why?"

"Why? What do you mean *why*?" Ashton scoffed. "That's insulting to even ask."

"You aren't even denying it now!"

He rolled his eyes, ignoring her statement and focusing on the question of why. How rude. "Seriously? 'Why?' What kind of question is that?"

"I mean, why are you hooking up with him? Is it casual? Is it love?"

"I never said we were hooking up," Ashton said slowly, his heart pounding.

*Was* it love? Well, yes. He was absolutely in total free fall over Walker Ronson and his cute smile and his steady gaze and his willingness to throw himself under the bus for his sister. And the way he gazed at Ashton like he was something special.

The way he'd taken care of him every single night even before they'd had sex: making dinner, bringing him a drink, lighting the fire, and tucking a blanket around him. And now, the way he kissed Ashton like he was drowning in him, and the way he fucked him like there was nothing in the world that could ever stop him.

Oh, heaven, the way Walker knew just how Ashton needed to be handled afterward: like he was precious, loved, and safe.

So safe.

"Walker's a good man," he offered carefully. "He's letting me stay with him while I look for a new place. Really, that's all that's going on." He considered reminding her how inappropriate it was for a receptionist to be grilling her boss in this way, but he couldn't bring himself to scold her. If he and Walker were being too obvious it was on them.

"Uh-huh," Kayla said skeptically. "When you're ready to be honest, I'm here for you and all the sweet goss." She stood and smoothed over her skirt. "Just so you know, no one in this office is going to believe you. So you might want to get your story straight—and fast." She grinned. "You two are so bad at hiding it. It's kind of adorable. Just think: two office romances in less than a year! Me and Joe, and now you and Walker."

Ashton rolled his eyes, waited until Kayla had left the room, and texted Walker with quick fingers.

*We need to talk*

The response was immediate: *Something wrong?*

*No, but we need to talk*

Seconds later, Walker shut Ashton's office door behind him and leaned back against it. He looked as good as he had this morning in his Christmas green golf shirt, looking like a worried, adorable snack. If snacks could look worried and adorable.

Regardless, Ashton wanted to eat him.

"What's up?" Walker asked, crossing his arms over his chest anxiously. "Uh, is it about this weekend or me or us…?"

"No, no, and no," Ashton said, rising to back Walker up against the door and reaching around him to turn the lock. "Well, a little."

Walker licked his lips, and Ashton's gaze followed his tongue. He remembered just what Walker had done with his tongue the day before and how nice that had been. He swallowed hard. His mind a total blank, what with Walker's mouth so close and his aftershave smelling so good. He leaned in, sniffing Walker's neck before kissing his earlobe.

"Really?" Walker whispered as Ashton brushed a kiss on his jawline. "Here? In the office?"

He sounded so scandalized that Ashton briefly remembered the first kiss he'd ever stolen from another boy—Marshall, a slightly older teen at his grandmother's church. They'd been playing hide-and-seek with the youth group and both of them had hidden beneath the same pew. The moment had grown taut with their mutual gaze until Ashton had taken the chance. Marshall had grabbed at his own mouth as if Ashton had punched him rather than simply pressed their lips together.

Marshall had hissed, *"You can't just kiss me here in the sanctuary!"* and never talked to him again. Instead, he'd helped spread rumors about Ashton that had reached his grandmother, and she'd—

He pulled away from Walker and the memory. "Maybe not? You just looked so worried, and you smell good, and I wanted to…" He waved his hands around, trying to rein in his babble and failing. "I don't know. Never mind. Who knows what I was thinking? But yes, of course, you're right. Not here at work."

Before Ashton could skedaddle across the room to the safety of his table-desk, Walker reached out and grabbed his wrist, hauling him back in. "But what if you smell good too, and I *want* to kiss you here in your office." He smirked. "With none of them out there any the wiser?"

Ashton's knees went weak, and he opened his mouth to correct Walker, to say that actually Kayla was apparently much the wiser and who knew how many others, but the kiss that landed on his lips was too delicious to interrupt. Heat rushed through him as he leaned into Walker eagerly, his pulse roaring and his dick growing hard.

A knock against the wood directly behind them jerked them apart.

"Uh, yes?" Ashton called out, running a shaking hand through his hair.

"It's me, Casey. Got a minute?"

They looked at each other wildly. A few pounding heartbeats passed before Walker broke away to step across the room to the windows, making a show of staring down at the street below. Willing his erection away, Ashton quickly wiped his lips with the back of his hand before yanking the door open.

"Hi!" he said way too brightly based on Casey's confused expression.

"Come in. Walker and I were just discussing a big project we're planning." He coughed. "Yeah. So we were just talking about that. To make plans. You know, for it."

"What big project?" Casey asked, stepping over the threshold and looking even more surprised when Ashton shut the door behind him. "I thought we'd wrapped up all the outstanding stuff for the year." He chuckled with some perplexity. "What've you two been hiding from me?"

"We haven't been hiding it. Not really. Have we, Walker?"

Walker turned around and Ashton's heart dropped into his stomach. With a burst of heat, his blood began to rush giddily through his veins, and he covered his mouth with his hand, trying to hold in his laughter.

*Heavens above, oh, heavens to **Betsy**!*

"Okay." Casey blinked rapidly. "I… Well, okay." He clapped his hands together. "It's not like I hadn't expected this in a way, but…" He cleared his throat. "When did it finally happen?"

Walker cocked his head. "What?"

Ashton gasped for breath behind his fingers, feeling dizzy.

"You know what." Casey gestured at his own mouth and swung his hand between Ashton and Walker.

"No?" Walker said, flicking his gaze from Ashton to Casey and back again. "What's so funny? Why are you laughing?" He looked down at the front of his pants like he was checking for a hard-on. "What's going on?"

Casey scoffed. "You're wearing Ashton's sparkle lip gloss, friend." He chuckled. "I've drawn some obvious conclusions."

"I was just—" Walker touched his lips and stared wildly at Ashton. "Trying it out? He's teaching me makeup? For men?"

Casey's smirk grew even more amused. "Not unless he had you smear it everywhere. And I mean everywhere."

Ashton rushed to his filing cabinet and pulled out his compact mirror and makeup wipes. Plucking one out of the package, he passed them to Walker who took one look at his reflection, grimaced, and started wiping.

"So?" Casey prompted, motioning between them again. "When?"

Walker nodded. "We're sort of…"

"Practicing," Ashton blurted. "For the wedding. That's our big secret project. That we needed to tell you about. Since you'll be there and all."

Walker's brows dropped in confusion, and Ashton didn't blame him. It wasn't like he was ashamed to confess about the two of them, but it seemed like now, when things were still so fresh and fragile, might not be the right time.

"You were practicing kissing for Walker's sister's wedding?" Casey scrubbed a hand over his head. "I don't get it. What's going on?"

"Operation Fake Boyfriend," Ashton said firmly. "That's what's going on."

Walker's expression flashed with momentary hurt, but Ashton rushed forward with his half-truth. He'd explain and make everything up to Walker later. He just wasn't ready to dirty the precious, newly fallen snow of their relationship. He wanted to keep it pristine and untrodden upon until they dirtied it themselves. Or until they knew for sure it was going to last.

And just how likely was that anyway?

How many times in his life had Ashton gotten his hopes up that someone might actually want him only to have those hopes trashed? His mother didn't want him, his grandmother despised him, no lover had ever really loved him, and no friends truly cared. If this thing with Walker was going to be short-lived, he'd rather his humiliation and heartbreak stay mostly private. Kayla's suspicions be danged.

"Operation Fake Boyfriend," Casey repeated. "Please. This makes no sense. Help a dumbass out, all right?"

"You should probably sit down," Ashton said, indicating one of the chairs across from his table-desk. "You too, Walker. It's a long story." He sat in his comfortable chair and waited for them to do the same.

Walker took the empty seat next to Casey, but he didn't look as relieved as Ashton felt at successfully distracting Casey from their kiss.

It took some time to lay it all out for Casey.

"So, to distract the shark-relatives and gossipmongers from Evelyn and Tom on their big day, you and Ashton are going to pretend to be boyfriends?"

"Yes," Walker said, shifting uncomfortably in his chair.

"And Ashton is going to be as outrageous as possible to gather all that negative attention onto himself?"

"Yes!" Ashton enthused.

Casey frowned. "And Evelyn's on board for this? Because, excuse me for stating the obvious here, but that seems like the most *dramatic* way possible to create a 'drama-free' wedding for herself."

"It'll work," Walker said. "Everyone will be fascinated by Ashton."

"I'm a fascinating person," Ashton confirmed with a twinkle.

Casey didn't dispute that. "Evelyn really doesn't mind that everyone will be focused on the two of you instead of her as the bride?"

"It's her dream come true," Walker said. "She never wanted a big wedding like this. It's Dad's plan more than hers. She just wants to get through it, and she thinks it'll be better for her—more romantic—if the gossips have something else to do that day than snipe about her and Tom."

"Your dad is going to lose his mind. He will absolutely shit a brick. Is Evelyn really willing for you to just toss whatever remains of your relationship with him out like it's trash? He's been cold toward you ever since you left the country club and even more so after you abandoned him to start SRS with us. Not to mention after you stopped golfing completely last year."

Ashton frowned. He had assumed that Walker wasn't doing his usual amount of golfing because it was winter. He wondered what had prompted him to stop. Walker had a lot of golfing paraphernalia in his office and some around the house, but he hadn't mentioned going to hit balls even once since Ashton had moved in.

*Have I moved in? With my lover? Wow! Good, cool, love that for me.*

Why had Walker quit? Did he stop enjoying the game? Or was it because of an ex maybe? The golf pro? Had Walker stopped golfing at the club due to lingering feelings for the guy? Ugh. Did Ashton really want to know?

Probably not.

"My dad will get over it," Walker said, but he did sound nervous.

"What about your mom? She's a sweetheart. She doesn't deserve to be embarrassed like that."

"Mom will survive it too." Walker looked a little sweaty, though.

"Did you even talk to Evelyn about how your mom will feel about you two making a scene at her wedding? And what about your grandfather? You know how much you owe him…" Casey darted a glance Ashton's way and lifted a brow at Walker.

"Look, you're making this out to be a bigger deal that it really is. We aren't going to push this thing so hard that Mom will be humiliated or that my grandfather will even notice what's going on. We're just going to distract the assholes. That's all."

"Right!" Ashton agreed. "It's a delicate operation, but I'm up for it. I can walk the line. I promise." He held up three fingers. "I swear I wouldn't hurt Mrs. Ronson for the world. She was so nice to me on Christmas Eve."

"You spent Christmas Eve with the Ronsons?" Casey's eyebrows rose again.

Ashton started to reply, but Walker cut him off. "He was there as my friend. He didn't have anywhere else to go."

Ashton flinched but didn't correct him. He knew he hadn't been invited as a pity case—had he?—but it still smarted to hear it stated boldfaced like that. And it smarted even more to hear Walker call him a friend when they were so much more now. But turnabout was fair play, and he had started it, after all.

"Oh." Casey looked mildly ashamed. "You could have spent the day with me and Joel."

Ashton shook his head and waved off the comment as Walker continued on, "As for Operation Fake Boyfriend, we're doing this. It's settled. We just wanted to let you know so you wouldn't be confused and think that we're…actually…together." He sounded so strained as he finished the sentence that Ashton was surprised Casey didn't call him on it.

"I see. Wow." Casey ran a hand over his hair. "Is there some way this can backfire on our brand? The firm can weather a lot. Most of our clients, if they found out about this, would be a little scandalized, but also amused. The question is: Is it fresh? Or is it a dick move? That's my main concern as your business partner."

"It's all down to the execution," Ashton insisted. "I can handle that. We'll keep ourselves just scandalous enough to provoke gossip, but we won't go too far."

"You'll just have to trust us." Walker sounded uncomfortable.

Ashton understood Walker's discomfort in asking for trust when they were outright lying to Casey at the moment. But it wasn't really a lie, was it? They were just withholding the complete truth. Besides, what he and Walker did together when they were alone wasn't really Casey's business or anyone else's. Not until he and Walker wanted it to be their business. And Ashton wasn't ready yet.

"I do trust you," Casey said, putting his hands on his knees and leveraging himself up to standing. "I'll leave you to it. Carry on kissing for, uh, 'science,' I guess."

"Practice," Ashton corrected.

"Right." He definitely sounded skeptical to Ashton's ear, but he wasn't pushing them on their deception and that was a win Ashton was willing to accept.

"Thanks." Walker sounded a little faint as Casey patted his shoulder and waved at Ashton across his table.

"I'll make my own way out. Might want to lock the door behind me. Wouldn't want Kayla or Damien busting in here and getting the wrong impression of your 'practice.'"

Okay, so he was busting their balls a little. Let him.

"Good idea," Ashton said, following him to the door.

Casey rolled his eyes as he left but said nothing more, and Ashton clicked the lock behind him. He leaned back against the door and groaned. "Heavens, that was close," he murmured. "You okay?"

Walker shrugged, covering his face with his hands before dropping them between his knees as he hunched down. Ashton hurried over, rubbing Walker's shoulders and skimming his fingers through his hair.

"It's all right," he cooed. "Casey believed us. Mostly."

Walker rose and turned to Ashton, taking hold of both of his hands. "He didn't believe us. He knows we were kissing."

"Obviously," Ashton said, laughing. "You should have seen your face! Oh heavens!"

"Yours wasn't much better you know. Covering your mouth and laughing like a hyena."

Ashton wrapped his arms around Walker's neck. "He believed us enough. He'll at least think *maybe* we really were just practicing."

Walker scoffed, lowering his face to nose at Ashton's neck and earlobe before pulling away and taking hold of his hands. "Look..."

"Yeah?" Ashton squeezed his fingers.

"Lying is..." Walker cleared his throat, obviously recognizing that their entire plan was a kind of lie. "Lying to Casey *especially*. That's a boundary I promised not to cross again, after... Well, a situation where I wasn't honest with him." Guilt lurked in his gaze. "I don't like the way I feel right now."

"Oh. I'm sorry. It's my fault, isn't it? Since I lied." He kissed Walker's knuckles and tried to collect his thoughts.

Walker sat and pulled Ashton onto his lap. It wasn't comfortable, but they were cuddled close, and he could smell Walker's aftershave.

"Why did you lie?" Walker asked.

"It's just that I wanted to keep this between us. Keep it precious and ours for a little longer. I mean, what if..." He broke off. His stomach tightened and he felt a little sick.

"What if, what?"

"What if this doesn't last very long?"

Walker held him tighter, his brows dropping again. "Meaning?"

Ashton shrugged. "Most people get tired of me? Or they think I'm not worth it? I don't have a lot of luck with people."

"Everyone loves you."

"For a little while," he said with a smile that hurt to fake. "Then they don't anymore. And that's okay."

"It's not okay!"

"It is. But if you decide that our original plan for Operation Fake Boyfriend is more your speed than what we've been doing, it'll be less embarrassing for me if no one else knows about us. You know what I mean?" Ashton babbled on before Walker could reply. "I mean, this thing between us is wonderful, great, I love it for me, for *us*, but you barely know me." He patted Walker's chest. "I'm surely a lot more than you expected or wanted, and you don't even know the half of it? Like the half of who I really am and what's happened in my life, and I think letting you off the hook when you get it, like really get it, will be so much less humiliating if—"

"I want to know the half of you! The *all* of you! Why would I run?"

"My life was a mess. I'm a mess." He wriggled, but Walker held him tighter, trying to get him to meet his eyes. "Let's just keep this..."

"Don't say casual."

"Oh, heavens, no!" Ashton jerked lightly. "I'm not interested in casual. But I'm not asking you to marry me either."

Walker flinched and started to move Ashton off his lap. Ashton wrapped his arms around his neck, unwilling to believe he'd already managed to make Walker ready to walk away. Couldn't he have a week or so first? "Wait, no, no, please, don't leave yet. This is what I mean. I'm not someone people stay with. Please, Walker. Please don't push me away yet."

"Shh," Walker murmured, kissing his cheek and then nuzzling his neck. "Forget I said anything. It's fine. We'll take our time." He pushed open Ashton's collar and kissed the knobs of his collarbones. "You're special, and you should be comfortable with how we're doing things. I don't want you to feel pressured to announce us to the world."

Walker gazed at him, stroking his fingers over Ashton's jaw so that he shivered. "I can't imagine ever getting tired of you. If anything, you'll grow tired of me or find out I'm not perfect and decide you're the one who has to go."

"Oh, you sweet overgrown puppy, I know you're not perfect," Ashton said softly, plucking at Walker's golf shirt. "I mean, you wear these shirts like they're in style for one, and for another, you let Bitsy lick your plate when you're done eating even though it makes her fart, and you can't carry a tune to save your life."

"When did you hear me singing?"

"In the kitchen. You thought I was already in the shower, didn't you? But I heard, and it was terrible. And I loved it."

"Yeah, but those are all superficial things," Walker whispered. "You could find out something worse about me—something you can't accept."

Ashton chuckled. "Like that your mom is a literal angel? Or that your father hates me because I'm not what he wanted for you? Or that you snore?"

"I don't snore."

"No, you don't," Ashton agreed. "But tell me, what could I possibly find out about you that would drive me away? If anyone walks, it'll be you." Ashton smiled, but his heart ached. "At least I know that going in."

Walker kissed him, and Ashton lost track of time for a while. When they broke apart, they were both stiff from making out in the uncomfortable office chair, and the lights in the rest of the office had been turned out.

Stepping out of the office building to walk to the parking garage for Walker's car, the streets were blanketed with snow. Pristine, pure, unadulterated.

Like them.

And Ashton knew it wouldn't—couldn't—last.

# Chapter Seventeen

T HE ROADS WERE dingy with dirty snow as they slowly made their way from Knoxville to Gatlinburg for the wedding. It'd turned to slush overnight in the shaded areas, but on the highway, it was just wet and more wet. Walker turned on the wipers to remove a fresh spray of crud from a passing truck, glad they were driving in daylight.

"According to this, we're being put up at The Inn at Christmas Place." Ashton affected a posh accent, glancing over the multi-page itinerary they'd printed out before leaving the house that morning. "That's the it's-Christmas-every-day-of-the-year hotel, yeah?"

"Yep. The whole wedding party will be there."

"I can't wait to see your mom again." Ashton grinned.

"She's looking forward to seeing you too." Walker hadn't talked to his mother since her post-Christmas texts declaring Ashton adorable after the awkward call with his father, but he felt sure she'd be happy to see Ashton again. She really had taken to him at Christmas Eve and if the "apology" call from his father was any indication, she wasn't opposed to Ashton being part of Walker's life for a much longer time to come.

"I hate that we're lying to her. I'm not a total asshole for dreaming up this plan? Or am I?"

"We aren't going to embarrass her. And it was my idea before it was yours. Besides, we aren't lying."

"Right. Things have changed," Ashton said with a cheeky grin. "Even if no one else at work knows, it's not a lie that we're together now." He froze. "Right?" His voice threaded with insecurity.

"Right," Walker agreed. "I don't sleep with guys who aren't my boyfriend."

"Really?"

He shrugged. "Not anymore."

Ashton laughed and reached over to squeeze Walker's thigh. "All right. Great. Love that for us." He sighed happily, and Walker's heart fluttered. "I didn't want to assume, but I'm glad you feel the same way. And see? This way we aren't lying really. We're very nearly being honest. Almost."

"Exactly."

After a beat, Ashton asked, "Are you sure Bitsy will be okay?"

"I'm sure."

Ashton hummed and squeezed Walker's thigh again before turning the music on the car stereo up a little.

Walker's heart warmed at Ashton's care for Bitsy. He'd taken the dogs to their regular boarder that morning and had been surprised at how concerned Ashton had been about leaving them there. He'd been so sweetly worried.

"I like this song. Who's it by?"

Ashton's question broke Walker's fond reverie. "I don't know. You'd have to ask Evelyn. She made the playlist."

Ashton pulled out his phone and tapped a few buttons. "We'll Shazam it. Ahhh, it's "The Sleigh in the Moon" by Sufjan Stevens. This guy again. Cool." He tapped a bit more. "Added it to my own Christmas playlist."

"Do you want to listen to yours instead?"

"No. This is nice. Evelyn has good taste."

When the song was over, Ashton turned back to the itinerary. "Once we check in, we have four hours of unscheduled free time, and then we have to meet Tom at Puckers for his party. Do you think they'll want to go see strippers after? I know you're bisexual, so maybe you might enjoy seeing a woman's body like that? But I have to admit I'd rather live my whole life without seeing a woman actively, seductively nude."

Walker laughed. "I think Evelyn would destroy him if he went to see strippers. I'm sure it'll just be a bunch of guys being guys at the sports bar."

"Great. My other favorite thing. Love this bachelor party for me."

"It'll be all right." He squeezed Ashton's leg again. "Remember Operation Not-So-Fake Boyfriend is the name of the game."

"Right." Ashton perked up again. "Okay, but who at the bachelor party do I need to needle? Anyone?" He deflated as he considered. "Won't it just be Tom's pals? And won't they all be bro dude tattoo artists? Or athletes? Or muscle pigs?"

"Muscle pigs? In your dreams," Walker said, laughing. "Tom's friends are mostly D&D geeks and musicians."

"D&D geeks are into tattoos?"

"Some? I guess? I wouldn't know. Never played it myself. But I'd say they're probably into tattoos more than your average golfer."

Ashton gasped. "What? You never wanted Tiger Woods' face tattooed on your chest right above your nipple?"

Walker snorted. "Of course. Right next to a Royal County Dawn club."

"That was just gibberish, wasn't it?"

"For you maybe. But about the bachelor party, you don't need to needle any of them—no pun intended—because they're all good guys. They're all on Tom's side in the divorce and the wedding. It's the extended family we need to focus on."

Ashton went back to looking over the papers. "Tomorrow morning is the wedding breakfast, then the wedding, followed by the reception, and that's where our real work begins. Evelyn has made it so easy with this spreadsheet—" he shifted the papers again "—but why don't we review it a little on the drive up? Okay, Aunt Brandy. She's your mom's sister and Morgan's mother, and she's pissed as fire about this whole situation."

"Yup."

"Why is she even coming?"

"To give Evelyn the stink eye during her ceremony I guess."

"Hm, so she's into cross-stitch and loves cats. She's pro-life—anti-choice, more like. Let me think…" He tapped his chin. "All right. I've got a plan for her. Next up, Uncle Raymie, short for Raymond," he read. "But he hates to be called that because his father's name was Raymond and they despised each other. All right, I'll 'Raymond' him into tomorrow then. Next!"

Ashton slowly gathered enthusiasm until he was nearly glowing with fun. Walker's heart tripped over itself when he glanced over and saw his smile, brilliant and beautiful, shining from the passenger seat.

Perfect.

"IT'S ALL SO extra," Ashton murmured, inhaling the scent of peppermint and fir tree. "The air even smells like Christmas!"

The lobby of the hotel featured every single bit of possible Christmas cheer and comfort: a relaxing carol piped in through invisible speakers, several Christmas trees, garlands strewn everywhere, red, green, and gold bows all about, and a big sign promising a sing-along story time with Santa Claus later. There were even Christmas cookies sitting out free for the taking. Ashton's mouth watered at the sight, and he carefully chose one while Walker checked them into their room.

"Oh, thank God."

Ashton turned at the familiar voice. Evelyn looked beautiful if harried and rather unlike herself in a conservatively cut pink sweater with frosted snowflakes and a wool skirt that came to mid-calf over high boots. "Everything okay?" Ashton asked as he accepted the cheek kisses she offered up and glanced to where Walker was showing the woman behind the desk his ID and a credit card.

"Yes and no. Brody and Layla are in the holiday crafts room, refusing to leave. And I get it. I mean, it's a lot more fun in there than going to a luncheon with my mom and Tom's grandmother, but *I* have to go to the luncheon and Tom's off with his folks having a last minute I-don't-know-what with them, and of course Morgan's family is being put up in another hotel closer to the venue, and—"

"Got it," Ashton interrupted. "We'll watch the kiddos. No problem. Just point the way."

Evelyn kissed his cheek again, and he wiped at the lipstick mark she'd no doubt left behind. "You're the best guy my brother's ever fake-dated."

Ashton's face grew hot, and he looked down quickly. "Thanks. Um, yeah."

"Ohhh! There's a story there," Evelyn said, brow raised. "But I really have to go. I want to hear all about it later. Um, I guess after my honeymoon! Ha!" She paled. "What the hell, I'm getting married. Wow."

"Yeah. It's pretty wow," Ashton agreed. He was happy with the way things were going with Walker, but marriage? That seemed like something that happened to other people for sure. It wasn't something he'd ever get to have for himself.

"I'll go tell the kids you're going to supervise them. Tell Walker I appreciate it."

"Of course."

Walker turned and caught his sister's eye, but she didn't wait, just waved as she rushed off toward the stairwell she'd just come up. Ashton assumed the arts and crafts room must be that way.

"What was that about?" Walker asked, wheeling their luggage over and handing Ashton a room key.

"We have to watch your new step-niblings while she bridal-luncheons with women of a certain age," Ashton said, feeling an absurd desire to kiss Walker's lips for no good reason. He held back. "Um, I guess I'll take the luggage up and then you can go be with the kids? She seemed in a big rush."

"I'll take the luggage." Walker nodded toward the stairwell. "You go on. I'll meet you there."

"Are you sure?"

Walker leaned in, kissing Ashton's temple. "I'm sure."

Ashton blinked in shock. He'd dated a number of men over the years, fucked more than a few too, but very few—read: *none*—had been casually affectionate in public and then usually only in a gay space like a club or bar surrounded by others like them. But here in the middle of this family hotel with wholesome Christmas everything all around, Walker had kissed his temple and claimed him.

*Maybe this could last after all?*

"Is that for Operation Not-So-Fake Boyfriend?" he asked quietly, checking to see if there were any potential aunts, uncles, or grandparents watching them.

"No, it was because you're cute," Walker said, taking Ashton's luggage in his other hand and wheeling both suitcases away. He winked over his shoulder. "Meet you in arts and crafts."

Ashton's pulse whirred wildly. He swallowed hard, trying to get rid of the weird and sudden lump in his throat. It was all happening so fast. Was it normal to feel this way about someone so quickly? Though he supposed it wasn't *actually* fast. They'd known each other for almost a year.

But they'd just discovered each other and now… And now…

A smile spread helplessly across his face. He couldn't remember the last time he'd felt so safe with someone. He'd never had this kind of comfort and stability in his life. And even though there was no way it could last, he could see the temptation of at least trying to make it permanent. Maybe the whole marriage thing wasn't so hard to understand after all.

He found Brody and Layla in the arts and crafts room busily making popsicle stick Christmas trees and eating candy canes. The kids greeted him like a long-lost family member, complete with hugs and excited babble. He studied their various creations (all hideous, all glittery) and sat next to them, taking up a stack of popsicle sticks to make a tree himself.

His life had never felt more perfect. It should have been terrifying, yet right now? It wasn't.

Maybe this temporary release from his doubts was the latest holiday miracle in a series of holidays miracles. He'd take it.

WALKER STOOD OUTSIDE the arts and crafts room, hands in pockets, a lump in his throat, and his heart fluttering wildly. Ashton looked so happy with the kids, dabbing glitter and sequins onto a wreath made of green-painted puzzle pieces. Three finished popsicle stick Christmas trees sat beside him, bedazzled with buttons, sequins, and more glitter. Walker loved how Ashton's beautiful face shone with joy and how his head tipped back whenever one of the kids made him laugh, which was often.

"He's a sweetheart."

Walker jolted, surprised to find his mother standing at his side, looking in at Ashton and the kids. "Mom, hi." He gave her a little hug, accepting her kiss on the cheek. "I thought you were having lunch with Evelyn in the hotel restaurant?"

"I visited the ladies' room and just happened to spot you here admiring your beau. He's such a wonderful young man. I admit, at first, I was shocked when you brought him home. But I'm so grateful you did. I'm happy for you, Walker. After all you've been through, I was worried."

"After what all I've been through?" When he compared his life and troubles to Ashton's, his was a walk in the park. Any darkness had been his own doing.

"You know."

"I didn't go through anything. I did all that to myself."

"Well, that's how your grandfather sees it, but I feel differently." She patted his arm. "We all have our reasons and you had yours."

Walker huffed a gentle laugh. "I'm not an innocent kid, Mom. I made my choices. They were bad ones."

She patted his arm again and said nothing damning, which was a reprieve he didn't deserve.

After a beat, he commented, "You never told Dad."

She shrugged again. "He wouldn't understand."

Walker swallowed, his heart skipping a beat. "Hasn't he wondered what happened to the trust fund money? Why I live at Grandpa's house? All of that?"

"I simply told him you don't want to touch the trust fund. I said you wanted to be your own self-made man, just like he was. He liked that."

"Oh, Mom." How long could the truth stay buried? From his father. From Ashton. His blood, so recently pulsing with sweet champagne-like joy, seemed to go sour.

"Walker, you made some mistakes, but you're on the right path now, and that boy is the proof of it. Look how he shines." She touched his arm and smiled up at him. "He's your reward for all the hard work you've done."

"Mom, he's not a trophy."

"Of course, I know that." She blew a small raspberry. "He has a lot to offer the world. He's very talented and intelligent. He's a boon for your little company, I hear. Evelyn adores him. The kids do too. Just look at them."

Walker swallowed hard. Layla threw her arms around Ashton's neck and kissed his cheek before presenting him with one of her creations. "Yeah."

"I just think it's worth noting that once you gave up that tricky vice he appeared on the horizon for you." She sighed happily and motioned at the window into the craft room again. "Sweet. Charming. Loving. He's a delight."

"He is," Walker agreed. He didn't know why, but his mother praising Ashton like that was making his throat tight again.

"Yes, he truly is." She squeezed his arm again. "I should get back to your sister and Tom's grandmother now. Enjoy him, sweetheart. You've earned this happiness. You and Evelyn both. It does my heart good to see my children happy. And at the holidays too. What a blessing."

Walker swallowed then kissed the top of her head. She headed away, her long pink skirt swaying. When he turned back to the window, he found Ashton looking directly at him, his eyes soft and his smile even softer.

With an echoing smile, Walker opened the door to the craft room and stepped inside. The kids looked up, calling him Uncle Walker eagerly, and for a split second he felt as though he'd walked into his own ideal life.

One he wasn't sure he'd truly earned at all, no matter what his mother said.

# Chapter Eighteen

THE WALK FROM the parking garage in downtown Gatlinburg to Puckers for the bachelor party was a short one. Luckily the sidewalks were well-salted, but the wind off the snow-covered mountains was cutting. Ashton buried his face in his knock-off Burberry scarf and shoved his gloved hands deeper into his pockets.

He wore a relatively simple outfit: a black sweater with some silver threads woven in over black jeans. He rarely wore something so plain, but for Tom's bachelor party, he hadn't wanted to look too out of place. The attention should be on the groom tonight. His and Walker's "reindeer games" wouldn't start until the reception, after all.

Walker wore a pair of khaki pants and a button-up shirt with a dark, tailored blazer and could not have looked more "country club" if he tried, yet Ashton found he rather liked it. Everything about Walker's style seemed much more attractive now that Ashton knew what was under it all: a beautiful heart and soul, and a sweetly sexy body that made Ashton weak in the knees every time he saw it in the buff.

In fact, he wished they'd decided to be late instead of early and taken some time to mess up the sheets on the king-sized bed in their hotel room. "I've never had sex on a king-sized bed," he said, the words making white puffs in the air.

"It's not really that different," Walker said with a surprised laugh. "I mean, unless you're a gymnast or something. There's just a little more room for rolling around."

"Hmm, maybe I should google 'different ways to fuck on a king-sized bed.' I bet the internet would provide some surprising guidance."

"*Surprising* being the key word there." Walker took hold of the back of Ashton's neck and shook him a little. "But feel free. I aim to please."

"Your aim sure pleases *me*," Ashton teased, biting into his lower lip and flicking a coy glance Walker's way.

The main drag of the small mountain town was dressed up in silver, gold, and colored lights. The entire place rang, sang, and glistened, and the scent of doughnuts, candy, bacon, syrup, and grease filled the air. It smelled like an amusement park and blinked like one too.

"Oh!" Ashton exclaimed as they approached the corner where they'd turn left to reach Puckers. He pointed across the street. "The taffy pull! Can we go look at it? Since we're early?"

"Sure."

No one grew up in the East Tennessee area without knowing about the mesmerizing taffy pulling machine residing in the window of the Ole Smoky Candy Kitchen. It was an all-ages favorite for its simple, old-timey entertainment. Ashton led the way across the lanes of traffic, and Walker rushed to keep up with his long strides.

Coming to a stop outside the window, they stood near the back of a small crowd of mostly children. All eyes were fixed on the candy machine inside. The taffy was stretched, tugged, and sectioned off by the machine. Then another machine cut the pieces into small logs and wrapped them in wax paper right in front of their eyes.

Walker stopped just behind Ashton. His slightly bulkier build made Ashton feel protected and shielded—from the wind, from the world. He relaxed and watched the vanilla-colored taffy being tugged into the right shapes and cut into tiny logs.

"I used to beg to watch longer when I was a kid," he murmured. "Grandma never had much patience for it. Sweets are the currency of the devil, you know, so we were never allowed to have them."

Walker slipped his hand around Ashton's waist, hooking his chin over Ashton's shoulder to hold him lightly. There in full view of the crowd. Grandma Hudson would lose her mind if she could see Ashton now.

"She sounds like a horrible woman to be raised by," Walker said.

"She was. Not that it made leaving her house any easier."

Walker wrapped his other arm around Ashton from behind, embracing him. There were a few looks from the folks around them, but no one said a word. "It was hard for you after you left?"

Ashton kept his gaze on the soothing, steady stretch and cut of the taffy. "Yeah, I had a few rough years. Did Casey ever tell you about it?"

"No."

"Casey's not much for gossip."

"He can be, but he's never gossiped about you."

"Or you."

Walker squeezed him a little tighter. Ashton's heart raced, but he wasn't going to pull away. He was grown and safe. He and his boyfriend—boyfriend? yes!—could share a back hug on the street just like any heterosexual couple. Like that woman and her husband over there.

"What happened?" Walker asked quietly.

"Well, I left without anything more than a bag of clothes and a fistful of dollars I'd made washing cars. I had no choice but to find and deal with my dad for the first time in my life so I could stay off the streets."

At a sharp double-take from a heavy-set man with a beard and a dark gleam in his eye, Ashton gave in and pulled away from Walker's full-on embrace.

Walker let him go but immediately settled his arm around Ashton's shoulder instead. "You and your dad aren't close, I know, but you think it's worth it to have him in your life?"

"Right now? I don't know. But in the past, yeah. He's not an addict like my mom, but he's always had his own set of expectations and manipulations. He didn't want me as a kid, and he doesn't truly want me now. He'll pay for some of my stuff and invite me to some family events, but it's just to soothe his conscience. We don't really click either.

But, then again, he's all the family I've got."

"I'm sorry."

"Yeah, well, that's life, isn't it? Love it or leave it. I try to love it." He sighed and huddled in closer to Walker again after the snake-eyed man trundled off down the sidewalk away from them. "I lucked out that he *could* help me and that he agreed to when I really needed it. But I don't need him now."

"You're a capable, strong person."

Ashton let Walker wrap his arms around him again. He loved the soft, warm huff of Walker's breath against his neck and cheek as they stood together. "The first time I came up here to Gatlinburg on my own, I was twenty. I'd bought this old clunker of a car—" he laughed. "Long dead and gone now. Anyway, I drove it up here, and I went into every single shop up and down this street. It's mostly trash, just so you know. But when I got to this shop, I just stood as long as I wanted watching the taffy being made. I remember they made chocolate, banana, and orange taffy that day. I bought three boxes. And I ate nothing but taffy for days."

"I'm surprised it didn't make you sick."

"Strong stomach," Ashton said, tapping his firm abdomen and laughing. "Seriously, I felt physically awful, but every bite of that candy was a huge eff you to my grandmother and my entire past. So it tasted delicious. Do you know what I mean? Have you ever felt like that?"

Walker hugged him close again, and Ashton felt him thinking. "I get it. Probably more than you think."

Ashton leaned back into Walker's chest, basking in the scent and warmth of him. Some of the families near them moved away as though trying to shield their children from the scandalous gay affection happening right next to them, but Walker didn't seem to notice, and Ashton tried not to care either.

"Honestly, I'm glad you don't *really* know. No one should ever really know. And that's why you're so you."

"How am I so me?" Walker asked.

"Are you fishing for compliments?"

"Maybe."

Ashton laughed, watching as an employee of the candy store came and switched out the taffy flavor on the machine. This one was yellow with thin brown stripes. "You're stable and easygoing. You help me feel…" He trailed off and cleared his throat, odd tears pricking at his eyes. "You help me feel truly safe." Embarrassed, he tugged away and started toward the door of the store. "Let's buy a box?"

Walker took hold of his hand. "Let's buy three."

After stashing the boxes of taffy in Walker's car, they returned to the main drag and hung a left. Taking some stairs down to a lower-level sidewalk, they approached the door of Puckers, the bar where the bachelor party was being held.

The sound of pool cues hitting balls greeted them on the sidewalk. Ashton's gut twisted nervously. To say this wasn't his scene was an understatement. When the plan for Evelyn's wedding had been to simply be himself—over the top and eye-catching—it'd all seemed like a great lark. One that might end with a fist to his jaw if he didn't tread the line carefully, sure, but a fun time all the same.

But now that he was falling steadily more and more in love with Walker, his boyfriend's soon-to-be brother-in-law's bachelor party suddenly felt like a huge test. One that he really needed to pass.

"Do you know these people?" Ashton asked, grabbing Walker's arm to stop him from opening the door quite yet. "Like, do you care what they think of me?"

Walker cocked his head, moving aside to let a big man with an eagle tattooed on his neck enter. "No. But even if I did, why would I care what anyone thought of you but me? Don't be nervous."

"It's just that this place isn't really my speed." Ashton eyed the bikers parking on the street and making their way down the steps to Pucker's door. "I'm having visions of that edition of Rolling Stone with the photo of Chris Colfer in a leather bar."

"Who?"

"You know Chris Colfer? From *Glee*?"

Walker shrugged.

"Of course you don't," Ashton said, a giddy anxiety rolling through him. "Ugh. What I mean is, look at me. And now look at them." He nodded at the bikers filing down the stairs toward them. "I don't exactly run with this crowd."

"Neither do I." Walker put his arm around him and tweaked his cold nose.

Ashton huffed.

"Look, don't worry so much. If it gets weird, we'll leave."

"Or I could go, and you could stay—"

"We came together. We'll leave together."

The reassuring masculine scent of Walker's cologne warmed him. "And if anyone picks on me?"

"I'll protect you."

Ashton fluttered his lashes. "Oh?"

Walker laughed and kissed his temple. "Always. C'mon."

Pucker's wasn't anything special. It was pretty typical as far as a dive sports bar went. Not that Ashton had been inside many, but he'd seen them on television, and this was absolutely the very picture of biker-chic: fluorescent signs advertising beers, stained-glass bowl lights over the booths, and pool tables lining the front windows for the competitive player.

Music pumped overhead with a steady, enjoyable beat—not pop of course, decidedly old school rock—but Ashton wasn't familiar with the song. The screens over the bar and in each corner hosted a football game. He wasn't a fan, but he didn't mind ogling asses if he was taken to a game.

Ashton didn't think he could get away with ogling asses here, though. Not without getting into a world of hurt.

The bar was loud with chatter, football, and music, and his ears ached from the sudden onslaught. He peered around looking for the party, wishing he'd begged off and stayed in the hotel room. Though then he'd have missed out on that taffy, and he did love taffy. And who was he kidding? He also loved a party. Just maybe not this one.

"Hey!" Tom shouted, standing up from a crowded table of men near the back of the room and waving. He wore a black T-shirt featuring a white noose and the words: *Help! I'm tying the knot, so buy me a shot!* emblazoned on the front. "Hey, y'all! Look!" He was clearly drunk already. He pointed their way. "It's my brotherrrr! And his loverrr!"

Heads swiveled all over the room, checking out Walker and Ashton. A few of the bikers who'd passed them on the sidewalk sneered, but a few others gave Ashton a *very* thorough once-over that implied a different kind of interest, and a lot more of it than he was comfortable with.

*Great. Love that for me.*

Tom launched toward them and hugged Walker, pounding his back hard, like all cis straight men seemed to do because no homo, dude, and shouted, "Tomorrow, Walker! Tomorrow you'll be my brother for real!" He giggled. "I love you, dude! I *love* you! You're the best."

"Thanks," Walker said, laughing and helping Tom turn back around to get to his table.

"Have you eaten anything? Or did you just chug alcohol for dinner?" Ashton asked as he followed. He tried to ward off a bear hug from Tom but failed. He smelled like whiskey…and cinnamon for some reason.

"Chug, chug, chug!" Tom laughed uproariously.

"Wow," Ashton said. "You're smashed and it's not even nine o'clock, bud. You might want to calm down. Eat a burger. Have some fries."

"Mmm," Tom said, nuzzling against Ashton's cheek. His beard was surprisingly soft. "Fries. Cheese fries!" And he broke away, turning back to his also clearly drunken pals, all tattooed and wearing shirts proclaiming them the Groom's Crew, shouting, "Cheese fries, guys! I need cheese fries! And milk!"

"No milk!" Ashton shouted, almost gagging. "What on earth? Who drinks milk after liquor. Bless that man."

Tom flung himself toward a new arrival at the edge of the crowded table. "Hey! Raul! Dude! You're here! You're really here! Yesss!" Tom beat against his friend's back, laughing and shouting. "I'm gonna be a real goddamn married man again, Raul. Me, a goddamn married man. Again."

The curse made Ashton flinch despite years of trying to deprogram himself from reacting to that kind of thing.

"C'mon, let's find a quieter place to sit," Walker said, ushering Ashton away from the rowdy, embarrassing core group.

"Wow," Ashton said as Walker directed him to a few empty chairs along the bar. It was close enough to the party they could still keep an eye on things, but far enough away they didn't have to shout to hear each other. Ashton removed his coat and sat a little primly, but he tried to smile. This was supposed to be fun, wasn't it?

"What now?" Ashton asked. "Normally at a party, I'd work the room, but as it is…" He winced. "Well, I'm going to sit right here for a bit until I get comfortable."

"I've never seen you like this," Walker said, taking the stool next to him and lifting a hand for the bartender.

"Like what?"

"Out of your element. Uncomfortable. Usually, you're like a fish in water everywhere with everyone."

He smirked. "I know. I'm such a good actor." He leaned in. "I guess I'm being an asshole. Judging books by their cover, you know? I hate when people do that to me."

It was Walker's turn to wince, and it took Ashton a moment to realize why.

"No, no." He patted Walker's arm. "You weren't judging me by my appearance, you were just waiting until the time was right to fully see me."

Walker snorted. "I wish that were the case. Truth is, I had some preconceived ideas about you." He shook his head, reaching out to cover Ashton's hand. "Doesn't matter. I see you now. And you're all I want to see."

"Whoa, slow down there," Ashton said, his cheeks heating as his heart flipped wildly. "I know I'm magical and amazing, but let's not leap too fast."

Walker leaned in and whispered, "I didn't leap. I fell."

He shoved at his shoulder. "You have the worst lines ever, Walker Ronson!"

"You love them." Walker winked.

"What can I getcha?" The buxom, middle-aged bartender asked, slapping down some square paper napkins.

"Spiced maple wings," Walker said, pointing at the item on the menu. "Is one order enough for two to share?" At her nod, he added, "And a Corona. Ashton?"

He grabbed the grubby cocktail menu and resisted the urge to cross himself—he'd never been Catholic, but he felt like it might protect him all the same. "The Banana Cream Pie Shooter?" He smiled. "Please?"

The bartender blinked at him, and he realized he'd probably over-shot it with the smile. He knew he was handsome, but sometimes he forgot how some people—usually women but sometimes men—reacted to him until they got used to his face.

"A'ight. Be right back with that," was all she said and turned on her heel.

"So much for Southern friendliness," Ashton said, baffled.

"She was blinded by your beauty. Can't blame a person for being stunned by you." He tweaked Ashton's nose. "So pretty it hurts."

Ashton rolled his eyes, shoving Walker's hand away from his face. He never would've guessed Walker Ronson would turn out to be such a sap. His insides frothed happily like an uncorked bottle of champagne going off. "Ridiculous," he murmured.

The bartender returned with Walker's beer and Ashton's bright yellow cocktail. "Yer wings'll be right up. Give it a minute." She approached the bikers motioning for refills.

Ashton sipped his cocktail and shuddered. "Ugh, so sweet."

Walker shoved his beer toward Ashton next. "Try this."

Desperate to get the sweet taste of out of his mouth, Ashton did. The deep, mellow beer was much better so he slid his cocktail toward Walker, saying sweetly, "Sure, we can switch."

Walker laughed and caught the bartender as she passed by with some empties in hand. "Another beer please." He pushed the cocktail toward her. "And you can take this. It wasn't to our taste."

She shrugged and wordlessly dumped the bright yellow contents into the sink behind the bar.

Ashton sipped at the beer, enjoying the fizz of it in his mouth. "But seriously, you never answered me before. What do we do now? What comes next at a shindig like this?"

Walker accepted the new beer from the bartender as she passed by again. "You've never been to a bachelor party before?"

Ashton shrugged. "I've seen them on TV, so I figure I know enough?"

"And what about a wedding? Ever been to one of those?"

He shook his head.

Walker laughed. "You volunteered yourself as my fake boyfriend for a wedding weekend even though you'd never even been to a wedding before? You're really not risk averse, are you?"

Ashton laughed. "I'm a daredevil at heart. What've you gotten yourself into with me?"

Walker slung his arm around Ashton's shoulders and whispered in his ear. "I don't know? Maybe a hell of a good thing?"

A big basket of savory-smelling wings dropped in front them. "There you go. Enjoy."

As the bartender skedaddled, Walker dug into the wings immediately. "Have some," he said. "They're good."

"You've been here before?"

"With some golfing friends last year. We were trying out the Gatlinburg course for a change of pace. Stopped in here afterward." He waved a hand to dismiss the whole thing. "No big deal."

Ashton ate one of the wings, the flavor melting in his mouth. It paired so well with the beer that before he knew it, they'd polished off most of the basket of wings and both of their drinks in a companionable silence. The laughter from the tables around them, the alternating low and loud chatter, the blaring screens, the clack of pool balls, and the strum of guitars through the speakers, kept them swaddled in a steady, almost soothing hum.

"Want to play pool?" Walker asked when they'd finished their food.

"Are you any good?"

"No, but I'm probably better than you."

Ashton scoffed and pressed a hand to his chest. "Excuse me? What makes you so sure?"

Walker tweaked Ashton's earlobe and then his nose again. Ashton rolled his eyes but found he didn't mind Walker's inability to keep his hands to himself. "Having been raised by your grandmother, I don't see you having gotten many chances to play with the devil's balls."

Ashton grinned and was just about to agree that Walker was probably better at *this* particular game of stick-and-balls when a gravelly voice interrupted.

"Well, damn, Walker Ronson! Long time, no see!"

Walker stiffened, and when he rose, took the man's hand, and said, "Michael Amos. Hey, yeah, it's been a while," he sounded strangely not himself.

Ashton gave the man a quick once-over, and the hair on the back of his neck stood up unreasonably. Michael looked to be Walker's age, so not that much older than Ashton. He had a blond birth mark in the midst of his very dark brown hair, and almost black eyes. His expensive-looking clothes endowed him with an elegance he might otherwise lack, but he was handsome enough and carried an air of insouciance that put Ashton on high alert.

Raising an appraising brow at Ashton, Michael sat at the bar next to Walker without being asked to join. "This your date?"

"Ashton, this is Michael Amos." Walker put his hand possessively on Ashton's back. "This is my boyfriend, Ashton Sellers."

"Nice to meet you," Ashton said.

Michael put out his hand. His fingers were dry and cold, and Ashton felt an odd temptation to crush them harder than necessary; he wished he could wipe his hand on his jeans as soon as he'd pulled it free again.

Was Michael an ex? Had Walker called Ashton "boyfriend" as a way to get a dig in with an old lover? Ashton didn't know, but something was definitely strange between the two of them. Michael seemed to be almost enjoying it, however. While his steady up-down assessment was thorough, his gaze seemed entirely free of jealousy or other animosity. Perhaps he wasn't an ex?

"Congratulations, Walker, you've caught a gorgeous one."

Ashton bristled. Ugh. Even the man's voice made him want to run away.

"Didn't know you played for our team," Walker said, picking up his beer and putting it down with a clunk when he found it empty.

Okay, Michael was definitely not an ex then.

"I don't, but an objectively beautiful man is still an objectively beautiful man."

Ashton gave a polite smile. Who was this guy? An unrequited love? An enemy? Who was he to Walker?

"Are you here to celebrate Tom's final night as a free man?" Walker asked. "I didn't realize you two were so close."

"No, actually. Came up for the wedding, obviously—wouldn't do to piss off your dad by not attending his daughter's wedding—but we didn't anticipate running into the groom tonight."

"He's wasted," Walker said, glancing fondly over his shoulder. "Hope he makes it tomorrow or my sister will murder him."

"Your father too, no doubt."

"No doubt."

"I'm glad to see *you* here, though," Michael said with a mischievous grin. "No one in my group—" he pointed toward a table of men about their age or slightly older "—is willing to play pool the old-fashioned way. With cash on the table and a jackpot to win."

Walker stiffened next to Ashton. "Sorry, I don't play pool."

Ashton frowned. Hadn't Walker just said he was pretty good? Better than Ashton at least? Not that it would be hard to be better than Ashton, but still. Why was he claiming not to play instead of just saying he didn't want to play for money?

Michael studied Walker a moment and flitted a glance toward Ashton before shrugging. "Not what I heard before heading over here, but I see you've got your mind on other things right now."

Walker smiled tightly.

"Michael, man! I love you, dude!" Suddenly Tom was draping over the back of Michael's chair, hugging him from behind. "Can't believe you're here too! Wanna join my party, man?"

Michael winced at Tom's pawing. "That's okay. The guys and I'll see you at the wedding tomorrow."

Tom's grin nearly split his face. "Tomorrow! Holy shit! I'm gonna be married tomorrow, dude. For real. To a woman who won't destroy my life this time."

"Low bar, but glad she clears it."

"She does! I'm so lucky, Michael. You're gonna be there, right?"

Michael guffawed and reached up to tousle Tom's messy hair. "I already said so, and I sent in my RSVP, dumbass. Your beard's itchy!" he cried, but he was laughing.

"No! You lie! My beard's soft." Tom purposely rubbed it all over

Michael's cheek and forehead, which didn't seem like entirely straight behavior to Ashton, but what did he know about it? He'd never been straight a second of his gay little life.

"Get off me, man. Ugh!"

"Say you love me too!" Tom said, hugging Michael even tighter.

"I love you too," Michael said, shoving at him. "Ugh. Get off." He shot Walker a look. "Your dad's gonna love having this one as a son-in-law."

Walker shrugged. "Yup."

Tom released Michael and whooped. "I'm marrying Evelyn Ronson!" He shouted to the room. "I'm the luckiest man alive."

Some folks shouted for him to shut up, but most people cheered and clapped and toasted him. Walker sighed and leaned over to Ashton. "He's out of his mind. I hope he can even stand up at the front of the aisle tomorrow."

"He will," Ashton said. "I have no doubt."

"He'll look like shit," Michael said, running a hand over his smoothed-back hair. "And I'll laugh my ass off at him." He turned back to Walker. "Sure you won't change your mind? Impress your pretty friend here with your pool skills—which I *know* you have. Joey told me you cleaned him out once a few years ago. Afterward, you could take this one back to your hotel to *celebrate* on a big ol' pile of easy cash? Think how fun that'll be."

Ashton bristled.

"If you're sounding so sure I'll win, then I'll definitely lose," Walker said, his voice tight. "I'll pass."

Michael studied him a moment. "We miss you at the golf course."

"I'm sure you do."

"Now, now, don't be like that." Michael raised a pacifying hand. "A little loss isn't anything you can't bounce back from. So long as you keep trying. Perseverance, friend. It'll all come out in the wash with perseverance."

Walker stood suddenly. "I just remembered. There's something I need to do before the wedding tomorrow morning. C'mon Ashton. Let's go." He put his hand out to Michael. "Good to see you. Give my best to Joey and the guys. I suppose I'll run into you again at the wedding tomorrow."

"Sure will." Michael didn't rise, just shook Walker's hand from where he was sitting.

Ashton abandoned his bar stool, confused and wanting to ask a lot of questions, but somehow he knew now wasn't the time. He flashed back to when he and Walker ran into Ashton's mom outside his apartment. He'd wished Walker had just followed his lead and ignored her, and he'd been so disappointed when he hadn't.

So he followed Walker's lead now as he tossed bills on the bar like he was in some kind of movie and headed over to the bachelor party table.

"Tom, buddy, we're heading out," Walker said, shaking Tom by the shoulders and leaning down to let his drunk soon-to-be brother-in-law give him another hug.

"But you just got here!" Tom cried, pounding Walker's back. "Stay and shoot pool with us."

"Sorry, but I remembered there's something I need to handle to-night."

"For the wedding?"

"Isn't there always last-minute stuff for things like this?"

"All right, all right," Tom said, turning to tug Ashton down into a hug too, all soft beard and liquor-breath. "Be good tonight, Ashton, but not too good."

"What's that supposed to mean?" Ashton asked.

"You know what it means." He winked.

"No?"

"Uh-huh, Evelyn said, and Evelyn knows," Tom said, touching his nose like that meant something, slurring his words. "She's brilliant. Sharper than a tack. No, no, sharper than tattoo gun needles. Sharper than—"

"She's smart," Ashton agreed.

"She says you guys are the real deal. I'm glad. I'm real, *real* glad."

"Okay, great. Love that," Ashton said, feeling oddly choked up as he patted Tom's shoulder. "Do sober up before tomorrow? Your bride will be much happier if you're not a sick mess."

"Nothing could make me sober like Evelyn," Tom said, all moon-eyed and like that even made sense. "Nothing."

"Okay," Ashton agreed again and looked toward Walker, who wasn't even paying attention but instead stared across the room at Michael Amos, still seated at the bar. "Walker? Ready to go?"

"What? Yeah, sure," he said, pulling himself out of wherever his weird reverie had taken him. "Let's go." He put his hand at the small of Ashton's back and steered him toward the front door.

Ashton felt the measuring gaze of men on him as he left. He felt safer exiting the bar on Walker's arm. If he'd been alone, he would have dreaded going out into the night, especially with the kind of attention he'd garnered in the bar behind him. He'd have startled at every dark corner. As it was, with a slightly distracted Walker by his side, he just paid extra close attention to all of them instead.

By the time they reached the parking garage, Walker's tension had ebbed, and once they were in the car Ashton finally dared to ask, "What was that all about?"

"Hmm?"

"That Michael guy," Ashton said, buckling his seatbelt and huffing into the cold air. "Why all the tension there?"

"I don't like him much is all."

"I noticed. But why?"

"I just don't."

"Did he reject you?" Ashton asked, getting his biggest fear out of the way first.

"No?" Walker gave him a curious look. "Michael isn't my type."

"He absolutely is! He dresses like that and looks all…" he circled his hand in front of his face. "Boring and yawn and cardboard."

"You think my type is boring and yawn and cardboard?" Walker laughed, starting the car and checking the mirrors. "What are you talking about?"

"I'm talking about the kind of men you fuck."

Walker swiveled in his seat, took hold of Ashton's chin with one hand and stroked his lip with his thumb. "Baby, you're the kind of man I fuck."

He scoffed and pushed Walker's hand off his chin. "Not usually."

"I guess I was fucking the wrong men before." Walker put the car in reverse, looking in the rearview as he backed up. "You're my type now."

Ashton's mind whirled. There was something he'd been trying to say or ask, and now Walker had him all off track, feeling giddy and cute and adored in a way that he'd never experienced in his life. *He'd* changed Walker's type. Single-handedly, he'd made Walker like men like him. Or maybe just him.

Oh wow. He'd made Walker like *just him.*

Wow.

"No buts. You're my type. No need to be jealous of Michael fucking Amos. Never in a million years," Walker said bitterly.

Oh. Right. That's what Ashton had been trying to understand.

"Why Michael effing Amos?" he asked. "Is there really no story there?"

"Let's just say he and I have some shared history I'm not too proud of, over which I have a lot of regret and he has none."

"If that's supposed to make me less curious, you failed," Ashton said, putting his hand on Walker's thigh as they made their way out of the parking garage.

"Please." Walker placed his hand over Ashton's and gently squeezed. "Let this go. He's not important to me and the problem is in the past. We won't have to deal with him anymore."

"He'll be at the wedding."

"Yes, but I doubt we'll even talk to him. He'll have more interesting people to try to get dancing on his strings, I'm sure."

"So he's a bully?" Ashton said, still trying to comprehend.

"In his way, but he's only successful with the weak-minded. I guess that was me. Once."

"Weak-minded? You?" Ashton blew a raspberry. He couldn't think of anything more absurd. "You're the most genuine, steady person I know. That's why I trust you so much. If he took advantage of that, it just makes him a bad person. You could never be weak, much less weak-minded, Walker."

Walker brought Ashton's fingers up to his mouth and kissed them, leaving behind a tingly feeling. Why did every single thing Walker did now make Ashton feel like he was on a tilt-a-whirl? He didn't even like those kinds of rides at the carnival, and yet with Walker he never wanted the feeling to stop.

"This has been the best Christmas season of my life," Ashton said, rubbing his hand up and down Walker's thigh. "Thanks to you."

"This has been the best few weeks of my life, period."

Heart thumping, he squeezed Walker's thigh. "Drive faster. I want to try out the king-size bed."

# Chapter Nineteen

"THIS IS WHAT you meant by trying out the king-size bed?" Walker said, laughing as Ashton rolled around in the scattering of taffy wrappers in the bed. "You're going to make yourself sick."

"Says the man who easily ate half the candy from these wrappers," Ashton said around a bite of licorice taffy. How he could stand the flavor, Walker didn't know, but apparently Ashton loved it.

He also claimed to love Sambuca in his weekend coffee, so Walker had added it to his notes in his phone and would be buying the anise-flavored liquor at his earliest convenience to surprise Ashton with. It was a thrill to think Ashton had agreed to stick around long enough that Walker could plan liquor-laced weekend mornings.

Speaking of…

"What's the plan for dealing with the things at your apartment?" Walker asked, rolling onto his stomach and resting his chin on the heel of his hand.

Ashton lay sprawled out, propped up by the headboard, his sweater pushed half up to reveal his treasure trail and his black jeans hitched up to reveal his black and pink socks. Walker wanted to kiss his prominent arches and then press more kisses up to his ankle bone, but he held back.

"I was just going to leave everything until I find a new place," Ashton said. "Surely it won't take a lot of time."

Walker picked up a taffy wrapper and flicked it off the bed. "You'll want to make sure you find the right place, especially since you don't have a car. It'll either need to be downtown—which is pricey—or near a bus line. You can't Uber everywhere. It's too expensive. Finding a place that's right could take a few months at least."

"I can rent storage space if it comes to that," Ashton said, unwrapping an orange taffy log and popping it into his mouth. "Mmm, so good." He flung his arms wide, letting the taffy wrapper fly up into the air and softly land on the carpet. "Love this. Love *all* of this."

Walker braved his next suggestion. "You could pack your stuff up and move it to my place. There's room in the office I already use for storage and more room in the basement. Maybe not enough room for your sofa, but you'll want a new one of those."

Ashton's brow popped, and he said around the taffy in his mouth, "Oh, will I?"

Walker wrinkled his nose remembering the second-hand, stained sofa. "Won't you?"

Ashton pondered Walker as he chewed and swallowed. "Maybe you're right. If I stayed with you a little longer, I could save up for some real furniture that I really want."

"Exactly," Walker encouraged. *Or you could just never leave.* "There's no reason to rush to find a place. This is an opportunity to make your life the way you really want it."

"What about you? I won't be in your way?"

Walker smirked and reached out to shake Ashton's foot. "Never."

"All right." Ashton relaxed back again, shoving the mostly empty taffy box off the bed. Taffy logs went rolling, but he didn't take his eyes from Walker's. "If you think it's a good idea."

"I think it's a very good idea," Walker said, climbing up to Ashton, pleased as Ashton slid down so that his head was on the pillow and his arms came up to catch Walker as he lay down on top of him.

Their kiss was sweet and flavored with candy.

Walker settled between Ashton's legs and moved to nuzzle his throat. The hotel room faded away as they kissed and clung to each other, taking their time moving on to the next stage, indulging in the sweetness of this one.

No rush.

No rush at all.

"SLEEP," WALKER WHISPERED, breaking away from their long, orgasm-free make-out session and kissing Ashton's head before tugging him close against him. "Tomorrow's a big day."

Ashton huffed. "Are you kidding me? You're stopping?"

Walker chuckled. "It's late, baby. You'll want to be rested in the morning."

"Yeah. But I want to get off right now."

Walker tugged him closer. "I know you do but I also know you're sore. Let's take a break tonight. Save it for tomorrow as a post-successful-Operation-Not-So-Fake-Boyfriend celebration."

Ashton groaned, but he was also too happy being held in Walker's arms to argue. There was no doubt that getting fucked by Walker was Ashton's new favorite pastime. Whenever Walker grew tired of him, whenever the time came he no longer wanted him, Ashton would miss a lot of things, but being held down to a bed while being relentlessly railed until he cried out and convulsed in orgasm would definitely be the thing he'd miss the most. He was sure of it every time they screwed.

But in moments like this, when he felt comfortable and adored, tucked up next to Walker's warm body, he knew this intimate gentleness and tender closeness would be the thing that kept him crying long after everything else between them had faded into a fond memory.

Tenderness was something he'd never had before and had never thought he'd ever truly receive. No matter what he'd told himself he deserved or dreamed he'd somehow find, he'd never believed deep down that he'd get it, much less from a man like Walker.

"What's wrong?"

"Nothing." He sighed. "I guess that's what's wrong."

"Mm?"

"I'm happy, Walker. Here with you and the dogs. I mean, not *here* since we're at the hotel. Not at your house. But what I mean is, with you? I'm actually happy."

"I'm happy with you too."

"When we're fucking do you ever wonder—"

"You wonder things while we're fucking? I'll have to work harder then."

"No, no, when we're doing *that* I can't think at all. But afterward, I wonder, and then I wonder if *you* wonder, you know?"

"No." Walker turned onto his side to face Ashton. "Explain."

"When you're inside me, do you ever wonder about what it means? To be joined like that? To mingle our bodies and feel that way together? Sometimes I think it *has* to mean something."

Walker's expression grew softer and even more fond. "What does it mean?"

Ashton squirmed. "It doesn't mean anything to you?"

"Of course it does. It's like with the ring." Walker touched Ashton's finger where he usually wore it, but he'd taken it off before bed. "It means everything to me."

"I want it to mean that you…" Ashton fell silent, his stomach twisting. "Never mind."

"Tell me."

"It's embarrassing."

"Fine, I'll tell you first." Walker stroked a hand over Ashton's hair. "I want it to mean that we're making love. How about you? Is that what you want?"

"Kind of. I want it to mean that you love me—really love me," Ashton said. "I know this is still new, but I want to think that we're growing love between us each time we do it. I want our love to be something we can create with our bodies and actions."

"I don't think we need to create it," Walker said. "It's already there."

"Is it?" Hope felt so dangerous and so beautiful.

"Love can be shown other ways. I show it by taking care of you. Making you dinner. Rubbing your feet. It makes me feel good, like a grown man—"

"You *are* a grown man."

"I know, and I feel that to my bones when I'm with you. Crazy as it is, fast as this seems, I've fallen so hard for you, Ashton Sellers. Your smile, your heart, the way you exist in the world." Walker smoothed a hand down Ashton's chest. "I can't get enough of you. How would you ever think I'd walk away?"

Ashton's heart wrung with hope. "I guess I'm not used to people who stay."

"Well, I'm going to stay." Walker reached for him.

"What about needing rest? And saving it for post-success celebration tomorrow?" he asked as Walker trailed his fingers down his back, between his buttocks, and slipped the tips of his fingers into Ashton's still slick and softly open hole. Ashton pressed down, trying to get them in deeper. He was tired and quite sore from all the fucking they'd engaged in the last few days, but he couldn't stop himself from wanting Walker to prove his words to him.

"I think we both need this more," Walker whispered and instead set about kissing Ashton all over, leaving a wet, sticky path in his wake that tingled in the cool air of the hotel room.

The heating and air unit roared next to the window, easing the temperature of the room up and down and covering the sounds they made—grunts, groans, and whimpers that Ashton had no doubt would otherwise carry through the hotel walls to their neighbors' rooms.

The cover of white noise allowed him to let loose a loud groan when Walker trailed his mouth over the top of Ashton's butt cheek and then dipped his tongue into his crack. Ashton went still, drawing his legs up and apart like a frog, and he put his hand over his own mouth to hold in his cry when Walker finally tongued his asshole with a greedy tenderness that drove them both wild.

How could this be a sin? He still wanted to know.

Why was it wrong to feel loved when a man was pressing his tongue into your body and moaning like he was starving for you? Why was it wrong to feel precious and adored? There was no way this wasn't the exact opposite of sin. Not when it made him feel all these things, and not when Walker—good, honest, strong Walker was the one who made him feel them.

Walker made him feel ready to toss aside his doubts and just believe.

Believe in love.

Believe he deserved this.

Believe Walker was going to stay.

When Ashton had been abandoned by love as a child, then told his kind of love was sinful as a teen, he'd thrown out all hope for this feeling, this leg-shaking, heart-aching feeling ever being something that he could trust in. But now...

Now...

"Oh, Walker," he whispered, tossing his head back and forth on the pillow, curling his toes and convulsing slightly. "Oh, I'm gonna come."

Walker drove into him harder, licking and sucking on his hole, and Ashton slid his hand between his body and the mattress, took hold of his own cock, and squeezed. He was close already.

"Walker," he gasped. "C'mere. Need you." He tugged Walker's hair and flipped over onto his back as Walker came willingly. He collapsed on top of Ashton, rutting their cocks together and kissing as urgent, undeniable need grew between them.

"Ah!" Ashton cried, his hips flexing up, tossing his head back. "I'm so close. So close. I miss you inside me."

Walker groaned and lifted up, elbows on either side of Ashton's head. "Wanna be in you, too. Feel you. Tight on my cock."

Ashton shoved Walker onto his back and climbed on top of him, reaching for the box of lubed condoms they'd put out on the bedside table earlier. "Fuck," he whispered, tearing one open. "Get this on. I need it. I *need* it."

Walker helped steady Ashton's hand as he rolled the sheath down Walker's rigid cock. Ashton's head spun as he positioned himself. Sore as he was, he should have used lube on his ass too, and he should have done a lot more prep than just some rimming, but he couldn't wait. He pushed down as Walker tensed beneath him.

"Sure about this, baby?" Walker asked. "We don't have to—oh, God, *fucking* hell."

Ashton smirked, his asshole smarting but the perfect pleasure of Walker's wide cock sinking into him more than making up for it. Taffy wrappers from candy they'd gorged on earlier crinkled on the bed as he shifted his knees to a better position and then drove his ass back and down, pushing his hole open to ease the slide.

"Ohhh," he whimpered as the base of Walker's cock finally pushed against his tender rim. "Holy heaven, you feel so big."

Walker held very still, the wrinkle between his brow betraying how much worry he still felt for Ashton's comfort. Ashton slipped his hands down Walker's chest to pluck at his tight nipples. Walker tilted his head back, his throat on display, begging for a biting kiss. Ashton bent down, sucked on his throat, then pressed a kiss to his clavicles.

"Your collarbones aren't bad either," he managed to tease between sweet little gasps as Walker's hips twitched up and down, fucking into Ashton lightly. "I almost see why you like mine so much."

"Don't. Talk. About. Your. Collarbones," Walker gritted out, the pink flush deepening in his chest and neck. "I'll lose my load, and this will all be over before you've come yet."

"Oh? These?" Ashton asked, sitting back with a gasp at the pressure against his tender rim. He ran his fingers over his own collarbones seductively and held his chin up, gazing down at Walker from beneath his lashes. "They're a problem for you?"

Walker groaned again and tugged Ashton forward and down, almost pulling him off his cock, and kissed his collarbones fervently. First he kissed with closed-mouth focus, and then with a sloppy, open-mouthed devotion that Ashton didn't understand but enjoyed just the same.

Walker's hips snapped up, thrusting his cock fully inside, and Ashton bit his lip to stifle a yell. As Walker mouthed his collarbones and fucked into him passionately, Ashton concentrated on relaxing his hole until the thrusts punched in and out easily, leaving him wide and gaping.

"Fuck, baby," Walker groaned. "Fuck, this is so good. You're so good."

Ashton whimpered, his cock tingling, his asshole thrumming, and his thighs, haunches, and buttocks shaking with effort and pleasure. Walker panted against Ashton's clavicles and grasped Ashton's hips as he fucked into him, shaking with every thrust.

Candy wrappers crinkled around them. The scent of sweat and sex rose in the air. Ashton squeezed his hands into fists, trying to hold back from touching himself. He wasn't ready to pull the last orgasm of the night from himself quite yet.

But Walker finished it, rolling Ashton onto his back and fucking into him with groaning, shaking abandon. Their bodies were wet with sweat, the sound of their skin slapping together mingled with their grunts. Ashton's asshole burned with the friction, but the electric pleasure coming from his prostate was maddeningly good, and his cock being rubbed between their bellies just…like…that—

"Oh!" he shouted. "Oh fuck! God! Help me, Jesus!" The forbidden curses left his mouth and his entire body seized. Cum pumped from his cock, and he shuddered like a wild thing, his heart pounding so loud that he couldn't hear anything but the rush of his own blood.

Walker shook over him, his hips stuttering and shoving hard. The thick pulse of his cock against Ashton's tender rim let him know Walker was coming, too—that and the way he whimpered in Ashton's ear, moaning sweet nothings that made no sense, and a particular sentence that did, but which couldn't possibly be true, no matter how Ashton felt when Walker was making love to him.

"I love you," Walker jittered out between his clenched teeth as he spasmed over top of and in Ashton. "I love you, fuck, *fuck*, I love you."

Ashton buried his face in Walker's neck, trembling all over as his body took in Walker's last brutal thrust, and his heart soaked up his beautiful words. They'd just talked about love and making love grow, but believing Walker loved him already was impossible. Maybe one day. Maybe soon.

"I…" Ashton tried to say the words back but couldn't get them out past the lump in his throat. Tears pricked at his eyes. "I…"

Walker kissed him, sucking the words out of his mouth and swallowing them down.

Ashton let his answering kiss speak them instead.

# Chapter Twenty

THE NEXT DAY, Ashton woke early to prep for the wedding. He wasn't part of the wedding party per se, but he was part of the wedding *plan*, and he had to look spectacular for it.

While Walker slumbered on, Ashton closed himself in the bathroom, gingerly pampered his sore asshole with A&D cream and began to work his magic on his face. By the time Walker tapped on the door and entered with a cup of coffee and a bleary expression, Ashton was almost done.

"Wow," Walker murmured. "You look gorgeous. Like you should be famous or something."

Ashton smiled at him through his reflection in the mirror, his perfectly painted lips shining in the blue-ish overhead lights. Truly, they could have sprung for better lighting in this hotel, but he supposed keeping a Santa on call was pricey. What did he know?

Before the trip, he'd done a test run and made certain the makeup colors he'd chosen wouldn't clash with his burgundy skinny suit. In the end, he and Evelyn had decided to ditch the BDSM chain idea in favor of a very floral tie and pocket-square. She thought Ashton coming to the wedding looking super-effeminate would be more than enough to get the guests' tongues wagging, and while that was super dang depressing, after a lifetime of being naturally femme, he was also sure it was true.

"Shower," Ashton ordered. "The wedding is in three and a half hours, and there are photos beforehand, right?" They'd skipped the wedding breakfast after fucking into the wee hours of the night.

Hopefully no one had missed them. The bride and groom hadn't planned to be in attendance, only the rest of the bridal party and family members had been invited.

"No, they're all after."

"Still, you'll want to be at the venue early for Evelyn and your parents in case any problems come up."

"That's what they hired the wedding planner for," Walker said, taking a bigger gulp of coffee and tugging off his robe. Ashton took a moment to admire his nakedness—had he really once thought he'd be unimpressed by Walker's body? Shame on him. "But all right."

Ashton left him to it. Unzipping the hanging bag Walker had let him borrow to keep everything nice and unwrinkled, he once again felt a thrill at owning such a nice suit. There was a time he'd never thought he'd be able to afford the clothes he enjoyed regularly now.

Shortly, he was fully dressed, and he sat on the bed trying to choose between burgundy socks with yellow ducks, cream-colored socks with multi-colored confetti-ish polka-dots, or black socks with burgundy roses, which was the direction he was leaning.

He looked up to see Walker standing in the doorway to the bathroom, his towel draped around his waist, and a little scowl between his brows as he studied Ashton. "You don't like the roses?" he asked. "I have some burgundy plaid socks if you think—"

"No, no, the roses are great. I was just... You know what? Never mind."

Ashton put the socks aside, walking barefoot over the tough hotel room carpet to where Walker stood. "Are you getting cold feet? I understand, but—"

"No, no, I don't have cold feet. Besides I think that's the groom's prerogative, not the younger brother of the bride's."

"I meant about Operation Fake Boyfriend," Ashton said with a giggle, but he sobered quickly. "Or maybe...about me? About being seen with me on your arm? Looking like—"

"Looking like a goddamn supermodel? Yeah, I'm horrified." Walker snorted. "Please believe me, there is *nothing* about you that could ever give me cold feet."

"Ah, ah, ah, you say that now, but—"

"But nothing." Walker rested his arms on Ashton's shoulders and leaned in, his towel dipping suggestively. "Listen, if there's anyone here who deserves to be anxious about someone getting cold feet over *us*, it's me. Baby, you have no idea."

Ashton ducked his head to meet Walker's downcast eyes, a shiver of concern running through him. "Then tell me."

Walker swallowed hard, opened his mouth, and said, "Later. I promise. Right now I need to get dressed."

Ashton crowded closer into Walker's space, touching the wrinkle between his eyebrows. "I know you do, but if you have worries, let me soothe them. What's wrong?"

"Nothing." He smiled, but it wasn't entirely sincere. "I guess I get a little cranky when I eat too many sweets and don't get enough sleep."

Ashton shook his head. His gut told him otherwise. "Tell me."

Walker groaned and put his hands on Ashton's shoulders, bringing him even closer but not quite entirely flush with his wet body, leaving him unrumpled. "Ashton, no matter what happens—today or any day in the future—always know that I admire you more than I could ever say. Do you understand? Tell me you believe me."

"All right. I believe you." He mostly did. He believed that Walker truly meant what he said right now, even if he might change his mind about it later when he grew tired of Ashton being so entirely *Ashton* all the time.

As Walker dressed, he said, "Last night, when we were watching the taffy pull?"

Ashton perched on the bed and pulled on the black socks with roses. "Yeah?"

"All I could think about was how spoiled Evelyn and I were as kids.

Three, four times a year, we'd come up to Gatlinburg with my folks, and my parents would buy that taffy for us like it was nothing. And every damn time, Evelyn would eat so much my dad would have to pull the car over on the way home so she could vomit. And she didn't gorge because she'd been deprived of it, but because she wasn't used to being told no, or enough, or *stop*. Neither of us were."

"Walker—"

"I'm embarrassed sometimes when I see how much you've lived with and endured, yet you're so amazing. Optimistic. Loving. Generous."

"You make me sound like a saint!" Ashton laughed, waving his hands to push the descriptions away. "I'm far from a good person. For heaven's sake, I've cut both of my parents out of my life! And why? For selfish reasons. For *me*. For *my* happiness."

"That's not true." Walker buttoned up his shirt and tucked it into his pants.

"It is!" Ashton took a slow breath. He couldn't afford to get too emotional. Tears would ruin his carefully applied makeup and then he'd have to start over, and no one had time for that. "What do you know about addiction?"

Walker flinched. "A little."

"You have a friend with a problem, right?"

"A problem probably describes it best, yeah. A *former* problem, really. He's doing great. I'd never call what he went through an addiction. He was, what did you call it? A binger." Walker continued dressing, putting on his suspenders and buttoning up his pants.

"All right. What I'm trying to say is that I know a *ton* about addiction. If there's a book or a study out there? I've read it. And do you know what most of the best studies say about the problem? They say addiction is best healed by social support—by having people in your life to love you. Nothing does more than that to help heal the wiring in an addict's brain."

Walker met Ashton's eyes in the mirror as he worked on his bow tie.

"Studies show most addicts recover spontaneously on their own in their thirties or forties when a time comes they no longer feel so hopeless and helpless and alone. There are other studies that focus on brain wiring, learning circuits versus reward circuits, and disease model versus other models. I know all about *all* of it, Walker."

"Of course you studied it. You needed to understand."

"Darn right, I needed to understand," Ashton said quietly, fighting the urge to rake his hand through his carefully styled hair. "I needed to understand how it was she left me. *Me*. Her *son*." His voice grew thick, and he blinked hard to keep tears from rising in his eyes.

"Ashton—"

"I read so many books about addiction because I wanted to understand how it was that I ended up without a mother to love me."

"Baby—" Walker reached out, but Ashton avoided his embrace.

"So I read and read. Every new theory. Every old one too." He counted them off on his fingers. "Choice theory, disease theory, self-medication theory." He tasted bile at the back of his throat and felt beads of sweat prick along his hair line. "And what I took away from all the theories was one fundamental fact: my mom *couldn't* stop using. It was out of her control."

He sat on the bed, wrinkles in his suit be damned. He couldn't stay on his feet any longer. "Whether it was because her brain was diseased or because of her choices or if she was self-medicating due to the pain of being raised by my abusive grandmother…"

Ashton gasped for air. He didn't want Walker to see him as a saint, as some angel. He was a human being, and he'd made his choices about his mother, and they were ugly ones. Some people would call him selfish. Some would say he was a dick.

Isn't that what his own father believed?

He plowed ahead. "Everything I've read has told me she's helpless to it. Whatever she did when I was a kid? It wasn't her fault. It was her addiction in control. But you know what all that really means to *me*? As her *son*? It means *I* didn't have a mom who loved me."

Ashton blinked away tears, refusing to let them fall. "You can say I'm so admirable if you want. But what's admirable in refusing to support your own mother when all the studies say you should? Where's the *empathy* in how I've chosen to treat her? Where's the *goodness* in what I say to her whenever I'm forced to see her? Where's the good person you claim I am? Where?"

Walker knelt before him, dressed now except for his suit jacket. He touched Ashton's chest with the palm of his hand. "There. It's in you because you think this deeply about it all."

Ashton shoved his hand aside. "Walker, stop idealizing me. I'm just a man. A human man. You're going to be so disappointed when you find that out."

He rocked back on his heels. "So will you. About me."

"No, because what I like about you is your humanity. The simple goodness of you. You're good at your work. You're loved by your family, and you know how to love. Like the dogs. You *love* the dogs. And they love you."

Walker tilted his head like he was trying to understand. "Yes, but you're saying that like they wouldn't love anyone who fed them and gave them treats."

"You don't really believe that. You know if something happened to you, the dogs would grieve."

"Yes, I guess I do."

"And you love your family and your friends."

"I meant what I said last night, Ashton. I love you."

He froze, his heart thumping hard. "I want to believe that."

"I'm going to make you believe it."

Ashton sighed. "Oh heavens, I shouldn't have brought all this up."

"Why? If not now, then when?"

"*Later.* For one thing, *you* have a wedding to get to, and for another, *we* have a wedding reception to scandalize." He rose to his feet and pulled Walker up with him. He leaned against him, taking a deep breath. Walker smelled like hotel soap and his familiar aftershave. "About love though…"

"Mm?"

"I think I could love you too." Ashton wished he could say it like Walker had, blatant and sure, but he just couldn't. He didn't trust it; didn't trust himself yet. Funny that he trusted Walker's love more than his own. At least Walker knew he had the ability to love and be loved.

"I know you can love me," Walker said huskily. "I've felt it."

"Heavens," Ashton whispered. "Well, right now, let's settle for something smaller, all right? You've got me in your arms, and it turns out that's pretty great, yeah?"

"More than great. Amazing."

"Don't be disappointed when I'm an actual human being," he warned again, heart thumping madly.

Walker kissed the side of Ashton's temple. "I promise. I'd ask you to promise the same but that wouldn't be fair."

Ashton rolled his eyes. "Don't be silly. Here—I promise to still feel the same for you when I realize you're a human being. Scout's honor. Feel better?"

Walker nodded.

Ashton smiled and pecked Walker's lips. "Good. Now let's go! Get your socks and shoes on! Evelyn's winter wonderland wedding will not wait for any man! Not even her brother!"

"As you wish."

"Ah, a Westley reference," Ashton said, smiling. "I guess that makes me Princess Buttercup? I'm fine with that." He tossed Walker his dress socks and checked himself in the mirror. He still looked great, if he did say so himself. "Let's go, buckaroo. I have some dazzling to do."

Walker smacked Ashton's ass as they left the room. "Dazzle away."

# Chapter Twenty-One

THE VENUE AT Greenbrier Estate was the smallest place Evelyn had been able to convince their father was suitable for her wedding. It still allowed for a guest list of over three hundred people, so it was a pretty grand affair even now. Walker could only imagine how big the other venues must have been.

"Oooh," Ashton murmured as they walked hand in hand through the decorated front doors and into the festooned main room that was meant to act as the chapel for the ceremony.

Rows of white cloth-covered chairs created an aisle that Evelyn would walk down to join Tom on the small riser placed before a wall of glass, boasting a beautiful view of the snow-dusted mountains drifting off into the glinting, shining distance. Red and white poinsettias paired with white, winter-blooming camellias were tangled together in floral arrangements throughout the room, and the scent of cinnamon was in the air, though Walker couldn't easily discern the source.

"It's fancy," Ashton said softly, clenching Walker's hand again. "Time for me to pretend I know what I'm doing."

"You'll be great."

Jutting off from the main space on either side were two rooms set up for dining during the reception. Buffet tables were already being laid in with cascading fruits, vegetables, and cheeses, and servers dressed with black bow ties scurried around perfecting the drape of each table cloth and the placement of each seat.

"Looks like they'll clear out the rows after the ceremony for dancing," Ashton said, nodding toward where a DJ was setting up in the right-hand side room opposite the location of the string quartet hired for the music during the service itself. "Evelyn won out over your mom on that front at least."

"Looks like."

"Yo, Walker!" Tom's voice greeted them from across the space, much more subdued than he'd sounded the night before. He squeezed past the knot of his groomsmen gathered by the cheese table, all of them looking at it longingly before being swatted away by the wedding planner's assistants. Tom sauntered over, handsome in a well-fitted tux, though his eyes looked tired and his skin tone was a little less glowing than it might have been.

"You survived!" Walker greeted him with a punch to the shoulder and then a hug. "You don't even look too worse for wear, I gotta admit. I thought you'd be clutching your head in-between puking everywhere."

"Makeup," Ashton murmured. "He's wearing makeup."

Tom groaned. "You've got good eyes. They swore to me no one would notice."

"It's not super obvious," Ashton said. "Let me guess: eye brightener, some skin color correction, and blush to get a rosy glow in those green cheeks."

"'Bout right," Tom agreed. "And some shit on my lips. Evelyn's gonna kick my ass for drinking so much."

"How's your stomach doing?"

"Your mom's friend is a doctor and she got me some antinausea stuff. Like the kind they give chemo patients. It's working, but I still feel pretty messed up. Why'd I drink like that last night?"

"Because you're an idiot?" Walker asked.

"I can't even argue it. I feel like such shit."

"Walker!" This time it was his mom's voice cutting through the growing hum of the crowd. "Come on, sweetie, your sister wants to see you before the wedding starts." She bustled over in her mother-of-the-bride dress seeming prettier and younger than Walker remembered her looking in years. She'd clearly had some professional assistance with her makeup too, though likely not for the same reasons as Tom.

"Ashton!" she exclaimed, her attention swerving from Walker and Tom to the shiniest one in the group. She took his hands in her own and smiled widely. "You look so handsome. Doesn't he look handsome?" she asked over her shoulder.

Tom waggled his brows at Walker as he replied, "He looks very handsome, doesn't he, Walker?"

"He does."

Walker saw his father approaching, dressed in a tux and looking like even he had not escaped the bride's makeup artist. Walker girded himself against whatever his dad might say or do. Ashton seemed to take a tense breath next to him too.

"Hello, boys," he said with a warm smile before patting Tom on the back, hugging Walker, and pausing in front of Ashton. He put his hand on Ashton's shoulder and squeezed. "Good to see you again, Ashton. Looking good in that suit. Thanks for coming."

"Of course. I wouldn't have missed it," Ashton murmured, surprise in his eyes.

His dad smiled and it didn't look entirely insincere. Progress. Walker would take it.

"Well, c'mon, the bride is waiting for you all." His raised his eyebrow at Tom, adding, "Not you. You wait here."

Tom saluted him.

Walker's mom smiled proudly at his father as if he'd accomplished something quite amazing by being not-so-cold to Ashton. "Come on you two," she said, looping her arm with Ashton's and starting to pull him across the room. "Let's go see Evelyn."

"Actually, if you don't mind, I think I'll stay here with Tom?" Ashton tugged his arm gently free of hers. "I feel like now is a time for family. Besides, I'd like to find some water before the ceremony, I'm a little thirsty."

"Oh, if you're sure?" She looked disappointed to have lost her grip on Ashton's arm, but he bent and pressed a kiss to her cheek and that had her lighting up like a Christmas tree again.

"I'm sure. Enjoy your family time before the wedding starts. I hear the whole day will go by so fast."

Walker pressed a kiss to Ashton's cheek and murmured, "Don't get into trouble without me."

"No promises," Ashton agreed, eyes flashing.

Walker's father didn't flinch at the kiss, which Walker considered another win.

In a spacious upstairs room reserved for the bridal party to prepare, Evelyn looked stunning in her white dress carrying a massive, red poinsettia flower bouquet. Her dark hair was pulled back into a bun with twirly curls by her ears and down at the nape of her neck where a beautiful, delicate tattoo of a camellia was visible. Tom's handiwork. He knew he was biased, but Walker thought his sister had never looked more lovely.

Just as they entered the room, their mother was pulled aside by the energetic and loud wedding planner who had a half-dozen questions for her as the mother-of-the-bride, apparently, leaving him alone to admire his sister for a long, unguarded minute. Spotting him, Evelyn turned away from her bridesmaids and rushed to his side.

Squeezing his arm, she asked under her breath, "You guys are ready for the reception? I told Ashton nothing is off limits. He can go all out. I just want to have every backbiting auntie or uncle looking at anyone but me."

"He's got it under control," Walker said, pulling Evelyn into a hug. "You look beautiful."

"Thank you." She leaned away to get a good view of Walker's face. "But seriously, he's really going to do this?"

"He's Ashton. He's really going to do it."

Her brown eyes glinted. "And you're going to let him?"

Walker laughed. "I'll let him do anything."

She punched his arm lightly, a grin taking over her face. "Yeah, I know."

"You know what?"

"That you're not faking it anymore. Either of you. But especially you." Evelyn took hold of his arms and tried to shake him lightly but only succeeded in shaking herself. "I think you're in love. For the first time ever." Her white dress swooshed around her feet as she swayed. "I *knew* it. I knew when you proposed this crazy scheme that it was all so you could get closer to him."

"No, it was to help you. Getting closer to him was a bonus."

"Ha!" She slapped his arm. "But it worked? And you're together? Really together? Not just pretending for the wedding?"

"We are."

She lifted up to whisper into his ear. "Do *not* mess this up. He's adorable."

"I know." Walker's stomach fluttered giddily and he knew he must look as smitten as he felt because Evelyn's smile grew even wider.

Suddenly, Evelyn's demeanor changed. With a furrow between her brows, she whispered, "Grandpa's here, you know. Dad said he's off smoking cigars somewhere."

"I haven't seen him." Admittedly, Walker had secretly half hoped that the old man just wouldn't come.

"He's in a good mood. Maybe he won't be hateful. As a kindness. For my wedding."

"We can hope."

She sucked air through her teeth. "Maybe just avoid him if you can?"

"Won't that make for awkward family photos? Me, trying to lean out of frame to stay away from an eighty-year-old man?"

"I just mean…" She crinkled her nose and bared her teeth in a grimace.

"I know. He's always been one to take a dig at me—or Dad for that matter—whenever he can. Ashton wants to meet him."

"Why?"

Walker rubbed his forehead. "Something about wanting to thank him for letting him stay in his house."

Her eyes widened. "Grandpa doesn't even know he's staying there, does he?"

Walker shook his head.

"Wow. Well, that fallout could be interesting. Use that if necessary. You know, to distract the vicious bitches."

"I don't care what Grandpa thinks of Ashton, but I do care what Ashton thinks of me."

"He doesn't know? About the house being Grandpa's?"

"He knows that much, but he doesn't know why I live there. He thinks I'm doing a favor for Grandpa."

Evelyn's eyes darkened with worry. "Ah. Walker, you can't move forward with him if you're keeping secrets."

"I know, but he…" Walker cleared his throat. He couldn't share Ashton's private business here in a room of eavesdropping bridesmaids. "He's special to me."

"I get that. He's a great guy, and you don't want to lose him. But lies always backfire."

"Everyone! Places! We have a wedding to put on!"

The wedding planner's voice cut into the room like a trumpet, high and loud, and Walker flinched. It was time to marry off his sister, not get into a heart-to-heart about his past mistakes and his new love.

"You look so beautiful," he said again, giving Evelyn a kiss on the temple. "I'll see you afterward for the family pictures."

"Bring Ashton up for them."

"No. If things don't work out with us—"

"Don't be negative."

Walker shook his head. It felt too much like tempting fate to ask

Ashton to be in the family pictures so soon. He'd ask the photographer to take a few special pictures of just him and Ashton in their suits as a memento of the day instead. Because wow, Ashton looked stunning in his well-fitted, burgundy suit with the bright, floral pocket square. How had he ever let Ashton's fashion choices bother him? He'd been an asshole. And afraid of what it meant to love a man like Ashton.

For fuck's sake, he'd been out as queer for years, and yet he'd somehow been living under the delusion that liking effeminate men meant he wasn't a man himself. How fucked up was that?

Walker shook those thoughts away and headed down to the now packed chapel. He recognized most people in attendance, even from Tom's side of the family. Morgan's parents, Aunt Brandy and Uncle Raymie, looked fit to be tied, but they'd chosen to come. If they were uncomfortable that was on them. Ashton would deal with them later.

Casey sat with his husband Joel, and near them Casey's father and mother sat with some of the other higher-ups of the oil company. Luckily there was no sign of Morgan in the crowd, which meant she really was going to keep her promise to Tom and the kids to stay away.

Layla and Brody were in the back with the bridesmaids being corralled until it was their time to walk down the aisle as the flower girl and ringbearer. Ashton had already taken a seat in the second row on the left side of the chapel. His glossy curls shone beneath the candlelight and stained glass, and just the sight of the nape of his neck made Walker's heart quicken.

As he hastened down the aisle to sit beside Ashton, out of the corner of his eye, he spotted Michael Amos and his brother Joey seated toward the back. Beside him were Hunter McMillan and his wife Bella, and next to them was goddamn Rupie Randolf—the man who'd won the final game of golf Walker had ever played and whose bank account now hosted the entirety of what had remained of Walker's former trust fund.

Heat rose up his neck, but he avoided eye contact with them all, taking his place beside Ashton quickly. Passing by to take his own seat in the front row, his grandpa gave him a tight nod, glancing curiously at Ashton. Walker braced himself for some sort of snide comment under his breath but none came.

Ashton gave him a bright smile. "Does she look beautiful?"

"So beautiful."

Ashton smiled softly, gracing Walker with a tender glance that made his stomach flutter with happy butterflies that overran the nervous ones.

Then came the sound of a few bows scraping against string, and after a few more tense heartbeats, joyful music flooded the chapel.

It was time.

As the double doors closed behind the last bridesmaid after the wedding party marched through, the music paused briefly before the bridal march began and the congregation rose. Ashton slipped his hand into Walker's and rubbed his thumb over Walker's knuckles.

Heart in his throat, Walker turned his attention to Ashton's bright gaze for a steadying moment. He wanted to kiss him but held back. There would be plenty of time for kissing later. The quartet started up again, and the doors swung open on Evelyn in her white dress looking stunning and his father in his black tux looking stunned.

The congregation breathed out as one. Ashton shifted in closer, and Walker slipped his arm around his waist. The scent of Ashton's aftershave mixed with the Christmas-y cinnamon in the air, and Walker's heart pounded with a thrilling joy. Perhaps he was foolish, and perhaps it was all happening too fast, but he believed one day he might be where Tom was now, waiting for Ashton to join him at the end of the aisle. Waiting for Ashton to make him the happiest man alive.

Walker glanced at Ashton's profile, surprised to see tears standing in Ashton's eyes as he watched Evelyn walk down the aisle. Seeing that Walker had caught him welling up, Ashton blushed but didn't bother wiping at his face as one tear slipped over the edge. "She's so gorgeous," he whispered to Walker, pressing a hand to his chest. "I'm so happy for her."

God, Walker's heart was going to explode. Ashton was too sweet. One day, one day, *one day* this could be them. His pulse thrummed the promise in an exhilarating rhythm, and it was only when the minister called the congregation to order that Walker realized he'd entirely missed his sister walking down the aisle because he'd been too busy staring at the man beside him.

It was all he could do not to watch Ashton throughout the ceremony too, every traditional word of it seeming more applicable and beautiful than ever before. And as Tom and Evelyn exchanged vows, their trembling "I dos" hanging in the air, he took hold of Ashton's hand and squeezed lightly, holding himself back from leaning over and whispering the phrase that permeated his mind.

*I will, Ashton. One day, I will.*

ASHTON THOUGHT THE ceremony had been beautiful, but he had to admit his favorite moment was when Walker had clenched his hand during the vows. He didn't want to make too much of it, but his heart had galloped wildly, and his mind had spun out fantasies of a future where Walker said similar words of promise to him in front of their friends, family, and heaven above.

But now the ceremony was over and done with. Time to set all of that aside. They had a job to do.

Operation Not-So-Fake Boyfriend was *on*.

"All right, let's get the gossip flowing our way before the bride and groom come back in," Ashton said, rubbing his hands together gleefully. Evelyn and Tom were out on the large deck area of The Venue having their photos made ten ways to Sunday with the wintery, white mountains in the background.

Walker still looked a little flushed and emotional, which was so adorable Ashton didn't know what to do with it. During the ceremony,

Walker had actually wiped at his own eyes twice. So cute. So loving. Ashton adored that his boyfriend was a big ball of silent feelings and affections. How had Ashton never known that before? How had he ever thought he was just flat, boring, *cardboard*?

"Okay, but first let's say hi to Casey," Walker said, steering Ashton across the room to where Casey and Joel stood peering out the windows of the reception hall, each clutching a champagne flute and looking a little wistful.

Ashton was curious to see Joel in a nice, if rather plain suit. The man lived in jeans, plaid, and T-shirts for obvious reasons—owning a home and garden store could be messy after all. But he cleaned up remarkably well. His dark hair sported some product to keep it in place, and his eyes sparked intelligently over his cheekbones.

He had an angular face, a little off-center in some way Ashton couldn't put his finger on, but he was a handsome guy. Every bit the opposite of blond, tall, muscular, all-American-looking Casey. Opposites did seem to attract, didn't they? In their own way, Ashton supposed he and Walker were opposites.

"You two look pensive. The ceremony bringing up memories of your big day?" Walker asked, hugging Casey and pounding him on the back in the most "bro" manner possible. Ashton smirked. Men. Both of his business partners were such dumbass *men*.

Joel was also apparently a man of that particular variety, because he punched Walker's shoulder and said, "Don't encourage him."

"Encourage him in what?" Ashton asked, keeping a sharp eye out for any clusters of gossip he should insinuate himself into and bust up.

"Nothing," Casey insisted.

"He suggested we have a vow renewal," Joel said with a grimace.

"Oh?" Ashton tilted his head. "But you just got married last year?"

"Exactly!" Joel said, tilting his champagne flute Ashton's way. "Besides why would a vow need renewing? Isn't that the point of a vow? That it's forever?"

"But this place is so beautiful," Casey said, gesturing around. "My parents would love it if we got married again here."

"Would they?" Joel asked. "Would they really? With me as the groom?"

"They love… well, they like you now. And they'd rather I marry you than someone else."

"You already did marry me, and there's no reason to do it again," Joel said, rolling his eyes. "I stand by my promises from that day. And I know you have too. So no. Just no."

Casey shrugged. "All right."

"That's it?" Walker scoffed. "You give me so much grief at work whenever you don't get your way, but when Joel says no to you, it's 'all right'? I see how it is."

"Believe me, he gives me plenty of grief when he doesn't get his way." Joel snorted. "All that easy capitulation means is that he just wanted to hear me say no."

Casey's lips twitched. "Is that what I wanted?"

"You like it when I put my foot down." Joel sipped champagne. "You think it's cute."

"I do."

"And you think my foot going down means something is negotiable if you really want it, and the subject is put to bed if you don't." Joel nudged Casey's arm. "The fact that you let my no stand means you weren't serious about the idea yourself."

"No vow renewal then?" Walker asked.

"It's a fun thought," Casey admitted. "But given how busy we are and how little he actually wants to do it, a vow renewal would mean letting my parents do most of the planning." Casey nodded across the room to where his cute, petite mom was chatting to some older woman with a pink scarf. "And they'd want to invite that crowd, so I'll just keep the memories of our quaint, homespun wedding in my heart and be happy with those."

"Yup," Joel said, clinking glasses. "Glad you came to your senses."

"It was just a fun fantasy."

"I know," Joel said, sliding his arm around Casey's waist and kissing his cheek.

"Anyway, today was beautiful. Evelyn seems happy."

"She is," Walker said. "And we like Tom, and obviously the kids are great." He nodded over to where the two children were tossing one of the bridesmaid's bouquets back and forth like a ball. No one stopped them. The pictures were mostly completed, and the bridesmaid in question was already digging into the fruit and veggie buffet. "They're all welcome additions to the family."

"Speaking of family, have you run into your grandfather yet?" Casey asked with what appeared to be a lot of sympathy.

Walker twitched, and Ashton frowned in confusion.

He'd noticed Walker's grandfather during the ceremony, of course. He'd been seated directly in front of them. The old man had been tall but stooped, with a fuzzy white beard and bright eyes that seemed to take in everything. It was like he'd been ready to insert a comment— probably a snarky one given his resting expression—at any moment during the ceremony. He hadn't of course, but he gave the impression that he was just barely holding his thoughts back.

Ashton hadn't met him yet. Everything had been so hectic since they'd arrived, what with the ceremony itself and tons of photos, which Ashton had refused Evelyn's invitation to take part in. He thought Walker's whole family was incredibly lovely, overall. Even his father, who clearly disapproved of Ashton for some unspecified reason, obviously loved Walker and Evelyn a whole lot, and that was evidence of enough goodness.

He wasn't sure what to make of Walker's tension at Casey's question about his grandfather or of the way Casey pointedly raised his brow when Walker said, "Not yet."

Walker's lips tilted in a smirk. "With any luck, I can avoid talking to him at all."

Casey chuckled. "Yeah. Maybe. Don't get your hopes up."

Joel interrupted. "Casey tells me you two have some sort of game afoot. What's the deal?"

"Oh, you know, a little bit of this and a little bit of that," Ashton said vaguely, not wanting to tip his hand with so many people around.

A woman passed close by, and Ashton clearly heard her say, "Can you believe she married him? Her cousin's own husband! Trash really. All of them."

Walker stiffened, and Joel stood up a little straighter like he thought those were some fighting words. But Ashton shook his head, putting his hand on Walker's forearm. "Ah, ah, ah. Operation Fake Boyfriend. Let's go."

Walker nodded and scanned the room. "There's my Uncle Darryl. We discussed him earlier." He nodded toward the open bar where Darryl snatched a glass of red from the bartender.

"We did indeed. And that's our cue," he said when Uncle Darryl started to make his way toward Morgan's parents. Evelyn had said that particular combination was always bad news, and Ashton knew what he had to do to make sure no petty arguments erupted before Evelyn and Tom could make their escape to their honeymoon.

The chairs were still being cleared away from the ceremony, but the DJ started playing some eighties music that had the children out in the middle of the cleared space doing a cute version of the twist while the adults watched with amusement. Observing from the sidelines, Morgan's mother stiffened as Darryl drew closer to her.

"C'mon," Ashton said, tugging on Walker's sleeve. "You have to introduce me before he starts a scene."

They dodged a few running kids who'd escaped their parents' clutches and scuttled past a few cousins on Morgan's side, all of whom they'd need to distract later. As they came closer to their first target, Ashton whispered, "I have a plan. Just tell him who I am and let me handle it."

"Uncle Darryl," Walker said, hugging the middle-aged man with reddish, graying hair and two stern lines between his brows from frowning all the time. "I wanted to introduce you to my boyfriend, Ashton Sellers." Walker gestured between them. "Ashton, this is Uncle Darryl, my father's brother."

"Wow, it's so good to meet you," Ashton said, sticking out his hand and pumping Darryl's arm enthusiastically. "You know, I was hoping to run into you today. I've heard a lot about you."

"You have?" He seemed stunned by that news.

"Yes! Evelyn says you're a financial advisor, right?"

"Yes," Darryl said, looking a little confused by Ashton in his entirety and not just by his eager interrogation.

"Great! Oh my goodness, I have so many questions. Do you have a moment?"

Darryl shot a glance toward Walker's dad and mom, who had come inside from the cold and moved toward the large, blazing fireplace at one end of the reception hall, taking up a smiling conversation with an old, blue-haired lady with crepe papery cheeks and a cane. Turning back to Ashton, Darryl sighed. "Sure, of course. What can I help you with?"

"First of all, I was curious. In order to advise people in your job, don't you have to... Oh, gosh, how can I put this?" Ashton tapped a finger on his chin thoughtfully and cocked a hip for effect. Uncle Darryl looked uncomfortable at this flamboyant display, but Ashton had to give him credit for not moving away.

"There are a lot of things I help people with in my line of work," Uncle Darryl said, handing Ashton a business card from inside his coat pocket. "We protect people from losses, help with investments for retirement, deal with—"

"Yes, of course, but to do all that don't you have to believe in money?"

Darryl blinked rapidly. "Excuse me? Believe in money?"

"Yes, you know. Don't you have to believe that it's real?" Ashton smiled winningly, pleased when Walker's uncle seemed to blink at the brightness of his grin—or the blindingness of his stupidity. Maybe both.

"That it's real…" he repeated like he thought he might be dreaming.

"I assume you do have to believe that and all," Ashton said sincerely, and he sensed Walker's body grow tight with his attempt to hold back laughter. He wouldn't look at Walker now. If he did, no doubt they'd both crack up and spoil the entire thing, so he pressed onward. "So, you can see how that's a problem for me. Can you explain to me, in say, two minutes or less, why money is real?"

Darryl shot Walker a disbelieving glance.

"I have to admit, I've always wondered why money is real myself," Walker said, and Ashton had to bite the inside of his cheek to keep from giggling.

Darryl cleared his throat and looked to Walker again. "I'm afraid that's a topic that will take longer than two minutes."

"Oh," Ashton said, letting the disappointment flood his voice and face. "I see. Five then?"

Darryl cleared his throat again and looked almost violently grateful when his wife (Ronnie, if Ashton remembered correctly) came up with a plate of food and said, "Darry, honey, let's get a table by the window before everyone gets the best spots."

"Excuse me gentlemen," he said with clear relief. "I have to go with my wife."

"I'll call you next week!" Ashton called, waving Darryl's business card in the air. "For that talk."

Darryl nodded at him and then put his hand at Ronnie's back, saying quietly, but not quietly enough, "Honey, Walker is dating a goddamn lunatic."

"But what a beautiful lunatic," his wife added, glancing back over her shoulder. "Look at his shoulders-to-waist ratio."

"Who cares about that? The man doesn't believe money is real."

"What?" Ronnie laughed. "Pretty and stupid? He must be good in bed."

Ashton clapped when they were out of earshot. "Perfect. Now they'll have plenty to talk about over there by the window with all their gossiping friends." True to his words, two couples joined them at the table and within seconds they were all peering at Walker and Ashton.

Clapping and cheers from near the entrance told them Evelyn and Tom had come back inside after completing the final photographs. "All right, now that they're back in the room, we'll have to work extra hard to keep the backbiters distracted."

Ashton's eyes clapped on to his next target, and he grabbed Walker's arm. "C'mon. I'll need an introduction again before I work my magic."

# Chapter Twenty-Two

"**B**UT HOW DO you deal, you know, *morally* with the fact that universities are a scam?" Ashton asked, all wide-eyed and innocent as he sipped his champagne, again cocking a hip.

Walker's heart beat hard, and he felt sweaty all over. He just knew that the wake of confusion and shock they'd already left behind them had the entire room buzzing about anything but Evelyn and Tom's history with Morgan. Which was what they'd wanted, and yet it was a lot more intense now that he was in it. The fear of being busted, of taking it too far—it left him shaky, giddy, and a little sick.

The rush of *that* was also familiar and disturbing.

This? Operation Not-So-Fake Boyfriend? This was a gamble. And not a pretty one either, no matter how much his sister had wanted them to pony up for it.

Ashton's current target, Samuel Jones, one of Morgan's cousins (and a distant cousin of Walker's too) was a dean at the local university, and, at the moment, he seemed a cross between offended and amused. "A scam? Just how, young man, are universities a scam?"

Ashton blinked like he was surprised that Samuel didn't know. "Well, because you pay tens of thousands of dollars, sometimes hundreds of thousands, for a degree that won't even guarantee you a job? You can come out of an education in a worse financial situation than when you went in. That sounds like a scam to me?"

Samuel scoffed. "That's not what a university education is for. You aren't paying for the guarantee of a job. That's trade school! University is for an *education.* You're paying for the improvement of yourself, your mind, and your understanding of the world."

"Well, like I said…sounds like a scam." Ashton smiled and clinked his champagne glass against Samuel's and took a long sip.

Walker was convinced his cousin was going to have a conniption fit, but instead the man simply stomped off.

"Was that okay?" Ashton asked, his voice tremulous with anxiety.

"It was perfect."

Ashton smiled. "Thank you. On to the next, then, right?"

"Right."

*Four encounters later…*

"POOKIE, WHY DON'T you kiss it and make it better," Ashton said with a pout, lifting his finger to Walker's lips. He'd caught it in his own teeth earlier when trying not to laugh too hard at a target's outrage, and he'd shaken it again and again like it really did hurt.

Walker leaned forward and gave his finger a tender kiss and then kissed Ashton soundly on the lips.

"Ah, ah, ah," Ashton said, pushing against Walker's chest as he tried to wrap Ashton into an embrace. "Not here, darling. Later. In our hotel room. Where you can have *all* of me."

Walker's homophobic cousins sat at the table beside them, eating wedding cake and looking utterly scandalized. Mission accomplished.

Take that, suckers.

*Two encounters later…*

"AH, I SEE," Ashton said, having inserted himself into a discussion between Morgan's mother, Brandy, and Evelyn's best friend from college, Jenna Leigh, and deftly twisted the conversation to the two women's different positions on abortion. "So, you're saying you think abortion is killing a baby?"

Brandy puffed up. "It is! It's murder!"

"Murder is a strong word for the destruction of a few cells early in a pregnancy," Jenna Leigh said, rolling her eyes.

"But she thinks you *are* killing something," Ashton said, indicating Jenna Leigh and chomping on a piece of cheese. "A very little something, but something all the same. Do I understand that right?"

"Well—"

"So would this be a compromise between your positions? Maybe it's murder, but it's not *bad* murder," he offered, looking for all intents and purposes like an absolute innocent. Walker was across the way loading up a plate with fruit and vegetables for them to share and leaving him to the madness of stoking this particular flame. He wanted nothing to do with it.

"All murder is *bad* murder!" Brandy exclaimed. "What on earth? What a thing to say!"

"But maybe not," Ashton said. "Like, don't you believe in the death penalty? I think you said something about that earlier, didn't you? When we were talking about pedophiles?"

Walker stopped in his tracks. Talking about pedophiles? At a wedding? Ashton must have brought that nightmare of a subject up while Walker was in the bathroom.

"Well, *pedophiles* aren't innocent little *babies*!"

"Ah, right. So they deserve it. I'm trying to fully understand your position," Ashton said with a nod. "Hm, but what if the baby grows up to be a pedophile and you could have stopped it with an abortion in the womb? What then?"

Jenna Leigh stared at Ashton like he'd grown a second head before she caught Walker's eye. She must have read something there, some glint of amusement or giddiness, because suddenly her own expression changed to conspiratorial, and she said, "Yes, what then, Brandy? What if every abortion prevents a pedophile from being born?"

"What if it's God's will?" Ashton asked, leaning down to look Brandy in the eye.

"Bull-hooey! You're both disgusting, amoral sinners. What do you know about God's will?" Brandy stomped away.

"I'm definitely a sinner," Ashton called after her. "Prayers accepted! Thank you!"

Jenna Leigh chuckled as Walker approached. "I don't know what game the two of you are playing here, but that was fun. Mean, but fun."

Ashton bowed to her with a flourish. "Thank you. You were a delight as well."

Jenna Leigh squeezed his arm happily before moving on to sit near the chocolate fountain and commandeering Layla to collect chocolate-covered strawberries for her.

"Now, is there anyone left?" Ashton asked, his cheeks flushed with success and his eyes glowing. "Or have I scandalized them all?"

"I'm sure there are a few people still in need of being boggled."

"Dazzled," Ashton corrected, taking an apple wedge from Walker's plate and chomping on it. "Let me fuel up, and then we'll tackle that knot of cousins over there. They look like they need to be appalled."


*Six encounters later…*

THE RECEPTION WAS a whirlwind of wide eyes, shocked gasps, and outraged whispers. And none of them were directed at Evelyn or Tom. In fact, Evelyn and Tom were nowhere to be seen, having taken off ten minutes before amidst ridiculous jokes about how eager they must be to start their honeymoon if they were leaving their reception so early.

But Evelyn and Tom hadn't seemed to care as they kissed the kids goodbye, hugged all the family, and climbed into Tom's shaving cream-covered Ford Ranger. Shortly thereafter, Walker's parents had departed with the kids, instructing everyone remaining to enjoy the DJ, the food, and the open bar for another hour until the end of their allotted time with the reception hall.

It was over. They'd done it.

Ashton was obviously proud of their performance, and Walker was too, though even he'd been shocked by some of the things that had issued from Ashton's mouth over the last hour and a half. But they'd succeeded! Together they'd pulled it off perfectly.

"I personally thought asking the CFO of your father's company about his planned increase in budget for green energy 'given that oil is responsible for most of the climate crisis' was fantastic. He nearly lost it trying to explain to me that there is no planned budget for green energy, while I kept insisting that he must have one since the world is on fire— literally—and he nearly foamed at the mouth."

"That was Casey's dad, you know," Walker said, elbowing him. "It wasn't necessary to needle him at all, actually. He's not family or a gossip."

"I know. I just liked calling him out as the CFO of the company. They need to make some changes and soon."

Walker laughed, popping a grape into his mouth and slinging an arm around Ashton's shoulders. "Oh, so you took a political break from the agenda?"

"Of course. Fake boyfriend's prerogative."

"But you're not my fake boyfriend anymore."

Ashton grinned widely. "No, I'm not."

"So just boyfriend's prerogative." Walker nuzzled his cheek and pressed a kiss there.

"Boyfriend. Wow."

"*You're* wow," Walker said, his heart thumping, wishing they were alone so that he could show Ashton just how *much* he made him feel. "*So* wow."

"Tell me more about that." Ashton giggled. "I'm all ears about the wonders of me."

"Most of what I want to say to you can't be said here." He waggled his brows. "But everything about today has proved to me how stunning you are."

"Like?" Ashton egged him on for details.

"Like when you handled my cousins so perfectly." He glanced toward the group of sort-of-relatives all talking and looking their way. "Pretending that you're my sub was a bit much, I admit, but they went wild with whispers when you obeyed every request I made like you were afraid I'd bring out the whip right then and there if you didn't."

"Gerald and that whole experience came in handy for something. Thank God."

Walker winced. He hadn't intended to bring up bad memories, and it'd been Ashton's idea to play up the BDSM speculation, but he never wanted to remind Ashton of bad times. Ashton was still shining with joy over their success, so he let his concern go.

"For the next group of backbiters we target, if we keep on with this, we should try playing it the other way. I'm the dom and you're the—"

A screech cut through the air, and all heads whipped toward the front of the reception area.

"Shit, it's Morgan." Walker's stomach lurched. All their work was about to be undone in a matter of moments.

"Oh!" Ashton gasped. "I hadn't pictured her looking like that."

Walker grimaced. Morgan had always been a beautiful woman, and not even her poor life choices took away from her ample bosom and apple-blossom eyes. Though he imagined it was only a matter of time before the partying took its toll. "Yeah. She's pretty."

"Where's that bitch? Where is she?" Morgan screamed. "Tryin'a steal my kids. Tryin'a steal my husband?" Her speech was slurred, and she was weaving as she pushed through the dwindled crowd, obviously drunk or high or both. "Where are you, slut?"

"Ah, man," Ashton said. "Hold my drink."

He shoved the drink at Walker and stalked toward Morgan. "Babe!" he cried. "Amazing! I'm so glad you're here! Sad thing is, you missed the ceremony and the bride and the groom and the kids too. They're already gone. Let me get you a ride home!"

She blinked up at Ashton, apparently dazzled by his shockingly beautiful face. When he took hold of her elbow and steered her right around and back out the front door of the reception hall, she simply went with him wordlessly.

The entire room went up in loud exclamations as Walker followed Ashton outside into the night. Hands grabbed at him and questions flew, but he didn't stop. When he stepped outside the double door and onto the gravel drive, he found his grandfather standing there with a cigar and a confused expression.

Aunt Brandy and Uncle Raymie exited directly behind him, heading across the drive and straight for their daughter. As Walker moved to join them, his grandfather grabbed his arm and pulled him around. Grandpa was stronger than he looked, and Walker was shocked at his hold on him.

"You're seeing that young man?"

Walker nodded, keeping his eye on Ashton, his aunt, uncle, and cousin. Anxiety shot through him. He needed to get over there and help.

Grandpa hummed, not letting go. "Interesting choice. He's orchestrated quite a lot of gossip today. Your mother is pretending oblivion to all of it, but your father isn't impressed with all this malarkey." He tugged at his beard and gazed at Walker. His blue eyes were steely like they'd been back when Walker had confessed his mistakes and subsequent situation to him last year. "Much of it is of a nature that could affect your business, young man."

"My business is fine." Walker wasn't about to explain that his business was founded on the idea that this kind of thing was…good for business actually? It was the antithesis of everything his grandfather and father believed about the world and what people wanted from the companies they hired.

"So you say," Grandpa said slowly. "But don't you care about your father's business anymore?"

Walker gave up trying to get away from his grandfather, settling for watching Ashton maneuver Morgan and her parents farther away from the reception hall and into the middle of the parking lot. He snorted at his grandfather's implication. "Is there anything that could really touch him?"

"His son being with a pervert could, yes."

Walker whirled on him. "Ashton might be effeminate, but he's not a pervert."

Grandpa blew a raspberry with his lips. "What's effeminate got to do with it? I'm talking about the kinky games, son." He rolled his eyes. "I've got no problem with a girly man. But the kinky stuff?" He wiped his mouth with the back of his veiny hand and chuckled. "Well, I guess I don't have a problem with that either." His brows waggled. "Your grandma and I played a lot of games in our youth too. But that's not the point. The point is what you do in your bed is no one's business but your own! Your beau was practically broadcasting it all to the room."

Walker's cheeks heated. He cleared his throat. "Grandpa, it's hard to explain, but Evelyn wanted us to—"

Aunt Brandy cried out from where she stood with Ashton and Morgan halfway across the parking lot. "You can't do that!"

Ashton just smiled winningly. "I can actually." Their voices carried on the winter wind.

"But, but...you!" She seemed to be trying to collect the worst thing she could say about the beautiful and calm man in front of her. "You approve of *murdering babies*!"

Ashton smiled cheerfully at Morgan. "Now, babe. This isn't the place for you. Let's get you home so you can see your kids this week instead of seeing the inside of a jail cell, which is sadly the direction I think you were headed just now. Don't you?"

"You can't threaten her like that!" Uncle Raymie exclaimed.

"Raymond, there was no threat involved," Ashton said with steel in his tone now. "I'm simply arranging for her—and you—to go home.

She's not fit to drive. Are you two?"

"We came with my *mother*!" Aunt Brandy screeched.

"Oh? Rosemary?"

"Yes," Aunt Brandy said and sniffed for emphasis.

"She's such a lovely lady."

Aunt Brandy paused. "Thank you."

"And, well, I think she probably doesn't need to see this mess, do you?" He indicated Morgan, which made Aunt Brandy huff, but Uncle Raymie's eyebrows twitched like he actually agreed. "We can arrange for her to make it home safe and sound, I promise. You three should go on ahead. There's nothing of interest here now anyway." He smiled again, heart-stopping and stunning in the moonlight with freshly falling snow dusting his dark hair. "I mean, yawn." He did yawn then, big and wide, with a hand over it to hide his teeth. "So much boring cheerfulness in there, all those good wishes being tossed around for the long-gone bride and groom. Gag. Gross." He leaned a little closer to Morgan. "Time to get out of here, don't you think?"

"You nasty little…!" Aunt Brandy huffed, cutting off whatever insult she'd planned to levy.

But Ashton seemed to have captivated Morgan, who just gazed up at him like he might have been an angel descended from heaven. Walker understood.

"Grandpa, I just need to—" Walker motioned toward the little group with Ashton dominating the center.

"Nah, you stay here. I think he's got this handled," Grandpa said, digging around in his pocket and pulling out a lighter and another cigar. "Smoke?"

He wrinkled his nose. "No."

"Suit yourself."

The wind had shifted, so Walker couldn't hear much anymore. Ashton had his arm around Morgan's shoulders. She gazed at him, obviously disoriented, as he jabbered to her and her parents and tapped at his phone with his free hand. Aunt Brandy and Uncle Raymie couldn't seem to get a word in edgewise.

When an Uber immediately broke free from the line waiting to deal with wedding reception guests, Walker watched in awe as Ashton maneuvered Morgan and her parents into the car and gave instructions to the driver, as well as a big cash tip. He waved the car off wildly, like a Victorian host farewelling family who were finally leaving after a very long, rather hellish, three-week visit.

As soon as the car was around the bend and off into the mountains, Ashton's shoulders drooped, and he sighed, clearly exhausted. Once he straightened up and turned to where Walker stood with his grandfather, a smile broke out over his face again, and he gave a victory arm pump.

Walker shot him a thumbs up and signaled him closer.

Near the door to the reception hall, a small huddle of people stood, half in and half out, clearly lingering there for the show.

"Well," Ashton said, dusting off his hands. "I think I earned my keep today, don't you?"

"You did," Grandpa said. "Explain yourself, young man."

"Ashton, this is my grandfather, Eugene Ronson. Grandpa, this is my boyfriend and business partner, Ashton Sellers."

"Ashton," Grandpa said, shaking his hand. "So what the hell, boy? You trying to stir up a bunch of gossip and drama here today or what?"

"That's right," Ashton said with a proud grin. "How'd you guess?"

"Simple observation. Doesn't take a genius."

"I guess not. Can we tell him, Walker? Now that's it's almost over? I mean, what could be worse than that?" He gestured over his shoulder where the Uber had pulled away with Morgan and her parents. "I figure our work has been completely undone anyway. All anyone is going to talk about now is how Morgan showed up and called the bride a slut. All our planning, all our shenanigans, down the drain." He laughed, passing his hand over his eyes. "I mean…wow. What a day!"

Grandpa chuckled too. "This has been some scheme has it?" He turned to Walker. "What was it? Another lost bet? How much are you out this time? Since you gambled away your entire trust fund already, I hope you haven't also gambled away my damn house."

Ashton's smile faltered. Ice hit Walker's veins. He cleared his throat, trying to think of a reply. "Your…your house is fine."

"Better be. Nothing left to bail you out with if it's not." He put the cigar out with the heel of his shoe, and slipped the unfinished half back into his suit jacket. "Well, grab one of those cars for me, young man. I want to get out of here tonight. Got a late flight to catch back to Florida, where the weather is accommodating and not bullshit cold like this." He slapped Walker's back. "Pet the dogs for me."

As Ashton led him toward the line of cars, glancing back at Walker with a pale, vulnerable expression on his face, Grandpa turned back around and shook his finger at Walker. "I mean it, boy. Don't gamble with my house."

"I won't. I don't…do that anymore."

Ashton's face tightened, and Walker hated the sound of his high-pitched, anxious voice as he instructed a regular taxi driver on where to take Grandpa. "Oh, all the way to the airport? That's quite the drive…you're sure? All right."

Walker watched, icy wind shifting through his hair and his heart feeling like a hard stone in his chest as Grandpa shook hands with Ashton, climbed into the taxi, and was carried away.

Ashton didn't move. He simply stood, hands at his side, a frozen, distrustful expression on his face. Walker's stomach roiled. He'd seen that expression before. The night they'd run into Ashton's mother.

The night he'd first seen Ashton's wounds.

# Chapter Twenty-Three

THEIR DRIVE VIA the hired car back down the mountain to the Inn at Christmas Place was brutal. Except for the awkward replies Walker gave to the driver, it was silent, and when Walker tried to reach for Ashton's hand, he pulled it away.

Walker didn't sense anger, though. Just confusion, fear, and a cold brittleness, like frost had settled over Ashton's skin.

He wanted to explain, but a hired car with a witness wasn't where he wanted to have this conversation. For his sake and for Ashton's, they needed some privacy. It would have to wait for the hotel at the very least.

His pulse pounded, his chest and throat tight. Tears pricked at his eyes. He needed to fix this, to have all the right words lined up by the time they were safely alone together, but all he heard was throbbing white noise, and all he could see was Ashton's expression as Grandpa's words had clicked into his understanding.

The winding of the mountain road made him nauseous, or maybe that was his guilt? He tried to swallow but found his mouth dry.

It took forever to make their way through the remaining traffic on Parkway to the hotel. Ashton jumped out without a word and headed inside as Walker delivered his thanks to the driver and opened the app to finalize payment. He caught up to Ashton at the elevators.

The scent of fir and peppermint sickened him now.

"Please," he said, taking hold of Ashton's elbow. "Let me explain."

"Oh, you'll explain," Ashton said tightly, tugging his arm away.

"When we get to the room. You'll explain."

It sounded like a threat, and Walker shivered. He tried to get a good look at Ashton's face, but he kept it turned down. When he finally did see him in the mirror in the elevator, his knees went weak with apprehension. Ashton's expression seemed to flit between rage and fear and hope. It was devastating, and that little bit of hope was more than Walker deserved but everything he needed to have hope himself.

"Now," Ashton said, sitting on the bed newly made by housekeeping, crossing his legs, placing his hands on his knees, and giving Walker a hard, angry stare. "Talk. Don't leave anything out. I mean it, Walker. Not a detail."

He swallowed hard and sat in a chair by the table, knowing that sitting beside Ashton right now wasn't the right move. "I don't have a good excuse for what I did back then. All I need you to understand is that I don't do it anymore."

"It?"

"Gambling. I don't gamble anymore."

Ashton swallowed hard, his Adam's apple bobbing. "But you did gamble." A statement, not a question.

"I did. It was a rough patch in my life—"

Ashton rolled his eyes and held up his hand. "Stop."

"I thought you wanted to hear it."

"I want to hear the truth, not excuses."

Walker swallowed hard, his head aching and his hands shaking. "It's not an excuse. I was hanging out with guys who—"

"Of course. It's someone else's fault. Let me guess, that Michael Amos from the bachelor party? He's the one to blame? That's why you hate him?"

Ashton sounded so disgusted, and Walker didn't know how to rein in his assumptions. "Let me explain."

"Did you really gamble away your entire trust fund?"

"I did."

"And Casey knows?"

Walker nodded.

Ashton's eyes grew darker, so that the green fairly glowed. "He knew this about you, and he let me get entangled with you anyway? Not this," he gestured between them. "Because he doesn't even know about this—but as business partners? He knew?"

"Yes, Casey knows."

"He knew…" Ashton blinked and whispered again, "Casey knew."

"Yes."

"And no one thought to tell me before I put *everything* I have into a business with a fucking addict as a partner?"

Walker winced. "Listen, that's not—"

"That's exactly what's happened here." Ashton's voice trembled. "I've tried so hard. So *hard* to get addicts out of my life. To be safe. Now I'm not safe." His mouth snapped shut. He had gone so pale Walker worried he might pass out. "Oh fuck, oh, heavens. Why?" He whispered as he dropped his head between his knees, hyperventilating as gasping sobs welled up. "Why? Why?" He said the word again and again. "Why?"

Walker moved toward him, but Ashton jerked up, shooting a leg out as if to kick him away. "Don't come close to me right now," he gasped. "Stay back. Stay away."

"Ashton," Walker whispered. "You're grown, and you *are* safe."

"Shut up!" he screamed, loud enough for Walker to jerk back. "Get away from me."

"Why? Just let me—"

"Why? Because you are *not safe.*"

"Please—"

"Get out," Ashton said, pointing at the door. "Go. Just go."

"It's not what you think. I haven't gambled in a long time, and I didn't gamble before that rough patch in my life, and—"

"Go! Get away! Get out! Leave! Just leave! *Leave!*"

Ashton was screaming the word with every breath, his PTSD clearly kicking in, escalating with each word Walker spoke, and Walker didn't know what to do except obey. He grabbed his bag with whatever was in it, abandoning the rest of his stuff strewn about the room. He stopped at the door.

"How will you get home?"

"Leave!"

"All right. But, please, Ashton…. Tell me you'll take an Uber. I can order you one now if you want? Or take a regular cab and I'll pay for it. Just come home, okay? I'll be waiting for you there. Please, just come right home to me. We can talk about it."

"Leave, leave, leave!"

Walker did as he was ordered, cold devastation rushing through him as he waited for the elevator alone. He could hear Ashton's sobs from the room all the way down the hall. He started to head back but realized he didn't have a room key on him. He'd left it on the table in the room.

Banging on the door wouldn't make Ashton let him in. Somehow, he knew it would simply send Ashton over the edge even more, so he headed down to the front desk where he made sure his credit card was on file and told them to allow Ashton to charge anything on it for as long as he wanted. Then he sat in his car in the parking lot for a long time in the darkness trying to process what had happened. How it'd all gone so wrong.

Sick with disappointment in himself and twisted up with fear, he texted Ashton. Small things like: *I'm still here. We could still talk.* No reply. *I'm worried about you.* Nothing. *I can't leave until I know you're safe* got an answer, though.

*I've ordered an Uber. Just go.*

Walker quickly tapped out: *Meet me at home?*

That went unanswered, of course, and he chewed on his lip, thinking of where else Ashton might go. His own apartment. His stepsister's place. A friend's house. The office. He sent one more message: *Please. I'll be waiting for you at home.*

Ashton left him on read.

The word *home* rattled around Walker's brain. His house had never felt like home to him before Ashton had come. Would it ever again?

Walker's hands shook as he pushed them through his hair. He moved the car to a vantage point in the lot where he could see the doors to the reception area. He waited until Ashton came outside still wearing his burgundy suit and looking like he'd been to war instead of a wedding. He climbed into a waiting Subaru, and Walker started his car again as Ashton's lift pulled away.

His attempt to follow was blocked by a huge truck that began backing up toward the hotel, attempting to make a late delivery of some kind. It was ten minutes before Walker could get out of the parking lot and start his journey home.

Alone.

# Chapter Twenty-Four

ASHTON HADN'T ACTUALLY planned to go to Walker's house. As he'd ridden in the Uber back toward Knoxville, he'd thought he'd just return to his old apartment—thank heavens they hadn't had time to move his stuff yet—but the idea of sitting alone in all that mess was more than his nerves could take. He'd considered going to Casey and Joel's house for comfort since they'd only come up for the wedding and weren't staying over, but rage rose in him again at the thought that Casey had known about Walker's addiction and simply not said anything.

Casey had *known*. About everything.

There was one more place Ashton could probably go, so he sent a quick text and got an urgent affirmative. But he couldn't go there right away. He needed his things, because he couldn't just live in this tight, burgundy suit that felt like it was strangling out what little life was left in him, and the suitcase he'd packed for the trip was full of clothes that would only remind him of the perfect, beautiful, wonderful day leading up to his horrible understanding that he'd been taken in by an addict yet again.

He gave the Uber driver a new address and fought nausea the entire hour-long drive.

In Walker's driveway, Ashton dropped his suitcase on the concrete and stared at the empty place where Walker's car should have been sitting, promising a confrontation he'd spent the entire drive preparing to have. The house sat dark.

So where was Walker anyway?

Probably off gambling. He'd probably pulled off the road and down-loaded a gambling app and was busy getting his fix. That's what addicts did. A little problem would come their way, make them uncomfortable, and their first move would be to go back to their drug of choice.

Fuck Walker. Fuck him and all of his excuses. Rough patch, his *ass*.

Still, Ashton hated the idea of going into the house—the place he'd so recently felt safe and secure—and he considered getting back into the Uber before it backed away. He didn't need his things, did he? He could always buy more clothes and toiletries and whatever else of his was tucked away in Walker's guest room. And he could just dump Walker's stuff he'd collected from the hotel room at the office come Monday. But no. He could do this. He could face this alone. Just like he'd faced every shitty thing in his life alone.

Even if he didn't have his own key buried deep in his luggage some-where, he knew where the spare was hidden. It was easier to get to, so he dug it out from the hole beneath a rock in the garden and keyed into the side door.

No dogs barked or came running out.

Right, they were at the boarders'. Safe from this storm that had blown in between him and Walker. At least he didn't have to fake happiness by greeting them. At least he didn't have to say goodbye to their sweet faces too.

Ashton walked as steadily as he could manage through the house and up the stairs to the room he'd stayed in so happily. The last few nights before the wedding trip, he'd slept in Walker's room, but all of his things were still here. He just needed to gather them and get out before Walker came back. It couldn't be that hard. Walker was probably going to be working on his gambling fix for a while.

He sat on the bed, trying to breathe against the tightness around his chest. Was he having a heart attack? Was it supposed to hurt like this? Ending something with someone he actually cared about? Someone he'd actually thought he could love?

"Come on, get it together," he whispered. "You can do this. You have to do this."

Ashton opened the closet and stared at the clothes hanging there. The suitcase he'd left out on the carport was full, and he had no other. With a trembling hand, he grabbed the wadded up black trash bag he'd thrown onto the floor beneath his pants and shook it open. He felt dizzy.

He was back to this again.

He could never escape this.

Ashton began to stuff the clothes down into the bag, not caring about the wrinkles or damage as he shoved them inside. His head ached, and his chest was so tight he really felt like he might pass out. With every clothing item he'd brought wadded into the bag, he headed to the bathroom, where he grabbed his toothbrush, cleansers, and razor blades. His hands shook so much as he tried to put the safety cap on the razor that he nicked himself. Blood welled and he ripped toilet paper from the roll, wrapping it around the end of his index finger, feeling faint.

Sitting on the toilet, Ashton was sweaty and sick. The entire drive he'd thought of all the things he'd say to shut down Walker's defense when he arrived, and instead he found himself alone sweating with nausea and absolute despair. He'd trusted Walker. He'd been so foolish. What was wrong with him? Was he permanently damaged from his childhood? Was his ability to detect bullshitters utterly broken? Was he doomed to be alone because anyone he gave his heart to was going to end up being a lying addict who was just using him for—

For what?

What had his mother been using him for? Money typically. But what had Walker wanted from him? Sex, obviously, but… That hadn't been the way it'd started. That wasn't what had brought them together. And Ashton had no money, not the kind Walker would need to feed an active gambling addiction, and Walker had known that; he'd always known that.

*Shut up*, he commanded his rebellious mind. *You don't get to hope. You don't get to try to convince me I'm wrong, understand? You just get to be glad we survived. So just shut up.*

His attention shifted over to the tub and the box of half-used bath bombs resting on the edge. All the suggestive names of the bombs. All the sweet hope he'd felt every time he used one. The way they'd made him feel cherished. Adored. Even before he'd fully understood what his feelings were, or what it could mean that Walker had bought these for him. He should leave them behind. Forget about them. Never use a bath bomb again, as ridiculous as that was.

He rose on shaky legs, clutching the black plastic bag. Before he could change his mind, he snatched up the bath bomb box and shoved it inside. The scents were nice, and he deserved everything Walker had given him, including the ring still on his finger.

The question was, did he want it?

Hot tears stung his eyes as he held his hand up, the spark and color of the opals catching even in the low light of the bathroom. He'd wanted the ring to mean something, but now, like everything else, it meant nothing at all. And yet the idea of taking it off made his heart crack open with pain. A tear slipped down his cheek, and he batted it away.

"Enough," he whispered. "Get your stuff and let's go."

A creak came from the doorway, and Ashton whirled around. Walker stood in the hallway, his body blocking the only exit from the bathroom. Ashton's heart pounded, and his throat ached. Walker had no right to be standing there looking like that, like he was the one wronged, like he was the victim here—all puppy-eyes and defeated, downturned shoulders. Fuck him.

"You came. I was afraid you wouldn't." Walker's voice shook. He put out his palms and begged. "Please hear me out."

Ashton swallowed hard and forced out his answer. "No."

Walker closed his eyes and gathered a breath before plowing ahead with his excuses. "I get that you're upset, but you don't understand the full context of what happened. I know it's a lot to ask right now, but I'd like it if you gave me a chance to explain. You'll see then how this situation is different from what happened in your past."

"That's what every addict says. There's always a reason they're different."

Walker ran a hand over his face. "Look, I'm not an addict."

Ashton crossed his arms over his chest and set his jaw.

"I'm not."

Ashton shook his head.

"What's the definition of an addict?"

"You tell me."

Walker said, "Someone exhibiting a compulsive, chronic, or obsessive need for a habit-forming substance, behavior, or activity—"

"Did you Google that on the way home?"

"In the driveway."

Ashton snorted and rolled his eyes. "All right. That's the definition—tell me how you don't fit it. Tell me why you're a special case."

Walker swallowed hard, sagging against the door frame, still effectively blocking Ashton in the bathroom. It made his heart pound to be so hemmed in, and yet he didn't want to touch Walker, not even to shove him out of his way.

"It wasn't a compulsion for me. It never was. It was defiance."

"Whatever," Ashton said, shoving off the counter, grabbing the plastic bag, and pushing his way past Walker after all. "It was defiance, sure. All right. You defiantly gambled away your trust fund and who knows what else."

"Just the trust fund."

"Great, just an entire fucking trust fund. Love that for you." He started down the stairs. He could make it out of here. He could get free from this and be safe again.

"Ashton, don't do this. It doesn't have to be like this."

He took the stairs two at a time as he fought down a sob. Flashes of memory screamed in his mind: needles, overdoses, lies, promises, black trash bags, shame…

His knees buckled as he passed through the living room, and Walker caught him, helping him to sit on the sofa. "I'm fine," Ashton gritted out, still gripping the trash bag tightly. "Just let me get my things and I'll go. It'll be over."

Walker knelt at his feet and said gently, "You know it won't be."

"It will," Ashton insisted. "It has to be."

"We work together."

He closed his eyes and shook his head. How was he supposed to go into the office now? Get work done? Look at Walker's face in meetings? Knowing that Walker had conned him, knowing that Walker had lied and stolen from Ashton something he'd never get back. Not just his heart, but his last bit of trust.

"Ashton…"

"I felt safe with you."

This close, Ashton could see that Walker's skin was blotchy, and his eyes shone with tears. "I'm sorry. I never meant for you to find out."

"That doesn't make it any better. If anything, that makes it worse." He whispered through chattering teeth, "That's addict talk, you know. That's what every addict wants to believe. 'This time it'll be different. This one time no one will have to know.'"

"That's not the reason I didn't want you to find out. I'm not… I mean, I don't…" Walker sat back and tore his hand through his hair. "I didn't tell you because it's not who I am anymore. All of that's my past, and I wanted you—I *still* want you—to be my future."

"Do you know how many times my mom told me that? How many times she said she was going to stop and put me first and—" Ashton's voice broke.

"I know, baby—"

"Don't!"

"All right." Walker's voice was so soft, so quiet, like he wanted Ashton to lean in and really listen. He was tempted to, but… "But this is different."

Ashton hissed. "Oh, I'm sure it is. It's always different with addicts."

"I'm telling you, and I need you to hear me: I'm not an addict."

"No matter how you want to twist the definition, people don't gamble their trust funds away without being addicts, Walker."

"Well, I did. I'm not saying I didn't have a problem, but the problem wasn't being helplessly hooked on gambling. My problem was how trapped I felt, how suffocated I was in my life, and—" He broke off and wiped a hand over his face. "Baby, I'm happy to explain it all to you, step by step, exactly what happened, and why I ended up in that situation—"

"Ha! 'Ended up in that situation.' Like you tripped and fell. Another sign of an addict is refusal to take responsibility for their choices."

"All right," Walker said grimly. "I'll tell you exactly what choices I made—*me*, because you're right, *I* made them—to get myself into that situation. But what I need for you to understand is that this *is* different from your mom or Justin. I'm different from them."

Ashton almost wanted to believe him. The hook in his heart was that deep, that strong. "How?"

"Because they promised to quit *for* you, or at least your mom did. I don't know about Justin's reasons for trying to quit." Walker rose up to his knees. "But I don't need to quit gambling for you or anyone else. Because I *already* quit—for myself. Over a year ago. It's over and done for me. This—right now, between us, whatever happens—isn't going to send me back to it. I have *no desire* to be that person again."

Ashton swallowed hard, his throat working.

"And I don't *need* you in my life to stay clear of gambling. Your mom said she'd do it for you, right? But I don't need you for my life to be okay, for *me* to be okay. I don't have to use you as some kind of inspiration to stay on the straight and narrow. I've already done that work. On my own. For my own reasons. And what I know is that I wasn't an addict, I was a miserable person, making myself more miserable until I got free. Do you understand?"

Ashton blinked away tears.

"I don't need you. I just want you. That's the difference." He put his hands out, pleading for Ashton to understand. "I want you as a lover and a friend. I *want* you."

"Ten hours ago," Ashton gasped out. "I'd have done anything to hear you say how much you want me, but now… It doesn't matter." He tightened his grip on the trash bag and stood up. "Because I don't want you."

Walker didn't stop him on his way to the door. He didn't come out to the carport and try to coax him back inside as he waited for yet another Uber to come and whisk him away to his always uncertain future.

It should have been a relief.

Instead, Ashton's heart cracked again and again with each ticking second. He straightened his shoulders, lifted his chin, and waited for the pain to pass. It would. It always did. He'd find a way through this.

But it hurt like hell that there would be no life with Walker waiting on the other side.

There was no home full of safety and trust in his future, not with Walker anyway. Because addicts lie. And Ashton was done with addicts. Forever.

IT WASN'T EASY to stay inside while Ashton stood stoically at the end of the driveway, his body rigid with emotion and his cheeks likely pink with the cold, but Walker also had a suspicion that if he ever wanted Ashton to hear him out in the future, then he needed some space to calm down.

Walker's biggest fear was that it would give Ashton time to solidify his version of events and relegate Walker to the pile of people who'd let him down. It wasn't shame that made Walker deny being an addict, because for a long time, he'd thought he'd been addicted too.

It was only when he'd seen a counselor for his problem that it became clear that the gambling had been a symptom, not the disease itself. And that the disease wasn't addiction or even compulsion, but depression, anger, and a lack of authenticity in his life. It was arguable, he'd been told, that these same issues were behind some folks' addiction issues across the board, but regardless, his counselor had insisted that he hadn't been so much an addict as a very angry man, acting out in a very self-sabotaging way.

Not pretty. Not a quality destined to attract a man like Ashton. But it was who he'd been for a short time, and it had nearly ruined his life. So, in that respect, he could relate to long-term addicts and compulsive personalities. But claiming the title of addict now meant something he couldn't identify with: an ongoing work to prevent himself from giving in to temptation and returning to the self-sabotaging behavior.

Recovered binger? Perhaps.

He did believe he had recovered from something dark and dangerous to himself and to others. And he preferred to keep himself away from the place and people he'd engaged in those behaviors with. But was he in danger of relapse? Did he need to guard himself constantly against temptation? Was he likely to shift his behavior to another compulsion or drug? No.

No way.

And that was hard to explain to anyone convincingly, especially someone who had gone through so much suffering from people in his life dealing with addiction. Walker understood that it all sounded like a lie. He couldn't blame Ashton for feeling betrayed. He'd never intended for him to know…

Which sounded awful. He got it.

He paced down the hall from the side door to the kitchen and back again. He watched as Ashton walked stiffly toward the Uber that had pulled into the driveway and climbed inside. Walker swallowed down a lump in his throat as the car pulled away, watching the red taillights until they vanished. He hoped without reason or certainty that at some point in the near future Ashton would let him talk, would really listen to him, and that maybe, just maybe, this could be repaired.

If not for the sake of the love they'd been shaping together, then for the sake of their business. They both had too much to lose to walk away from that. As unlikely as it was, Walker couldn't entirely dampen the hope that burned in his heart. There had to be a way to regain Ashton's trust. Maybe not with words, but with actions.

He just needed to prove to Ashton how safe of a bet loving him could be.

# Chapter Twenty-Five

"COME ON IN," Angel said, holding the door open wide and shoving aside a laundry basket of folded clothes with her bare foot. "You look like hell. I'm glad you texted me. After what happened last time you were here, I thought maybe you never would again."

"Honestly, so did I," Ashton said. "But it turns out there are bigger betrayals in the world than you going along with whatever my father asked of you." He swallowed thickly. "And, heaven help me, but I really don't want to be alone right now."

"Here," Angel said, guiding him toward her couch. "Sit down. You look like you're going to pass out."

Ashton let himself fall onto the lumpy cushion of the sofa and clenched his giant, black plastic bag of stuff to his chest, breathing shallowly.

"You can put that down," she suggested gently.

He shook his head. He really couldn't quite yet. It felt like safety to hold on to it, familiar and horrifying, yes, but it meant he was on his way out of an unsafe situation.

"Let me make some tea," Angel said, heading behind the counter that separated the kitchen area from the living room. "I have a calming blend that'll help. My mama gave it to me for Christmas."

Ashton said nothing, letting her clank around behind him heating water and getting down mugs. He took in the room, noting that the pink and black Christmas decorations had been taken down already, and in their place were gold and black New Year's Eve decorations. He hadn't realized Angel was so into the holidays.

When she returned with a steaming white and purple mug for him and a green and yellow one for herself, he had no choice but to release his hold on the plastic bag and let it fall to the floor at his feet. The tea was some mix of herbs that included chamomile and lavender, and it wasn't bad, but it wasn't good either. Still, he sipped it and tried to steady his mind and hands.

"So…" Angel sat cross-legged beside him on her ratty couch. "What happened?"

Ashton took a few more sips before he felt steady enough to tell Angel about Walker, about the romantic turn their arrangement had taken, the wedding, and the miserable discovery that Walker was just another liar like everyone else.

"Ah," Angel soothed when he was finally done, wiping a tear from his cheek with fingers still warm from the mug she held. "And you're sure he's a liar? Maybe he just didn't think it mattered to you, since it's in his past and all."

"He knew it mattered."

She sat her mug aside and squeezed his arm. "Ashton, maybe now isn't the time to say this, but not everyone who's ever made a really bad mistake in their life is a disaster of a person."

"I know."

"Do you?" Angel sighed. "Look, I made a mistake the last time we were together, and if it weren't for this situation with Walker, would you even be here now? Or any time soon? I sent apology after apology, all unacknowledged."

Ashton put his mug down on the coffee table and crossed his arms over his chest. He didn't know what to say. Angel had hurt him, betrayed his trust, and it's true that if Walker hadn't betrayed him even more, he'd probably have put off any sort of reconciliation with her for some time—maybe even forever. And yet when he'd texted to say he needed a place to stay for the night, she'd immediately responded that her couch was his for as long as he wanted it.

"I'm not mad about it," Angel said. "I deserved what I got, as far as your anger goes, but I'm not a bad person. And if you'd have just given me a chance to apologize…" She sighed. "I don't mean to guilt trip you. I'm just saying, did you even listen to him? Really listen?"

He shook his head.

"Don't you think, given everything, maybe you should?"

Ashton's throat felt like it was full of sharp rocks. "I don't know if I can."

"Why?"

"I'm afraid I'll believe him." He pressed his fingertips to his eyelids and tried to breathe. "I can't afford to believe, Angel."

She was quiet for a long moment, but then she scooted even closer, sliding her arm around his shoulders. "Have you ever done something you're ashamed of?"

"I haven't gambled away a hecking trust fund."

"Okay, that wasn't my question."

Ashton sighed, his throat tight. "Of course I have."

"What?"

"You want me to confess? To the worst thing I've ever done?"

"Sure. Tell you what, I can confess the worst thing I've done if you want to hear it first."

Ashton gritted his teeth. What was happening? What was she trying to do? Why did she care if he gave Walker a second chance or not? "I don't want to hear it."

"I took a cat back to the shelter to keep my asshole father from hurting it."

Ashton blinked at her. "That's…complicated, not bad, Angel."

"No one adopted her. I called and called, and no one took her."

"Angel…"

"Now you. What's the thing you're most ashamed of."

Ashton's stomach twisted, and he covered his face.

*"Fairytale of New York" played as his mother's eyes dropped shut, and her breathing slowed. He drew close to her, touched her cold cheek, and whispered, "I hate you. I hope you die. I hate you. I hope you **die**." His heart pounded in his chest. Vomit rose in his throat. He reached for the phone and dialed 911.*

"I wanted her to die," he whispered. "I was just a kid and I wanted her dead. I still…" He shook his head. "I don't know. I can't care. About her. About Justin anymore. About…him."

"You don't know if you can care about Walker. You didn't listen. You don't know if he's worth your forgiveness or not. Maybe he's really not! I left a cat at the shelter, good reasons or not, even though I'd promised to take care of her! I let your father set a trap for you at Christmas! Maybe I'm not worth your time and attention either. No one's innocent. No one."

"I can't have an addict in my life."

"You said that he said he's not an addict."

"Addicts always say that, Angel! All of them!"

"Maybe this time it's true. I also say I'm not an addict. And I'm not."

"Heaven help me, I don't know if I should slap you or cry," Ashton whispered, his voice thick and tears pricking his eyes. "Why are you doing this to me? Why do you care so much if I give him a second chance to convince me he's worth the risk?"

"Because you just told me that you loved him. When have you ever said that to me before about anyone?"

"I said that?" He scanned his memory of what he'd said to Angel as he'd poured everything out about the last few weeks. "I said I loved him?"

"Don't you?"

His throat tightened so much he couldn't speak. He covered his heart with his hands and tried to keep the pain inside.

Angel patted his arm. "Yeah. That's what I thought. Let me get you some more tea."

"Got something harder?" Ashton asked. "To take the edge off?"

"Maker's Mark?"

"Perfect."

She rose, and the sofa shifted with her movement. Ashton licked his lips and gazed down at the huge plastic bag of stuff by his feet. Everything he had was in there. Except his heart. It was still with Walker, whether Walker deserved it or not.

THE NEXT MORNING, Walker unhooked the dog seatbelts on Nina and Simone and watched as they followed Marble and Bitsy onto the carport, darted into the yard for a quick piss, then stood panting and excited by the carport door.

He thought he could better handle the absence of Ashton from the house if the dogs were there trotting around, barking, nuzzling, and asking for food and treats and trips outside. But it quickly became evident that the dogs missed Ashton too.

They returned to his place on the sofa again and again with confused expressions and quiet huffs. Bitsy actually cried at the bottom of the stairs, as though she thought Ashton was upstairs and just not coming down. Walker took her up and showed her the empty closet, and she snorted sadly before going downstairs to sit with her butt to him, staring at a wall.

Dinner was rough as well. Walker wasn't hungry, and there wasn't much in the fridge, but some masochistic part of himself still flipped open the recipe book Ashton had given him for Christmas, running his eyes over Ashton's bubble-writing and the various recipes they'd tried together.

Sick, really, to do that to himself, and yet he couldn't stop. He ran his fingers over the words and tried to imagine Ashton's hand moving across the page as he'd put the recipes down and explained their reactions and opinions to each in the notes. What had Walker done? Had he really lost someone as loving as that?

The dogs were nearly as restless as he was, but they eventually settled in their beds and on the sofa with worried expressions and tense bodies. Walker couldn't concentrate on a TV show and resorted to scrolling Twitter on his phone. When he realized he'd seen all the trending topics without registering any of them, he opened Facebook instead.

He gulped as his eyes caught on the first post on his feed. It was doing quite well with over two hundred and fifty reactions and nearly thirty comments.

Christ.

The post lacked the sincere cheer of Ashton's earlier shitpost that had started this whole mess, though he was clearly trying to fake it. Reading the paragraphs Ashton had typed, written in an epistolary style, made Walker dizzy.

*Dear friends, clients, and fans,*

*Red alert! Red alert! This is a general notice for everyone who attended the beautiful and touching wedding ceremony between Evelyn and Tom Barstow yesterday in Gatlinburg. I have an important announcement. (Well, after congratulating the bride and groom once again on their happy union, of course.) It's time to come clean and clarify that Walker Ronson and I are **not** dating. In fact, he was a client of mine.*

*Some of you may remember my now-deleted post offering to pose as anyone's boyfriend for the upcoming holidays for the small price of a place to stay for a few days. Well, Walker took me up on that offer. Yes, I was his Boyfriend for Hire at the wedding. The various shenanigans we indulged in there were part and parcel of that gig and nothing more. The bride and groom had reasons to wish for a dis-*

*traction at the reception, and Walker and I acted as such. Again, we are not in a relationship and everything you witnessed was faked.*

*I know, I know! You're shocked! We seemed so in love. I get it. But hey, I'm just that good of an actor! And it seems that Walker is even better than me!*

*So, disregard all you heard either of us say or do during our fake boyfriendship. (Yes, that's a word! I just made it up! Cha-ching, coined and submitted for copyright!) Please hold any disappointment at this news. I know we made an attractive pair, but some things are just too good to be true.*

*Lastly, I regret to announce that I'm retiring from the Fake Boyfriend business permanently. I might be very good at it, but it takes a surprising emotional toll.*

*Congratulations again to Evelyn and Tom! May you be happy forever! And finally let me wish a happy New Year to everyone else.*

*Loads of love from your former Mr. Jingle Bells,*
*Ashton Sellers*

Walker was reading over the post for what might have been the fiftieth time when a text notification popped up on his screen.

It was from Casey and it attached screen shots of Ashton's post with the comment: *This doesn't pass the sniff test. Call me.*

Walker poured himself two fingers of whiskey before sitting back down and obliging.

"Hey, dude," Casey said calmly.

"What's up?"

"I'm not an idiot, Walker."

"Meaning?"

"Meaning Ashton talks a good game—he's a great salesman, and I went along with it because he seemed desperate for me to believe that you two were not actually making out in his office the other day. But I'm not a fool, and there was no need—fake boyfriend for Evelyn's wedding or not—for you two to be kissing in his office that day except the obvious. I was going to let you both tell me on your own time, but now he's made this post, and well… What the fuck went wrong? You guys were so into each other at the wedding. That wasn't acting. So what the hell? And is this gonna be a problem at work?"

"I really don't know."

"You don't know what went wrong?"

"No, I know exactly how I fucked things up. I don't know about work."

Casey was quiet for a moment. "Are you okay? Is he okay?"

"I'm okay. He's… I don't know. I hope he's okay."

"You're not okay either," Casey murmured. "You were really into him. At the wedding, whenever you looked at him…" He whistled. "Never seen you like that, friend."

"I'm not ready to call it a lost cause yet. But I don't know if I can fix it."

"What happened?"

"He found out about the gambling, losing my trust fund, and all that. Now he thinks I'm an addict."

Casey sighed. "Shit."

"I know. He wouldn't even listen to me try to explain. It's all or nothing for him."

"Because of his family."

Walker felt a twinge of jealousy that Casey had known about Ashton's family situation before he had but let that go. "Yeah. He's got…"

"Issues."

"No, he's got every right to be angry—at me, at them."

"Walker, you're not like his mom or his brother."

"Cousin."

"Right. Cousin. You went through a bad patch and—"

"That's what I told him!" Walker exclaimed, rising from the sofa to go to the window. It was chilly in the room and he should have started a fire earlier, but he hadn't had the energy, especially when he knew it would just make him miss seeing Ashton all cozy and warm on the couch. "I told him exactly that, and he wouldn't hear me. He said all addicts say things like that."

"I'm sure they do."

"But I'm not an addict!"

"I know, but from the outside, you have to admit that denial sounds sketchy."

"Fucking hell, what am I supposed to do? Go back in time and undo it? Stay working at my father's firm, ruining my life and being miserable?"

"Whoa, whoa, you're reading me wrong. I'm just saying be patient. Give him a minute to process this."

"I'm afraid he'll just cement me in his mind this way and never let me actually talk to him."

Casey sighed. "You're not going to let that happen."

"I can't exactly make him listen to me."

"No, but you can let him know you haven't given up."

"I'm not like you. He's not like Joel. If I push him, he'll just shut me out. I've seen him do it."

"To who?"

Walker rubbed a hand over his face. "His mom."

"But you're not her."

"His stepsister. His father."

"There's history there, Walker."

"But his history with them informs his present with me, and I'm scared, all right? I've never felt like this before. The thought that he's out there hurting because of me? I hate it. And thinking that he'll never forgive me? It's tearing me apart."

"Give him a few days to process. You'll see him at the office tomorrow at the very least. In the meantime, get clear on what you want to say to him. You might not get another chance." Casey cleared his throat.

"Sorry, dude. Have to go. Joel's got Bruno leashed and we're taking him jogging. He's gotta trim down."

"Right. No problem. I understand."

"You're not a bad man, Walker. He'll see that eventually. Just give him some time. You were moving awfully fast. Some space will make you both see more clearly."

Walker didn't want space. He wanted Ashton sipping wine and reading on the sofa. He wanted Ashton laughing in the kitchen. He wanted Ashton in bed next to him, warm and sweet-smelling in sleep.

He ended the call and tossed his phone on the sofa before kneeling to start a fire after all.

He was going to need something to keep him warm.

# Chapter Twenty-Six

ASHTON COULDN'T SLEEP.

Angel's couch was terrible, and there were strange clanking noises coming from the pipes, not to mention an odd gurgle in the toilet that he could hear all the way down the hall. He hadn't slept a wink the first night after he'd arrived either, and even though he should have been exhausted enough tonight, he just couldn't get settled.

The black plastic bag full of his things crinkled from time to time as though it were a living thing getting settled into a new place. He hated that he could taste panic is his throat when he thought about carrying it a few streets over to his apartment in the morning—because there was no way he was staying another night on this horrible, threadbare sofa, as grateful as he was to Angel.

He picked up his phone and opened Facebook. The replies to his most recent shitpost ranged from: *You're crazy, man* to *Oh, no! you two were so cute!* to *Methinks he doth protest too much*. He hadn't replied to any of them after the first few. He didn't have the heart.

A text notification popped onto his screen, and he almost dismissed it and blocked the number. At the last moment he clicked cancel and opened the message instead.

*The gambling took place over four months when I was very depressed and willing to do almost anything to feel excited again.*

Ashton didn't reply, but he didn't go back to blocking Walker either. Another message came through.

*It was a bad kind of excitement. The thrill wasn't from gambling, but from doing something that my father would hate. Even when I lost, I was happy.*

Ashton stared at the message, letting the words sink in.

*My father and I don't have the best relationship. We don't have the worst either. Back then, it was worse than it is now, though he thought it was better. I resented him so much. Down to my bones. Because I didn't know yet how to tell him that I didn't want what he wanted. I'd internalized what he told me about myself to the degree that I didn't even understand what I found attractive in a man. But that's another story.*

Ashton cocked his head, thinking back to what he knew of Walker's love life before Ashton had come along. He'd dated those men to please his father? Weird. But people did weird things because of their parents. Just look at his own life and choices. Just look at the state of his heart.

*Michael Amos headed a little group my father approved of because they had money and connections, and he believed I was finally showing interest in friendships with the right kinds of people. Little did he know that Michael is a gambling fiend and to hang out with him is to eventually get sucked into it as well. And gambling with Michael is never small wagers. He bet big and often. So I did too.*

Ashton's stomach churned. This was when the excuses would start. He braced himself.

*I gambled like I wasn't going to live to regret it.*

He stared at the single line of text for a long time as the bubble appeared and disappeared beneath it.

*I guess some part of me hoped I wouldn't. Live, I mean, not regret it. I wasn't seeing clearly. I was angry, and hurting myself to hurt my dad made sense at the time.*

Ashton swallowed thickly.

*Losing my trust fund was the best thing that ever happened to me. The day it was done, completely finished, was the first day I knew what my goal in life would be: to stand on my own two feet. To be out from under my father's thumb. To breathe freely. To love myself. But even then, I didn't know how to do it, just that I wanted to.*

Ashton could relate. He wanted to be free of the weight his family had hung on him like trauma ornaments on the tree of his life.

*I can see you're reading this, so I'm going to continue on. That's where you and Casey came in. Well, Casey to start, and then you, and suddenly with SRS, I had my way out. My dream career with people who prized authenticity over everything else, and that was it for me. I never looked back. You can ask Casey if you don't believe me. I still miss golf, but I don't miss gambling.*

Before he could second guess himself, Ashton typed in: *Why don't you golf, then?* He chided his own weakness as he hit send.

*I don't believe I'm an addict, but why risk it? I have new hobbies now.*

Ashton sent: *So you're scared that you could fall into it again?*

*I will never gamble again. Golf reminds me of what kind of person I let myself become and why. I don't need it. I'm not that guy.*

Ashton didn't reply. He didn't know if he was glad he'd replied at all, actually. He should have just let Walker have his say and left him on read. Believing him was so tempting, and he could feel his resolve slipping already.

*I love you, Ashton. You're good, kind, loving, beautiful, and brilliant. I don't want you to say goodbye over this. We have a good thing. If it takes ten years, I'll prove to you that you're safe with me.*

He licked his dry lips and adjusted the lumpy cushion under his head. He wanted to believe Walker. He really did. *How?* he typed and almost deleted it, but then sent it through.

*With how I live and how I love you. You'll see. You won't ever doubt.*

Ashton covered his face with his hand as tears welled and a sob started in his chest. Could he trust this? Could he really?

*I won't push you. Just come to me when you're ready. I'll be waiting.*

# Chapter Twenty-Seven

ASHTON ATE COLD cereal at Angel's place for breakfast, thanked her for letting him stay, and lugged his giant, black plastic bag several blocks over to his old apartment. The lease was set to run out in two days, and he and Walker had planned to rent a U-Haul to move everything into storage until Ashton had found a new place. *If* he'd found a new place.

They'd only talked about it vaguely. Given how things had been going before it all went to hell, he'd started to let himself entertain the idea of living with Walker in that beautiful old house forever, all cozy and safe and letting himself be loved.

Now...

Well, now he didn't know what to do.

Sitting on his sofa in the torn-apart room, he considered his options. There weren't many. In the end, and despite still feeling bitter about a lot of things, Ashton called Casey to ask for advice and help. Within two hours, Casey arrived with Joel, a truck, a stupidly big SUV, and a ton of unconstructed boxes from Joel's home and garden store.

"Where do you want to start?" Casey asked, hands on his hips while Joel began taping the boxes together for packing.

"Anywhere, I guess," Ashton said, looking around at the mess of his place. "It really doesn't matter much."

Casey's brows flicked with concern, and he shared a glance with Joel before taking one of the boxes and starting to fill it with the contents of the bookcases still pulled out from the walls for the exterminator's treatment.

"You really don't mind me moving into your old trailer?" Ashton asked Joel as he created more and more boxes. Joel had lived in it for several years before he and Casey had built their cabin on the land a bit closer to the lake. "I thought you were going to make it into an office for your writing work?"

Joel shrugged, his hands moving expertly to crease another box into form. "Turns out I like the view out our guest room window better than the views from the trailer. You're welcome to stay as long as you want."

"Thank you. I know it's really short notice, and you've dropped everything to help me because I didn't have anything else lined up. I *could* have had somewhere lined up already if I hadn't..." He shook his head. "Never mind."

Joel and Casey exchanged another look, but neither of them pressed, and Ashton was grateful. They had a lot to do today if they were going to get all of his stuff out of the apartment and unloaded into the trailer.

"I'm not usually this big of a slob. It's because of the bed bug treatment," Ashton said as he moved stuff in off the balcony and into the living room to pack. "But the landlord said they didn't find any traces in here. They examined my bed and sofa and everything."

"We know," Casey said, taping up a box of kitchen supplies. "You don't need to explain. We understand."

It took four solid hours of the three of them working nonstop to load up the truck with everything Ashton wanted to bring, including his sofa, mattress, and bedframe. There were some items—a cabinet he'd claimed from the trash when he'd first moved in and some old books— he decided to leave behind and let his landlord deal with as he saw fit. Otherwise his entire apartment was packed up and transferred in less than a day.

Some part of him was pleased by that, and some part of him was horrified. How easy it was to just pack up his entire life and move it somewhere else. It made him feel rootless, ungrounded, like maybe he didn't matter or even really exist outside of his own body. He'd never had a home, and he hadn't even made one for himself. Home was his skin. No more, no less.

"You're in a dark place, huh?" Joel asked when Ashton climbed into the truck's passenger seat to drive his things over to their property. Casey was in the SUV with a bunch of boxes and a lamp in the passenger seat, leaving no room for Ashton to ride with him.

"That obvious?" Ashton asked, buckling his seat belt.

He lifted a brow. "Wanna talk about it?"

"I don't know how much there is to say. I'm still trying to figure it out myself."

"Understood."

They rode in silence for several minutes, but by the time Joel had launched the trunk onto the interstate headed west, Ashton found words pushing at his lips wanting to be let out. Pressing his hand to his chest, rubbing where his heart still ached with confusion and hurt, he decided to go with it. What was the worst that could happen? Joel might tell Casey, and Casey might tell Walker, but it's not like any of this was a secret now, was it?

"My mom was an addict," he said gruffly.

Joel nodded. "That sucks. I can relate. My dad was a mean drunk. And he drank a lot."

"Oh yeah? I'm sorry. My mom wasn't mean. Just..." He shook his head. "Heroin. Pills. Whatever she could get her hands on. I watched her overdose. More than once."

Joel whistled low. "Tough stuff for a kid."

"Tough stuff for anyone."

Joel huffed agreement.

"I had to harden my heart to get away from her." There was so much he was leaving out. His life with his grandmother. His attempts to help Justin. His research. His dashed hopes. His fears. His PTSD. His trauma. But he didn't want to talk about those things. He wanted to talk about Walker. "I'm worried that maybe, on one hand, I've hardened my heart too much, and maybe, on the other, I haven't hardened it enough to be safe."

Joel flicked on the blinker and edged the car toward the exit ramp that would lead to the road toward their property. He said nothing.

"Walker texted me last night. He said he's not a gambling addict."

"Mm."

"What do you think?"

"About what?"

"Do you think he's a gambling addict?"

"I think he lost a shit ton of money during a pretty dark time of his life, but I haven't seen him do anything like that since. He's a calm guy. Vanilla. I mean that he's personally vanilla, not in bed. I have no idea what he likes in bed."

Ashton chuckled. He knew what Walker liked in bed, and vanilla was a fair description, but as it turned out, vanilla was what Ashton liked too. Passionate, safe, vanilla love. That's what he craved. Which led him to a question he'd been pondering since his last exchange with Walker: "I've been thinking, what do you think it means to be safe?"

"Seems like it must be different for everyone."

"What's it mean for you?"

"Hm, being home with Casey—that's safe. Not smoking anymore—that's being safe. I don't know. What's 'safe' mean to you?"

They turned down a road that would lead to the lake. Gray tree limbs were scrawled against an even grayer sky. Tennessee in winter—gloomy, miserable, wet, but home. "I don't know. I'm trying to figure it out. After all I went through as a kid, feeling safe is the most important thing to me."

"More important than feeling loved?"

Ashton winced. How had Joel hit the nail on the head so perfectly. "Can't I have both?"

"Love isn't safe," Joel said with a crooked little smile. "It's dangerous. Everyone knows that."

"Do they?" Ashton wasn't sure. He'd always imagined love as the one emotion that, once he found it, would make him feel safer than anything else. And he'd experienced that with Walker, hadn't he? Until…until…

"Love means having your heart torn out eventually. No way around it."

Ashton blinked.

"Think about it. What's the most painful experience in life? Grief and loss, yeah?"

Ashton nodded.

"Well, you can't love and not have grief. You're seeing that now, aren't you? You loved Walker—or thought you did—"

Ashton winced again.

"And now you're grieving the loss of the idea of him. You know, the man you thought you were loving."

"Yes."

"Even if you were lucky and never had this… Hmm, how can I put it?" He thought for a moment. "Even if you never had this reality check of loving a flawed human being, in the end, the person you love dies or you die." Joel nodded. "Pain—it's always the end of love. Some would call it the price. But it's more like the shadow of love. Inescapable. Can't cut it off. None of us are Peter Pan."

Ashton was quiet. It was true, wasn't it? There was no love without pain. Though he could vouch for there being plenty of pain without love in the world. Maybe he wasn't cut out to have love. Maybe that was another thing his mother took from him.

"Is it worth it?" he asked. "Knowing that you're going to lose Casey one day or he'll lose you. Is loving him worth it?"

Joel's hands tightened on the steering wheel. "I think you know the answer to that."

Ashton was quiet for the rest of the drive to the trailer. He said little as Joel and Casey motioned him into their cabin for some food before they began unloading everything he owned into the trailer sitting at the top of their property. As he sipped the beer they'd opened for him and put chips into his mouth and forced himself to chew them, he ran his fingers over their dog Bruno's silky ears and pondered whether or not he was cut out for love or if he was better off alone.

Was it safer to love? Obviously not. Was it better? The expected answer was yes, but he wasn't sure. Never let it be said that he, Ashton Sellers, didn't have trust issues galore. Including when it came to trusting himself.

The first thing they did was set up the mattress and bed in the biggest bedroom in the trailer. He'd have a place to rest tonight, at least. Then they moved in the sofa and stacked boxes in the living room, dusted off their hands, and sighed.

"Come to the cabin for dinner with us," Casey said. "We'll order delivery. You don't have anything here."

Ashton knew he should say yes. Not only that, but he should buy the food after all they'd done for him today and on such short notice. But he already felt like he was going to come apart if he couldn't be quiet and alone with his thoughts. If he went to the cabin with them, he'd let himself be distracted from what he really needed to figure out. And while a distraction sounded nice, it also meant he was only delaying the inevitable.

"You want to get settled," Joel said. "No worries, man. We're good on our own."

"Let me pay for your—"

Casey scoffed and rolled his eyes. "Don't you dare. We're friends and business partners. You'd have done the same for us."

Ashton nodded. He would have, and when they'd finished up the cabin, he'd helped them move furniture around until they'd gotten it just right. "If you're sure. I can't tell you how much—"

"Bah, enough of that," Joel said, taking Casey by the arm. "Let's go.

I'm hungry and Bruno needs his dinner."

As Ashton watched them walk down the yard to their cabin, he felt reassured that they were so close. He could change his mind and go join them later. For now, he just wanted…

He didn't know.

He should be hungry, but he wasn't. He should be tired, but he was jittery with unspent panic. How to feel safe again? How to know what to believe? He looked around at the empty rooms of the trailer. How to make this hollow place a home? Maybe he should start with that.

He opened the boxes but was too tired to unpack them.

WALKER STARED AT the popcorn ceiling of his living room, the sofa feeling so empty and big without Ashton taking up half of it. The dogs slept on their beds, seemingly at peace with Ashton's absence now. While their pacing and looking had driven the knife in Walker's heart deeper, their casual acceptance of Ashton's absence wasn't much better.

It made the last few weeks feel unreal. Like maybe they'd never happened at all. Maybe Ashton had never been on this sofa with him, never laughed in the kitchen with him, never arched under him in bed…

Walker stretched out, wishing he felt comfortable instead of just sad and lost. Tomorrow he'd have to go back to the office and face the reality of his life after-Ashton while staring right at Ashton. It was going to suck. It was also his only hope of winning him back. Proving to him that he was a safe person to pin his heart to.

Walker's phone pinged, and he rolled his eyes. It was probably his mother again, wondering about Ashton's Facebook post. Wondering about a lot of things he didn't want to have to explain. He could barely explain it to himself.

Another ping.

Another.

"Fine," he grumbled, grabbing his phone. "Can't I mope for ten fucking minutes?" He sat up when he saw the message preview on his home screen.

*I've moved into Joel and Casey's trailer on their property. We transferred all my stuff out of the apartment today. I didn't want you to worry.*

Walker swallowed hard. He *had* been worried actually. He knew Ashton didn't want to stay in that old apartment any longer, and he'd worried that Ashton would sign another year's lease in desperation.

*Thanks for letting me know. You deserve a place where you're comfortable.*

A few long seconds passed with no reply bubble, and Walker was just about to give up when one finally popped onto the screen.

*I was comfortable with you.*

Walker's throat tightened. *I know. I'm sorry I let you down.*

Another long delay and then: *We were probably moving too fast.*

Walker fought the reflexive denial but eventually gave in to it. He needed Ashton to understand how he'd felt, how he still felt. *Some might say that, and it's okay if you think so, but I thought what we had felt just right.*

Ashton's reply: *Had? Past tense?*

Walker's heart jolted. He thought carefully before replying: *That's up to you. My heart hasn't changed.*

There was another long silence, and Walker put his phone aside, paced the length of the living room as the dogs watched with curious eyes, and stopped in front of the Christmas tree. He hadn't taken it down yet, but he hadn't turned the lights on since Ashton left either.

He swallowed hard. Bent and plugged the tree in. The illumination hopeful in a way nothing had been since his grandfather's fateful words at the reception.

*Ping.*

He rushed to pick up the phone and collapsed onto the sofa.

*I don't know what I want. I'm sorry.*

It was hard not to be disappointed, but at least Ashton was still talking to him. At least he wasn't shutting him out entirely like he had at first. Walker replied: *Like I said, you don't have to rush it. I'll be right here waiting. I promise.*

Another long moment passed, and Ashton acknowledged his message with a thumbs-up emoji and nothing more.

Nina jumped up onto the sofa next to him. They both stared at the phone for a long time, but when it was clear no more messages would be incoming, Walker put the phone aside. He ran his hands over Nina's soft head and stared at the Christmas tree and the shimmering star at the top.

Hope was a terrifying thing, and yet it was all he had. He clung to it with both hands.

# Chapter Twenty-Eight

"I FEEL LIKE we should talk," Casey said as he drove them both toward downtown and their office building.

Ashton took a sip from the travel container of coffee Joel had pushed into his hands that morning. Living in the trailer would definitely require that he get his own car sooner rather than later. He couldn't rely on Casey to get him to the office every day. Between rent and a car payment, he was going to be spending just as much money monthly as he had when he'd been paying for Justin's rehab.

"What about?" he asked disingenuously.

Of course he knew. It just felt exhausting to consider it. He'd had a rough night, tossing and turning in his bed, alternately too cold and too hot with the space heater kicking on and off throughout the night. Plus he'd heard weird noises from the woods near the trailer and convinced himself it was a serial killer waiting until he fell asleep to break in and murder him.

Because that made sense.

Like he was worth killing.

It'd probably been a possum or a wildcat. And he was probably just heartbroken and exhausted. A recipe for paranoia if he ever knew of one. Great, good, loved that for him.

"About Walker."

"Ugh." Ashton wiped a hand over his face, his stomach flipping over in a sick twist. "Do we have to?"

"Yeah. We kind of do. For the sake of our business, I need to know what's going on and if things are going to be okay in the office."

"Things will be fine." He didn't have much choice on that front, did he? Everything he had was tied up in their business. "I just wish you'd told me about him from the start."

Casey flicked a surprised glance Ashton's way. "Told you what?"

"That he had a gambling problem."

"Had being the operative word," Casey said firmly. "Look, I didn't tell either of you a lot of things about each other. I didn't tell Walker about the addiction history in your family or why you were always broke, and I didn't tell you about that dark period in Walker's life. It wasn't a pretty time. But he's fine now."

"You sound awfully sure about that."

"I couldn't be surer of anything if I tried. He's never made another risky move in all the time I've known him." He shot Ashton a glance. "Well, except for you. Starting something with you was definitely risky."

Ashton flinched, unsure if he should be offended. "What's that mean?"

"It means SRS is in deep trouble if either of you decides to bail because your relationship fell apart. And I suppose all those shenanigans at Evelyn's wedding were risky, but that was more you than him. In my experience, you're definitely the one more likely to pull a wild idea out of the hat and run with it, collateral damage be damned."

Ashton sat still a moment, casting his mind back over the last few years of his life: taking on the role of a submissive in Gerald's kinky sex, bringing a Grindr hookup to his grandmother's for Christmas, diving into ownership he could barely afford with SRS, and pushing the envelope with every client's marketing.

He did like to take risks. It was true. Risks like that thrilled him. Compared to Walker's typical boring approach to things, Ashton *was* a thrill-seeking monster.

"I'm not going to tell you how to feel," Casey said, which made Ashton fairly sure he was definitely going to tell him how to feel. "But

Walker is a sure bet. If you let yourself trust him, he won't let you down."

"Did he pay you to say that?"

"He wouldn't have to. He's a good guy, and I've never seen him look at anyone the way he's been looking at you recently. Don't let his past mistake ruin something precious."

"You're awfully opinionated."

"You're the risk-taker, Ashton. You're the gambler, not him. All I'm saying is that if your feelings for him are real at all—take a chance on him. He deserves it."

Ashton deliberately sipped his coffee and remained quiet. He had no energy left for pointing out how terrified he was of trusting what Casey said to be true. He just had to get through the awkwardness of the day and then he'd be back, safe and sound, in that tiny trailer with his myriad of boxes to unpack.

Both physically and emotionally.

He had a lot of work to do before he could feel steady enough again to be ready to decide how he felt about Walker.

WALKER WASN'T HIDING in his office so much as he was camping out in there for fear of his life. He knew Ashton had come in with Casey because he heard their voices in the hallway before he'd leapt up from his desk and pre-emptively shut his door.

He hadn't locked it, though, and that said more than he wanted to admit.

Maybe Ashton would come to him.

Maybe he'd want to talk.

Or maybe Walker was a fool with a growling, angry stomach who was hours past lunchtime, pacing alone in his office with nothing to hope for and nothing to lose either. Because all was already lost.

*Ping.*

His phone had been silent most of the day. It was like even his assistant and the rest of the office knew that he was trying to lie low. Grabbing it now, he swallowed hard.

*Meet me at Coffee & Chocolate.*

His heart hurt. Like actually hurt. Was it hope or despair? He wasn't sure. But this was the chance he'd been waiting for, wasn't it?

The weather sucked. Post-Christmas haze and drizzle combined with a cold wind made the walk of four blocks rather miserable even with his scarf and thick, woolen coat. He walked quickly, his mind racing.

Meeting in public was a bad sign. It meant Ashton wanted an audience—and not one made up of their fellow employees. But meeting at all was a good sign. It meant Ashton was willing to look at his face as they talked. Maybe...

His heart couldn't handle maybe today. It was in despair. This was it. This was Ashton telling him it was over for good, but they'd have to make the best of it at work, and for him to man up and stop hiding in his office like he was the victim when they both knew Ashton was the one who'd been done wrong.

The cafe was entirely empty except for the guy behind the counter. He nodded at Walker as he came in, then flicked a glance Ashton's way before going into the back room.

Ashton looked beautiful if exhausted. He wore a casual outfit—jeans and a purple hoodie—completely atypical for his usual office apparel, but Walker figured he probably hadn't unpacked his stuff entirely or ironed out his clothes or hell, maybe he just felt too sad to dress up like usual. Walker could relate. He wondered what their office mates thought. He'd never seen Ashton like this except in the cozy comfort of his home, snug on the sofa, cuddling with dogs, and being...his.

Fuck. What had he lost?

"I got you a coffee the way you like it," Ashton said, pushing a paper cup with a plastic lid his way. "And some chocolates."

Walker sat and looked at the four chocolates on the plate in the middle of the table. They were marbled and beautiful, seeming more like jewels than treats. He didn't want one. The thought of eating made him feel sick. But he took the coffee and sipped it before muttering, "Thank you."

Ashton leaned back in his seat. The light from the window illuminated his drawn features and highlighted the moss-green of his eyes. The dark circles under them were stark. Walker wanted to apologize for them, for everything, but he kept his mouth shut. He'd told Ashton he'd wait for him. He wasn't going to push. Not even now.

"You look horrible," Ashton said finally.

Walker shrugged. "I feel pretty horrible too."

Ashton huffed, and Walker wished he could take the words back, shove them far into his throat and swallow them down. He shouldn't make any of this about his feelings. He was the one who'd let Ashton down. He was the one who had to prove what he was made of.

"Are you okay?" Walker asked.

Ashton gazed at him steadily. "I've been better."

"The trailer… Is it going to be all right while you look for an apartment?"

Ashton's jaw tightened. "I might just stay there. Get a car instead. The rent on the trailer would be less than most of the places around town."

Walker nodded, his fingers convulsing on the paper coffee cup. He wanted to reach out and wipe a fallen black eyelash from Ashton's cheek, but he didn't have the right to touch.

"Did Bitsy do okay at the boarders'?" Ashton asked quietly.

"Yes."

"She had fun with her friends?"

Walker nodded.

"I miss them."

"They miss you."

Ashton's lips twisted. "Do they?"

"Yeah. And I miss you too."

Ashton let out a low sigh and looked at his watch. "Do you have appointments this afternoon?"

Walker shook his head.

"All right. I'm ready to listen. Tell me your side of it then. I want to know everything. From the beginning. I won't interrupt you or argue this time, all right? I promise."

Walker's heart thudded wildly.

"I want to hear it all from you, from your point of view. Just please leave nothing out. Even if you think it doesn't matter or isn't important. I want to know."

"Everything?"

Ashton's jaw clenched and released. He whispered, "Everything."

Walker scrubbed a hand over his face. "This could take a while."

"I have all night." His beautiful lips twisted up in a haunted version of a smile. "Love that for me."

Walker closed his eyes and began.

# Chapter Twenty-Nine

TWO DAYS HAD passed since Ashton had spent four hours listening to Walker's long, winding, and seemingly faithful confession of his darkest time, and yet he was still weighing the vulnerable sincerity of it against his own past trauma and wells of fear.

There was no way he could just jump back into Walker's arms, home, and bed. But he couldn't deny that Walker had laid it all bare for his examination, and it had taken everything in him not to hug Walker as they'd parted. Not to make promises he wasn't sure he could keep just to take that hopelessness from Walker's eyes and wipe the misery from his face.

It wasn't that Walker had said anything entirely unexpected. Once Ashton got back to the trailer and started unpacking boxes while thinking through what Walker had revealed, he wasn't surprised by any of it. He'd met Walker's family, seen the way his father treated Walker, and witnessed the discomfort the man had had with Ashton at Christmas.

There was no doubt in his mind that Walker's father expected to dominate him, and that Walker had, for most of his life, been fairly easy to control. Until he hadn't been anymore.

And that was where the gambling had come in.

The entire four months of gambling like a fiend, at least how Walker had described them, had been a childish tantrum, a flailing fuck you with big, eternal consequences. Not unlike Ashton's own gamble of bringing his Grindr date to Christmas.

Except that the thing Walker had been trying to escape wasn't his family's abuse but the suffocating thumb he'd been under. The control and expectations. Losing his trust fund, throwing in with Casey and Ashton, leaving his father's company—it'd been everything Walker had needed to wrestle his way out of submission. Without giving up his family entirely in the process.

And Ashton understood that.

He understood Walker's regret at the way he'd done it too—at the loss of the money, at the twisted way he'd hurt himself to break free. Sometimes cutting yourself free meant cutting *yourself* in the process. Ashton had hurt himself plenty, hadn't he?

Sometimes on purpose, like with Gerald, and sometimes by accident, like with Justin, but he'd hurt himself in some cruel, scarring ways. So who was he to judge Walker for taking a shit ton of money with him into that dark underworld before being reborn to life?

Now it was New Year's Eve, and he was no closer to knowing what he wanted to do. Casey and Joel had left to go downtown to Market Square for the local ball drop and to watch their friend RJ's new band play at the Preservation Pub. They'd invited him to go, but what was he going to do at a pub with happy couples and their happy friends?

Angel had texted him too, inviting him to a party at her friend Tobias's place, but that had sounded even worse. Drunk twenty-year-olds who still thought the best fun in life was being loud and obnoxious in as many ways as possible? No thanks.

It was brutal to know that for him the greatest fun in life had been sitting on his now ex-lover's sofa with dogs at his feet and knowing that there was a chance, a very real one, that he'd never have that back again. And that he'd been the one to choose to lose it.

He gazed out the window at the Christmas lights reflected on the lake below the trailer, just visible through the trees. He knew Casey's parents' house was just across the way, up on the bluff. Joel had pointed it out to him that evening when they'd taken Bruno for a post-dinner romp in the woods while Casey had done the dishes. He stared at the lights all over their deck and the way they reflected in the water below.

Ashton didn't give much thought to the religious side of Christmas anymore. Not since he'd sworn it off and left Grandma Hudson's hellish home. But the thought bubbled up all the same: return of light, rebirth, new life, generational trauma healing in the light of a new hope. Taking all the Christianity out of it, there was no doubt that a newborn babe, coming in the heart of darkness, represented something bigger than the twisted faith of his grandmother.

Something tender and fresh that should be nurtured on faith.

Maybe he'd been too hasty in throwing the baby out with the manger, so to speak. Maybe he needed to slow down and really feel his way through this. Nurture this small spark of love he'd held in his hands and trust Walker to nurture it too.

Maybe faith was something he could cultivate. Maybe, just maybe.

*HOW DID YOU screw things up with Ashton?*

Evelyn's first text from her honeymoon in San Francisco wasn't very reassuring to say the least.

*Happy NYE to you too,* Walker replied.

*I saw that post on FB from him. What went wrong?*

*You said it yourself: secrets don't stay hidden*

*Oh damn, Walker*

*Yeah. Damn*

*There's no hope he'll change his mind?*

Walker paused before answering. He wanted to tell Evelyn all about the hope he nurtured like a flame in his heart, but he didn't want to get *her* hopes up only for them to be dashed later. She should be enjoying her honeymoon, though, and would pessimism really bring her joy? Would misguided optimism? Ugh. He tried for a middle ground. *He hasn't cut off all contact with me. But I wouldn't hang your hat on his getting over it any time soon.*

*Fuck*

*Look, don't sweat it. You're on your honeymoon. You should be happy.*

*I am happy, but I'm allowed to be worried about my brother, aren't I?*

*I'll be okay*

*But you're in love with him. I could see it in your eyes.*

*I'm not dead & he's not dead, so who knows what the future will bring*

*Your optimism is touching but don't you think you should be fighting for him?*

*Now?*

*Yes, now*

*It's NYE*

*Exactly*

Walker sighed. *What do you expect me to do on NYE?*

*You need to be with him at midnight. That way you'll be sure to spend the year together.*

Walker shook his head. *Superstitious nonsense*

*Do it. It'll mean a lot to him.*

*What seems to mean a lot to him right now is me keeping my distance.*

*Walker, you're such a pushover. Go get him. GET. YOUR. MAN.*

Walker rolled his eyes. *This isn't a rom-com.*

*I'm telling you. Don't give up.*

*I haven't!*

*You have!*

Walker didn't bother sending a reply, and when Evelyn sent another message an hour and a half later it was a photo of her and Tom on what looked like a frigid rooftop with champagne, a picnic, and watering, red eyes from the wind that ripped through their hair. *Cheers,* her text read. *We love you. Get your dude.*

*Happy New Year & I love you too*, was his only response.

*New Year's Rockin' Eve* played from the TV, and he set about taking down his Christmas decorations finally. He always felt there was something especially pathetic about decorations on the morning of January first.

The dogs mainly stayed out of his way, though Nina chased a few of the plastic ornaments he dropped as they rolled across the hardwood floor. It always seemed to take so much more time to take the decorations down than it did to put them up. He assumed it was a measure of the enjoyment he took in it and the sad resignation that the celebrations were now over.

This time, he also felt grim misery, because he couldn't help but imagine how it would have been taking the decorations down with Ashton. How they'd laugh and tease and how he'd explain the different ornaments to Ashton—where he'd bought them or who'd given them to him—and they'd probably take a break for hot chocolate and to make out on the sofa. Or disappear into Walker's room...

He cut his thoughts off firmly there. It was possible that was never going to happen again. He couldn't dwell on it. At this point, he'd be happy if Ashton just wanted to be friends with him or business partners like they had been. Okay, *happy* was an overstatement.

Walker had just returned from dragging the nearly-dead tree out to his wood pile when his phone rang. He sighed when he saw the name on the display, but he couldn't keep putting this off.

"Hi, Mom."

"Sweetheart, are you all right?"

"I'm doing fine. Just putting away decorations. Getting ready for the ball to drop at midnight." He tried to sound cheerful, but he didn't think he succeeded. He felt a little dizzy. How was he going to admit to his mother how he'd screwed up? She'd liked Ashton so much.

"Your sister tells me Ashton left you over the trust fund situation."

Walker cleared his throat. "More like the behavior that led to the trust fund situation. He didn't care about the money."

"Right. Of course he wouldn't. He's a sweet boy."

Walker swallowed hard.

"Well, what are you going to do to win him back?"

He laughed. "You and Evelyn are too alike sometimes."

"We just don't want you to lose the best man you've ever been with over something as silly as that rough patch you went through."

"It wasn't silly, Mom. It was a dark place. I get that it scares him to think I could make such a mistake. I get that *I* scare him now."

"Pfft. You're fine. It was just a spell. You're over it."

Walker ran a hand through his hair and kicked aside the final box of ornaments he still needed to carry up to the attic. Was this how Ashton had felt listening to him downplay what he'd done? Probably. God, he hoped he'd at least sounded like he took some responsibility for his situation instead of just shoving it beneath the rug like his mother wanted to do.

"Mom, I need to go."

"Oh? Do you have plans for the evening? Evelyn made it out like you were moping alone at home."

"I'm not moping. I just—" The doorbell rang. The front door, which he almost never used, and which often jammed when he tried to open it. The dogs went wild, scrabbling over wood floors and barking madly. He grabbed the excuse eagerly, calling out over the wild barking, "Sorry! There's someone at the door."

"Are you having guests over?"

"Probably a pizza guy at the wrong house," Walker yelled over the woofing. "Look, I need to go. Happy New Year. I love you."

"Love you too!"

He hung up before she could say anything else, reaching the front door and jerking it a few inches open while trying to hold the dogs back with one foot. "Enough!" he said sternly to the dogs. "Enough!"

They continued to bark and keen, but they stopped jumping quite so much. He turned toward the cracked open door without really being able to see through into the darkness of the front stoop. "Uh, wrong house."

"Walker." Ashton's voice was strained, and he panted like he'd been running. "Can we talk?"

The dogs went utterly berserk, and there was no way he could keep them from pushing him aside and barreling out to the man on the front stoop. Ashton yelped and stumbled down on his butt, the dogs circling him like he was a long-lost pack member finally returned home.

Walker finally found the switch to turn on the rarely used front porch light and saw Ashton now on his knees fielding kisses and cuddles from Nina, Simone, Marble, and Bitsy. It was a mad moment with all the dogs yipping and crying in delight.

"They missed you," Walker managed to get out around the lump in his throat. "Sorry. Let me try to get them back inside, and I'll come out."

"No," Ashton said breathlessly. "Uh, can I come in?"

Walker whistled. The dogs came back inside, looking over their shoulders to see if Ashton followed, obviously delighted when he did. Ashton looked thinner than even the last time they'd talked at Coffee & Chocolate, and his green eyes were darker than usual, an almost muddy color.

"You're…" Walker reached out, wanting to run his hands over Ashton's arms and down his chest to make sure he wasn't wasting away over in that trailer. He held back. "Are you eating enough?"

"I've never been much of a cook. I don't suppose you have any leftovers?" He sniffed the air. "What country are you working on now? Weren't we going to do Cuba?"

Walker didn't bother telling him that he'd given up on the Food Tour of the World project since returning from the wedding. He couldn't bring himself to spend much time in the kitchen. It seemed so meaningless just feeding himself. There'd been so much more to it when he'd been feeding Ashton too. Nourishing and caring for the man he…

Loved.

Yes, the man he loved and could love forever if he got another shot at it.

"Come on," he said, pulse racing. "Let me take your coat and get you something to eat."

Ashton handed it over and wrapped his arms around his torso. He still wore just a hoodie—this time a navy one—and jeans. Walker hoped he'd get to see him looking comfortable on his sofa.

Ashton sat at the table and watched as Walker pulled open cabinets and started pasta going with some meat sauce. He said nothing—about the fight, the holiday, the trailer, or what he'd been thinking about—until Walker placed the food in front of him and took his own seat across from Ashton to watch him eat.

Three bites in Ashton said, "The traffic getting here was horrible. There's a party at the end of the street with so many cars they've got the road blocked. The Uber guy couldn't get through, so he let me out and I ran the rest of the way."

"New Year's Eve can get out of hand," Walker agreed, his heart twisting in his chest with a horrible, hateful hope. "I thought you might have plans with Casey and Joel or something. Or Angel."

"Joel and Casey invited me out with them, but…" He shrugged. "I wasn't in the mood for live music. And Angel invited me to go with her, but her idea of a good time is *a lot.*"

Walker laughed cautiously and waited. He wasn't going to make assumptions. He wasn't going to let his hopes rise too high. Never mind that his blood was rushing through him like it was carbonated.

Ashton ate until the plate of spaghetti was half gone. "This was great. Thank you."

"It would have been better if I'd been able to let the sauce simmer for a while, but it got the job done."

"I've missed…" He cut himself off.

"My food?"

He laughed, looking sheepish. "And the dogs. And…you."

Walker took a slow breath. "You know I've missed you too."

Ashton glanced away uncomfortably, but then he brought his gaze back to meet Walker's. "You have a surprising number of people on your side, you know."

"My side?" Walker frowned in confusion. "I don't know what that means. I don't have a side in this. I was wrong, and you have every right to feel how you feel, and—"

"I mean Casey, Joel, and hell, even Angel tried to talk me into giving you another chance." He smirked. "Kayla harassed me all day today about whether or not my Facebook post was hiding the truth, basically begging me to consider a real relationship with you if it wasn't because, and I quote, 'you'd be so cute together and Walker deserves a guy like you.'" He smiled wryly. "I asked what I deserved, but she was less effusive on that topic."

"Ashton—"

He held up a hand. "Give me a minute. I'm not here because I'm over it and ready to recommit. I'm here because…" He cleared his throat. "It's the new year. Do you remember that super old cartoon about Baby New Year?"

"Sure."

"Every year is fresh, like a baby." Ashton frowned. "Heaven help me, I don't know what I'm trying to say. I keep seeing it in my mind's eye, and thinking about it, but I can't put it into words."

"Describe it."

"It's a jumble. There's the Baby New Year, right, but there's also the baby in the manger in the Christmas story." Ashton leaned back in his chair, scrubbed a hand over his face, and huffed. "It's just that babies are precious, aren't they? And they require a lot of care, a lot of trust that they can grow, and a lot of love. A whole lot of love."

Walker stayed quiet. He had no idea where Ashton was going with this, but it seemed important to listen.

"When I think about certain parts of myself, I think those parts of me are still in their infancy. Like trust. My ability to trust is just a baby." He sighed. "That doesn't make a lot of sense, though. Babies trust easily."

"I understand. The ability is an infant. It's not grown and mature and able to take care of itself, so you have to protect it. Keep it safe."

"Parent it," Ashton added, his eyes lighting up. "You understand what I'm saying."

"Yes. I get it."

"When I felt that part of me—the part that's so young and tender—being threatened by what I saw as a clear monster from my past, I grabbed the baby and ran with it."

"You had to keep it safe."

"Yes. To keep me safe."

"I understand, Ashton. I really do."

"I know, and that's part of it. You're not a monster from my past. Like you said when I first found out about it all: you're not my mother or my grandmother or Justin. You're not even Gerald—who wasn't a bad person, just a bad fit. You're a human being who's made some mistakes but learned from them and changed his life accordingly. Heavens, isn't that the kind of man anyone should trust? That maybe I should practice learning to trust?"

His beautiful lips trembled as he went on. "You never promised me that you'd been perfect or even always good. But I've worked with you; been your business partner. I've listened to you argue for what's right for your clients' marketing and branding and for our employees and office. I've seen how you were willing to put yourself out on a limb to protect your sister. I know how you love your mother and how you spoil your dogs. And how you tried to spoil me. I know you."

Walker's throat was too tight to say anything. Tears pricked his eyes, and he wanted to pull Ashton into a tight embrace and kiss his neck, ears, and those damn collarbones that even now peaked out of the top of the stretched-out neck of his hoodie. But he held back. This was Ashton's time to clear the air. He owed it to him to listen. There could always still be a "but" coming that would ruin everything…

"But—"

Here it was.

"But I'm not ready to jump back in with both feet."

"Of course not."

"*But* I'm not ready to walk away either."

Walker's heartbeat leapt, and the flood of relief gave him double vision for a moment. He pressed his hands to his face and tried to breathe, shocked as a weird sob broke out. Was he crying? He thought he might be crying.

"Oh heavens, don't cry," Ashton whispered, falling to his knees and scooting over to take hold of Walker's hands and pull them from his face. "Don't cry."

Walker's heart wrenched. Tears slipped over his cheeks, and he wiped at them with the back of his hand. "I don't know what's wrong with me. I don't do this."

"You don't cry?"

"Not usually. Not like I've cried lately."

Ashton laughed. "Wow, that's very bro of you and something we'll have to work on."

"You're saying we're not over? Really?" Walker needed to verify that his ears hadn't deceived him. "You want to try again with me?"

"Yes, but slower this time. I'll stay at the trailer for the time being, and we can date. Take it easy."

"Yes," Walker agreed easily.

"No sex, no sleepovers."

Walker tipped his head to the side. "No sex?"

Ashton's lips twisted wickedly. "That a problem?"

"No, uh, no, that's fine with me."

Ashton's eyes narrowed. "We could make my Grandma Hudson proud with our slow courtship. No sex before marriage. All that Christian goodness."

Walker's throat clicked as he swallowed. "No sex before marriage?" Was he hearing this right? Surely he was hallucinating this entire conversation. He was asleep on the sofa and would wake up any moment alone and even sadder than before. There was no way Ashton was asking them to get together and be celibate, right? Had to be a dream.

"Walker," Ashton said softly, sliding his fingers over Walker's cheek and gazing into his eyes. It felt very real. The entire dream felt incredibly real. Maybe it wasn't a dream? Was he really about to agree to celibacy before marriage? "What do you think?"

"Uh, well, I'm willing to slow things down, but no sex until marriage seems a bit grim, to be quite fucking honest."

Ashton's smile was like lightning, and it cut to Walker's quick. "Ah, there you are. I was wondering if you were just going to agree to everything I suggested. I was going to say we had to get rid of the dogs next and get only cats in their place."

Walker gawped.

"I mean, there has to be a limit on the groveling. Don't get me wrong, I wanted you to grovel. More than that, I just want you to be as real and honest with me as possible. I want to share this infant trust with you and hope you don't damage it, hope it grows until I don't feel like I need to protect it anymore. To do that, you have to be honest with me."

"I don't want to go slow," Walker said. "I want to go back to how we were. I loved taking care of you. It made me happy to cook dinner for you, rub your feet, and give you a home. It made me happy to make love to you, and hold you, and—"

"It made me happy too."

"Then how will this infant trust grow between us if that all just stops?"

Ashton smiled fondly, rubbing his thumb across Walker's cheekbone. "You make a good argument. But I need a place of my own, something that's only mine. Somewhere I can run to if I need to leave."

"I promise you'll never need to leave."

Ashton's pulse throbbed visibly in his neck, his heart clearly beating so hard. He took a shaky breath. "I want to believe you. Having the trailer will help me believe you."

Walker licked his lips, desperate to kiss him. "Okay. I understand. So how do you want to do this? How do we move forward?"

"Day by day," Ashton said. "Some days I'll stay here with you, and some days I'll go to the trailer. Some days I'll be at the trailer and wish I were here with you, and maybe sometimes I'll be with you and wish I'd chosen the trailer."

Walker huffed a laugh.

"But I want to try. I want to believe that the man I've been loving these last few weeks is the real Walker Ronson. Tell me I'm not wrong."

"I'm the real Walker Ronson. The most real I've ever been is when I'm with you."

"Same. I feel the same." Ashton swept his fingers over Walker's eyebrows and down the sides of his face. "You're beautiful, did you know?"

Walker snorted. "I'm fine. You're the beautiful one."

"I used to think so too," Ashton said, and Walker couldn't help but laugh. "I even told my hairdresser that you were... Never mind."

"Never mind?" Walker laughed. "How am I supposed to let that go?"

Ashton ignored him. "But now... Now I think you're just *wow*."

He couldn't resist another moment. Ashton's lips were soft and warm, and Walker tugged him up to sit in his lap, angling his head up to continue the kiss. The dogs, sensing that there were leftovers they might be entitled to, pattered into the kitchen, and Ashton broke away to look down at them, smiling fondly.

"I've missed you little beggars so much," he whispered as they all sat at Walker's feet and stared up at Ashton with saliva pooling at the sides of their mouths. Ashton put the spaghetti plate on the floor and they scrambled for the leftovers, making a small mess, while Ashton laughed.

"How do we do this?" Walker asked when the plate was licked clean, and the dogs had departed the kitchen for the warmth of the living room again. He gripped Ashton closely and buried his head in Ashton's chest. "It's New Year's Eve. Should we seal it with a toast? I have some champagne. We could—"

Ashton broke his words off with another kiss, this one rougher and full of hotter intentions.

"But you said slow," Walker murmured when they broke apart again.

"Then come make love to me slowly." Ashton stood and pulled Walker up. "I'm not in the mood to play hard to get tonight. Let's meet the new year the way we intend to go on."

"Trusting each other."

"Yes," Ashton hissed, tugging Walker past the dogs and toward the bedroom. "Love that for us."

Walker loved it for them too.

ASHTON HADN'T THOUGHT he'd ever be back in Walker's warm bed, wrapped in his strong arms, sharing kisses, rolling around in bed desperately, both of them rutting against each other like they'd never get enough.

As they finally pulled apart to grab some air, Ashton shook with anticipation as Walker reached into the bedside drawer for the box of condoms and lube.

"How long has it been since you were with anyone else?" Ashton asked, the word *trust* still echoing in his mind.

"Over a year. You?"

"Five months. A hookup. I've had a checkup since, and it was all clear."

Walker swallowed visibly and asked with a tremulous voice, "Are you saying…?"

"We're working on trust, right? And, when it comes to this, I trust you completely, Walker. So I should exercise that trust, shouldn't I? Make it stronger?"

Walker let out a slow breath. "Only if you're sure."

"I am. I want this. I want you inside me with nothing between us."

"Have you ever done it like this before?" Walker asked as he put the condom aside and took up the lube with shaking hands. "Gone bare?"

Ashton shook his head. "No. Never."

Walker groaned. "I'll be the first to mark you inside?"

Ashton pushed Walker back to the bed, taking the lube from him and opening it. "First to come inside me. First to leave part of yourself behind."

"*Fuck.*" Walker groaned and squeezed his eyes closed. "This isn't a dream. I'm not dreaming."

"No," Ashton murmured as he warmed the lube on his palm and took up Walker's thick, hard cock. "Not a dream. I'm here. We're together."

Walker's stomach trembled as Ashton worked his hand up and down his dick, getting it thoroughly slicked. Then he moved astride Walker's hips and positioned himself. He quickly added lube to his asshole and took hold of Walker's cock again.

He stared into Walker's eyes as he sat back, letting the pressure build and then exhaling slowly as Walker's cock slid inside hard and fast. Ashton threw his head back, his breath coming in gasps at the sudden stretch and fullness. He lifted slightly before easing himself all the way down again, taking Walker all the way and squirming at the feel of Walker's rough pubic hair against his tight rim.

"Oh baby," Walker gasped, straining for control. He gripped Ashton's thighs and held very still like he might tumble over into orgasm immediately. "I've missed this. I've missed you so much."

"I know," Ashton murmured. "I've missed you too."

Walker groaned. "You're so hot and slick inside. It feels so good." He shivered and convulsed slightly. "Don't move or I'll come, baby. Shh, shh, hold still."

Ashton bit into his lip, looking down at Walker through his lashes, admiring how Walker scrunched his eyes, trembled, and fought for control, so turned on by Ashton, so adoring of him, so needful. "Open your eyes," Ashton whispered. "Watch me."

Walker whimpered but complied. When Ashton started running his fingertips over his collarbones sensuously, Walker gritted his teeth and issued a string of curses that made Ashton laugh. That seemed to undo Walker even more, and he dug his fingers into Ashton's thighs to hold him steady, throwing his head back against the pillow, reaching for control.

"I can't believe I'm feeling you. Really you. Skin on skin. I can feel it all," Walker gritted out. "Your pulse on my cock. Through the walls of your body. I feel like I'm gonna lose my mind."

"Mm." Ashton held very still again to let Walker calm down. But he didn't want him to calm down too much. "Look at me. Watch."

Walker groaned but flicked his gaze back to Ashton as he grinned and started playing with his collarbones again. "You're a menace," Walker ground out. "A cruel, teasing menace."

"Mm, you love it."

With a hard grip on Ashton's hips, Walker surged up and flipped them over, keeping his cock buried deep in Ashton's body as he did. Gasping, Ashton clung to Walker's shoulders and wrapped his legs around his waist to hold him inside. Walker's weight pressed Ashton into the mattress, and the reckless force of his first thrust knocked another laugh out of Ashton.

"You'll pay for that," Walker murmured, kissing Ashton's neck before turning his attention to biting lightly along his collarbones. "It might not be today, or tomorrow, or the next day. But some day soon I'll tease you until you lose control."

"Threaten me with a good time. Go on."

Ashton shrieked with laughter as Walker tickled him for a split second before giving up so he could mouth Ashton's collarbones deliriously, moaning like he was going to come from just kissing them alone. He'd certainly done that before, and Ashton had no doubt he could do it again, but not today. Not before Ashton got everything he wanted first.

"Enough of that," Ashton commanded, raking his hands down Walker's back to grab his ass. "Move now. Fuck me. Make me come."

Walker abandoned Ashton's neck and collarbones to gaze into his eyes. "Ready?" he whispered.

He gulped at the heat and lust he saw in Walker's expression and the determination in his gaze. "Yes. I'm ready."

Walker kissed him thoroughly as he started thrusting at a slow-but-steady pace, but shortly he broke the kiss, getting up onto his knees and hitching Ashton's legs back, holding him open for his cock by hooking Ashton's knees over his arms.

Ashton gripped the sheets, familiar with this position from their nights together after Christmas, and he knew just how perfectly Walker's cock would hit. Bracing himself, he met Walker's gaze again and nodded.

Walker's lips curled into a sweet smirk, like he knew just what he was going to do to Ashton. He drew back slowly, stretching out the withdrawal of his cock before he fucked back into him with hard and relentless strokes.

"Yes!" Ashton cried out, eyes rolling back, his prostate singing like a struck bell, the pleasure rippling all over his body. "Like that. Just like that." He squirmed with each thrust in, and eventually released the sheets to grasp at Walker's waist, shoulders, and ass, trying to get him in further, deeper, harder. "Please," he begged, legs shaking and asshole spasming around Walker's plunging cock. "I need it. I need you."

"You're so tight and hot," Walker whispered, trembling as he moved inside Ashton again and again. "Thank you for being here. Thank you for letting me… Just thank you."

Ashton clung to Walker harder. "I love you. I trust you."

Walker shivered and kissed him again, their bodies sliding together, trapping Ashton's cock and providing delicious friction. "Wanna come with you in me," Ashton groaned, breaking their kiss to mouth Walker's earlobe and whisper his desires. "Wanna feel you shoot inside me. Want you to load me up."

"Oh, baby—fuck!" Walker grunted and lifted up, getting back into position to tag Ashton's prostate relentlessly. He pushed Ashton's legs back, held him open, and stared at where his cock entered Ashton's body. "So hot. Bare. Slick. Fuck, baby." His pupils blew wide. "I'm so close. But... Not yet. You come first."

Walker was so beautiful this way—hanging on the precipice, dying to give Ashton what he needed before he reached his own climax. It was tempting to urge him to wait longer, to see if he could hold out despite his trembling and desperate shivers of lust.

But Ashton was too needy, so he took up his own cock, squeezing and releasing around the head, a technique he loved while being fucked. "Go on. Hit my prostate, please. Get it." Ashton gave his cock a few sharp jerks.

Sweat broke over him as Walker obeyed, hunching hard into him, slamming against his prostate so that sparks shimmered in his periphery vision, his heart pounded, and he felt as though he were levitating off the bed. One perfectly aimed stroke had him shouting.

"Close," he groaned. "I'm gonna... Just... Yes! There! Fuck!"

Ashton's toes curled up and his breath grew shallow. Walker stared down at him avidly, the blue of his eyes glowing with lust and heat. His hips didn't stop their inexorable rhythm, and each thrust was another hitch closer to the promise of that perfect shattering. Ashton's eyes rolled back just as his body tightened all over, and—

"Holy fuck!" he shouted, his orgasm exploding through him, pumping cum onto his chest and splattering his cheek. "Fuck, Walker... *Fuck!*"

That was all it took for Walker to come too. He grunted and shook, his hips losing rhythm and spasmodically thrusting deeper, seeking to get as far into Ashton as possible. Ashton felt the warmth of Walker's cum paint his inner walls, loved the desperate jerks of Walker's cock as he struggled with the intensity of his orgasm, and clung to his wild ecstasy as he unloaded all his pleasure and love into Ashton's body.

The true intimacy of the exchange, the pure trust and belief in it, left Ashton reeling as he jerked through another small, shivery orgasm while Walker bucked again and kept on filling him up.

Eventually, they lay sweating and sticky together. The evidence of their reconciliation was everywhere: Ashton's face, the sheets, between their bodies, and leaking slowly from his ass. Ashton's cock throbbed between them in spent satisfaction, and his asshole remained stretched around Walker's still sturdy thickness.

"Wow," Ashton finally gasped. "You were… That was…"

"So hot."

"Yeah. Amazing."

Walker chuckled. "Too fast, though. We didn't last long at all."

"We've got time," Ashton murmured, holding Walker's quaking, trembling form tight and sliding his fingers into Walker's hair. After-shocks coursed through Walker's body, and Ashton relished in the pulses of his cock still thick and straining against Ashton's asshole. He didn't want this moment to end. It was too human, too real.

But he also knew it wasn't the best they could do together. There was so much more potential between them. More love to make and grow. More trust to exercise and share. More to prove. This was just their first quick orgasm of reunion, solidifying their promises to each other and their desire to be more to each other, to forgive and find a way to be together.

"Stay there," Walker whispered as he reluctantly pulled free. "Don't move." He took hold of Ashton's ankles, lifted them up to his shoulders, and canted Ashton's body backward.

Ashton laughed. "What are you doing?"

Walker was gruff as he muttered, "Want to keep it inside you. All of it." He slid his fingers down to scoop any cum that had escaped back inside Ashton's slightly gaping hole. His touch was tender, and Ashton felt his ass grab at his fingers as he pushed the jizz back inside. "Want you to absorb me. Wanna be part of you forever. Inside and out."

Ashton almost laughed. Walker was so whimsical sometimes. So romantic and magical.

Walker reached out and slid his finger through the streak of jizz on Ashton's cheek before sucking it into his mouth, instantly swapping Ashton's urge to laugh with a wash of heat and renewed desire.

"I love you," Walker whispered as he pulled his finger free from his lips. "Everything about you."

"Tell me more. You know I love to hear about the wonders of me." Ashton tried to sound loose and glib, but the softness of his voice betrayed him.

"Wonders of you? Everything. Your taste, your smile, your laugh. How you cry out when you come. The way you…" He trailed off, waving at Ashton's whole person. "The way you are. So beautiful. I can barely understand how beautiful you are."

"And?" Ashton shouldn't be greedy, but he was. He wanted more.

"And I missed you—" His voice broke. "I was so scared."

He collapsed onto Ashton, suddenly sobbing against his throat.

Stroking Walker's back and wrapping his legs around his hips, lining their still semi-hard cocks up together, Ashton cooed and hummed. "I missed you too. I was scared too."

"I'm so sorry."

"I love you, Walker. I trust you. We're going to be all right."

He nodded against Ashton's neck, and they lay together quietly until the flood of emotions passed.

Once Walker was calm, they made love again. More slowly this time, more tenderly, with less dirty talk and more awe. They whispered pledges and oaths. They kissed and touched, they whimpered and shook. They shared each other's cum and saliva, promising to never lie or withhold, to always be honest, to always be true. They promised to be better men for each other. To trust and grow. To love.

As they made their pledge, distant cheers went up from neighboring houses and quite loudly from the party next door.

"Happy New Year," Walker whispered, nuzzling his cheek.

"Thank you for adoring me."

Walker drew back, and they shared a smile and kiss.

Everything wasn't perfect. Ashton knew their problems couldn't all be solved with just words and a couple of orgasms. But this moment was beautiful all the same. There were a few things Ashton knew without a doubt: life wasn't fair, some of the best things came with a great deal of risk, and love was undoubtedly the riskiest thing of all.

But Ashton had chosen this gamble freely. He believed Walker would be as safe a bet as he would ever find in a truly passionate love. Together, he believed they could win the jackpot: home, happiness, lust, and love.

And he knew, right here, right now with Walker—he was grown and he was safe.

A new year had begun. For them both.

# Epilogue

"Your mom adores me," Ashton said as he put down his phone after having exchanged a flurry of texts.

*How could she not?* "She does," Walker agreed, smiling as Ashton turned the Christmas music up even louder on their wireless speaker so that Sufjan Steven's voice rose dramatically in their kitchen.

Ashton grinned and went back to putting the final touches on the cookies they were decorating to take with them to the Ronson Christmas celebrations the following day.

Marble, Nina, and Simone milled around at their feet waiting for them to drop something. Walker had already "accidentally" dropped three entire cookies, and, Walker had noticed with fondness, Ashton had dropped a few too.

"Were you just texting with her?" Walker asked.

"Yup. And with Evelyn too."

Walker smiled, wondering what his mom must have sent in the text message to Ashton that had him so giddy and confident in her love of him, but he didn't pry. Ashton and his mom had been sharing secret texts all week, and he supposed it probably had something to do with a Christmas surprise. He liked surprises, so he'd just have to wait and see.

"And your dad finally likes me too," Ashton said loudly over the music. "You know what he said to me yesterday?"

"You were talking with my dad yesterday?" Now *that* was news.

"Yes, I was, and he said I was good for you! Can you believe it? And then he said he was glad I came into your life." Ashton pressed his hand to his chest, his big green eyes growing wet, and his voice sounding a little choked up. "Honestly, he could just say nothing else to me for the rest of all eternity, and I'd be happy enough with that."

Walker put his arm around Ashton's shoulders and kissed his stubbled cheek. "You *are* good for me. He's right. I'm glad he sees it."

"We're good for each other," Ashton corrected. He turned the music up more and danced at the counter as he put the final touches on a few more cookies.

Walker watched, amused and a little hopeful that this part of the Christmas Eve plan—apparently there was an extensive one—might be finished soon and they could have a long enough break to indulge in a different kind of celebration for a little while.

"So…" Walker said, turning down the music and sidling up to Ashton, who glanced toward the living room with an odd expression that quickly passed. "Are you almost done with these? They look perfect you know. And we don't want to make so many that no one has room for the jólakaka."

"Yes, I'm excited to try the Icelandic Christmas cake!"

"Me too." They'd been working through traditional recipes of Iceland for the last few weeks, and many were hit or miss. They were both optimistic about the Christmas cake, and planned to make one for tonight to have for their one-on-one Icelandic Christmas, and one for tomorrow to share with their family. "But before we start on that…" He wrapped his arms around Ashton from behind. "Want to celebrate our one year Sex Anniversary again?"

They'd already started out the day with an orgasm in bed, but looking at Ashton's collarbones exposed by his loose-necked T-shirt, seeing his eager smile and excited eyes, and watching him get all pinked up from the heat of the ovens and the effort of making the perfect cookies had Walker ready for another round.

Ashton blushed and rolled his eyes. "Later," he whispered, like someone might hear them talking. "I, uh, wanted to do presents first."

"Oh? So early in the day?" Walker grinned.

"Yeah. This particular present can't wait." Ashton looked so nervous all of a sudden that Walker had a good idea of just what kind of present it might be.

Over the last year, Ashton had really put in effort to find exciting new toys for Walker's ass to "make up" for not enjoying topping, and while Walker always insisted Ashton didn't need to "make up" for anything, the toys were always fun. "Baby, let me guess: You have a very naughty present in there for me? A thick plug, maybe? If so, I'm all for this early present plan, and my ass is all yours."

Ashton's neck and face flushed even redder, his green eyes glowing oddly. "Shh!"

"What? You know I love your taste in toys."

He gulped wildly and pressed his hand over Walker's mouth. "Oh heavens, shut up."

Walker dodged Ashton's hand and laughed. "Why so shy? Who's gonna hear? The dogs? You know they've heard worse."

"Well, I haven't." Evelyn's voice came from the kitchen doorway. How or when she'd arrived and come into the house, Walker didn't know, but now the dogs went wild, forgetting all about possible dropped cookies to greet her in a frenzy.

Ashton also burst into a jumble of excited, embarrassed, jittery nervousness. He quickly covered the cookies with the wax paper he'd cut earlier and positioned himself at the counter between Walker and Evelyn.

"It's here?" he asked her with wide eyes.

Evelyn nodded, bending to pet the dogs before she stood, snapped her fingers once, and commanded them to sit. Somehow they all did.

"You *have* to teach me how you do that," Ashton said in awe.

"You say that every time, and every time I tell you both that you just have to mean it. But neither of you ever do, and that's the problem."

Tom's voice called from the living room. "Hurry up, y'all. I can't hold it much longer."

"Hold what?" Walker asked. "What are you even doing here? What's going on? I thought you're supposed to be with Tom's family for Christmas Eve?"

"We are, which is another reason why we need to get this show on the road."

"Ashton?" Walker asked, turning to see that Ashton was almost vibrating out of his skin. Nerves? Excitement? Joy? All of the above as far as Walker could tell. "What's going on?"

"It's your present. It's been almost five months since Bitsy—"

Suddenly a blond furry thing with giant paws bounded into the kitchen.

"Sorry! He's a squirmy one!" Tom called, appearing in the doorway beside Evelyn, his bearded face red from exertion.

Marble, Nina, and Simone began barking and sniffing, and the puppy—bigger than Marble by far and not that much smaller than Simone—fell onto its back, offering its tummy to the small pack. They circled him, investigating, and Walker gaped.

"It's been almost five months," Ashton repeated. "And a few months back Joe at the office said his brother's golden-doodle had a surprise litter on the way, father unknown, and..."

"You got me a puppy?"

"Yes?"

Evelyn nudged Nina away from the puppy and bent to scoop him up. He was almost as big as her torso. She held it out to Ashton, who took him into his arms and cuddled him close before pushing the fluffy, furry, licking mess into Walker's arms. "There was a brown one too, but I liked the looks of this one," Ashton said softly. "Evelyn and Tom have been keeping him for me the last few days. The kids love him. He's good with them, right, Ev?"

"Great with them, actually," Evelyn said, going to take Tom's hand. "And speaking of the kids, now that we've delivered this rascal to you, we're gonna grab them from Morgan and get on the road." As an aside she added, "Thank God things are still going better with her. She's really shaped up since she started dating that new guy."

"*And,* thanks to Ashton, a second one from the same litter is waiting at my Mom and Dad's house for the kids' gift from Santa," Tom said with a grin. "They were so great with Polo here—"

"Polo?" Walker asked.

"That's what I've been calling him," Ashton said. "You know how you kept teasing me for being so stressed about your Christmas present? You said I should just get you another boring old Polo? So...yeah, I thought it was cute. But you can name him something different if you want."

Walker stroked the fur from the puppy's eyes and gazed at his adorable, happy, puppy-face. The other dogs leapt up trying to sniff at his butt. "No, Polo is perfect."

"Do you like him?"

"He's...he's..." Polo twisted in Walker's arms, and he had to put him down for the other dogs to inspect some more. Walker tugged Ashton close and hugged him, his throat going tight and sore. "He's so cute, and so are you."

"Let's go," Evelyn said, tugging Tom's hand. "Love you both. Merry Christmas. Happy Sex Anniversary."

"Heavens," Ashton murmured, still wrapped up in Walker's arms. "Forget he ever said that."

"Alas," Evelyn moaned. "I will remember it every Christmas Eve for the rest of my life now. I'll always think, 'Today is the day Walker and Ashton boned for the first time' even when I'm eighty."

Tom scoffed. "C'mon. We've got to get to my folks' place. Later!"

The dogs skittered and scattered as the puppy bounded around, trying to play. Walker clutched Ashton close, feeling his heartbeat against his chest and wondering why he felt so near to tears.

"This is okay, right? I wanted him to be a surprise, but I know a new puppy is a lot to handle, and maybe I overstepped because this isn't really my place, and—"

"Of course it's your place. You live here." They'd collected his last few boxes from Joel's trailer the week before after Ashton had slowly migrated through the year and stayed for good after Thanksgiving.

"But it's not my house."

"It's as much yours as mine." Walker held Ashton far enough away to look into his eyes. "You know Grandpa said he'd sell it to me."

"Yes, but—"

"And I told him I wanted him to sell it to *us*. I want your name next to mine on the title. I want your name next to mine on a bank account." Walker swallowed hard. "I'd planned to do this tomorrow, but…"

He dropped to his knees and took hold of Ashton's hand. "The ring's in a box under the tree, but Ashton—"

"Get it."

"Get what?"

"The ring." Ashton's eyes were wet, but his smile was enormous. Joy was so beautiful on him. As if he could get anymore stunning…

Walker laughed and hefted up to his feet again. "Okay, come on." He took hold of Ashton's hand and led him into the living room. The puppy and the other dogs followed, wrestling and playing. Marble even growled a little, but no fight broke out. Walker's heart hammered as he found the box beneath several others under the tree.

He turned to find Ashton already on his knees with a box held out in his hand. Walker's throat went tight again, but he knelt before him. He opened his box, and Ashton did the same. The two gold rings sat gleaming in their respective dark velvet. The dogs tussled behind them on the floor.

"Walker Ronson, will you—"

"Ashton Sellers, will you—"

"Yes."

"Yes."

The rings were forgotten at first in the kiss that followed and the pile of dogs that rubbed up against them until they tumbled to the floor. The dogs rolled with them and on them, and they finally broke free enough to slide the rings on each other's fingers, laughing and crying and kissing between yips and nips from the dogs.

Walker pulled Ashton and Polo up onto the sofa. They cuddled close, holding hands and gazing at the rings on their fingers while patting their new puppy. Nina, Simone, and Marble came and went, up and down, sniffing their new family member.

Walker said, "A year ago, I remember how I felt with you sitting out here on the sofa while I made dinner for you. I felt like a grown man for the first time in my life. Tonight, with you and the dogs and this new guy—I feel like I'm not only grown but starting on the biggest journey of my life. The most important one. Building forever with you. I don't want to mess it up."

"You won't. I believe in you. In us."

A few minutes later, Polo stopped squirming and seemed to simply pass out against Walker's thigh. As he collapsed into puppy-sleep, Nina, Simone, and Marble seemed to relax too, going to their beds and lying down.

"Walker?"

"Mm-hmm?"

"Do you think I'm a good man?"

He took Ashton's hands in his, stroking over the opal ring on his right hand and the new engagement band on his left. "Yes. You're a deeply good man."

"I hope so."

"Why are you asking a question like that?"

"I got a letter yesterday. From my mom. I almost didn't open it, but then I did. It was a long list of things she's sorry for."

"An attempt at reconciliation?"

"No, she's trying rehab again. It's one of her steps—making

amends."

"How did you feel about it?"

"I don't know. I don't want her in my life, but I started wondering if I can forgive her in my heart. There's a difference isn't there? Between inviting her back into my world and forgiving her for not being the mother I needed her to be."

"Of course."

"But I don't think I'm a good enough man to forgive her yet."

"That's okay too."

"Is it?"

Walker gathered Ashton close. "Baby, you don't have to forgive her to be good."

"She mentioned Justin in the letter. He's still living with Grandma. Still using."

"I'm sorry."

Ashton clutched Walker closer. "Me too. I'm sorry for them both. I'm sorry for the relationships we all lost with each other. I truly am. But they almost broke me so much I couldn't trust you enough to have this. I might be able to forgive them for what they did to little Ashton, to past-me, but realizing how much they'd injured my ability to believe in another person, in you, is damage too fresh for me to forgive them for it yet."

"I was never going anywhere. I was going to win your trust back no matter what it took."

Ashton buried his face in Walker's neck and took a slow, deep breath. Then he bent low and nuzzled sleeping Polo. "I know you were."

"Mm."

They held each other for a little while, just being together. Ashton sighed. "I love how dogs smell when they sleep. Popcorn goodness."

"Corn chips," Walker corrected.

Ashton huffed. "Corn products, then."

Walker nuzzled his hair, content.

The Christmas tree twinkled in the corner, and the dogs snoozed on. The day was still early. It wasn't even lunchtime yet, and they had the rest of the afternoon for their other presents and the entire evening to celebrate together with their Icelandic Christmas dinner. But right now, with just the two of them and their dogs—plus a ridiculously cute new puppy—Walker was utterly content.

Did he deserve this beautiful life? He didn't know, but it didn't matter.

He was never letting it go.

*Dear friends, clients, and fans,*

*This is your one and only Mr. Jingle Bells reporting to you with tidings of comfort and joy! Four years ago I ended my relationship with my homophobic family by bringing a shirtless Grindr date to the family Christmas party. At the time, I thought that was the biggest surprise I'd ever get or give for Christmas.*

*But last year on a whim, I made a silly shitpost offering to pose as anyone's boyfriend in exchange for a place to stay for a few days while they fumigated my apartment. Little did I know that post would change my life.*

*First Walker Ronson asked me to stay with him and stop being ridiculous on Facebook.*

*Then Walker asked me to pretend to be his boyfriend at his sister's wedding for *hand wave* reasons.*

*Shortly after that? Walker gave me a ring that meant, and I quote, "nothing."*

*Then that self-same Walker Ronson—that cutie-pie Polo-shirt wearer of my heart—changed his mind, said the ring meant "everything," and asked me to bed. (I know he's dying that I posted that, but it's true.)*

*It wouldn't be the full story if I didn't also tell you it wasn't long before Walker and I hit a pretty big crisis, and I thought things were over between us for good. I'm pretty sure he thought so too.*

*But love prevailed, and we decided to give it another try. Over the last year, Walker has proven to me again and again that he's the right man for me. And this Christmas? I surprised him with a puppy… And we surprised each other with a proposal.*

*That's right! We're getting married!*

*So I think the moral of the story is this: make more shitposts, win more prizes.*

*No, no, that can't be it. ;)*

*The moral of the story is: I love Walker Ronson and he loves me, and thank heavens for shitposts and for fake boyfriends and rings that mean everything and nothing, and for this last year of our life. Thank heavens for forgiveness and trust and learning that people can grow. Thank heavens for Christmas, for new beginnings, for the return of the light.*

*Thank heavens for faith—in the better side of people, in each other, in love.*

*Oh, yes, thank heavens for love.*

*Happy Holidays and Happy New Year to everyone from your forever*
*Mr. Jingle Bells,*
*Ashton Sellers*

## THE END

Love Ashton and Walker? Want more? Go here to join my newsletter and access three bonus scenes!
https://dl.bookfunnel.com/7fasjax62s

If you or a family member suffer from issues of addiction—alcohol, drug, gambling, or other—and you're looking for help, call 1 (800) 662–HELP in the U.S. (they have operators in English or Spanish) or another crisis hotline in your country. You can also link through to SAMHSA. For gambling issues, you can also reach out to National Problem Gambling Helpline in the U.S. at 1 (800) 522-4700 or link through.
www.ncpgambling.org/help-treatment/national-helpline-1-800-522-4700

Please know you can beat addiction and problematic binging behavior. There's a different, brighter future waiting for you.

# Letter from Leta

Dear Reader,

Thank you so much for reading *Mr Jingle Bells*! 2020 was a difficult year for so many of us, and it was no different for me. I began writing this book in January of 2020 fully expecting to have it ready to release by December of the same year. Life sure did throw some surprises our way, though, didn't it?

Retreating into this book was a beautiful break from the chaos of 2020. Imagine my horror when I realized in February of 2021 that the nearly completed draft of this book had been deleted from my computer! My blood ran cold! Luckily, I was able to retrieve it via a miracle worthy of a Christmas book (thank you, DropBox Tech Wizards! forever grateful to you!) and, for that reason, I believe this story was meant to be out in the world.

It was a joy to write this holiday novel for readers, and I love Ashton and Walker's story. I hope you enjoyed reading it as much as I loved crafting it. I'd like to express my thanks again to PC for discussing his gambling issues with me, and to my many friends and family members who have shared with me over the years their stories of pain and triumph around drug and alcohol addiction.

If you or a family member suffer from addiction issues or gambling problems, please scroll back a page and reach out to one of the hotlines listed. There are people ready and willing to help you! You deserve a brighter future!

Flip on through to get a gander at the first chapter of *Mr Naughty List*, the second book in this series, featuring a teacher who wants to be spanked by his hot former student.

Be sure to follow me on BookBub or Goodreads to be notified of new releases. And look for me on Facebook for snippets of the day-to-day writing life, or join my Facebook Group for announcements and special giveaways. To see some sources of my inspiration, you can follow my Pinterest boards or Instagram.

If you enjoyed the book, please take a moment to leave a review! Reviews not only help readers determine if a book is for them, but also help a book show up in site searches.

Also, for the audiobook connoisseurs out there, *Mr Jingle Bells* (as well as all the *Mr. Christmas* books) are available now, narrated by the amazing John Solo (*Mr Frosty Pants* & *Mr Naughty List*) or the wonderful Nick Hudson (*Mr Jingle Bells*). Check for the books on Audible!

Thank you so much for being a reader!
Leta

Mr. Naughty List

(Mr. Christmas #2)

# Chapter One

FRESHLY SCRUBBED AND eager, Aaron fairly skipped by the glittering storefronts in Market Square. Knoxville was all done up for Christmas with lights and ribbons and wreaths, and he hummed along to "Jingle Bell Rock" as he passed the outdoor ice rink on his way to the cozy, familiar pub where he usually met his hookups.

He paid Scruffy City Hall's leather-clad bouncer the $10 cover charge for the night's band and headed inside to find the dim, wood-lined interior already packed with people. Needing a drink sooner rather than later, Aaron forced his way through the crowd and up to the bar to put in his order with the hipster, bearded bartender and was gratified by a glorious whisky sour within mere moments.

An unfamiliar and yet very Christmas-y song rang around him, emanating from the next room. Visible through an arched doorway, the small, crowded stage flashed with spangled lights from a disco ball.

The holiday spirit was evidently rampant amongst the patrons, a mix of college students and single thirty-somethings, dancing and singing along to the catchy, Christmas-themed chorus. Silver, gold, and red decorations hung from the pub's ceiling, adding a sparkle and shine that lifted the room out of mediocrity and into joy. Aaron's spirits rose even higher.

Gazing around, hoping not to see any familiar faces and pleased to find nary a one, Aaron moved into the room where the band responsible for the jangling array of Christmas tunes amped up the excitement of the drunk and adoring crowd.

Dodging elbows and squeezing between dancers, Aaron sought out a place where he could watch, listen, and drink. The rock-n-roll carols vibrated his bones, a cheering, holiday-infused hum that made his eardrums ache, but Aaron didn't plan to be here long enough to worry about his hearing. Fingers crossed, anyway.

He'd already been blown off once that evening by a potential hookup. In his desperation to secure an end to his current spell of celibacy, he'd been less choosy than usual in arranging this one. Aside from a photo of a handsome, if rather cruel-looking face, to identify the guy by, Aaron only knew his screenname—CaptainKY—and wasn't even sure if that referred to the state or the lube.

Aaron had resisted the lure of hookup apps for almost six months. He'd been proud of himself for making good use of the Internet and his right hand to satisfy his needs instead of requiring the sexual services of a stranger. Not that he *wanted* to be celibate. It was just that it was so damn hard to find no-strings-attached fucks in a town the size of Knoxville. Not as a teacher trying to keep his sexuality quiet.

The last thing Aaron needed was to find himself face-to-face with a student's closeted dad on parent-teacher night, or discover he'd screwed the older brother of one of his current students, or to trip and fall into some other horrible situation that could cost him his already tattered reputation and maybe his job.

Thus, his usual preference was to pick up men passing through town: business travelers for the most part, though truckers would do just fine if he was looking for a certain *expérience spécifique*. That'd been the plan tonight, actually. A tough-looking man who'd been trucking through town had offered to meet him for drinks and a long, slow blow job, followed by a nice, hard spanking. But the trucker had backed out at the last minute for an unspecified reason.

Which, okay. Fine. Whatever.

Aaron sometimes backed out of hookups too. It happened—second thoughts, or some protective instinct warned him against a particular rendezvous, so he flaked. But he'd *needed* it tonight. He'd been aching for it for weeks now. So, no sooner than the trucker had ditched him, Aaron had been back on the apps, scrolling for a new catch.

And he'd found one.

Cruel face. Baseball cap. In town for a monster truck show.

Aaron could totally *not* relate to that interest, but all the better. It was so much less likely they'd have to spend a lot of time talking. Instead, he'd test CaptainKY out here at the club, make sure he felt safe with him, and then go back to the hotel where the guy was staying. Probably not the Hotel Oliver, since that was a bit posh for the stereotypical monster truck fan, but maybe the new business-class Marriott, which was right around the corner from his apartment. Aaron wouldn't even be tempted to spend the night.

Sipping his cocktail, he meandered closer to the stage, attracted by the glow of the fake stained-glass windows on the balcony above the room and the optical illusion of the castle-like hall behind the stage itself. The sound was tight, and the performers were dressed up in Christmas glitz—reindeer antlers, wristbands made of tinsel, and the girls wore shimmery hair and makeup. Entertainment, Knoxville style.

Aaron was meeting CaptainKY between nine and nine thirty, but he'd been too anxious and horny to wait at home, so he'd come out a little early. He figured a drink in advance would soothe his jitters and make him looser all over. For whatever happened in the hotel. God, he hoped the guy was hung. He needed a cock in his ass more than he needed air.

Aaron drowned that desperate thought with another mouthful of whiskey. Fixing his attention on the band, he noted that it was made up of two girls and two guys: a glittering, probably Korean woman on drums, a pixie-looking lady with blue hair seated at a decorated, stand-up piano, and two fine, wiry pieces of man-flesh on bass and guitar. Both of the guys weren't too precious to play up the Christmas theme either. One wore jingle-bells on reindeer antlers, and the other had tinsel bracelets and necklaces shimmering with every move.

Aaron's gaze hung on the lead-singer-slash-guitarist. Beneath the reindeer antlers, the man wore his light brown hair shorn close to his scalp, and he possessed an easy sexuality that made Aaron's nipples tingle and his overeager cock rush hot with blood.

Aaron rolled his eyes at his own horniness, annoyed to be like a raw nerve, needy and twinging with every semi-arousing stimulus in sight. Like this tall, handsome singer with his beautiful, angular body. *Damn.* Nothing *semi*-arousing about him. More like a total hard-on.

Finally finding an empty corner to lurk in while he waited for CaptainKY to arrive, Aaron stared at the stage, chewing his bottom lip and nearly drooling over the lead's muscled arms and attractive hands. It was like a poem, the way the tendons of his forearms moved with each chord change. Aaron's skin felt alive just watching.

As minutes passed and Aaron slowly sipped his whiskey sour, letting the alcohol relax his high-strung nerves, he admired the singer's strong jawline and the wiry ligaments of his neck as he sang Christmas songs both strange and familiar. His voice was a scratchy baritone that sent shivers down Aaron's spine.

Aaron licked his lips again, spinning out a fantasy where he got this man on a bed somewhere, straddled his long legs, and unwrapped the nice package showcased by the tight fit of worn jeans.

Flushing with want, Aaron fanned himself. He shouldn't have worn a sports coat. Christ. Given that he'd been horny as hell before he even arrived at the pub, it wasn't surprising that he was steaming hot in here now, or that his imagination had taken such a dirty turn when faced with a man exactly his rough-looking type. This was the kind of man who clearly knew what to do with his hands—based on the work those fingers were doing on the fretboard, anyway.

Standing there, sporting wood beneath his sports coat, Aaron was unprepared for the effect a certain toss of the lead's chin would have. That quick move, followed by his piercing gaze raking over the crowd, triggered Aaron's memory.

In a flash, he knew him.

RJ Blitz, former high school senior, sat in the back row of Aaron's very first English Composition class as a teacher. He'd glared at Aaron like he'd wanted to turn him inside out, or beat him up, or do something else that had left Aaron feeling eternally anxious for that whole school year.

*Fuck.*

Even now Aaron battled the fear that a student would guess his sexuality and use it to hurt him—either professionally or physically. He only needed one more strike and he'd be out. Even five years ago, before the mistake and the humiliation, RJ Blitz had been a student Aaron had avoided interacting with.

RJ had been just as tall and lanky as he was now, but he'd also radiated an intensity that had shaken Aaron to the core. Violence. Attraction. Aaron didn't know, but he didn't risk reaching out, even when RJ's grades had been subpar despite his clear intelligence.

Once RJ had graduated, not only had Aaron been glad, but he hadn't ever anticipated seeing him again. Well, maybe on the local news, arrested for God only knew what. Drugs probably. Though, to be fair, that had been a mostly subconscious opinion he'd formed of RJ's possible future based on the anxiety RJ had always made him feel, the lack of effort he put into his work, and classist biases that Aaron was ashamed even now to admit to.

He blinked at RJ on the stage, all coiled sexuality and shimmery Christmas-coated lust. How was his former student the total hottie he was hungering for as he owned the small stage at Scruffy City Hall? A student. *His* student. And here Aaron had been ogling him for nearly thirty minutes. *Hard* for him even.

Fuck.

Based on the friendly smiles shot out to the giddy audience, as well as the affectionate, happy glances sent toward his bandmates, RJ was no longer the furious young man he'd once been. But there was still some underlying *something* in him that sent a shiver through Aaron's body, riled him up, and, at least tonight, engaged his lust.

Maybe it was because on stage, all of RJ's formerly pent-up, hostile energy was transformed into pure sex. No matter what song he pulled out—a rock version of an old Christmas standard, or a cheesy rendition of "Frosty the Snowman"—sexuality simply rose from him like a glowing aura of hotness.

Yes, his former student was quite possibly the most delicious thing Aaron had laid eyes on in ages. At least since the last Cocky Boys porn clip he'd jerked off to several days before.

RJ tossed his head again, and Aaron groaned. Definitely even yummier than porn.

Aaron stayed in his corner, sipping his drink. Watching. In the dark privacy of his mind, he allowed himself to imagine all sorts of dirty things: RJ shoving him against the alley wall behind Scruffy City Hall, RJ's hand against his neck as he jerked Aaron off, huffing small growls in his ear like the ones he'd just let loose in the middle of an artsy rendition of "Rudolph the Red-Nosed Reindeer." RJ plowing him as Aaron cried with joy.

He squirmed against the wall and took slow breaths. He wished CaptainKY would arrive already so he could get fucking laid. And he also hoped CaptainKY took his time, so he could watch RJ's whole set. He didn't want to miss a single, sexy minute.

*Jiminy Christmas.* What was wrong with him? He seriously needed to get fucked tonight. That was the only explanation for the appealing wrongness of wanting a former student—one wearing tinsel on his wrists, jingly reindeer antlers on his head, and a sexy smirk on his face—to fuck him silly. As messed up as it was, there wasn't much Aaron wouldn't do to get a chance at RJ Blitz. *Just look at him, for God's sake…*

But Aaron had never been quite that good, or quite that bad. Santa didn't give out presents like that. At least, not in his experience.

CaptainKY would just have to do. Now where the fuck was he?

READ MORE

# SMOKY MOUNTAIN DREAMS

by Leta Blake

**Sometimes holding on means letting go.**

After giving up on his career as a country singer in Nashville, Christopher Ryder is happy enough performing at the Smoky Mountain Dreams theme park in Tennessee. But while his beloved Gran loves him exactly the way he is, Christopher feels painfully invisible to everyone else. Even when he's center stage he aches for someone to see the real him.

Bisexual Jesse Birch is a single dad with no room in his life for dating. Raising two kids and fighting with family after a tragic accident took his children's mother, he doesn't want more than an occasional hookup. He sure as hell doesn't want to fall hard for his favorite local singer, but when Christopher walks into his jewelry studio, Jesse hears a new song in his heart.

Smoky Mountain Dreams is a heartfelt gay romance with a single dad, winter holiday highlights, found family, and steamy scenes to warm even the coldest heart!

*Full-length novel featuring winter holiday scenes*

# TRAINING SEASON

## by Leta Blake

Can a cowboy's firm hand help discipline this feisty figure skater—on and off the ice?

Matty Marcus fears he doesn't have what it takes to achieve his Olympic dream. His self-esteem is at an all-time low after figure skating coaches and skating judges have told him he's not skinny enough, good enough, or masculine enough to win.

Matty wishes he could afford the kind of coach he needs, a top-notch one who specializes in keeping their skaters focused. But those coaches are ridiculously expensive, and Matty is financially strapped.

Until a lucrative house-sitting gig brings him to rural Montana.

And to Rob.

No one has ever looked at Matty the way rural cowboy Rob Lovely looks at him. No one has ever touched him, loved him, and healed him from the inside out. No one has ever made him feel so valuable and adored. Worthy. Strong.

No one has ever taught Matty how to fly. Or how to lose.

Rob might be a cowboy and a single dad who knows nothing about figure skating, but after only a few months, he's trained a new kind of bravery into Matty's soul.

But to achieve his Olympic dream, Matty will have to face the ultimate test. Has he truly learned what it means to win—on and off the ice—during his training season?

Training Season is a MM romance with a feisty, flamboyant figure skater and an easy-going dominant cowboy, opposites attract, hurt-comfort, single dad, winter holiday highlights, love beyond reason, multiple steamy scenes, and a well-earned happy ending. *This book contains some BDSM elements.*

## Gay Romance Newsletter

Leta's newsletter will keep you up to date on her latest releases and news from the world of M/M romance. Join the mailing list today.

## Leta Blake on Patreon

Become part of Leta Blake's Patreon community in order to access exclusive content, deleted scenes, extras, bonus stories, rewards, prizes, interviews, and more.

www.patreon.com/letablake

# Other Books by Leta Blake

Any Given Lifetime
The River Leith
Heat for Sale
Smoky Mountain Dreams
Angel Undone
The Difference Between
Omega Mine
Bring on Forever
Raise Up Heart

**The Mr. Christmas Series**
Mr. Frosty Pants
Mr. Naughty List
Mr Jingle Bells

**The Training Season Series**
Training Season
Training Complex

**Heat of Love Series**
Slow Heat
Alpha Heat
Slow Birth
Bitter Heat

**Stay Lucky Series**
Stay Lucky
Stay Sexy

**'90s Coming of Age Series**
Pictures of You
You Are Not Me

**Co-Authored with Indra Vaughn**
Vespertine
Cowboy Seeks Husband

**Co-Authored with Alice Griffiths**
The Wake Up Married serial
Will & Patrick's Endless Honeymoon

**Gay Fairy Tales**
**Co-Authored with Keira Andrews**
Flight
Levity
Rise

**Audiobooks**
Leta Blake at Audible

**Free Read**
Stalking Dreams

**Discover more about the author online**
Leta Blake
letablake.com

# About the Author

Author of the bestselling book Smoky Mountain Dreams and the fan favorite Training Season, Leta Blake's educational and professional background is in psychology and finance, respectively. However, her passion has always been for writing. She enjoys crafting romance stories and exploring the psyches of made up people. At home in the Southern U.S., Leta works hard at achieving balance between her day job, her writing, and her family.